I0836192

THE DEAD MAN AND THE CEO

Also by Ian O'Regan

Denton Rourke Mysteries

For Whom the Curtain Calls

The Dead Man and the CEO

Reader Praise for
FOR WHOM THE CURTAIN CALLS

"Funny, heartfelt, witty and very creative. An amazing piece of work."

—*Amazon.com reviewer*

"This book becomes one that can't be put down. Enjoy sleepless nights as you keep turning pages to find out what's next."

—*iTunes bookstore reviewer*

"Denton [Rourke] is one of the best characters I've read in a long time. Reading this book was FUN."

—*Smashwords.com reviewer*

"Quirky turns and laugh out loud moments. Light and fun and hard to put down."

—*Amazon.com reviewer*

FOR WHOM THE CURTAIN CALLS
Available in paperback and for Kindle at
www.amazon.com

THE
DEAD MAN
AND THE
CEO

A DENTON ROURKE NOVEL

IAN O'REGAN

THE DEAD MAN AND THE CEO. Copyright © 2012 by Ian O'Regan. All rights reserved. No part of this book may be used or reproduced in any manner whatsoever without written permission except in cases of brief quotations embodied in critical articles and reviews.

This is a work of fiction. Any similarities to actual places, people (living or dead), or events are unintended and strictly coincidental.

Black Castle Press
San Antonio, TX

Cover design by KJ Feder Delgado
kreativejunkie.blogspot.com

ISBN-10 0615737854
ISBN-13 978-0615737850

For Evan and Mackenna

Now go finish your homework.

A Note From the Author

After the release of *For Whom the Curtain Calls* I received a lot of what one might call, "typical" questions: "How long does it take to write a book?" and "Where do you get your ideas?" and – most often – "Are you *sure* you don't want that mental health insurance supplement?"

But as I closed in on this, the second Denton Rourke novel, one question came up far more often than any other: "Do I have to read these novels in order?"

Well … you don't *have* to do anything. But I do recommend the Denton Rourke mysteries be read in.order. Each has its own mystery/adventure, but there are larger storylines for some characters which readers will get more out of if they go in order of publication.

So if you haven't read FWTCC, put this down and get a copy. I mean it – stop reading this … *now*.

CHAPTER 1

Denton Rourke watched Phillip Anderson's administrative assistant as she blinked rapidly and gazed wide-eyed at her bright white blouse which now sported streaky, dark-red stains. He wondered if he should cover his ears before she screamed, but she appeared stuck in an endless cycle of staring at her ruined top, then at her boss, and then back at her clothing.

Phillip Anderson offered no apology or explanation for his actions. In fact, as Denton frowned and surveyed the ridiculous scene playing out in front of him, *no one* seemed able to find a single word worth saying. He turned his disapproving stare to stunned police officers Tim Sowell and Russell Carlson in search of … *anything.*

Silence.

Denton sighed. Though the entire group deserved his disdain, he decided to let Anderson off the hook. After all, the man had skipped the, "I'm really very sorry," strategy and cleverly jumped straight to, "I'm really very dead." So as Denton looked at Phillip Anderson's lifeless body sprawled across his office desk, his neck adorned with a tightly wrapped yellow telephone cord which stood out against his blue-gray body, he could not help but excuse the man's lack of verbosity. And since Denton felt strongly that deceased people should most definitely *not* speak up to offer insights into anything – ever – he moved on quickly.

"Well," Denton started, "redecorating alone may not draw the eye away from—"

The woman in the red-stained blouse started screaming.

"Finally," Denton muttered.

Carlson clapped his hands over his ears and chuckled as the woman deafened the room. Sowell took off his oversized glasses and wiped them on his tie. He approached Denton and stared at him with dark, expressionless eyes.

"So you'll take the case?" he asked in a tone that seemed more like a confirmation than a question.

"I never said that," Denton replied. He watched Carlson attempt to hug the shrieking woman. She swung her hands at him violently and continued to wail in the direction of Anderson's corpse as though she were attempting some sort of resurrection via auditory assault therapy.

"Ma'am!" Sowell raised his deep voice and caught her attention. She stopped and stared at the aging officer.

"Please desist. You are *not* injured, and you are drawing unneeded attention to this situation."

The woman looked at Sowell for a moment, digesting his words. Finally, she nodded quietly.

Sowell turned back to Denton and his eyebrows flashed upward.

"Looks good, doesn't it?" Sowell asked.

"I'll think about it," Denton said.

Apparently not pleased with the room's return to some semblance of peace and quiet, Anderson's body chose that moment to roll off the desk and land with a grotesque thud at the feet of the momentarily calmed secretary. As he hit the ground, a small mobile phone popped out of his mouth and bounced forward, coming to rest next to her high heel.

The woman stared at the curious device for a minute, and then resumed her screaming.

Sowell watched the scene for a second before turning back to Denton.

"Think quickly, if you would," he urged. "Happy Monday."

Denton watched Carlson's hopeless second attempt at being a

calming influence and shook his head.

"And I thought Friday had been bad," he said.

# # #

"FRIDAY MORNING, UNITED ALLIANCE BANK, nine twenty-three," Denton said quietly as he scribbled in a small black notebook. He snapped it shut and peaked out from his hiding place and again found the hallway empty. After a few more minutes, he heard something. He inched out once more and looked down the corridor.

He saw her.

"I've got you now," he said. "I know what you're doing, lady, and I am on the case."

Denton's eyes rolled upward at his choice of words. He reopened his notebook and scratched a few more words. Then he leaned out and watched his suspect again as she went about her business. It wouldn't be long now.

For three weeks he'd tracked his target. He memorized her schedule and noted her every move. She looked innocent, but behind that smile something ominous hid – Denton felt it in his bones. And he would make her explain herself.

He heard movement from the hall once again. His muscles tensed. He had to act fast to catch her in the act.

Denton popped from his inconspicuous spot between two desks whose occupants were thankfully either late or had called it a day after finishing their first cups of coffee, and stepped into the aisle. Then he sprinted to the end of the aisle and walked quickly toward the hallway, trying not to count the number of colleagues who seemed to have Friday off.

"Slackers," he muttered.

Or maybe not.

"One case at a time," he said to the air.

Denton hit the hallway at full stride and came face to face with the suspect. He pulled up and watched as she made no effort to hide her activities from him.

"Lo siento, Señor Denton," she said as she hung a CLOSED sign on the door of the men's restroom. She pointed to the sign as though Denton were a kindergartener.

"Closed," she read it to him with an overly slow pronunciation.

The sign taunted him with bright yellow glee, and Denton stared hard into the woman's dark eyes.

"So," he said as he flicked the sign, "time to clean this restroom, huh?"

The cleaning lady looked back at him with hardness.

"Si."

"Uh huh, uh huh," Denton nodded. "So you haven't cleaned this restroom already? Like, ten minutes ago?" he accused, ripping his notebook from his pocket and brandishing it like a weapon.

"Well, well, well," a deep, commanding, and tired voice surprised Denton from behind. "Isn't *this* a shock?"

Denton turned around and found himself caught in the disapproving gaze of his boss, Don Fowler.

"Denton Rourke," he said, "investigating something. Whodathunk?"

Denton pocketed his notebook and turned to face the man. As he did, the cleaning lady entered the men's room and closed the door. Denton looked back at the sign, then back at his supervisor.

"Don, I am onto something here," he said, his eyes flashing excitement.

Don's eyes signaled boredom.

"Denton, when are you not 'onto something'?" he asked.

He grabbed Denton by the arm and led him around the corner away from the restroom. When a good distance separated them from Denton's target, Don let him go. Denton turned to his boss.

"This is serious!" Denton said in a frantic whisper. Then he smiled. "You know you want to know."

"No, I don't," Don said.

"Yeah, but you do."

Don Fowler looked at his employee for a minute, wondering if hitting him with a file folder would be considered "unproductive" by

Human Resources. In Denton's case, they'd probably make an exception. Denton waved his notebook in front of Fowler and teased. Fowler finally sighed.

"This had better be good," he said.

# # #

DON FOWLER USHERED DENTON into his office and closed the door. Denton sat without invitation and opened up his notebook. Fowler let his large but solid frame fall into the cushioned chair behind his desk and watched Denton leaf through pages like an excited kid flipping through a new comic book. Denton stopped and dropped an index finger forcefully on to a particular scribble. "September third," he announced. "Ten twenty-five in the morning, twelve noon, and three thirty-seven."

"Okay," Don nodded for no particular reason.

"September fourth," Denton continued. "Nine fifty-three, twelve twenty-nine, and three fifty-four."

"Uh huh," Don got up and walked over to his coffee pot.

"September fifth," Denton said, flipping a page. "Nine nineteen, eleven forty-"

"Denton," Fowler turned. "Will you please get to the point? What are you reading to me?"

"My restroom breaks," Denton said, continuing to flip pages and scan his notes.

Fowler stared at him. He ran a hand over his dark-blonde widow's peak, pushed his glasses up on his nose and opened his mouth to speak. After a couple of quiet moments of contemplation, Fowler closed his mouth and walked to the door of his office. He opened it and smiled.

"Denton, get the hell out of my office, please."

Denton turned. "This is for real, Don!" he pleaded.

"Oh, I don't doubt that for a moment, Denton," he assured. "I believe that you are reading me the actual times of day – every day – that you visit the little boy's room."

Denton suppressed a snort. It always made him laugh when his no-nonsense, manly boss used that phrase to describe a bathroom. Don continued.

"So let's just get you out of here now before you start giving me a list of ones and twos, okay?"

"Don, the times are relatively random."

"I don't care."

"But the janitorial staff keeps to a rigid cleaning schedule."

"Not listening," Don shook his head.

Denton stood and walked over to him. "Even though I use the restroom—"

"*Really* wish you'd stop saying that," Don said, looking upward.

"— at varied times each day, the men's room near my desk has always just closed for cleaning when I arrive. Now, the cleaning crew can't possibly be there legitimately every time I have to … go."

Don lowered his gaze to meet Denton's.

"Uh huh. And that means?"

"That means the cleaning lady is closing the men's room on purpose."

Don stared at Denton for several seconds. Finally, he closed his door and returned to his desk. He dropped back into his chair and began to rub his temples as Denton sat back down in front of him.

"The cleaning lady … is closing the men's room … on purpose."

"Yes."

"Well, I apologize for the stupidity of this question, but … why is she doing that?"

Denton shrugged and turned another page in his book. "I don't know, but it doesn't happen on her days off. The cleaning crew comes every forty minutes, like clockwork."

"You've stalked the whole crew."

"Well, that's a bit of a poor word choice. I … *monitored* them."

"I can't believe I'm even having this conversation," Fowler said, rising again. "Do you have any idea what would happen if someone caught you spying on the cleaning crew?"

"*Monitoring*," Denton corrected.

"Call it whatever you want – do you understand the trouble you could get in?"

"I think it's fairly obvious that I do not."

His boss shook his head and reached into his desk drawer, retrieving a thin manila folder. He opened it.

"Will Johnson," he read from the file. "Denton Rourke proved Johnson was the 'Lunch Lifter' who'd been stealing people's food from the break room refrigerator."

"Yep," Denton nodded.

"By putting this sign on the fridge door," Fowler added, holding up a bright orange sign.

EMERGENCY!
MISSING FROM FRIDGE:
ARSENIC-LACED TURKEY SANDWICH
FOR SON'S SCIENCE PROJECT
IF YOU ATE THIS, PLEASE CALL ME
THEN IF STILL CONSCIOUS, CALL A HOSPITAL.

"Worked like a charm," Denton said.

"Yes, until he sued us for the panic attack your little stunt caused."

Fowler flipped the page before Denton could retort.

"Denise Jamison in Accounting: Filed for – and received – paid mental anguish leave.

"That wasn't my fault," Denton said.

"I sent you to cover the executive council meeting, during which you accidentally proved her involvement in an affair with the vice president of sales. That one almost got you fired."

"I'm still not sure how we ever got that far off the agenda," Denton said.

Fowler continued to flip pages. "There are four – four different reports you've filed which have implicated employees in nefarious plots."

"And I've been right every time."

"That's starting to matter less and less," Fowler said. He closed the file and looked at Denton.

"Denton, I know this adjustment hasn't been easy – I didn't expect it would be. But you've been here six months now. I think I've cut you a lot of slack."

"You have," Denton acknowledged.

Fowler nodded. "You're a good employee, and I think you have a lot of potential."

"Thank you."

"Wait – I'm just getting to the 'but' part of this."

Denton waited. His boss pointed at him.

"But if you don't leave the cleaning crew alone, I'm going to turn this over to HR and let Rompeaux deal with you."

Denton shuddered at the name. "But this is a solid lead."

Fowler stood up and pounded his index finger down repeatedly on Denton's file.

"You see a dozen solid leads around every corner, Denton. You've got something on everyone, don't you? Tell me, what have you got on me?"

Denton straightened in his chair. He opened his notebook and flipped through a few pages. He ran his finger down a page before finally stopping.

"You played hooky on a Thursday three weeks ago. Said you were going to the doctor for a prostate exam, but you played golf and then went to the movies."

Fowler continued to stand and stare at his employee.

"How do you know that?"

"Because the day you were out it was sunny and ninety degrees. The next day you showed up and your right hand was sunburned, but your left hand – your golf glove hand – was white. Plus, you used the prostate exam excuse the first week I was here. The company's health plan only pays for one a year, and you're too much of a cheapskate to pay for a second one out of your own pocket, no matter how much you enjoyed it the first time."

Fowler added a scowl to his stare. He put his hands on his hips.

"And the movie?" he asked.

Denton shrugged. "That's just a guess. What else would you do with half a day to kill in the middle of the week?"

Fowler worked hard on his frown, but could not hold it. He sat back down and looked down at his files, hiding his grin.

"Speaking of Rompeaux, you're missing his meeting." he asked.

"Yes. Why?"

"Get in there. It's important," Fowler said.

Denton rose and headed for the door. As he opened it, he turned back to his boss.

"I know what it's about," he said.

"Do you?" Fowler asked, eyebrows raised.

"Yes," Denton said. "And if you trust me so much, you should have told me first."

Denton exited without waiting for a response, closing the door quietly as he departed.

CHAPTER 2

Marcus Rompeaux blotted his brow with an already overly damp napkin and tried to ignore the single drop of cool sweat he felt trickling down his spine and into his pants. He took a deep breath of stale air. The room felt like a sauna.

"And, at the end of the day, it is what it is," he said.

He stared out from behind the podium at the expressionless faces and wondered if his audience noticed the thick, suffocating temperature as well. How could he perspire so much? He knew the sweating made him look dishonest. The fact that he worked in HR didn't help, either. He knew the odds of these people trusting him were on par with the odds they'd allow their children to be babysat by a lion.

Rompeaux shifted his remarkable girth forward and inhaled deeply, trying with all his might not to look like a sweaty blowfish in the process.

At a solid five-foot, two inches, his frame found the three hundred-plus pounds he asked it to support a problematic task. And while some people carried their extra weight in their gut, or their calves, or their backsides, Rompeaux's excess had managed a rather perfect distribution so that so that every part of his body looked fat.

His fingers looked like Vienna sausages. His face appeared filled to maximum capacity so that even his eyes seemed to bulge out due to hidden pockets of flab. His bulbous nose, round glasses, and perfectly round, bald head ensured that not a single crisp angle could be found anywhere on his person. His bushy gray-brown mustache matched the hair around the crown of his head, which was cut too short and stood up in sharp, angry spikes.

And, sadly, when he took a deep breath, eyes wide in terror, he most certainly looked like a sort of floundering puffer fish or some other graceless sea creature.

He exhaled and tried again to pat away the sweat running down his forehead. He clicked a button on his pointer and watched the slide behind him change. He spoke as confidently as he could.

"And teamwork is the one thing we, as a team, can work on."

Rompeaux pointed at the big, boring graphic behind him which repeated the preposterous phrase. He gauged the expressions of his audience members, relieved at his apparent success at lulling them into a dreamlike trance.

No one asked questions, because no one paid attention – presumably to avoid the risk of collapsing into a protective coma. And as the HR leader for several lines of business in the United Alliance Bank family, Marcus Rompeaux considered that a success.

Nobody liked Human Resources, which meant for the most part everyone left him alone. And while this worked for Rompeaux, United Alliance's Senior HR people found the lack of employee participation very disconcerting. With budgets already tight, HR needed to prove its use beyond filing paperwork for new hires and terminations, and producing employee informational videos on the dangers of touching one another, farting too loudly in cubicles, and the like.

Marcus Rompeaux didn't care one way or the other, and half-hoped someone *would* scuttle his department, preferably in the next twenty minutes. He clicked the button on his pointer once more and gestured toward the screen as it changed again.

"After all, there is no *I* in *Team,"* he said as though the statement ranked among the most profound ever uttered in civilization's history. "And here at United Alliance Bank, there is no *Team* without *U*."

Audible groans erupted throughout the room, though quiet enough that the presenter could not pinpoint their specific locations. He found this good. Very good.

Hooray for the plan!

The bloated lecturer aimed his pointer toward the screen for another round of enlightening platitudes. Then a door at the back of the room opened and Rompeaux turned to glare at the latecomer. But his expression changed to chagrin and mild panic as Denton Rourke came through the door.

Rompeaux felt his shoulders sag and his excitement deflating.

"I thought Fridays were supposed to be easy," he muttered to himself.

# # #

GAVIN SPINCER TURNED THE KEY in the lock and pushed the front door open, lifting up on the handle to keep the warped bottom from scraping against the floor.

He waited in the doorway a moment, allowing his nose to adjust to the foul stench escaping from inside. Most people would instantly assume the smell came from some *thing* that had died inside of some *other* thing which had itself perished by falling into a pot of boiling cabbage several months earlier. Spincer just knew it as the smell of home.

Most days he didn't give much thought to his living conditions beyond the most basic precaution of making sure the house wasn't actually on fire before he went to sleep. But this Friday morning represented a new beginning for Gavin Spincer. So on this special day, he cared even less.

"At last," he said in a whispered tone which might have concerned anyone who accidentally got close enough to him to hear. "It begins."

The white plastic bag in his left hand crinkled excitedly as Spincer made his way to his computer. He sat down, pushed a mountain of magazines, old pizza boxes, and empty energy drink cans onto the floor and placed the bag on the brown, sticky desktop.

"Gadsden the Mighty," he announced, "prepare for your rebirth!"

He ran a hand through his greasy blonde hair and smiled at the bag. After a brief moment of reverence, he grabbed the bag, ripped its contents from inside, and hoisted it skyward.

"To the Genesis!" he cried out.

He lowered the box and ran his fingers over the raised gold lettering as he read.

WIZARD QUEST CRAFT: THE GENESIS

For most in the online gaming world, the debut of Wizard Quest Craft simply offered *another* new online "world" where people from all over the globe could sort of come together and kind of embark on magical quests, fight goblins, uncover treasure, and – most definitely – wear shiny armor.

Recent sales figures from across the planet showed online fantasy worlds generating millions in monthly subscription fees from approximately eighty bazillion men and nearly fourteen women.

For the past six years, Gavin had dedicated a disturbingly large portion of his life to the most popular of all online worlds, "Warlords and Wizards." Between game play, game discussions, and game planning, Spincer had spent roughly as much time on W2 (as its followers called it) as a medical student spent to get a degree, join a hospital staff, save lives, and retire.

Spincer considered himself a W2 God. His character, "Gadsden the Mighty" boasted considerable power as a 140th level Ranger and – all things considered – should have enjoyed immense popularity among other W2 fans. Unfortunately, Spincer's complete lack of social skills in the real world translated near perfectly in W2 as well. Spincer upset everyone he came into contact with in the online world via his constant taunts, provocations, and purposeful abandonment of team mates during battles so he could watch the other players get killed and laugh at them after their characters regenerated.

But after more than half a decade of getting away with alienating residents of the premier online universe, Gavin Spincer finally went too far.

After months of work, he managed to hack the game's code and promptly gave his character the power to decapitate priests – the game's only character class who could not fight and thus did not take damage. Not stopping there, he also gave himself the ability to disrobe female characters and grope them repeatedly.

The immediacy of the retaliation surprised and pleased Spincer. Less than three hours after he began his perverted, bloodthirsty quest, the Warlords and Wizards administrators froze Gadsden the Mighty inside an empty cavern. They then allowed players to line up and hack him into very small bits.

Gavin enjoyed watching the spectacle, until he realized that Gadsden the Mighty, though laying in a hundred bloody pieces on the ground wasn't losing health points, and therefore could not regenerate. When he tried restarting the game, Spincer found he could only return to Gadsden's remains, next to which a large white board had been built so players could write the most obscene epitaphs to their loathsome colleague.

Incensed, Spincer restarted the game and created a new Gadsden. Then he watched as his new Ranger appeared – frozen in place – right next to the original Gadsden's mound of parts. As players once again lined up to make another neat pile, Spincer noticed that the online administrators had changed Gadsden the Mighty's name. He read the new moniker in horror:

GADSDEN THE BANNED

The following two months marked a low point in Spincer's life, as he split his time between lying under his computer table in a ball, cursing and crying, and lying in his bed, cursing and crying. Occasionally he would try another W2 login, get the same result, and then return to the darkness and despair of the real world.

But the announcement of Wizard Quest Craft changed everything. The all new fantasy world touted as bigger, bolder, and better than W2 could ever be, promised Gavin Spincer a new start. He had barely slept in the last days before its official release and felt no guilt about calling in sick to his IT job at United Alliance Bank so that he could camp out at the store overnight and ensure he received one of the first copies when they went on sale the next morning.

Now, desperately sleep deprived and frantic to restart his online life, Spincer tore through the cellophane packaging, pulled the box apart and removed the shiny CD from its sleeve. He turned toward his computer and prepared to load Wizard Quest Craft, but stopped for a moment to focus on something peculiar which caught his eye.

He cocked his head as he looked closely at his telephone answering machine. He narrowed his eyes in suspicion. The machine, as benign as any other answering machine, didn't really deserve such paranoid scrutiny. It merely wanted its owner to know that while he'd been out purchasing his fancy new game, someone had called and left him a message.

Spincer understood this. However, since no one *ever* called him, he had no choice but to respond to the machine's efforts with severe distrust.

Finally, he clicked the button and listened to the message. Slightly more than forty-five seconds later, the machine clicked off and Spincer's expression remained unchanged. He pressed the replay button and listened again. And when the machine clicked off, he pressed the button and listened to it a third time, his face reddening.

Spincer sat and quietly continued this ritual until he'd heard the message 31 times. Finally he let the machine click off, and sat and stared at nothing. After ten minutes of careful contemplation he stood up, placed the game CD back in its sleeve, put it back in the box, and wrapped it back up in the white crinkly bag. Then he threw it against the wall and watched it drop onto the drab, brown carpet.

Spincer reached into a laptop case on the floor and pulled out his work computer. He lifted the lid and began the login process.

"New game to play," he hissed.

# # #

MARCUS ROMPEAUX GATHERED HIMSELF and pointed at Denton.

"Mr. Rourke, you are *very* late," he scolded. "You missed nearly the entire presentation!"

"Well then my timing is getting better," Denton smiled as he grabbed a bagel off a plastic tray. Rompeaux noticed the chuckling around the room and bristled.

"Yes, yes, Mr. Rourke. I think we've established – on numerous occasions – that you are a very funny person. With that out of the way, would you be kind enough to find a seat so we may continue?"

"Sure," Denton said as he poured himself a cup of black coffee from a decanter.

Then Rompeaux watched in horror as the late arrival made his way up the middle aisle and took a seat on the front row directly in front of him.

No one ever willingly sat on the front row during an HR presentation. Worse, no one ever smiled during his meetings – especially not with an idiotic grin like Rourke's. Sweat appeared once more on Rompeaux's shiny head. The air – somehow – got thicker. He took another deep, blowfish-like breath, and turned to the screen.

"Now—"

"I have a question," Denton's bagel-filled mouth announced with a raised hand. Rompeaux did his best not to allow his eyes to bulge, and instead rolled them skyward.

"Yes, Mr. Rourke?"

"You said earlier that there was no team without you," Denton began.

Rompeaux smiled and spoke as though he were humoring a child.

"It was just a metaphor, Mr. Rourke," he explained.

"Actually it was just a cliché, Mr. Rompeaux," Denton replied. "A metaphor is like, *The long arm of the law*, or *A sea of trouble*, or *The shocked stare of the sweaty man-walrus.*"

A chorus of gasps and quiet laughter sucked more air out of the room as Denton smiled and took another sip of his coffee and shrugged.

"I'm not sure that last one is legitimate," he said. "It just came to me for some inexplicable reason."

Rompeaux's mouth dropped open and his eyes shifted to full bulge as he stood frozen at the podium, staring in the direction of the awful man in the first row who sat back and drank his coffee. After several awkward moments, someone in the audience cleared their throat loudly. Rompeaux blinked, but did not move. He continued to stare at Denton. Finally, his lips moved almost imperceptibly.

"What," he spoke slowly, "is your question?"

Denton put his coffee down and stood up.

"Uh, I was just wondering what percentage of this department you were laying off today."

All eyes turned toward Denton. Then, in an incredible feat of synchronization, they turned in unison to stare at the profusely moist Marcus Rompeaux.

"Mr. Rourke, you know we do not comment on rumors and speculation," he tried.

"And that is a very good policy," Denton said with a nod. "But I'm not speculating. You've got 36 employees in here, and nobody who isn't in here is at their desk. So I figure you're in charge of giving us a great little *teamwork wins* speech while your crew hands out severance packages to the rest of the department."

Though the room had fallen deathly silent, Rompeaux felt he could hear anger and fear emanating from his audience. Denton continued.

"So, how many? Ten percent? Fifteen?"

"Twenty-five," Rompeaux heard himself blurt out.

The crowd met the sudden admission with angry murmurs and a few non-murmured expletives. Denton smiled, waved and sat back down.

"Okay. So the whole, *It's not a team without you* is really more like, *It's a team without them*," he corrected.

The murmurs and agitation grew louder. Rompeaux smiled uncomfortably at the crowd. In an effort to extend an olive branch, he made a big deal of turning to the PowerPoint presentation and shutting it off. Then he turned back to the podium and smiled at his audience.

"I'd like to point out that there are job eliminations in a variety of areas today, not just yours. And of course, the bright side is that all of *you* are still employed."

Only one person smiled back as he drank his coffee and gave the man a big thumbs up.

As a member of the Human Resources team, Rompeaux had been trained not to hate people. He'd been to countless seminars on dealing with uncooperative employees and conflicting personalities, each encouraging the seeking of common ground and common goals. But at that moment, Rompeaux truly believed it would have been far more productive for him to have spent all those nights and weekends attending classes on lethal Karate instead.

Rompeaux tried to smile at his audience.

"Well, I believe this is a good spot in which to end the session, so you're free to go. I'd like to ask that you think of your colleagues in this difficult time, and try to keep the farewells simple and quiet."

"Screw you, Rom*putz*!" an anonymous voice offered. Rompeaux lowered his head.

"Yes, well, done and done, I'd say," he replied, looking back at Denton.

Denton stopped smiling. He began to speak, but Rompeaux turned and made his way slowly toward a side exit.

As Denton watched the man lumber away, Frederick Maxton dropped into the seat next to him. He grabbed a piece of Denton's bagel and popped it into his mouth.

Well," he said between chews, "this will not help sales of your book, *How to Not be an Ass.*"

"Shut up, Fred," Denton said, still watching Rompeaux's disappearing figure.

Fred smiled. "Hey, come on," he said. "Feel bad later. Remember – we still have jobs."

Fred rose and moved toward the back auditorium exit. Denton sighed, got up, and followed him, trying to prepare for a series of uncomfortable handshakes and best-of-luck wishes to his new former colleagues.

As he walked toward his department, he told himself it was still better than being punched and shot by thugs or harangued by asinine community college administrators. By the time he turned the corner into his area, he'd pretty much convinced himself he was right.

Then he heard the crying. And he knew he was a damn idiot.

CHAPTER 3

Two hours later, with the building clear of all "impacted" employees, Denton sat in an empty break room drinking a cup of the scorched coffee which the company generously made available throughout the day at no charge. He stared at the television and tried to focus on the business report. Across the short hallway, the sound of a toilet flushing interrupted another sip of his acidic java. He cast an unkind eye toward the men's and women's restroom doors and wondered for the nine hundredth time why the architects of the United Alliance Bank building had placed the room where food and drink were consumed directly across from – and within unfortunate earshot of – rooms visited for starkly opposite motives. It certainly didn't make either set of patrons very comfortable, knowing each could hear the other from where they respectively stood and/or sat.

Denton shook his head and returned to the television. A serious-looking man read his serious script with intense seriousness. The graphic below him reinforced the non-trivial theme.

SPECIAL REPORT:
UNITED ALLIANCE BANK'S WOES MOUNT

Denton stood and turned up the sound.

"…and with several board members now resigning, it seems

United Alliance Bank's troubles just won't stop piling up," the anchor reported. Denton thought the man's grave tone seemed tinged with just a hint of pleasure, like he'd just reported that his ex-wife had been run over by a cement truck, thereby negating future alimony payments.

"Sources close to the struggling bank say its next earnings report will once again show the company losing money – a lot of money – even as their cross street rival, Huntsman Bank, reports continued growth under the majestic leadership of Chief Executive Officer Joseph Handel."

Denton shook his head as Fred Maxton entered, grabbed a cup of coffee and took the seat next to him.

"He just said, 'majestic,' didn't he?"

Denton nodded as the television anchor continued.

"...while sources close to United Alliance indicate another round of layoffs may be in the planning."

"Wow, these guys are really up to speed," Fred cracked. He looked at Denton. "Be glad you got in here when you did."

"I'm trying," Denton said, having not yet classified the major changes of the past six months as either good or bad.

Fresh off solving his biggest, his most glamorous, and – as luck would have it – his first major case, Denton had hoped to quit his job as a community college teacher and open up shop as a full-time detective. He figured saving iconic rock-and-roll band The Dash from a grisly on-stage death would generate some serious buzz and allow him to pick and choose high-end cases instead of waiting on the police department to dole out jobs which more often than not fell in a category somewhere between insignificant and criminally mundane.

So Denton had smiled for all the television cameras and answered all the pointless questions during the "local hero" pieces on the morning shows. He took care to speak slowly and clearly, and made sure to mention he would be accepting new cases immediately.

But as the details of Denton's success played out in the media, one minor item he'd requested they not focus on became the source of great amusement: the small, insignificant fact that he'd kind of blown up his last client.

Of course, no one blamed Denton for the fact that the man who'd hired him to uncover the mysterious happenings in the Palladium Music Theatre turned out to be the same man plotting to kill off a beloved rock band. However, potential clients didn't seem keen on the idea that Denton might implicate and/or off them during an investigation. As such, the anticipated work offers never materialized.

Adding to Denton's troubles, the dean of Powell Community College read some of the in-depth reporting on Denton's adventures and realized rather quickly that the school had been paying their part-time English professor to work on his alternative career. He fired Denton via a form letter.

The police department had reacted in a similar fashion. Sergeant Tim Sowell's Captain, embarrassed by the public revelation of the amount of responsibility his department had put on Sowell without promoting him to Lieutenant, and angered by an amateur's access to police resources, expressly forbade the further hiring of Denton.

So with no job, a non-existent client list and very existent bills, Denton had no choice but to join the mainstream work force. To his surprise, he found United Alliance Bank eager to bring him on board. The move also came as something of a surprise to the bank's parent company, United Alliance Insurance, given that Denton's big case had implicated one of its high-ranking executives in a large-scale fraud scheme. Most on the board expressed concern, explaining that the company didn't normally award those who cost them millions in fines with full-time jobs and health benefits. But after the presenter's fifteenth PowerPoint slide explaining the goodwill such a move would generate, the board, having already forgotten the original topic and eager to argue about lunch venues, approved Fred Maxton's proposal and sent him away.

So Denton took his hyper-speculative, overly keen mind to the card fraud department and found almost instantly that most cases resolved themselves with just a little advice like, "Don't give your credit card to your ex-husband," or, "Free trial offers don't require your Social Security Number."

Now, half a year later, Denton found himself far from the bright lights of celebrity sleuthing as he sat in a dull, drab break room with bad coffee, unfortunate lavatory acoustics, and a good friend.

Fred nudged Denton.

"Look!" he urged as he pointed at the screen. Denton refocused on the network, which had shifted to a live report from the street. Denton recognized the front of their own United Alliance Bank building rising tall behind the ridiculously handsome reporter.

"And we're on TV," Fred noted. "With Russell Banfield – again."

"I'm sure it won't be as bad as last time," Denton said.

Fred shrugged. "As long as Peanut isn't taking a break downstairs, I suppose."

Weeks earlier, 67-year old Telephone Banker Virginia "Peanut" Reilly watched Banfield's live report while she ate her yogurt in a break room just off the main lobby. As the reporter attacked her company for the fourth day in a row, the 4' 11" grandmother of seven walked out of the building, strolled directly over to Banfield, and expressed her displeasure with him by tossing vanilla yogurt on his jacket and pants during the live broadcast. In an interview later with a rival network, Peanut simply shrugged and said it seemed like the fastest way to submit her feedback.

Denton smiled. "I heard she brought clam chowder today."

"Shut up," Fred said with a slightly worried grin.

When UAB brought Denton on, Fred sought him out so he could make sure the mid-level employee with the highest profile knew what to expect around the office. Finding they had similar tastes in music, movies, and humor, they hit it off immediately and started spending most lunch and break times together.

With his thick black hair, dark eyes, and effortless style, Maxton fit the public relations mold perfectly. Denton marveled at Fred's ability to sound as cool as he looked in every situation – mostly because he knew how the guy acted the rest of the time. For his part, Fred Maxton grew up a huge fan of The Dash, and marveled at Denton's heroic history almost daily. And after meeting Denton's fiancée, Beth, and hearing their story, Fred told Denton that he once again believed in the miracle of romance. Denton suggested Fred hold off on that faith until he himself actually found a girlfriend.

Hair unmoved by the morning breeze, Banfield continued his somber assessment.

"...which is why, as I take a pause and think back over the last two years, I'm in awe of the quickness of the turn of fortunes of United Alliance Bank."

"Horrible sentence structure," Denton commented.

"God-awful tie and jacket combo," Fred added.

A few moments later Fred bolted upright, leaned forward in his seat, and focused hard on the television. Denton looked at Fred, then back at the TV. He watched as his friend slumped back in his seat and buried his face in his hands.

"Is that ...?" Denton asked, trailing off.

"Yes," Fred's muffled voice came through his fingers. "Tell me when it's over."

Denton looked at the TV again. In the background of the shot, a tall, thin man with wiry salt and pepper hair approached Banfield. He wore a light-tan suit, a white shirt with a red tie, and a positively sublime smile.

Denton kept watching as the man moved smoothly across the screen and somehow ended up right next to the talking head. For more than half a minute the entire viewing audience – except for Fred – watched as United Alliance Bank CEO Ohnemus Parker quietly and happily stood next to the oblivious reporter and listened to him insult the company's structure, efficiency, and management.

"What's he doing?" Fred asked, still hiding his eyes.

"He's holding a cup of yogurt," Denton said.

Fred dropped his hands and shot a scolding look at his friend.

"This isn't funny, Denton. He could get everyone in trouble if he says something that's not approved for public dissemination."

Denton pointed at the television and Fred turned in time to see Banfield finally notice Parker at his side. The audience also witnessed something they hadn't seen in the five years Banfield had covered business news: five seconds of Banfield not talking.

After a couple of uncomfortable laughs, Banfield collected himself and smiled for the camera.

"Well, ladies and gentlemen, this is certainly a surprise – joining me right here live is none other than UAB's CEO Mr. Ohnemus Parker!"

"Please don't speak, please don't speak," Fred begged toward the television. The television refused to lend a hand.

"Hello, Russell," Parker said with a relaxed and easy going kindness. "How are you?"

Banfield smiled for a moment. Few executives he ever spoke with bothered to remember his name. But he recovered quickly from the kindness and turned serious once more.

"Mr. Parker we've all heard the reports, the rumors and the second guesses about United Alliance Bank's solvency and stability. Let's hear it from the horse's mouth, as they say. Is UAB in trouble?"

As Fred held his breath, Denton looked around and realized the once empty break room had filled almost to capacity, with all eyes quietly focused on Parker's smiling face.

"Russell, like a lot of companies these days – and a lot of banks specifically, we're dealing with some bad assets that are holding us down. Now the good news is that we've got a lot of *good* assets as well. We've got a great commercial deposit business, and our parent company is strong, too," Parker said as he continued to smile.

"And what of the rumors that there will be another round of layoffs?" Banfield asked.

"You mean besides the one today?"

"Oh God," Fred muttered. He fell back into his seat.

On the television, Banfield stared, dumbstruck.

"Uh … the one today?" he asked.

"Yes. Well, Russell, we don't anticipate any further reductions in staffing. We consider them a painful, difficult way to do business. But we are pursuing all our options as we work to keep UAB moving forward."

"How do you respond to shareholders who say that management is the problem, and that you, for one, have allowed things to go so wrong for a bank that as recently as two years ago was one of the strongest in the country?"

Parker's smile didn't fade or waver. "Russell, that's a fair question. And that's really why I'm out here today. I and my entire staff have been working tirelessly to find smarter ways to do business so we can keep people employed and turn our profits around. So today I'm announcing a special hotline where stockholders and concerned citizens can call and talk to my personal assistant, Joe. Joe will take down all your questions and make sure I receive them post haste."

"What the hell is he doing?" Fred asked. Denton simply continued to stare. Having only been with United Alliance a short time, he found himself able to watch more out of curiosity than concern. So far, he liked Parker.

On screen, Parker reached into his pocket and removed a folded piece of notebook paper. He opened it up and held it in front of the camera, showing the television audience a ten-digit phone number neatly written in black marker.

"Now, if you will call this number and talk to Joe, he'll take care of all your needs and questions."

Fred pointed at the numbers, counting them off silently. Then he reached into his pocket and produced a small, black notebook. He flipped furiously through it and stopped on a page near the middle. He looked down and then back up at the television just in time to see Parker shake Banfield's hand and wander off. He closed the book and bolted from his seat.

"What's up?" Denton asked. Fred stopped and turned to him.

"That's not Parker's personal line at UAB he just gave out to a million viewers," he said.

Fred's head sunk. "It's Joseph Handel's personal line – at Huntsman."

Without another word, Maxton turned and left. Denton stood up and approached the coffee maker. He smiled as he poured another cup.

Now he *really* liked Ohnemus Parker.

# # #

PHILLIP ANDERSON ALSO LIKED OHNEMUS PARKER, but found himself wondering if he should blame the quirky CEO for his current predicament.

A few minutes earlier, Anderson sat in a dive bar as just another anonymous customer sipping watered down vodka tonics and watching Russell Banfield on the television. He rolled his eyes as Banfield shook his head gravely and used words like, "disaster" and "crumbling," – all with "United Alliance Bank" as the preface.

He sighed and returned to his terrible drink, which he did not find quite terrible enough to complain about. Also making his list of not worth mentioning to management: the room's impressive collection of dirt, grime, and discolored stains he felt fairly certain were blood. When you wanted to drink that early in the day, you couldn't afford to get picky.

The bartender watched the television a few seconds longer before turning away with a shake of his own head.

"Can you believe these guys?" he asked, jamming a thumb toward the TV. "How do you drive a multi-billion-dollar bank into the ground without someone noticing until it gets *this* bad?"

"Very carefully," Anderson quipped and took a long draw from his glass. He wiped a napkin over his balding head and signaled for another round as he tried to push from his mind the number of UAB employees receiving their notice.

The bartender returned with a different glass – *different*, Anderson noted, not being the same as *clean*.

"I think about all the bad decisions these guys made, and all the men and women they're now putting on the streets," the bartender said.

Anderson's eyes popped open and he stared at his server. Did the man know *nothing* about proper bartender etiquette? Anderson wanted words of pithy wisdom. He needed empty platitudes and placations. Instead, he now found his drink tainted with visions of breadlines, soup kitchens, and desperate people forced to eat their own shoes.

Anderson shook the increasingly ridiculous images from his head. It wouldn't be at all like that. Most of them would keep their jobs, he knew that. He smiled uneasily.

"We don't really make good or bad decisions," he said. "We simply make *decisions*, and we leave the 'good' or 'bad' of them for others to determine based on outcomes."

The bartender nodded. "Like the football coach who goes for the win instead of the tie on the last play of the game. If they win, his decision was good. If they lose, it was bad."

Anderson took a sip and nodded. "Precisely," he said, wiping his lips on his sleeve.

He looked back at the television. Russell Banfield now stood in front of a giant financial chart which sported a bright red arrow plummeting downward. Anderson shook his head and wished very earnestly that someone would throw something at the pompous talking head much stronger than vanilla yogurt. Like volcanic lava.

He stared into the bottom of his glass and listened not to Banfield, but to his own words. Then with a purposeful nod, Anderson stood up and retreated to a table. He pulled out his phone and typed furiously. After a good ten minutes of his thumbs flying around the keyboard, he pocketed the device once more and returned to his stool.

"The point is," Anderson continued, "there's no reason to ask if a decision was good or bad. If you made the right decision, the outcome means very little."

"You're getting pretty deep for this place," the bartender said with a smile.

Anderson chuckled. "Sometimes, things go too far. Outcomes blur your focus and before you know it the success of that outcome means more to you than whether your decisions – your actions – were the right ones. Sometimes you don't see that until it's too late."

Anderson finished his drink. He rose, put on his glasses and handed the man his credit card. The bartender slid the card through the reader and looked at his customer.

"Sounds like you're wrestling with a decision yourself."

"Not anymore," Anderson smiled. "Just wondering about the outcome."

The bartender smiled and looked at the television report again.

"You know, I used to work at UAB, if you can believe it – for six years. My entire team got let go a couple of months ago."

Anderson looked at him grimly. Then he reached into his pocket, retrieved a handful of $100 bills and deposited them in the tip jar.

"I can believe it," he said.

The bartender put up his hands. "Hey, hey. You don't have to do that. I got a decent package—"

"It's not charity," Anderson cut him off. "It's payment for information."

"What information?"

Anderson headed for the exit. At the door he turned back and smiled through sad eyes. "The confirmation of a decision."

He gave the bartender a friendly nod, and disappeared into the street.

Now, under the dull hum of a pale blue neon bar sign, Phillip Anderson found Ohnemus Parker slipping from his thoughts. And the rain that drenched him from head to toe didn't register as even a minor concern. In fact, all his troubles had faded so that he could focus his attention solely on the rope that, no matter how he twisted, continued to constrict around his neck. The edges of his vision darkened and his head bubbled with pain and pressure as his eyes instinctively closed for fear of bursting. In the final moments of helpless thrusting, Anderson's mind wandered away from his body's dismal position. He wondered how he could feel so light and warm. He wondered whether he knew his assailant. He wondered if his murder would eventually constitute a correct decision, or just a successful outcome.

Then he didn't wonder anything at all.

CHAPTER 4

Denton sat at his desk and carefully reviewed his Friday productivity. So far he'd irritated his boss, failed to bust the crazy cleaning woman, foiled Rompeaux's efforts at an orderly layoff, and explained to a high-revenue UAB customer that the hotel charges on his credit card were courtesy of his wife. And he'd also mentioned to the man that she was probably *not* using the rooms by herself.

All in all, he'd accomplished a lot for one day, and it seemed more than reasonable that he should sneak out and go see Beth at her apartment during lunch.

As he tread quickly toward his car using Fred's newspaper as an umbrella, Denton's good friend self doubt stopped in for a chat. By the time he'd pulled out of the parking lot, his surprise visit to Beth sounded like a slightly worse idea than eating the exposed foam sticking out of his cracked passenger seat for lunch.

Denton thought about the wedding date he had yet to come up with and how sore a point it had rightfully become for his ultra-patient fiancée.

He wanted to marry her and he made sure to tell her as often as possible. But his sudden loss of employment prospects following his first case forced a complete change in his thought process. Now, with his current company's financial position looking about as stable as an intoxicated giraffe, Denton worried about marrying Beth and then immediately losing *another* job. He wanted to feel secure in his work and confident about his ability to take care of her properly.

Denton had shared the basics of this concern with Beth, and following some light laughter she had shared with him the basics of independent women and a reminder of the millennium they currently occupied. He knew what she said made sense, but it did little to ease his mind. Denton also knew that the longer he continued down his current road of indecision, the more likely he'd find himself driving off a cliff.

So naturally Denton detoured onto a course even more dangerous as he vetoed suggested dates by citing his work schedule, bad weather fears, and even conflicts with his father's availability.

Of course, Connor Rourke knew nothing of his son's dastardly use of him as an excuse to delay picking a date. And if he found out, Denton knew his reaction would involve the phrase, "my Irish boot," the location, "your arse," and a colorful strategy of placing one very far inside the other.

For the remainder of the drive, Denton worked very hard at thinking of more pleasant things, such as large numbers of his colleagues being unemployed, his boss suspecting him of being insane, and a malicious cleaning woman hell-bent on giving him a bladder infection.

He parked at Beth's apartment complex and walked quickly to her door. He unlocked it and knocked as he entered.

"Hello, Beth?" he called out as he closed the door.

Beth Ingraham came out of her bedroom, looking as dazzling as ever to Denton. Her straight blonde hair hung across her face and dropped onto her shoulders perfectly. He smiled and marveled at her sense of style. Her jeans in a perfect color of blue hugging her hips and a white top with a subtly dropped neckline made her look like she just came from a department store photo shoot. Denton noted yet again the great shape she kept herself in, and then remembered his "engagement diet" for the first time all week.

Beth smiled at him, her blue eyes sparkling.

"Oh, hello, Fraud Officer Rourke," she toyed in her British accent, "Have I done something wrong? Are you here to interrogate me?"

Denton narrowed his eyes at her and smiled. "Well I certainly hope it comes to that, Ms. Ingraham."

"*Miss* Ingraham," she corrected. Denton thought he heard a small reminder in her playful tone, but didn't follow that path. He kissed her and smiled wearily.

"Have you seen the news this morning?" he asked.

Beth shook her head. "No, right now it's still 'All thesis, all the time,' I'm afraid."

Denton nodded. The end of Beth's academic career stood just weeks away and she spent most of her free time working to complete her MBA in International Business.

"We had another round of layoffs this morning," he said.

Beth's mouth fell open. "And you …" she didn't want to ask.

Denton shook his head. "No, no – I'm safe. But it's been a rough day and I needed to get away for a few minutes. I couldn't think of anything better than seeing you."

Beth smiled and gave him a long hug. When she released him, she winked.

"How could anyone ever let *you* go?" she asked.

Denton smiled as he made his way to the fridge and opened it to survey his options.

"Cute," he said. "If only you were in charge of my career."

"Give me another year or so," she said. She backed up toward the bedroom. "I need to finish getting ready. I'll be right out. Make yourself a sandwich or whatnot. And don't leave – I need to talk to you about this weekend."

Denton closed the refrigerator.

"So, you're expecting company. Who is it?" he asked.

Beth stopped dead. She turned slowly.

"Excuse me?"

Denton began to point around the room.

"You've dusted the ceiling fan blades, hung up a generic picture of *boats* – which I know you hate, so I'm guessing it was a gift from the surprise guest. And you've cleaned the fridge from top to bottom and stocked it with a bunch of weird meats and cheeses you and I have never bought. And there's English tea next to the stove."

"I *hate* when you do that, Denton," she said with a pout.

"I'd say he's British, and coming in *from* the UK tonight. And, of course, that he's a *he*."

"How could you know *all that*?" she demanded.

Denton tapped the freezer door. "You've got British Airways flight information written down."

Beth smiled and slowly walked towards him.

"Denton, would you like to know who's coming in?" she asked in a rather enticing whisper.

"Uh, yes?"

She stopped directly in front of him, their bodies nearly touching. She put her soft hand on his face, pulled him to her, and kissed him for what Denton estimated was about eleven hours.

Finally, she pulled away and bit her bottom lip.

"I'm not telling yet. Maybe when I come back out," she teased.

"I *hate* when you do that, Beth," he said.

"No, you don't." And with a wink, she trotted off to her bedroom and closed the door.

Denton shook his head with an uneasy grin. He reopened the fridge and spent the next few quiet minutes happily humming as he built a marvelous capicola and mozzarella sandwich. When he deemed it complete, he placed it on the table and smiled. He tried to gauge how much of the joy of the sandwich stemmed from the glorious ingredients and how much from the idea he that was going to eat some other guy's food.

As he sat down in front of his masterpiece, the doorbell rang. Beth did not appear from the bedroom, so Denton shrugged and walked over to the door. He opened it wide and made eye contact with a tall, thin man in a brown checked suit. His bald head and narrow eyes looked down at Denton past a somewhat pronounced nose.

"You're not Elizabeth," the man said with an English accent and a disapproving tone.

"*Well done*, sir," Denton replied. "You'd be surprised how many people confuse us at first glance."

"Where is Elizabeth?" the man asked.

"May I ask who is inquiring?"

"You may."

Denton stood and looked at the man. The man looked back in silence. A half a minute went by before Denton sighed.

"*Who* is inquiring?" he said with a roll of his eyes.

"Archibald Ingraham," the man replied.

Denton felt his muscles tense.

"Ingrah—"

"Her father," the man nodded his confirmation.

"Of course."

"And now," Archibald said, "may *I* inquire as to why an unkempt man is answering my daughter's door in the middle of a workday?"

Denton looked down at his Friday outfit, and then back at the man.

"I think *unkempt* is a bit harsh," he said.

"Really? I thought I was being kind."

"Daddy!" Beth's excited voice erupted from behind Denton. He moved aside as she bounded past him and hugged her father.

"You're early!" she said, breaking away with a smile and a nervous laugh as she ushered him into her apartment. "I didn't expect you until this evening."

Archibald smiled. "I caught an earlier connecting flight and thought I'd surprise you."

"Of course you did," Beth said. She looked at Denton. "Daddy loves his surprises."

"As, it would seem, do you," Denton said, still holding the door wide open. He turned to Archibald. "I didn't know you were coming *at all*, Mr. Ingraham."

Beth laughed uncomfortably. "Daddy, this is Denton."

Denton extended his hand to Archibald, who shook it slowly.

"Hi, sir. Denton R—"

"Denton stopped by to say hello on his lunch hour and was just heading back to work," Beth blurted out.

Denton looked at her. Her eyes bored through him and telegraphed very clearly that anything less than emphatic agreement with her last statement would most certainly lead to his death.

"Uh, yes! I don't like to be gone too long from the office," Denton said. "But it's important to take a break now and again to see Beth."

Archibald's face showed no expression.

"Indeed," he said.

Indeed? Is that good?

Beth laughed and led Denton to the door. "Thanks for coming by, Denton, have a great weekend and I'll talk to you on Monday, okay?"

"Monday? Beth, what the—"

"I'll explain, I promise," she mumbled quietly to him through nearly closed lips. "Please, just go."

Denton stood dumbfounded as he watched the door close and listened to the lock turn.

Monday? What the hell was he supposed to do all weekend? And what about his sandwich? He sighed and turned away. The sandwich belonged to Archibald now.

"Stupid Friday," he muttered as he trudged toward his car.

CHAPTER 5

Monday

Ohnemus Parker stared out his office window and tried to enjoy the view. The Huntsman Bank building, truly United Alliance Bank's cross street rival, loomed large in his window, serving as a perpetual reminder of what most certainly awaited his company.

For twenty-one years, Parker had led United Alliance Bank with a simple idea: work hard, have fun, and leave the egos at home. It had worked well for him and for UAB, and as a team Parker's employees had faced the thick and thin of every economic cycle imaginable. Time and time again the bank would emerge a little battered, but never beaten, and always headed toward recovery.

But the latest cycle of boom to bust had left the bank in rough shape, and no matter what strategy and structuring Parker employed, UAB continued to hemorrhage money.

Parker thought about a buyout/takeover scenario with Huntsman Bank. Some on the board seemed almost eager to cut a deal with the once-hated competitor. Of course, the employees – for the most part – would have jobs, though some would have to move on. But most would be saved by a buyout. He felt better knowing that.

"Mr. Parker?"

Ohnemus Parker turned from the window and smiled at his assistant, who had poked her head inside the door. Her tightly pinned black hair matched her tightly pinched expression. She looked like a babysitter getting ready to scold a mischievous child.

"Hello, Tina," he spoke with genuine kindness. "What's going on?"

"Phone call," she said. "It's Joseph Handel."

Parker's eyebrows rose with his grin.

"Well, how does he sound?"

"Perturbed, sir."

"Perturbed," Parker repeated the choice of words. "That's all? He doesn't by chance sound … angry?"

"Possibly," she replied. Parker furrowed his brow.

"What about … vexed?"

"Potentially," Tina said, still staring at him.

"What about …. Pissed? Does he sound pissed?"

"American or British definition?" Tina asked, as the term meant *angry* in the states, but *highly intoxicated* across the ocean.

"American, my dear," said Parker with a scolding laugh.

"Yes," Tina smiled finally. "He sounds plenty pissed."

Parker grinned. "Then we'd best not keep him waiting."

He winked and shooed his assistant out of the room as he picked up the desk phone. He leaned back in his chair and stared out the window at the Huntsman bank building.

"Hulloh, Joey!" Parker exclaimed with the most genuine pleasure possible. "To what do I owe the honor of this call?"

Parker winced as the earpiece exploded in a fury of expletives and threats. He bit his lip to prevent laughter and held the phone a distance from his ear to avoid going deaf. When the line quieted down, Parker summoned all his focus and will and spoke.

"Joey, I'm sorry, these darn phones have been going in and out this morning. Why did you say you need my phone number?"

As the earpiece erupted again Parker quietly muted the receiver, placed it on his desk, and went back to reading email.

Tina's emotionally unblemished face popped back in from the doorway.

"Mr. Sheppard is here," she said.

Parker raised an eyebrow.

"Well, well," he said. He hung up the phone. "Send him in, of course."

Tina disappeared with a nod and Parker rose as John Sheppard entered with a tired smile. He strode over to Parker and shook his hand and both men sat down.

"Good morning, John," Parker said. "What on earth brings the Chairman of the Board here so early on a Monday?"

"Ohnemus," Sheppard started, and then looked down at his feet. He blinked a few times and then leaned forward and rested his arms on Parker's desk.

"You need to go," he said.

"I see," Parker said with a slow nod. "When?"

"Today," Sheppard said. "Call it a vacation – Lord knows you deserve one. Just do it immediately. Make yourself scarce."

Parker nodded as he thought through the man's orders.

"John," he said. "It was a little harmless fun. You and the board voted me out over that?"

Sheppard shook his head. "I'm no longer chairman. We lost two more board members just last week and I resigned this morning."

"John, no."

John Sheppard waved off the protest.

"The sell-happy contingent keeps growing and that's not something I can support. But that's not why I'm here. There's been no vote on your tenure here. Not yet, anyway."

"Then what's going on?"

Sheppard rose and looked at the office door. After staring at it for a few seconds, he turned back to his friend.

"Something's happened downstairs, Ohnemus," he said. "Something bad."

###

"DO YOU HEAR ME, PARKER? Do you understand what I'm telling you, you …?"

Joseph Handel stopped, realizing he'd actually run out of expletives and had no new variances of his general "Parker, I hate you" theme to share with the feisty CEO. A moment after that, he realized Parker hadn't said a word in some time.

"Parker? Are you there, you old … Parker!"

Handel slammed the phone down then swung around in his chair and glared out the window at the UAB building. He knew Parker was in there, enjoying a good laugh over his clever prank. Handel cursed himself for continuing to let the man's ridiculous stunts get under his skin. He turned back to his desktop and imagined the day when he would march that unbalanced old fool out of his own building in front of every news station in the city. He'd wipe the stupid smile right off Parker's face that day.

Handel's ears perked up at the sound of his assistant's phone ringing yet again. His eyes burned as he heard her politely explaining to yet another caller that they had not reached Ohnemus Parker's office.

"Kelly, just hang up and unplug the damn thing," he ordered. A few moments later the incessant ringing ended. Handel let out a breath and relaxed in the silence. He furrowed his brow again, remembering a photographer from Banker magazine planned to call him that morning. He had to approve the photo shoot locations for his "Banker of the Year" spread, and the photographer's first suggestions had been, in Handel's opinion, "pedestrian."

Kelly entered noted office and laid some notes on the dark mahogany desk.

"When is IT going to get this fixed?" Handel demanded. "I don't want to have to take calls from my toilet," he gestured toward a door on the far wall of his office.

"They're working on it right now," Kelly said.

Joseph nodded and shifted some papers on his desk with a visible pout.

"Do I look bloated today?" he asked with distinct seriousness.

"Not at all, Mr. Handel," Kelly replied in the same tone. His admin had learned from her predecessor to avoid gushing answers full of empty compliments.

Handel smiled lightly and nodded. He turned back toward the window and tried to catch a glimpse of his own reflection. His perfect, gray hair seemed less perfect. The bags under his small brown eyes looked bigger. He *felt* bloated. And angry.

"What's on our website today?" he asked. Kelly pressed a button on her PDA.

"Joseph Handel directs Huntsman Bank to donate one million dollars to plant trees in urban community parks," she recited. "Also, there's a sidebar piece on your visit to Buck Williams Elementary."

"With the video of me reading to the children?"

"Yes, sir."

Handel nodded, and thought about the six takes the camera man had needed to get the shot right and how he kept making Handel mess up the reading. And those noisy and unappreciative children seemed completely incapable of understanding the need for him to recite the same passage half a dozen times. Still, as long as the video looked good, the company news machine would have their story and the entire twenty-five minute ordeal would have been worth enduring.

Huntsman employees had for years watched their company site turn into a shrine dedicated to reporting the wonders their fearless leader performed on a daily basis. From branch visits, to donations to schools, to his frequent visits with political leaders, the site displayed Handel's every captivating moment for all the employees to enjoy. The running joke at Huntsman was that if cancer were to be cured, within minutes the Huntsman intranet would announce that Handel himself had cured it over the weekend while simultaneously saving dozens of drowning puppies. Oddly missing from the Huntsman news network were stories regarding his $25 million bonus and the company's numerous hostile takeovers of smaller banks.

But the current day's stories detailing Handel's greatness could not lift him from his funk. He looked like a fool – again – in front of Parker. His mind turned back to the "merger."

"Kelly," he said, looking up at her with a wink. "Get him on the phone, please."

"Yes sir, Mr. Handel," Kelly said and walked out of his office.

Handel leaned back and smiled. It wouldn't be long now.

At her desk, Kelly plugged the phone line back in and was greeted immediately by a fully lighted display of calls. Handel bolted forward in his chair as the telephone system once again commenced with its harmonious, high-pitched song of irritation.

The smile vanished from his face and his eyes darkened as he grabbed his mobile phone and stormed into his bathroom. Though well out of earshot, Kelly worked very hard not to laugh as Handel made a flamboyantly demonstrative performance of slamming the door in rage and disapproval.

# # #

IN MOST SITUATIONS, DENTON considered getting excited over the beginning of a new work week clear evidence of a mind in need of either counseling or a lobotomy. But after spending the entire weekend alone, staring at the rain and wondering what was going on with Beth and her father, the first sounds of a corporate Monday made him smile. Sort of.

Denton sat in his chair and looked intently at his monitor, trying to make a face that would convince people walking by that he found his work both fascinating and challenging.

"That works better when you turn it on, super-genius," a woman's sarcastic voice said from behind him.

Denton didn't turn around. He put a finger up and continued to stare.

"Please do not disturb the expert when he is deep in study," he scolded.

"Oh, I didn't realize it was so important," she said with amusement. She pointed at his blank screen. "What do you have there, oh great one?"

"I'm looking at the full list of successful, long-term relationships experienced by one Miss Candace Coving—"

Candace Covington slugged him in the arm and sat down on his desk with a smile. Her straight blonde hair fell in a ponytail out the back of her ball cap. Denton noted her torn black denim jeans and her white t-shirt with The Blood Flies logo smeared across it in crimson. He smiled and turned on his machine.

"And good morning to you," he said. "Glad to see my favorite IT computer fixer lady made it through Friday's cut."

"I am, too, mostly," she said. "But IT got rid of a few more folks too, so now I'm picking up extra work while at the same time trying to finish the new automated escheatment tool project."

Denton shook his head and shrugged his complete ignorance to what that meant. Candace looked at the ceiling and thought for a moment.

"Customer opens an account, and for whatever reason stops using it for a long period of time. If we can't get hold of the customer, then eventually we have to send the money in that account to the state to hold in a kind of giant lost and found. That's escheatment – more or less."

"Okay," Denton said. "And you're automating it."

"Yup. Caldwell's baby. It'll cut down time and paperwork and should keep us in the government auditors' good graces."

"Well," Denton said, "that's about all the fascinating bank talk I can take for one day. Tell me – what could I possibly have done already this week to upset the IT department? I haven't even logged on to this thing yet."

Candace pulled a small silver flash drive from her pocket and smiled again.

"This is a preemptive strike," she explained. "Corporate downloaded some programs onto a few PCs by mistake – yours included. Most folks will get an email alerting them that the programs will be deleted overnight. But since you take those emails to mean you need to hurry up open all the programs before they go away, I'm here to remove the files before you do something stupid … again."

Denton shrugged. "I just like to know what they do."

Candace rolled Denton and his chair away from the keyboard. She plugged the jump drive into his PC and clicked through some screens.

"Good weekend?" she asked with her back to him.

"Not my best weekend," Denton said. He always used that response when weekends turned out poorly. He found it simple, and factual – since his *actual* best weekend involved almost dying in an alley at the hands of a semi-giant with a handgun, then nearly dying in the back office of a concert venue at the hands of a quasi-mobster with a verbal food fetish, and then narrowly escaping dying while stuck atop an inflatable nylon bovine. Then of course, he completed the weekend by finally getting engaged to Beth.

Denton pushed the contradiction-laden memory away. "I didn't talk to Beth all weekend," he said.

Candace continued to read the screen, clicking the mouse every now and again. "What'd you do now?"

Denton's face moved into full frown.

"Why do you immediately assume *I* did something wrong?"

Candace turned her head around and let her amused eyes lock on him for a moment. "Uh, because I've met Beth, and I *know* you," she laughed and turned back to the screen. "You two fight about the date again?" she asked.

"Thankfully, no," Denton said. "We *might* have, for all I know. But her dad is in town and I guess she spent the whole weekend with him."

"Ooh, you met her *father*," Candace's eyes bulged and she performed a dramatic shudder. She smiled, "Were you nervous?"

"Not at all. Because I didn't know he was coming."

Candace cocked her head at that tidbit and quit the act.

"She didn't tell you?"

"Nope."

"Huh," she said. Then she turned back to the computer. "Maybe you didn't do anything."

"Thank you," Denton said.

"Hello, Denton," a familiar voice said from behind him. Denton and Candace both turned to see a tall, well-dressed black man with a shiny police badge hanging from the pocket of his tan sports coat. Next to him stood a shorter, larger officer in plain clothes. A genuine grin shown through his bushy brown mustache.

Candace turned back to Denton's computer and grabbed her flash drive.

"Or maybe you *did* do something," she commented as she moved quickly past the two men and disappeared around the corner.

"Where are you going?" Denton called out as she exited. "It's everyone's favorite superhero, Tall Black Police Cop and his burly sidekick, Captain Burrito Stain!"

He continued to watch the corner for a moment, then shifted his eyes to his guests and shrugged.

"Well, *I'm* a huge fan, he said. "Can I get your autographs?"

"How are you Denton?" Tim Sowell asked.

"Peachy," Denton replied as he switched off the fun and games mode. "What do you guys need? Did the bank forget to give you a toaster when you opened your joint checking account?"

Russell Carlson's smile disappeared into his upper lip's hairy companion.

"Hey, come on, Rourke," Carlson said. "A lot's changed lately."

Denton nodded. "I can see that. Carlson, you've lost about 10 pounds and gained a Sergeant rank – good job. And our dear Sergeant Sowell is now *Lieutenant* Sowell. Quite the jump in just a few months. Congrats."

Sowell and Carlson looked at each other. Sowell pushed his oversized glasses up and smiled.

"Denton, please," he said.

Denton rolled his eyes and swiveled back toward them.

"Is *that* how I sounded when I was asking for cases for months on end so that I wouldn't end up ... *here*?"

Sowell's dark eyes focused in on Denton. "I wish it could have been different, Denton. I hope deep down you know that," he said. "And as it is, perhaps everything worked out exactly as it needed to."

Denton's jaw tightened and his eyes narrowed.

"Why are you here?" he asked.

"We've got something we want to show you," Sowell said.

"I'm sure. Just tell me it's not Carlson's disco-era prom pictures," Denton said. "Because there's no solving the mystery of the powder green tux and mullet combo."

"Five bucks says you stayed home playing Dungeons and Dragons during *your* prom, Rourke."

Denton tilted his head and smiled at the burly cop.

"Touché," he said. Then he nodded. "You're getting better at this, Carlson."

Sowell rolled his eyes. "Denton, we just need five minutes of your time. Can you spare that?"

Denton leaned back. He desperately wanted to help investigate anything not related to yet another UAB customer who gave her credit card number to a complete stranger on the phone because he "sounded so honest." But he still harbored ill will toward the police department for forcing him into his current version of employment hell.

After spending another few seconds trying – and failing – to figure out a way to screw their station captain without punishing Sowell and Carlson, he let out a sigh and looked hard at the two men.

"Animal, vegetable, or mineral?" he asked.

"Animal – human," Sowell specified.

"Dead, missing, maimed by ducks, or other?"

"Dead."

"Foul play?"

"We don't know yet. We're hoping maybe you can help."

Denton sighed again. "Look, Lieutenant, I'd love to help you, I really would. But this is my job now. And however much it may at times make me want to kill myself with a stapler, it's how I make a living. I can't run off to a crime scene any time I want anymore."

"I know that," Sowell said.

Denton stared at the man. Then he rose.

"So, if you know that, then your request for five minutes of my time wasn't figurative," he said.

"It was not."

Denton spoke slowly as he turned his stare toward Carlson. "Which can only mean one thing."

"I think he's on to something, boss," Carlson said.

Denton closed his eyes tightly and put up his hand.

"No," he said. "No, no, no, no. Go away, please. Now."

"It won't take long," Sowell said.

"Jesus Christ, Sowell," he screamed in a whisper. "*The crime scene is in my building?*"

Sowell nodded slowly. The slightest grin escaped the corners of his mouth.

"Are you enjoying this?" Denton asked.

"Sometimes things work out just as they—"

"Stop that," Denton demanded.

"Five minutes, Denton," Sowell said. "That's all I'm asking for."

"No, it's not," he replied, thinking back to their first "simple" case together which sent Sowell to the hospital and Denton to within knocking distance of Death's front door.

As Denton continued to shake his head in quiet protest, he caught the bulbous figure of Marcus Rompeaux exiting the elevator and heading his direction. Then he turned to Sowell and smiled.

"Make it ten minutes," he said, "but let's take the stairs."

Denton ushered Carlson and Sowell to the corner of the building, waved his badge in front of the stairwell access pad, and almost pushed them inside. He closed the door quickly.

"Okay, what floor?" he asked.

"Executive Row," Sowell said.

"*This is an executive issue?*" Denton blurted out.

"That's right," Carlson chuckled. "Now, what floor do you work on, Rourke?"

Denton rolled his eyes.

"Six," he said.

"Uh huh, uh huh," Carlson nodded as though in earnest. "And Lieutenant, which floor are *we* heading to?"

Denton glared at Carlson who, for reasons still unexplained by science had the lung strength and stamina of an Olympic athlete crammed into a body slightly less fit than Jabba the Hut.

"The 28th," Sowell replied.

Carlson chuckled and started upward, taking two steps at a time.

Denton and Sowell followed behind for exactly one flight, and then exited the stairwell on seven and headed for the elevators.

The two men entered the elevator. Denton pressed a button and turned to Sowell.

"I didn't say I was taking the case," he said.

"I know that," Sowell nodded.

"I'm serious. I'm going to look – as a *favor* to you. Then I'm going back to my desk to do paperwork."

"Understood," Sowell continued nodding.

The two men remained quiet for most of the ascent. Finally, Denton shook his head.

"Shut up," he said.

"Understood," Sowell replied, still nodding.

CHAPTER 6

As Denton Rourke and Tim Sowell rode the elevator toward the plush offices and power ties of the revered twenty-eighth floor, Tonya Garza awoke to a far less impressive reality.

She rubbed her temples and tried to shake a series of very unpleasant nightmares from her thoughts. Her mouth felt dry and her head pounded rhythmically. She tried to recall how long she'd been asleep, or even *when* she'd gone to sleep, but then something else started to creep inter her subconscious. When it arrived fully, Tonya froze. Her eyes shot open wide as she realized she had a far bigger problem than not knowing how long she'd slept.

She had no idea where she was.

Tonya bolted upright and collided head first with a hard wooden fixture. She cursed in Spanish and flopped back down on to the strange bed.

"Hello?" she called out, trying to sound more irritated than scared. No one answered.

Tonya wrinkled her nose at the smell of the place and tried to piece together the most recent activities she could remember. She recalled pushing her cleaning cart at work and her latest run in with Denton Rourke as he tried to convince his boss that she was "out to get him." She did feel slightly bad for him. What if they decided he'd lost his mind and fired him?

She snorted. That would be his own fault, anyway.

She thought back to her first meeting with Denton. His smile upon seeing her looked natural, not like the sad, "Oh, you poor creature," smile most people gave to a person cleaning bathrooms. No, she could tell a sincere smile when she saw one, and his looked more sincere than most. And he was cute. Sure, he was a little pudgy, and he dressed like he didn't own a mirror – but she could work with that. They had their routine: she'd push her cart past his desk, he would look up and smile and say hello. She'd smile back and say hello, and move on quickly. No, it wasn't a relationship, per Tonya's own rules, but it was … *something.*

Then he ruined everything.

Tonya had pushed her cart by his desk one Monday and as she prepared to say, "Good morning, Señor Denton," with a thick, sexy accent on *Señor*, she noticed a new picture. The heavy brown wood frame displayed the photo of a skinny blonde woman whose smile taunted Tonya and clearly declared, "He's all mine, sucker."

Denton smiled like nothing was wrong. "Hi, Tonya," he said for the millionth time.

"Hola, Señor Denton," she repeated with a half smile. "What a beautiful girl," she said. "Your … sister?"

Denton had chuckled. "No, no. My fiancée," he had said.

"She is *very* pretty," Tonya had said in a tone that would have sounded more appropriate had she suggested the girl in the photo be drowned in a nearby river, or fed to wolves.

Stinging from a slap only she felt, Tonya had sworn from that day forward to make Denton's life miserable. And now she took great joy in the daily consternation he displayed when he reached his destination and found it closed – as usual.

But her successful torments of Denton Rourke now seemed insignificant. Fully awake but still no closer to knowing where she was, Tonya fought the very strong urge to scream out to the heavens for assistance. She tried to figure out who could be behind her current situation.

Her ex-boyfriend? Not likely. Tonya figured the man who could not be dragged away from The Court TV Channel long enough to fill out a job application would not have the mental fortitude to plan and elaborate kidnapping.

Before she could dive deeper into her pool of suspects, a blazing light filled the room. Tonya closed her eyes tightly and raised a hand to block the glare.

As her eyes adjusted, she saw a single bulb hanging from a thin wire, illuminating a very small and very bare room with no windows. The drab, green paint adorning the walls now, after years of neglect, enjoyed the protection of several layers of dust and dirt.

Tonya looked at the door which faced her from across the room. The wood looked old, heavy, and impenetrable. A new, shiny brass locking knob had been installed just above the original keyhole – which seemed large enough to be used as a peephole from outside the room.

The pale blue eye staring at her through said keyhole agreed.

Tonya screamed a Spanish expletive and pulled herself as far back against the headboard as possible. She stared hard at the lone eyeball, and then threw a pillow at the door. The eye vanished during the pillow's flight, and reappeared when the attack ended.

"Stay on the bed," a voice located somewhere just below the peeping eye commanded.

Tonya repeated her very uninviting Spanish expletive.

"I don't know what you're saying, but if you want food and a chance to use the restroom, then stay on the bed."

Tonya wanted very badly to unleash a record-breaking string of curses. However, her mind suddenly made her keenly aware of something else: she was only wearing her tight halter top and her underwear.

"Where are my clothes, weirdo?" she demanded. "If you touch me, I will kill you."

"As interesting as that might be to see you attempt, you can relax. I'm washing your clothes – there was a bit of an accident during your acquisition. You can have them back when this is over. And believe me, I have no plans to touch you, abuse you, torture you, or even *keep* you."

A pause developed between them for a moment. Then the voice came back.

"Actually, *one* of those things isn't exactly true. Care to guess which?"

The voice followed its question with a high-pitched giggle which went on for several seconds and then ended with a nasal snort.

"Sorry, sorry … just a little humor," it said.

Tonya stiffened. "You are not funny."

"Okay, but seriously, I'm on a very important quest, and I'm really not interested in harming you in any way. However, I *do* have to keep you here for a little while. You'll see cuffs and a blindfold on the table next to you. Please don't be afraid – they're precautionary, just to make sure you don't … I don't know … try to attack me? Not that you'd try anything, of course."

"Of course," she said flatly.

"Great, so if you could just cuff yourself to the headboard frame and then get the blindfold on, I'll bring in some food and water. Then later I'll lead you to the restroom."

Tonya wanted very much to kick the eye right through the keyhole. But hunger, thirst, and the call of nature had the upper hand. She turned her back to the keyhole and put on the cuffs, making sure to only close them to the largest size. She then grabbed the blindfold with her free hand and worked it over her head until it covered her eyes.

"Thank you," the voice said. "Oh, and, listen, it seems only fair to let you know that my quest requires that I kill a few people. You're *not* on that list, but if you try anything at all, I'll have no second thoughts about leaving you in this room to slowly starve to death."

Another pause filled the room for an uncomfortable few seconds.

"I don't mean to sound like a downer," the voice continued. "I just don't want any misunderstandings between us. Open communication is the key to any successful partnership, don't you think?"

"Of course," Tonya said with a nervous smile. As nonchalantly as she could, she tightened her cuff down another notch.

"Awesome," the voice said. "This is going to be quite the adventure!"

Tonya swallowed hard as she heard the door opening.

# # #

DENTON AND SOWELL EXITED the elevator into a world visually unique in the UAB building.

Sowell walked across the marble floor and surveyed the long line of oil paintings decorating the main hallway, each depicting a United Alliance CEO from history.

"Impressive," he remarked with a raised eyebrow. He turned toward their destination and Denton fell into step with him.

"You realize my boss is *never* going to approve of me spending my work time on this case," Denton said.

"He already approved it," Sowell said without losing a step.

"He ... *what?*" Denton stopped.

"Oh yes," Sowell replied, still walking. "He was – oh, what's the word ... *insistent.* I believe he said something about you possibly hitting your potential for once."

Sowell turned a corner and entered a thickly carpeted hallway.

"Cute," Denton said, jogging to catch up. "But that doesn't mean I can spend all my time—"

Denton cut himself off as he rounded the corner and found Sowell shaking hands with a short, pasty man in a dark blue suit and light gray tie. The man smiled unhappily as he pushed his small, wire rim glasses higher up on his small nose and took quick sips from his premium coffee cup. His grey eyes appeared tired and possibly ready to burst into tears.

Sowell turned to Denton.

"Denton, this is Kevin Kahneman."

Denton shook his cool hand and the man smiled.

"Hello, Denton," he said. "Kevin Kahneman, AVP of Accounting. If I can do *anything* to help, please let me know."

"Hello," Denton said. "What happened to your hand?"

Kahneman looked at the bandage around his left hand and chuckled.

"I tripped and fell in the grocery store parking lot," he said. "Believe me, this isn't near as bad as what happened to my suit."

Denton smiled. "Mr. Kahneman—"

"Please, call me Kevin."

"I really can't do that, but thanks. So, what's your relationship to this case?"

"I work for Phillip," Kahneman said, his words softening. "*Worked*, I guess. I still can't believe that he's really … gone."

Denton smiled politely.

"Okay, let's all pretend that five minutes ago I sat twenty or so floors down completely focused on how to deal with my fiancée's father and had absolutely no clue about what goes on up here. *Who* is Phillip?"

"Phillip Anderson," Sowell began, "is the Executive Vice President of Accounting for United Alliance Bank."

Denton nodded and looked at Kahneman.

"And you report to him."

Kahneman nodded. "For many years now. He taught me all I know about corporate accounting. He was a truly great person to work with and to know."

Kahneman looked back at Sowell. "People loved Phillip. I can't imagine anyone wanting to hurt him."

Sowell looked at Denton. "Mr. Anderson's administrative assistant found his body this morning. Building security locked it down immediately."

He shifted his gaze to the AVP.

"Mr. Kahneman, are you sure you're okay to do this? Denton and I can review the scene ourselves and come find you later to get your full statement."

"I appreciate that, Lieutenant," Kahneman replied. "But I feel like I need to see him. I guess that probably sounds weird."

"Not at all," Sowell said. "Follow me, please."

The three men turned off the main hallway and into a large foyer area decorated with big leather chairs, exotic plants, more lacquered wood, and chrome accents to everything. A receptionist's desk sat in the center of the area, clearly positioned to oversee the two large offices hidden behind frosted glass at the far left and right corners.

Kahneman pointed to his left.

"That's his office."

Denton looked over at the doorway guarded by one of Sowell's officers. Two women sat on a couch outside the door, one crying quietly, the other providing tissues as needed.

Sowell nodded to the officer and turned the handle.

"Mr. Kahneman, if you'll give us just a few minutes, I'll call you in momentarily."

Kahneman nodded his understanding and remained outside looking slightly relieved. Sowell led Denton through the door and closed it behind him.

Denton surveyed the immense office and its current residents. Several uniformed officers busied themselves taking photographs and filling out forms. Another officer stood by the large window and dusted for prints.

And on the edge of Anderson's desk sat a grinning Russell Carlson, delicately sipping his coffee while his doughnuts rested on the dead man's desk calendar.

"What took you so long?" Carlson said with a chuckle.

Denton shook his head and turned his attention to Phillip Anderson's body, which hovered above the desk, suspended by what looked like an old phone cord. His body swayed slightly in the air conditioner's manufactured breeze, making it difficult for Denton to stare at his key target without getting dizzy. Or grossed out.

Denton whispered something in Carlson's ear. Carlson nodded.

"Can I have everyone's attention? Anyone I see trying to take a picture of this room with their phone or any contraption other than a police department-issued camera will be shot on sight, and then fired and then arrested."

He turned to Denton. "Good enough?"

"Perfect," Denton nodded. "The crying woman outside – Anderson's admin?"

"Claudia Brothers," Carlson said. "She'd been with him for fifteen years or so."

"Suspect worthy?" Denton asked.

Carlson shook his head. "I don't think so. She's pretty attractive, and he's really not. At all."

"Well, he *is* dead."

Carlson shrugged. "Either way, I doubt there's a romantic angle here. But you be the judge. She said she'd come back in if needed."

Denton nodded. "Let's go ahead and bring her and Kahneman in for a few minutes."

He motioned to an officer.

"Brothers and Kahneman, please," he said.

The man moved quickly to the door and within moments delivered both parties to the room.

Denton watched both of them, looking for any subtle actions that might tell him a story. Claudia Brothers, as expected made her way toward the desk with her eyes firmly fixed on the floor.

Kevin Kahneman, however, took one step into the room, looked up at Anderson's body, and froze in wide-eyed shock.

"Oh my God. Oh my God. What …? What …?" he stammered as he tried to get the sentence out. Finally he pointed a frantic finger up at his dead boss and made eye contact with everyone in the room.

"What in the hell is this?" he screamed in a high-pitched panic. "WHAT IN THE HELL IS GOING ON HERE?"

He then proceeded to hyperventilate, and Sowell put an arm around the man and led him back outside.

Denton turned to Carlson.

"I don't think he did it," he said.

Carlson did an excellent job of not laughing as he turned to Anderson's admin and spoke softly.

"Ms. Brothers, I'd like to introduce a friend of ours. This is Denton Rourke. He's helping us with this case."

"No, I'm not," Denton said. "Hello, Ms. Brothers."

Brothers looked up at Denton, slightly confused. Denton pointed to the diamond and ruby brooch accenting her white blouse.

"That's beautiful," he said. "Mr. Anderson has excellent taste."

Brothers' eyes widened.

"How did you …"

"Husbands and boyfriends buy necklaces, bracelets, rings. They don't buy brooches, and they don't normally notice when a new one appears out of nowhere."

Brothers paled a bit. "It … it was a gift for fifteen years of service – that's all. I don't want you to think—"

"I don't," Denton waved his hand as though batting the idea away and changed subjects.

"Ms. Brothers, I know this is impossibly difficult, but would you look around quickly and tell me if anything seemed out of place in the office when you found Mr. Anderson? Anything at all that's been moved or taken?"

Claudia Brothers nodded and after a scan of the room she shook her head.

"No, it looks the same. Mr. Anderson kept his office very organized at all times."

"Did you leave work on Friday before Mr. Anderson?"

The woman shook her head. "No, he left before lunch and didn't come back. I left around six."

Denton nodded. "Did Mr. Anderson ever—"

Without so much as a polite warning, Anderson's body, officially tired of being on display in a piñata-like position, broke free from the phone cord harness and came crashing down on top of his desk.

The sound and the visual of a two hundred-pound cadaver dropping in unannounced would likely have been enough attention for most non-living objects. But Anderson's body possessed a secret flair for the dramatic. So when it hit the desk, it landed on Carlson's doughnuts at the precise angle required to fire raspberry filling across Claudia Brothers' bright white blouse.

The room fell silent as all eyes turned to Anderson's reckless and ill-behaved corpse. Denton closed his eyes tight, pinched the bridge of his nose, and waited for the screaming to start.

And so it did. And then Sowell restored the quiet. And then Anderson fractured that fragile peace with a final triumphant crash which he topped off by coughing up a tiny phone for his audience to stare at.

So while Claudia Brothers screamed some more and Sowell tried to make the case for Denton's service, Denton himself looked skyward and wished for the run-of-the-mill type misery the past Friday had provided.

CHAPTER 7

Denton and Sowell watched as Carlson worked to get twice-frantic Claudia Brothers out of the office. Sowell looked at Denton.

"Denton, I'm all for letting you think about it, but this obviously requires immediate handling. We could really use your help."

Denton stared at Phillip Anderson's body, now sprawled sideways across the floor. Satisfied the man had no further thrills up his sleeve, he knelt down and eyed the impossibly small phone which had exited the EVP's mouth during his climactic plummet. He reached into his jacket pocket, retrieved a pencil, and used it to flip the phone over.

"Uh, crime scene," Sowell said, walking toward Denton. Denton returned the phone to its original position and stood.

"Anything?" Sowell asked.

"Of course," Denton replied as he walked around the desk.

Returning to the body, Denton reached into Anderson's jacket pocket and retrieved a slip of paper. Then he rubbed Anderson's pant leg.

"*Crime scene*," Sowell repeated a little more harshly.

Denton rose, looked at the slip of paper, and then sniffed his fingers.

"Relax," Denton said. "I doubt my smudged fingerprint on his pant leg will raise an eyebrow while Forensics tries to figure out how he got jelly doughnuts smeared into his clothes post-mortem."

Carlson reappeared with a much calmer Kevin Kahneman in tow. They approached Denton and Sowell just in time to see Sowell's eyes rolling up into his head.

"Besides," Denton said, "there's no crime here, anyway. He killed himself."

Kahneman blanched further. "I don't understand any of this. It's not possible. It just *isn't*. He just couldn't have hung himself."

"Mr. Kahneman, it's natural to feel like this. Suicide is always very difficult for those close to the victim to fathom."

"Claudia said he had a phone in his mouth!"

"Which is not illegal, I don't believe," said Denton.

"Well, no … but it's very *weird*," Kahneman protested.

Denton stared at the assistance vice president and narrowed his eyes. Then turned and addressed the entire office.

"I need this room cleared," he said.

The room stared back at him without movement. Carlson stepped closer to Denton.

"Would you like me to take a stab at this?" he asked.

Denton looked at his shoes. "Yes, please."

Carlson nodded at the officers in the room, and Denton watched as they quietly made their way to the exit. Denton burst into a wide grin.

"Okay," he said, "that's kind of awesome."

"Thank you," Carlson said.

With the room emptied, Denton's smile gave way to irritation, which he aimed at Kevin Kahneman.

"Let me tell you what's *weird*, Mr. Kahneman" Denton said. "What's weird is a seasoned executive loudly arguing a murder angle in a room full of people, thereby risking the spread of wild rumors of a homicide across the building during the worst financial crisis in the company's history."

Kahneman's mouth opened slightly.

"I didn't—"

"But that's not as weird as the fact that Anderson didn't die in this office, but outside a bar last Friday around noon, that he's recently been in the trunk of a car, and that – in spite of the incredible difficulty involved – someone brought him back to his office and strung him up with a telephone cord."

"But—"

"But that's not the weirdest thing?" Denton asked. "You're right. The weirdest thing, the most impossible thing, is that someone did this without being seen."

With that, Denton stopped talking and walked over to the window. The three men watched him, Kahneman the most dumbstruck.

"So … you agree that he didn't hang himself?" Kahneman asked, fascinated.

"That yellow phone cord," Denton replied. "Every phone cord between here and the elevator is black or brown. If Anderson had decided to hang himself in his office, wouldn't he just use the one on his desk phone? He wouldn't go out and get a specialty one for the job."

"Reasonable, but not airtight," Sowell said. "You're assigning logic to a man who may have believed killing himself made perfect sense."

Denton nodded. "Fair enough."

He walked around Anderson's desk, then backed up a few paces and looked at the spot in the ceiling where the man had previously hung.

"So, let's forget logic and go with physical logistics," he said.

"Meaning?" Kahneman asked.

Denton pointed at the desk and then the ceiling.

"Anderson was hanging directly over his own desk. If he did this himself, he couldn't have tied the cord short enough to suspend his entire body above it without standing on something. So what did he use, where did it go, and how did the process *not* make a mess of the man's incredibly tidy desktop?"

Everyone quietly scanned the room in search of an item they knew did not exist.

Sowell smiled. "That's a little more convincing."

"Mr. Rourke," Kahneman began, "how do you know he died

elsewhere? And why did you say it was near a bar?"

Denton shrugged. "He's mildewed, has sticky cuffs, and was at a bar shortly before he died Friday."

Kahneman looked at Sowell and Carlson, wide-eyed.

"I don't … I'm not sure … he says such odd things."

Denton handed Sowell the slip of paper from Anderson's jacket and turned to Kahneman.

"It's a receipt from Friday," Denton said.

Kahneman looked at the paper over Sowell's shoulder.

ORD	50304290930	$6.00	11:02
ORD	50304290930	$6.00	11:20
ORD	50304290930	$6.00	11:39
ORD	50304290930	$6.00	11:59
ORD	50304290930	$6.00	12.22

Kahneman stepped back. "I don't understand. It's nothing but numbers. You're right about the time, obviously, but how do you know it's a bar?"

Denton made a face and looked toward the ceiling.

"Because that is the order number for a vodka tonic at Jimmy's, which its owner technically calls a Bar and Grille."

"And how do you know *that*?" Kahneman asked. Then almost immediately he added, "Ah … uh …"

"No, no – I don't have one of their Frequent Bender cards, or anything," Denton said. "It happens to be close by, and I've known the owner – whose name is not Jimmy – since we were kids."

Sowell refocused the group and turned to Denton.

"It's only rained once in the last week, and that was on Friday, between eleven a.m. and one p.m. And his clothes are damp."

Denton nodded. "And the sticky residue on the cuffs of his shirt probably matches the stuff on the arms of his chair."

Carlson put his hands on his hips. "So you're saying someone killed him and then went to the trouble of bringing him back to work?"

"Yep," Denton said. "Taped him to his own chair and wheeled

him back to his office in the dead of night."

"No one could pull that off without getting caught on camera," Sowell said.

"An executive could," Kahneman replied.

All eyes turned to the AVP of Accounting. He scratched at his neck and shook his head.

"There aren't any cameras in the executive parking garage. Privacy complaints," he explained.

Sowell turned to Carlson.

"Get with UAB security anyway and gather up any footage they do have from Friday night."

Carlson nodded and wrote something in his notebook.

"I just don't understand," Kahneman whispered. "Why would someone kill Phillip?"

"And why would they steal his computer?" Denton added. "Oh – yeah. It's gone … which also is weird."

Kahneman's head lurched hard around toward the desk. Carlson leaned over and placed his hand gently on the PC sitting on Anderson's desk.

"I know I'm going to hate asking this," Carlson said, "but what do you call this, Rourke?"

"That, my observant doughnut diva, is a computer."

"Ah, good." Carlson said.

"It's just not *Anderson's* computer."

"Of course not."

Denton wandered over to the window as Kahneman's pasty complexion lost another shade of pigment.

"Oh my God," he said quietly. "He's right."

He looked up at the group.

"All the executives recently received upgraded PCs from our vendor. Faster, more secure, overall better. But while the vendor improved the insides, the outside stayed almost the same, except the new boxes have fan vent cutouts on *both* sides."

Denton tapped on the solid metal side.

"Old model."

Kevin Kahneman's short hyper-breathing returned, and Denton started to worry that the man might actually pass out at any moment. Sowell seemed to share Denton's concern, and he once again helped the distraught AVP out into the foyer.

Denton watched the two men disappear, and then dropped onto a couch near the window. Carlson followed and stood, admiring the view.

"All right, hot shot," he said. "What *else* did you pick up?"

Denton stared straight ahead.

"Why should I tell you? You didn't even save me a doughnut."

Carlson pointed to the desk. "I can still hook you up with some of that tasty desk snack."

"Pass," Denton said.

"Come on," Carlson said, dropping down on the couch next to Denton. "I know there's more. Tell me and I'll buy you a dozen tomorrow morning."

Denton shook his head. "No, thanks."

He rose and stared out over the city. When protected by a large pane of glass, Denton found high-level views of city skylines calming. Something about the macro-level of everything from that distance made it very difficult for him to scrutinize minutiae.

"You guys abandoned me, you know," he heard himself telling Carlson. "I mean, I know you had to. I know that. But that doesn't make it feel any better."

"I know, Rourke, and we hated it. Believe me, Sowell is doing his best to make it up to you – you don't even know how hard he's trying."

"Meaning what?"

Sowell wandered back into the crime scene.

"I sent Mr. Kahneman back to his desk with a bottle of water," he said, staring at the two men through his glasses. Denton worried sometimes that the overly large lenses gave the clever Lieutenant the power to read his thoughts.

"Denton, do you have more information you'd like to share?" he asked, looking at him over the top of his frames.

"See?" Denton said to no one.

"Of course," Sowell said, "the only reason *not* to share what you've learned is if you're taking the case, and need to keep a few things to yourself while you investigate."

Denton chuckled. "You guys don't get it. Even if I *wanted* to take this case—"

"You do," Carlson said.

"That doesn't matter. They will *never* let me take it on. Once word spreads out to the senior execs upstairs, I'll be back on six, reviewing a backlog of fraud claims while this is brushed off as a tragic, yet highly uncomplicated suicide."

A knock from the doorway interrupted the discussion. Denton turned toward the noise, and then smiled.

"Well if it isn't Marcus Rompeaux, head of HR for my area," he announced loudly. "Gosh, Mr. Rompeaux, what brings you up here?"

Rompeaux cleared his throat and took a few small steps into the room, his eyes working hard to avoid the entire desk area of the room.

"Gentlemen, please pardon my interruption," he said. "Mr. Rourke, Daniel Caldwell has asked to see you."

Denton's faux-shock and surprise ratcheted up another level.

"Daniel Caldwell, Chief Operations Officer of United Alliance Bank?"

Rompeaux sighed heavily. "Yes, Mr. Rourke."

Denton looked back and Sowell and Carlson with a shrug.

"Can't imagine what he'd want to see me for," he said. Then, sensing the moment for levity had passed, he turned serious.

"Sorry, fellas," he said. "But I have a job to protect, too."

Sowell nodded without changing his expression.

"Understood."

Denton turned to exit, passing by the disapproving gaze of Marcus Rompeaux on his way out.

"Officers," Rompeaux started, "thank you for taking time out from your busy schedules to review this tragic suicide. The funeral home will pick Mr. Anderson up shortly, and the company will make the remaining arrangements. Naturally, we'll be reaching out to Captain Levine to let him know how much your cooperation has meant to everyone during this difficult time."

Denton slowed his pace, jaw clenching.

Keep walking.

"Of course," Rompeaux continued, "I imagine it goes without saying just how much UAB appreciates all of our local law enforcement – what, with the hundreds of thousands of dollars we give every year to organizations that support police causes. And with so many of UAB's board members being close friends with Police Chief Robinson, I'm sure he hears of our satisfaction all the time."

"Well, you're too kind, Mr. Rompeaux," Sowell said with a soft smile.

"Ah, good," Rompeaux backed up toward the doorway. "Then we understand each other."

Denton's head popped into view from the doorway.

"Well, *I'm* still unclear about a few things," he said, squeezing past Rompeaux and back into the room.

Rompeaux took a startled step backwards and made a throaty, guttural protest to the intrusion.

Denton smiled at Sowell and Carlson. "Don't mind him, he swallowed a seal at lunch."

"Now, look—!" Rompeaux sputtered.

"You know what's *really* weird, Carlson?" Denton asked, walking back toward the center of Anderson's office. "What's *really* weird are Kevin Kahneman's hands."

Rompeaux stumbled back into the office.

"His hands?"

Denton nodded without turning around.

"Yes, Marcus - *hands*. You'll recognize them as the meaty things at the ends of your arms which help smear chocolate pudding on your chest at the 'anything goes' massage parlor on 14th Street."

"Mr. Rourke!"

Denton continued. "Well, just Kahneman's injured hand, really. And I'm not sure why it's weird yet. But it'll come to me."

Rompeaux bristled. "I don't think you—"

"But what I also really, definitely, find peculiar," Denton pointed a finger at Rompeaux as he walked toward the window and started again.

"Kahneman felt compelled to ask *a lot* of questions. '*Who* would kill Phillip Anderson?' '*How* do you know he died near a bar?' '*Why* does Marcus Rompeaux smell like Pop-Tarts when he sweats?'"

"All right, that's quite enough!" Rompeaux's pink face seemed ready for a transition to full crimson.

"Yes," Sowell said, trying to ease the tension. "Mr. Kahneman was quite inquisitive."

"Inquisitive about a lot," Denton agreed. "But not about *everything*."

Denton walked back over to Anderson's desk with his head down, eyes piercing the floor. He paced as he spoke again, still without looking up.

"Kahneman's feelings for his boss are genuine. His need to understand how Anderson ended up dead is real."

Denton stopped talking and stared at the ceiling. A full minute later he grimaced, scratched the side of his head, and looked at Anderson.

"When Kahneman saw Anderson's body hanging from the ceiling, he freaked out and insisted there was no way the man could have hung himself."

"Seems pretty natural," Carlson said. "He didn't want to believe his boss would take his own life."

"Agreed," Denton said. "But that's not what he said. He never mentioned suicide at all – and he never asked why his friend might have taken his life. He just insisted he couldn't have *hung* himself. He said it was *impossible*."

Denton's audience stared at one another. Denton resumed his pacing, though with faster steps.

"And he's right," he continued. "But why did he know that?"

Denton paced his way to the doorway and turned back to the three men.

"When I said Anderson had been killed near a bar, had been transported here in the trunk of a car – *and* had his computer stolen, he only asked for an explanation of my bar theory. Why would a man desperate to understand what happened to his friend *not* demand I provide even cursory explanations of the other bizarre suggestions I made?"

"Because he already knows the answers," Carlson said.

Denton smiled and gave him a wink.

Rompeaux's sweat glands shifted into high gear.

"Oh my God," he stammered. "Okay, we can lock down the building – quietly of course …"

"Relax," Denton said. "Kevin Kahneman didn't kill his boss. He's scared of something. It could be nothing, so I wouldn't move in on him at this point."

"But … I don't …" Rompeaux trailed off.

Denton nodded as he walked out of the room.

"I know, I know," he said. "I don't, either."

He slapped the HR lead on the shoulder.

"Come on, Rompeaux-meister, let's go see Caldwell."

"*Please* stop calling me that," Rompeaux demanded. "And he wants to see you alone."

Denton turned to look at the HR Director. Instead of a smug look of satisfaction, Denton saw solemn seriousness in Marcus Rompeaux's face.

"I read your file, Mr. Rourke," Rompeaux said. "I'm aware of your … *talent.* But how did you figure out that Mr. Anderson had been in someone's trunk?"

Denton smiled and shrugged. "That one's easy," he said, walking backwards toward the elevators.

"How *else* would someone cart a dead body around town – strapped into the passenger seat?"

Rompeaux stared for a moment before giving a light chuckle and a nod to Denton. Then he put his back to Denton Rourke and marched his stubby legs away, leaving him to make the trek upstairs alone.

CHAPTER 8

Denton stepped off the elevator on the 40th floor and noted the supreme silence with some concern. He'd always expected that decibel levels would shrink progressively the higher one ascended in a corporate building. The offices on the 28th felt quiet enough to make the 6th sound like a slightly elevated wine bar during happy hour. But now Denton wondered if he'd walked off the elevator and directly into space. He figured if folks inhabiting *this* elevation ever stepped off on his floor, they'd believe they had somehow ended up in a biker bar on "Blood Brawl for Beer" night and immediately dive under the nearest desk in fear for their lives.

As he made his way toward the large administrator's desk, he tried not to convey his amazement at the expanse of crystal, marble, dark wood, and a couple of opulent-looking materials he didn't recognize and suspected were not yet available to most of the human race.

He walked slowly wondering how many employees find themselves needing to convince the COO that an exec found hanging in his office didn't kill himself, but rather died at someone else's hand, in some other location, somehow made the arduous trip *back* to work only to then get strung up above his desk for all his effort.

Still not the dumbest thing you've ever attempted.

He arrived at the admin's desk and smiled at the well-dressed, attractive brunette sitting behind a row of monitors. He wondered if he should have borrowed Sowell's tie.

The woman smiled back at him.

"Hello, Mr. Rourke," she said. "Thank you for coming up on such short notice."

Denton stayed very still and for a moment just as silent. Finally, he spoke.

"Hi."

The woman chuckled. "It's okay to breathe, Mr. Rourke, I promise."

Denton tried to relax.

"Sorry. First time up here," he explained.

"Well, you have nothing to worry about. Daniel is as normal as the next person," she said as she stood up. She extended her hand. "I'm Rachel."

Denton shook her hand and nodded. Rachel sat back down and flicked one of many switches on a large panel and pushed a button.

"Daniel," she said.

"Yes – hello, Rachel," Daniel Caldwell's crisp, confident voice emanated from ... *somewhere.*

"Hi. Denton Rourke is here to see you."

"Oh, excellent – that was fast. Hi, Denton, come on back," Caldwell said.

"Will do," Denton heard himself saying in a tone he knew made him sound like an excited nerd accepting a surprise invitation to the prom from the leader of the cheerleading squad.

Rachel laughed at Denton's rolling eyes.

"Okay, you're up," she said.

"Thanks," he smiled. "Any last tips?"

"Yes, don't call him 'Mister Caldwell.' He *hates* it."

Denton thought about his insistence on using appropriate formalities with senior leadership, and swallowed hard.

"No problem."

He thanked Rachel again and moved past her desk toward Daniel Caldwell's office.

"Good luck," Rachel called out.

Denton didn't hear her as he wrestled with his last-minute talking points.

"Something is wrong here. Important not to ignore this," Denton whispered as he walked. "We can't afford for it to get worse in this financial environment. Don't call him Mr. Caldwell."

Denton stopped in front of two 10-foot brushed nickel doors with large, frosted panes of glass accenting the sides.

Something is wrong here. Important not to ignore this. Shut up and pay attention.

Everyone has secrets. Everyone lies. Shut up, sit down. Pay attention.

He pushed Connor Rourke's mantra way, took one more deep breath and opened the door with a knock.

Seated at a long glass desk at the far side of the long office, Daniel Caldwell smiled at Denton's presence and rose.

"Denton Rourke!" he announced as he moved from behind his desk and headed directly toward Denton, right hand extended.

Denton smiled and waved. On the inside he swore to his brain that he'd give it a good kicking if it didn't stop making him look stupid. He made a somewhat graceful segue from wave to handshake. The COO's grip had a perfect firmness that projected sincerity and confidence.

Perfect seemed to fit Caldwell's entire being. His dark blue suit fit him perfectly and the light blue silk tie added a perfect accent. A perfect smile revealed perfect teeth. His skin held a perfect tan from his neck all the way up to his very perfect hairline, of which Denton found himself perfectly jealous.

"Hi, Mr. – Daniel," Denton said, eyes looking upward at his skull.

Caldwell winked. "Rachel warned you, didn't she?" He chuckled as he crossed the thick decorative rug and stopped in front of a chrome and glass wet bar.

"It's not a rule that's set in stone, or anything," he continued. He picked up a silver pitcher and poured ice water into two crystal tumblers. "I just don't like people to think I expect special treatment because I've got some obscure letters following my name."

Caldwell handed Denton a glass and gestured him into one of the black leather chairs which faced his desk.

Both men took their seats as Caldwell threw a hand up as if to stop an argument.

"Don't get me wrong," he said. "I *know* there are levels of authority and supervision, and that people will act differently in front of me. I just don't want people to see me as someone they should bow to or avert their eyes from when I'm getting a sandwich in the cafeteria."

Denton nodded, and took a drink, still going over his talking points.

Something is wrong. Important not to ignore. Financial … this is the best water I've ever drank. 'Drank'? 'Drunk?' 'Dranken'? Oh God, I've forgotten how to talk.

"… but one can try, right?" Caldwell asked.

"Absolutely," Denton replied, praying he hadn't just volunteered to do something weird like introduce him to the sixth floor lunatics. He raised his glass and changed the subject.

"*This* is not from our water fountains," he said with an impressed smiled.

"It's not even from our *country*," Caldwell replied with a smile. Then his face changed and his lips pressed together and downward.

"Denton," he said. "Phillip Anderson's death presents us with a problem."

Something is wrong.

Denton nodded. "Yes sir, I can see why."

This is too important to ignore.

"And it's not just the timing," Caldwell continued, "or the fact that Anderson and I were close. No, there's something … *wrong* with all this."

This is not a suicide.

Caldwell took a quick sip from his glass and returned his eyes to Denton's.

"I just find it impossible to believe this was a suicide," he said.

Investigation. You can't believe … wait, what did he say?

"I'm sorry, what did you say?" Denton repeated.

Caldwell rose and made his way to the large window once more.

"Denton, our stock price sits on the edge of the truly abysmal, our shareholders call for our heads on a daily basis, and our CEO has decided to take a 'leave of absence' – presumably because he's losing his mind."

"He's not losing his mind," Denton interjected.

Caldwell turned toward Denton. "I pretty much agree with you, but he chose the worst possible moment to pull his little stunt. However funny it might have been."

Denton wondered if he should stand also, or scoot his very heavy chair around to face the man, or just keep craning his neck around until he lost feeling in his extremities.

"The point is, Denton, Phillip – for whatever his faults – didn't kill himself. I just know it. And if I'm right, to ignore this would mean risking something much worse. Someone *must* look into this."

"Agreed," Denton said, tossing his unneeded talking points to the back of a dusty closet in his head. With some effort and noise, he scooted his chair around to face the window.

Caldwell turned and made his way back around his desk. Once again misaligned with Caldwell, Denton simply got up and switched to the other chair. Caldwell smiled.

"The question is, of course … are *you* that someone?"

"I am," Denton replied with confidence. Caldwell nodded.

"I know this goes without saying, but here I go anyway: This requires a very high level of discretion. The police are willing to keep this as quiet as possible and not pursue this as a murder – for now. But we must maintain that quiet."

"Understood," Denton nodded.

Caldwell nodded in return. "Understood, yes. But achievable?"

Denton opened his mouth to reply, but stopped as Caldwell removed a manila folder from a desk drawer and opened it. Even upside-down, Denton recognized the employee photo staring out from the corner of the page.

He frowned at the picture, remembering very well the day he'd been photographed for his UAB badge. Upon receiving the badge and looking at the picture which made him look even rounder and balder than he already was, he taped a picture of James Bond over his own and went about his business. So far, no security guard had said a thing.

Caldwell smiled. "You should see Rachel's, though she'll never show you. Somehow, they made that sweet and very lovely woman look like a man with measles."

He flipped past the page and put his finger on a paragraph. After a moment, he looked up at Denton with a bit of a grin.

"Your last case culminated in a series of explosions and fire which demolished the interior of The Palladium Theatre."

"Yes, but they weren't my explosives," Denton offered.

"And the *death* of your employer," Caldwell continued.

Denton shifted in his chair.

"In my defense, he was an insane person hell-bent on murdering three innocent people to protect a legacy that existed only in his mind."

"I care about *my* legacy," Caldwell said. "Though I'd prefer not to kill anyone over it."

Caldwell closed the file and looked at Denton.

"So you don't foresee the same kind of high-profile resolution strategy here?"

Denton shook his head. "That case dealt with a rock 'n roll band and ended at a concert," he said. "This is the corporate office of a financial institution. I don't foresee anything occurring that would bring UAB anywhere near those decibel levels."

Caldwell appeared content with Denton's answers. He opened the drawer and tossed the file back in.

"Okay," he said. "What would your first move be?"

Denton leaned in. "What do you know about Phillip Anderson?"

"Quite a lot," Caldwell said with a shrug. Then he smiled.

"What do *you* know about him?"

Denton sat back, surprised by the question.

"I'm sorry?"

Caldwell leaned forward.

"Obviously I've read your file. I know what your personality test showed and the peculiar attention to detail you possess. You've been to Phillip's office. You saw everything the police did. So, impress me. What do *you* know about Phillip Anderson so far?"

Denton stared at Caldwell for a moment, and then stood up so he could pace.

"Phillip Anderson was efficient," he said. "He had a no-nonsense practicality about him. Everything either had a purpose or it didn't exist for him."

"And you base that on what?" Caldwell asked.

"His desk," Denton replied. "A full-sized desk calendar, with nothing but specific appointments and deadlines written in their corresponding squares. Not a single scribble, or doodle, or random thought scrawled into the margins. No coffee mug or other container with a dozen pens and pencils jammed into it – just a single, black pen."

"He could just be a neat freak," Caldwell challenged.

"Oh, it's more than that," Denton said. "No plants, no souvenirs from vacations, no family pictures. The books on his coffee table were accounting reference guides. No picture books of Hawaii, or exotic cars, or whatnot."

Caldwell nodded. "Not bad. Anything else?"

"He was funny," Denton replied. "The small framed sign on his wall that reads, 'Eschew Extraneous Promulgation,' was more than just an irony for him. It amused him, but he *believed* in it."

"Very good. Is that all?"

Denton returned to the chair and sat.

"He was right-handed, had a secret yet innocent crush on his secretary, loved sunsets on the beach, and once auditioned for American Accounting Idol."

Caldwell smiled gently at the obviously invented additions.

"Denton," he said, "the man *is* dead."

Denton felt his face getting hot. "Right. Of course. I'm sorry – sometimes I say things I shouldn't when things get tense."

Caldwell waved a dismissive hand.

"It's all right. And you're pretty much spot on. Phillip was practical – almost diabolically so. If something gave off even a hint of redundancy or uselessness, he made it disappear."

Caldwell looked toward the ceiling and chuckled.

"I remember once – many years ago – when he and I worked in the insurance division, another colleague set up a two-hour meeting to review a document that ran twenty-eight pages."

"That sounds fun," Denton said.

"Phillip thought so. He spent the afternoon poring over the doc and removing anything he considered a 'timewaster.' Then he sent the new version out to the team. We ended up in the meeting room looking at seven bullet points on a single page. The meeting took less than ten minutes."

"Nice," Denton nodded.

"For us, sure. But our colleague with the publically eviscerated presentation felt a little differently."

"Ah."

"After awhile people stopped inviting him to meetings … which I suspect was part of his plan in the first place."

"Eliminate the origin of the timewaster," Denton said. "The meeting itself."

Caldwell nodded his agreement. Then he pointed at Denton and smiled.

"Now, there was one peculiar thing about Phillip that would be hard to know from a look at his office. For someone who liked things, 'to the point' at all times, he had a fondness for riddles."

"That does seem odd."

"Yes. He *loved* them. And he took great pleasure in annoying people with them – especially me."

"Really?"

Caldwell tilted his head. "Don't give away my secret, but my brain is wired for straightforward and literal processing – I'm just not good with word games and riddles. Phillip knew that, so at least once a week would send me a locked document and some ridiculous riddle or brainteaser in which he'd hidden the password. I'd spend a few minutes trying to decipher it, and then just call him and yell. He loved it."

Caldwell stopped. A far off stare developed in his eyes.

"I guess in a way, I did, too," he said.

Denton drank his water to keep his mouth too busy to even consider another idiotic utterance. A knock at Caldwell's door relieved him of any need to come up with a clever yet non-offensive segue. Caldwell looked up and smiled.

"Ah, Peter, come in," he said.

Denton followed suit and turned toward the visitor.

"Peter, please meet Denton Rourke," Caldwell said. "Denton agreed to help us with the Phillip situation."

Peter approached Denton. In his late 40s or early 50s, Peter's chiseled jaw, close-cut gray hair, and grim expression looked very out of place in the inviting and relaxed atmosphere of Daniel Caldwell's office. His strong physical build filled out his light grey suit perfectly. As Peter approached and extended his hand, Denton noted how the man's bright yellow tie matched the yellow fitness bracelet around his giant wrist. He reached out and prayed the man would not crush his hand in some attempt to signal his alpha-male dominance over him. Denton figured the obviousness of that fact did not require broken bones.

Peter clearly agreed, and Denton sighed internally at the standard firmness of the man's grip.

"Peter Markung," he said. "Assistant to Mr. Caldwell, Logistics Manager, and Iron Man Triathlon finisher."

"Denton Rourke," Denton replied. "Fraud Analyst, HR Annoyance, and Iron Man Collector's Edition DVD owner."

Peter stared at him, eyes flashing a slight concern.

"Iron Man *DVD* owner," he repeated.

"*Collector's Edition*," Denton corrected. "Robert Downey, Jr. is awesome."

Caldwell chuckled. "Denton, Peter is greatly downplaying his role here. I can't tell you how many times he's saved me from professional and personal crises. Whether it's resolving department conflicts, gathering research, or making sure I remember my nephew's birthday, he's a lifesaver."

Peter eyed Denton warily for another moment before turning to his boss.

Caldwell nodded. "Peter is fully briefed on the issue, so feel free to reach out to him if you need anything."

Peter smiled at Denton.

"Make no mistake, Denton," he said. "This is *your* investigation. You do it *your* way. If I can help, let me know. Other than that, I don't need updates, and you don't need approvals. It's your show."

"Great," Denton said. "Question one – for both of you: How did I get here?"

Caldwell smiled as he looked over at Peter.

"I told you," he said to his colleague.

Peter smiled as well. He looked at Denton.

"You came highly recommended."

"By?"

Caldwell sat back. "By Phillip Anderson."

Denton paused to weigh his next words carefully.

"Huh?" he said.

Caldwell pointed at his computer.

"About a month ago, a brain teaser went out via email to most of the accounting lines of business via email. It came from a generic Accounting email address."

"I remember," Denton nodded. "The bear and the spoon riddle."

"Exactly," Caldwell nodded. "Of the fourteen correct responses Phillip received, yours was the only one he received in the same hour he sent it out, and you were the only respondent who did not try using the internet to get the answer."

"I don't want to know how you know that," Denton said.

"You're right," Peter smiled. "We have no idea what he was up to, but he included both of us when he sent it out and taunted us with the results after we both failed to figure it out. So when we saw Phillip's email from Friday, we thought of you immediately."

"What email?" Denton asked.

Caldwell stared at Denton for a moment, before moving his gaze to Peter, who looked downward.

"It's probably nothing," Caldwell said.

"No doubt," Denton said, again shifting his eyes left and right to try and stare at both men. "But let's have a look anyway."

Caldwell turned to his computer. He clicked his mouse twice and his printer hummed into action.

Denton watched as a single sheet of paper made its way into the tray. Caldwell picked up the page and extended it to Denton.

"Phillip sent this to me Friday," he said. "Peter and I were en route back from a company retreat in the mountains of New Mexico, where none of the UAB folks could get signals on their devices. So I didn't see it until Sunday afternoon."

Caldwell's eyes shot toward the ceiling as Denton took the paper from him.

"Just a standard resignation email, if a little verbose."

Denton scanned the note.

Daniel, my dear friend,

I hope you find my final words of some use. What we envisioned for a future is not the future I wish to see. I've included attachments you'll need soon, though I firmly believe you can succeed without them, no matter what they may reveal.

What I've become is not what I want to be. With this decision, my anxious soul is once again calm and still. I now know this is for the best. And I feel better than I have in a long time.

I hold you in high regard and I will think of you no matter what fate I go to. I always enjoyed our debates about patience over speed, and I hope you may yet convert.

--Phillip

Denton looked at both men before refocusing on Caldwell.

"Have you ever *seen* a resignation letter?" he asked.

"Denton, please—"

"Because this looks more like a *suicide* note," he finished.

Caldwell remained motionless as he stared at Anderson's email on his screen. He shook his head.

"How can that be possible?"

"Well that's the wrong question, isn't it?" Denton said as he turned to exit.

"What is?" Peter asked from behind.

Denton stopped in the doorway and looked back at the two men.

"What's *possible*," he said. "*Everything* is basically possible – except ordering the cafeteria's fish special and then actually eating it."

"You believe it's possible someone murdered him?" Peter asked.

"I think it's very possible."

"Yet you also think the victim may have written a suicide note beforehand."

Denton looked at Peter quizzically.

"Sure," he said.

"That seems pretty ridiculous," Peter replied.

Denton grinned. "Well, we've just moved Anderson's situation from impossible to ridiculous. That's progress."

Caldwell smiled weakly. "Okay, Denton … what now?"

"Can I see the attachments Phillip sent with this email?" Denton asked.

Caldwell shook his head. "I'm afraid not, Denton."

Then he leaned forward and pointed to his screen.

"Phillip locked the attachments with one of his riddles," he explained. "I don't know what he sent, and if it's confidential company information, I could get both of us in a lot of trouble by handing it out to unauthorized personnel."

"We're hoping maybe the note is a clue," Peter said. "Originally we thought it might tell is where he was and what he was doing, but now … now we just don't know."

Denton felt his brain flashing through a hundred thoughts. He pulled one out to focus on.

"How can a dead man wander into his place of work and hang

himself in his office without security picking up *any* evidence on video?"

"He *can't*," Peter said. "There are multiple cameras on the entrance where his badge was used to enter the building. They feed into a digital recorder in the central security room."

"But?" Denton asked.

Peter nodded his confirmation of Denton's suspicion.

"But the security office has no footage during the time Anderson went through those doors. They say it's likely a system glitch."

"No doubt. And can guards in the central security office transfer captured footage to other storage media – like a DVD, or a flash drive?"

Peter nodded again and turned toward Caldwell.

"Yes, which is why I've been pushing our executive committee to abandon the outsourcing of security to low-bid enterprises with no true investment in UAB's protection."

Caldwell put up his hands. "Your stance has been duly noted in the past and the time for 'I told you so,' is no doubt coming. But let's stay focused on the issue at hand."

"Sorry, sorry," Peter said. He turned back to Denton. "Sometimes it just feels like I'm never right about anything *good*."

"I know that feeling," Denton said, jamming the email into his pocket.

"Well, we've got the What, Where, and When," he said. "I'll get to work on the How and the Why ..."

He smiled at the two men.

"And the *Who*," he said.

Denton gave a quick wave and backed his way out of Caldwell's office.

Peter Markung and Daniel Caldwell watched as Denton strode confidently away and turned not toward the elevators, but into the hallway which housed the Ladies' Executive washroom. After they watched him reappear and blaze toward the elevators, Peter turned to his boss.

"And you're *sure* he can help?" he asked.

Caldwell broke off his stare and looked at Peter.

"Forget what you *see.* He's smart, motivated, dedicated to UAB, and – very importantly – he strikes me as a good person. He'll come through."

"I guess I'll trust you on that," Peter said, heading for the door.

"And make sure you do whatever you can to help him. We *need* to understand what happened, why it happened, and what Phillip put in those files."

Peter nodded quickly. "Yes, sir."

Caldwell dialed a number and gave Peter a quick thumbs-up thank you as the door closed.

While the phone rang, Caldwell stared at the email still glowing in his monitor, and shook his head slowly.

"Phillip, you stupid bastard," he whispered. "What got into you?"

Without waiting for a response, Caldwell returned his attention to the phone.

"Hello, Don Fowler, this is Daniel Caldwell. How have you been?"

CHAPTER 9

Denton took a detour on his way back to six, stopping a couple of floors above to pay a surprise visit to Fred. He peaked through his friend's office window before knocking and saw him studying something on his computer screen with amazing focus. Denton's eyebrows rose, and barged through the door.

"Busy?" he called out loudly.

Fred jumped in his chair and clicked a button on his keyboard. Then he turned to the door. Seeing Denton's grinning face, Fred rolled his eyes and glared.

"You *do* understand the concept of a door, correct?" he asked. "When closed, you knock."

Denton closed the door behind him. He dropped into a chair and kept smiling.

"Do *you* understand the concept of closing your blinds or getting a privacy screen for your monitor so you don't show the world your … well, let's just call it 'non-standard' internet use?"

Fred waved off the suggestive tone.

"I'm just doing a little fact finding in preparation for some communications to one of our target demographics."

"I know what it was," Denton said. "You do keep secrets, don't you? Oh, and that's a *very* nice response you've composed. Very natural."

"Thank you," Fred acknowledged. "What do you want?"

Denton looked shocked. "Can't I just come for a visit?"

"Should I base my answer on theoretical possibility, or historical record?" Fred asked with a smile.

Knowing a review of said historical record would do nothing to help his case, Denton moved forward without addressing Fred's question.

"I just left Daniel Caldwell's office," he said.

Fred smiled.

"Did you, now? Well how is Mr. Caldwell today?"

"He prefers you call him Daniel," Denton corrected.

"I'm sure. Well, next time the two of you are hanging out, will you put a good word in for me? Maybe get him to put me in charge of global communications."

Denton looked at Fred, eyes wide.

"You don't believe me," he said.

Fred rubbed his chin for a moment before looking back at Denton.

"No. Now, in spite of what you just saw, I really am busy today. The rumors are already starting and the press is implying that Phillip Anderson's death marks the beginning of a huge corporate cover up."

"A cover up? Of *what?*"

Fred shrugged. "Of pretty much anything. These days, they're not really that interested in specifics when it comes to large financial institutions. If someone finds an executive at The Gap's corporate HQ dead in his office, it's a tragedy. At UAB, it's automatically a sign of something nefarious."

Denton nodded and rose. "Good word. All right, I'll leave you to your work. We still on for tomorrow morning? Breakfast in the break room? Julian's cooking again."

Fred nodded. "Heck, yes. I'll see you there."

Denton turned for the door and found himself staring into the scowling face of his boss.

Denton's smile brightened. "Hi there," he said.

"Do you know who just called me?" Fowler asked through his

scowl.

"An eccentric millionaire who wants to buy your mustache," Denton guessed.

"Daniel Caldwell," Fowler replied.

"Ah."

"Do you know *why* he called me?"

"Yes."

Fowler stared at Denton some more. Denton always found himself impressed at his boss's ability to convey varying levels of irritation without moving a single facial muscle.

"Your 'special assignment'," Fowler said.

"Right," Denton agreed.

Fred tuned in. "Wait, you were really in Caldwell's office?"

"Oh, I'm sure that's impossible," Denton replied as he walked out with Fowler. "See you in the morning, Fred!"

Denton closed the door quickly behind him, drowning out the continued protests and questions from within. He followed Fowler to the elevator and waited without comment. Fowler stared up at the floor indicator, watching the numbers retreat toward them.

"Good for you," he said without looking at Denton.

"We'll see about that," Denton replied.

The elevator chimed its arrival and opened, allowing the two men to enter. Denton hit the button for six and leaned against the back of the elevator.

"Do us both a favor, will you, Denton?" Fowler said.

Denton turned toward him. "What's that?"

"Make it a *good* thing that Caldwell knows our names."

As the doors closed, Fowler's mustache twitched slightly in the formation of what Denton thought looked slightly like a smile.

# # #

"YOU'RE MORE THAN AN HOUR EARLY, Mister ...?"

"*Zot*," the man said. "Niklas Zot, photographer extraordinaire. You have no doubt heard of me."

"No doubt."

Jim Chambers, security guard – extraordinarily bored, eyed the aging German wearily. "Nee-claus," wore all black – black pants, black t-shirt, black linen jacket, and a black beret. Only his gold-rimmed sunglasses with their blue lenses escaped the manic dearth of color. He had a tripod under his arm and a large black duffle bag strapped across his back. He smiled as he tapped the large, very professional camera hanging around his neck.

"Ze lighting," he said. "Meester Handel is very particular about his lighting – of course you know zat, I'm sure."

"Of course," Chambers said as he looked again at the Huntsman Bank guest directory for the day.

"Like I said, Mister Zot, you're very early. Mr. Handel won't be back for at least an hour."

"Ya, I know dizs very well, of course," Zot nodded. "When he arrives, I want everyzing just right so that he will not have … oh, how shall I put it … a … *man tantrum*?"

Zot winked at Chambers, who couldn't suppress a slight grin.

Chambers recalled a previous incident in which the sandwich Joseph Handel had ordered arrived at the lobby desk four minutes late. Handel had demanded the delivery man stay there while he made his way down from his office so he could personally chastise him for his gross dereliction of duty. The delivery man, a young Italian named Joe Turino, had been in the country less than a month and had learned only two phrases before his arrival: "God Bless America," and "I want to work, please." This had helped him secure a job within a matter of minutes, and – unbeknownst to him at the time – insulated him from the dramatic verbal assault Handel felt the lateness of his sandwich deserved.

Sensing his diatribe was not having the intended effect, Handel grabbed his sandwich off the lobby desk, shook it at Joe Turino, and then threw it to the floor and used his foot to repeatedly stomp it into a gooey mess.

Though unclear on Handel's words, Joe knew anger when he saw it. And while he did not quite understand Handel's fiery assault on his own lunch, Joe wanted very much to help make his customer happy. So he reached into his backpack, and retrieved a small yellow bag, which he shook at the CEO of Huntsman Bank with a smile.

"It come with chips," Turino helpfully offered. "I kill for you!" He then threw the bag on the floor and proceeded to mimic Handel's foot-stomping motion over and over, crushing the chips into a fine power, all the while smiling at his near-incendiary customer.

Shuddering at the memory and not wanting even a remote repeat of that day – especially one involving expensive cameras and a German diva, Chambers smiled at the photographer.

"Okay, Mr. Zot, I'm going to send you up," he said and handed him a visitor badge. "This will give you access to the 43rd floor. It expires in sixty minutes, so you'll need to come back down before then and sign in again if you need more time. Do you need help with your equipment?"

Zot took the badge with a smile. "No, I am fine. Zank you for your help, Officer Chambers. You've been very patient and polite wiz me."

Chambers smiled. "You're welcome. Good luck up there."

Zot gave Chambers a quick wink and a nod and headed for the elevators. Chambers chuckled and reached for the phone. His stomach gurgled, demanding lunch. He found the number for Pincole's Pizza, and dialed.

# # #

"SO, WHAT ARE YOU ALLOWED to tell me?" Fowler asked as he and Denton entered his office. Denton stood as his boss walked behind the desk and sat.

"Probably not much," Denton said. "Daniel wants this to remain very discreet."

Fowler chuckled. "Well, that's certainly the first word that comes to my mind when I think of you."

Denton smiled. He sat down across from Fowler.

"Don't worry. I won't withhold anything from you unless I absolutely *have* to."

Fowler put up a hand. "Actually, I'd rather you didn't tell me anything *unless* you absolutely have to," he said.

Denton looked at him quizzically. Fowler shrugged.

"In spite of whatever precautions Caldwell takes to keep this quiet, it *will* be the talk of the building sometime in the next … ten minutes or so," he explained. "That means Martin will show up in my office, desperate for the details so he can pretend to be in the know."

Denton thought about Fowler's relationship with his boss, Martin Rampart. A gaunt, unhealthy looking man with dark hair and beady eyes sunk too deep into his skull, Rampart represented the kind of supervisor every employee would choose to work for if they couldn't get a job reporting to Attila the Hun or Adolf Hitler.

Rampart employed a weasel-esque management style aimed at disguising his own ineptitude by setting impossible goals for his employees and then deriding their work so that *they* seemed incompetent. But where most weasel managers had a sense of where to draw the line, Rampart didn't, and so had also gained a reputation for submitting other people's work to his superiors in the name of "the team," thereby taking credit when things were received well and providing him a scapegoat if something fell flat.

Fowler had previously defended his boss's management style, citing the man's unfortunate split personality.

"He's an idiot *and* an asshole," Fowler had explained.

Denton leaned forward in his chair.

"I can't see you telling him anything about the case in any circumstance."

Fowler snorted. "I wouldn't give him a heads up if his shirt were on fire, much less tell him anything about the case," he said. "Still, it's just better if I don't have to lie."

"Got it," Denton said. "It's probably best for you to keep a low profile right now, anyway. What – with the job interview and all."

Fowler stared at him stone-faced. Denton shifted in his chair.

"Don't worry, I'm not going to say any—"

"How did you know?" Fowler cut him off. Without letting Denton respond, he gestured wildly from side to side.

"Is it my office?" he asked. "Damn it, I knew I should have been more subtle. You knew because my office is clean."

"No, because your tie is," Denton said.

Fowler stood up. "How do you do it – seriously?"

Denton sat back in his seat and dropped his eyes.

Everyone has secrets. Everyone lies. Shut up. Pay attention.

"Never mind," Denton said. "Look, it was obvious. You're not happy working for Rampart, you're ridiculously qualified for the position, and it's a VP title, which you need as insurance in case Huntsman really does take us over."

Fowler stepped out from his desk and paced the floor.

"That pretty much sums it up," he said.

Denton rose and turned to his boss.

"It might be better if you *did* have information to give Rampart if he asks," he said. "As it is, he won't believe you if you tell him you don't know anything."

Fowler scoffed. "I'm not going to risk your hide by giving anything to that brainless duck fart."

Denton's eyes went wide. "Whoa there, potty mouth," he said. "That's no way for an aspiring executive to talk."

Fowler waved him off. "I've done his work for him, I've let him take credit for my work, and I've let him blame the team for his mistakes. But that's it. I've done enough … I deserve this chance, and he's going to come through!"

Denton had watched Fowler's face redden and his voice rise through his rant. Now both men stood facing each other in an awkward silence.

After a moment, Fowler seemed to recognize the position he'd put Denton in, and he turned toward his desk with a laugh.

"Hey, sorry," he said. "You know how he makes me."

Denton smiled. "Yeah, I hear doctors actually prescribe working for him to patients with low blood pressure."

Fowler dropped back into his seat with a light chuckle.

"Any advice?" he asked.

"Yes," Denton said. "Get a manicure."

"I don't know what I expected you to say," Fowler grumbled.

"I'm serious," Denton replied. "The folks you're meeting with – they're senior executives. They *all* get manicures – even the guys. A nice suit and tie are great, but everyone will wear one. A manicure will send an unspoken message that you get it – that you're executive material."

Fowler looked at him straight faced.

"You may be seriously deranged," he said. "But I have to admit that sounds pretty sensible."

Denton's jacket pocket erupted in a clatter of technological noise. He reached in and fished out his phone.

"So you *do* know how that works," Fowler said.

Denton looked at the number.

"It's Beth," he said. "Are you going to be okay?"

"Of course," Fowler said. "Please take that call – outside."

Denton winked and snuck out the door.

DENTON ANSWERED THE PHONE, trying hard not to sound desperate.

"Hey there," he said. He looked off with a distant start for a moment, before realizing she couldn't actually see his attempt at nonchalant behavior.

"Hello, Denton," Beth said. Denton tried to gauge her tone for some hint of her state of mind. "Did you have a nice weekend?" she asked.

"*Did I have a nice weekend?*" Denton blurted out, trying to muffle his rising voice. "Well, I suppose I had a nearly glorious weekend – if you consider it the epitome of a good time to sit around your condo watching golf and wondering what your fiancée is up to with the Earl of Sullen Buttocks."

Beth giggled. "Why did you choose to watch golf?" she asked. "You *hate* golf."

Denton fell silent for a moment. He rolled his eyes and answered.

"I was trying to sound pathetic," he said.

"Well, I'd say that's a bull's-eye, Mr. Rourke. Well aimed."

"Thank you. Still, I *did* spend the weekend alone, you know."

"I do, yes," Beth agreed. "Do you have time to come over for a chat?" she asked. Denton still couldn't tell anything from her tone. He decided to play it cool.

"It's been a busy day, so far, but I'll probably have time in a couple of hours," he said.

"Really?" she replied. "Well, I guess I could see if my father wants to come over while I wait."

"I'll be there in twenty minutes," he said, already walking to the elevators.

"Are you sure? I don't want to be a bother."

Denton could now hear the tone of good-natured taunting very clearly.

"Yes, yes, I'm sure. See you shortly."

He hung up the phone as he entered the elevator and ordered it to the lobby.

"Golf?" he said to himself as the doors closed. "What an idiot."

# # #

NIKOLAS ZOT EXITED THE ELEVATOR and whistled his way through the lobby.

"How'd it go, Mr. Zot?"

Zot turned to see Officer Chambers smiling from the security desk. Zot returned the smile and approached.

"Oh, Officer Chambers, every-zing iz perfect!" he exclaimed. "Zee lighting iz just right, zee background iz … vell, exquisite."

"Glad to hear it," Chambers said with a nod. "But, you're leaving?"

"Ya," Zot said. He tapped his camera. "I do not have the right lens cleaner for my camera. And my friend, zis lens iz worth more than I'm getting paid for zis job, ja? So I vill be right back."

"No problem, Mr. Zot," Chambers said. "If you'll leave me the visitor's badge, I'll get you a new one when you come back in."

Zot smiled again and retrieved the badge from his pocket. He placed it on the counter. "Zank you very much. You are most helpful."

Chambers nodded and took the badge. "Don't be too long," he warned. "Mr. Handel can be a bit … severe about time."

Zot smiled and made his way out of the building.

Chambers smiled as he dropped the badge into the card recycler behind him. He stopped smiling as he turned back to the front desk and looked directly into the face of Joseph Handel.

"Good afternoon, Mr. Handel," Chambers said in what to him sounded like a fairly natural tone.

Handel did not smile. Dressed in a deep blue suit with a bright red tie, Handel had at his side a young, attractive woman in business attire.

"Good afternoon," Handel said as he glanced quickly at Chambers' name badge. "Officer Chalmers, this is Regina …"

Handel turned to the young woman. "I'm sorry, dear. Tell me your last name, please?"

"Hanson," the young woman said for – by her count – the fourth time since lunch.

"Hanson," Handel repeated to Chambers. "Ms. Hanson works for *The Daily* and she's doing a piece on me for the Wednesday edition. I believe you'll find her on the list."

Chambers nodded. "Yes, sir. I have a badge ready for her. Here you go, Ms. Hanson."

Handel intercepted the plastic card and extended it to his guest. "Thank you, Chalmers," he said without looking at him. "Now, is Mr. Niklas Zot here yet?" he asked.

Chambers swallowed. "No at the moment, sir. He's—"

"All right," Handel interrupted, looking at his watch. "Delete him from the visitor list."

"Sir?" Chambers could feel his heart beating hard in his chest. Handel turned to him, surprised.

"It's five after one," Handel announced. "Zot was asked to be here at one o'clock sharp. Now, *I'm* here, and Ms. …"

"Hanson," Chambers and the reporter said together.

"Ms. Hanson is here. If he can't be bothered to arrive on time, then we don't need him. I have a Nokama Elite Z1100 in my desk. Kelly can shoot the pictures."

"Your assistant is out today, Mr. Handel," Chambers reminded him.

"Yes, of course," the CEO replied. He turned to his guest. "Well, the camera is simple enough to use. I'm sure you can take the photos."

Without another word, Handel led Ms. Hanson toward the elevators as he launched into a discourse on how all successful CEOs stay focused on "the little things."

Chambers watched them move away, noting how Handel carried himself very much like a person of royalty – minus, of course, minor things like grace, refinement, and basically everything else.

Shaking his head, he stepped over to his computer and started erasing the curious yet kind photographer's name from the system.

Finishing his update with a final, determined click on the keyboard, Chambers nodded with satisfaction and looked up to see a man waiting patiently.

Chambers heart jumped into his throat and attempted to strangle him. The guard tried to calm himself as he looked at the man's black duffle bag, his tripod, and the camera around his neck.

"Hello … name please?" Chambers asked.

Don't say Zot. Don't say Zot. Say Angel of Death, or IRS, or Amway, I don't care. Just don't say –

"Zot," the man said. "Niklas Zot. I have an appointment with Mr. Handel."

A bundle of nerves went off in Chambers' stomach. He felt sweat breaking out on the back of his neck.

"Uh, I'm sorry, Mr. Zot, but I think you might be a tad late," he said using a tone most people reserved for slightly more alarming news like, "This country doesn't have bail," or, "That wasn't chicken in your sandwich."

"I most certainly am *not* late," new Zot announced. "Mr. Handel's office called me this morning and asked to change our time from one o'clock to one fifteen. It is now ten after."

Chambers tried to remember how much money he had in his savings account.

"I'm very sorry, Mr. Zot. There seems to have been some kind of mix up. If you can wait there just a moment, I'll check into—"

"Nein, nein!" Zot said. "I keep a strict schedule and I expect the same from those who wish for me to photograph them."

Chambers jumped back as Zot stomped one foot loudly onto the floor and stiffened into a very upright form. "I will *not* photograph Mr. Handel today. Perhaps tomorrow … perhaps never."

With a clipped bow to Chambers, the second Zot turned and marched out of the building.

Jim Chambers watched the man walk past the windows and down the street. Then he returned to his computer to make damn sure he'd erased any mention of "Zot" from the system's memory.

"What in the hell was he doing in Handel's office?" he asked himself quietly.

An hour later, Chambers watched Handel and the reporter step out of the elevator. They shook hands at the entrance and left in opposite directions. The moment they both disappeared from his view, Chambers ran to the elevator and made his way to Handel's office.

Approaching slowly, he slid his security card through the reader and opened the door just enough to peek into the CEO's palace.

"Jesus *Christ*!" he exclaimed as he flung the door wide.

He blinked twice to make sure he wasn't hallucinating.

"Why … why would you …?"

Chambers trailed off. Then he closed the door and made his way quickly to the janitorial closet.

"I can remove it, I can remove it," he told himself. "And if I can't, I'll just play stupid."

Chambers rifled through the closet and practiced his look of utter ignorance.

CHAPTER 10

Denton drove through the rain-soaked streets and tried to ignore the persistent, very loud rattle coming from the dashboard of his old and increasingly cranky Nissan Maxima. He added the noise to the bottom of a long list of problems with the aging vehicle and finally admitted to himself that the time had come for him to either try and sell it or just push it into the ocean.

He cast an unhappy gaze at the spot where he believed the rattle originated – a long, ugly crack in the dashboard which curiously only came into existence after his previous attempt to silence the noise by beating the entire console to death with his fist.

Denton refocused on the road and his destination. While visiting Beth normally put him in a great mood, today's impending "chat," which would inevitably turn to talk of potential dates on which their wedded bliss could start, had his stomach doing flips.

Nothing had changed for Denton. He still wanted to marry Beth, but the fear of losing his job continued to gnaw at the back of his mind. And with the arrival of her dad, the gnaw now felt more like a full-on buffet behind his eyeballs.

Why had she not said anything about his trip? And why did Archibald seem so surprised to see Denton? Why had Beth sent him away without a decent introduction? The corners of his mouth dropped downward as what remained of his devoured brain forced its opinion into the discussion.

Her father is obviously successful. You are – obviously – not.

"Shut up," he muttered.

Before Denton could dive deeper into his funk, another random thought fired in his head, and he felt his mood lighten for a moment.

The COO of United Alliance Bank asked me for help. I'm important to the Executive Office.

Yes! Not only did Daniel Caldwell seem to like him, the man put him in charge of getting to the bottom of Philip Anderson's peculiar demise. If this went well, Denton might earn himself a spot in Caldwell's organization. And in the event of a UAB takeover, Caldwell would make sure he took care of Denton … right?

Uh … sure, why not?

Denton ignored himself. He knew no guarantees existed, but this did present him with a great chance to establish a case for keeping him long-term.

Long-term stability. That sounded really nice to Denton.

Of course, he did recognize the one glaring issue with his entire plan: he had no idea what had happened to Phillip Anderson. How could this man have endured his own murder, and then – if you believed the official line – still found the energy to go back to work and hang himself in his office?

Denton smiled. He liked peculiar and impossible. He nodded to himself and declared the plan straightforward and doable. Solve Anderson's death, save Caldwell and the company from trouble, establish self as part of "key personnel," marry Beth … set fire to ancient Maxima.

Slowing in front of Beth's place, he punched the dashboard again, lengthening the crack but not dampening its enthusiastic chirping.

He didn't care. He turned off the car and enjoyed the silence for a moment. Then he winked at the dashboard's scarred outer coating.

"Piece of cake," he told his ride. His ride remained characteristically uninterested in its driver's commentary.

Denton turned up his collar, hopped out, and trotted toward Beth's door.

# # #

"I SUPPOSE *YOU* WOULD HAVE reacted better if you'd found a dead person in *your* trunk?"

Kevin Kahneman followed his accusatory statement with a defiant glare at his PC's monitor and then further followed it with a few deep breaths into a paper bag. The monitor, unmoved by the taunts of UAB's Accounting AVP, continued to display a full color and quite clear film featuring Kahneman and his famously dead boss, Phillip Anderson.

He read the note which accompanied the DVD and watched as Anderson continued to play the role of "Corpse in Man's Trunk" with conviction. Kahneman found his own performance as "Man Pulling Corpse out of Trunk" less impressive.

Oh my God … I look so fat.

Something in Kahneman's brain sprung to life and refocused him on the fact that the average viewer (or jury member) would likely find "fat," the least important word in the phrase, "Hey, that fat guy is committing a major felony."

Kahneman sucked air through the bag once more and resumed his frantic pacing and hand-waving.

"But, I didn't *do* anything," he said for at least the sixth time. He looked at the screen. "I mean, of course I did *that* … and *that* – and hell, obviously whatever else is on there. But it's not what it looks like!"

Kahneman lunged at the mouse and clicked out of the viewer. The screen went black and fell silent.

"Jesus Christ, Phillip," he said quietly. "What *else* did you get yourself into?"

He sat back down and stared at nothing. He thought about that night, and how stupid his plan now seemed. But he'd had no time to prepare, or plan. And really, who prepares for finding you can't put groceries in your trunk because your boss's dead body is taking up all the space?

"Nobody," he replied.

Kahneman punched a button on the keyboard and the DVD popped out. He picked it up and tossed it on top of the desk, and then looked around the room without focus. He poured himself another bourbon and drank it down. The warmth of the drink helped him relax a little.

He thought about his *real* plan, and how close he'd come to piggy backing off Phillip's scheme. But the man had gotten himself killed – and now some two-bit hood wanted hush money? How could his plan go from a smoothly running machine of six months to a colossal comedy of errors so quickly?

Kahneman couldn't argue with his inner voice which continually told him that his plan for handling Anderson's body had – for lack of a better word – sucked. But he hadn't had time to come up with anything brilliant. He just knew the dead man had to go back to his office – period.

Take him back to his office ... dump him ... leave. Employees and police would probably assume he died from the stress of the current UAB situation. Anderson's physical condition would actually help sell that idea, since he never exercised and had a cholesterol score Kahneman figured fell into a range more appropriate for an adult elephant.

But the deceased EVP had not helped *at all* when he found a way to go from lying on the floor in front of his desk where Kahneman left him, to swinging from the rafters. Dead people rarely displayed that kind of determination without assistance.

Now the police and that very strange Denton Rourke wanted to volley back and forth between suicide and murder? Let them – that didn't worry him.

But the blackmailer ... the blackmailer concerned him. He read the note again. The man wanted $10,000 delivered to a drive-in? Lovely.

Kahneman breathed into his paper bag again and then had another bourbon. He did not need the added trouble of some third-party sleazebag demanding a reward for catching Kahneman's ridiculous antics on camera.

And would $10,000 really be enough to make this guy go away? Kahneman doubted it, and he could not have someone coming back for more and more money.

He relaxed a little more. He could handle this scumbag - he could make the guy leave him alone. After all, he'd carted a dead body across town and dumped it in an office building. That gave him street cred ... whatever that was.

He picked up the disc and dropped it into his shredder, smiling grimly as the gears loudly tore it to pieces.

# # #

A FEW MILES AWAY, GAVIN SPINCER read a very similar note and watched a very similar DVD. But while both discs featured the deceased yet highly photogenic Phillip Anderson, this one featured Spincer, not Kevin Kahneman, as the best supporting actor.

He restarted the video and watched as he and Anderson carried on in a manner neither man would call complimentary. He furrowed his brow at the note he found taped to the DVD.

The police don't have to see this.
$5,000 cash ... Mayan Drive-In Theatre
9am tomorrow

Spincer wanted to laugh at the idea that someone thought he had $5,000 in *any* tradable tender, much less cash. But this unforeseen twist in his clever plan confused him and would not allow a moment for humor.

Though he'd carefully prepared his missions, he had not considered the possibility of new players forcing their way into his quest – especially not like this. Gadsden the Mighty had not been ready.

He wandered upstairs, chiding himself for the fact that – like he'd done so many times before in Warlords and Wizards – instead of approaching his missions in a straightforward and practical fashion, he'd gotten "cute," planning complex and grandiose ways to dispatch his enemies. And now it would cost him time.

"Stupid!" he yelled as he walked the hallway.

"What's the matter?" Tonya taunted from behind the door. "Is the murdering adventure not going well?"

"It's not an *adventure*," he fired back at the closed door. "It's a *quest*."

"Quest, shmest," Tonya retorted. "Whatever you want to call it, it sounds like you're failing."

Gavin pulled a key from his pocket. He already regretted trying to explain any of this to her, as his efforts to put her at ease had only scared her more. And now she saw fit to *mock* him?

He jammed the key into the lock and burst into the room.

"Quests are made up of multiple tasks!" he yelled. "And I have *not* failed!"

Tonya's eyes shot wide open at the forceful entry and the way Spincer spit his words at her. She watched in silence as he paced the floor in front of her, barely aware of her presence.

"All quests have obstacles to overcome," he said, looking at the floor. "And all good games offer non-linear play, which adds layers to the …"

Spincer trailed off, lost in thought. Tonya remained as quiet as possible, hoping that gave her the best chance at not being killed during his rant.

After contemplating the ceiling for a quiet eternity, Spincer finally shifted his gaze to Tonya. He smiled at her.

"It's a *side mission*!" he announced.

Tonya felt compelled to respond.

"And that's … good?" she tried.

Spincer stared at her as though she'd just asked the difference between DC and Marvel Comics. Then he nodded profusely.

"Yes! All the best games have side missions! Side missions help you develop your skills, and they help you gain experience you can call on when the time comes to complete the main goal!"

Tonya stared in horror, and murmured something.

Spincer's smile faded.

"What? What did you say?"

Tonya looked away for a moment, but could not stop herself from bringing her eyes back up to meet his.

"This isn't a game," she blurted out.

Spincer laughed. "Don't be stupid – of course it is," he said. "This whole thing is a game. I know the rules, and I know when – and *how* – I can break them."

Tonya had no idea how to respond, so she just sat quietly.

"I'll be back later," he said. "Wait here."

Tonya rolled her eyes as he wandered out of the room. She rattled her cuffs against the bed frame.

"Ya think?"

CHAPTER 11

Beth smiled as she opened the door.

"Hello, ma'am," Denton leaned against the doorframe and spoke in a smooth, authoritative tone. "I received an anonymous tip earlier that someone at this address might be in need of a stuffy Brit extraction."

"Did you, now?" Beth said with an eyebrow raised.

Denton nodded. "That's right. Thankfully, we here at Stuffy Brit Extraction Conglomerated excel at this type of thing. Normally we just lay down a few blocks of really disgusting cheese and a copy of *Boring Tea Monthly*, and they come running."

Beth nodded. "Interesting," she said. "I don't suppose this anonymous tip came from a cranky man of Irish descent who wished to abscond with the stuffy Brit's daughter."

Denton scoffed. "That hardy seems plausible, but I'll look into it."

"Good." Beth giggled. They shared a kiss as she turned to let him in.

"I missed you," she said, closing the door. "Are you okay? I saw the reports about the man who killed himself in your building."

"I'm okay," Denton said. "And he didn't kill himself."

"What?"

Denton shook his head at his own stupid self. He sat on the couch and looked at her.

"Sorry, I shouldn't have said that. Please don't repeat it."

"Of course not," Beth said as she joined him.

"I'm really sorry about the weekend," she said.

Denton tried to act slightly amused.

"Yeah, what *was* that? I'm no detective, but it seemed like the Duke of Dippy Britches didn't really know who I was."

"He's *not* a dip," she argued.

Denton titled his head at her. "That wasn't *really* the part I hoped you would refute."

He got up and walked to the refrigerator. He grabbed a Coke, popped the tab, and took a seat at the breakfast table as she followed him over.

"Do your parents know about me, Beth?"

Beth paused her approach for a moment, and then sat down next to him. She put her hand on his and looked into his eyes.

"They *do* know about you, Denton. I swear," she said.

Denton shook his head. "I'll watch an entire soccer game with you if your parents know how long we've been together, what I do for a living, that we're engaged, or even my last name."

Beth broke eye contact. "It's a *match*, not a *game*."

Denton shook his head again and took another sip. Beth squeezed his hand.

"Denton, you mustn't think this is in any way because of you," she said. "My parents are … oh, how do I put this … *difficult* people."

"Ah, yes," Denton said. "Well, it's no wonder I'm in complete confusion over all this, what with my parents being the most simple and amiable people ever."

Denton thought briefly about his father's penchant for outrage and iron-clad grudges against all sorts of living and non-living things if a case – however flimsy – could be made that said thing had wronged him in some way. His mind started to wander to his mother's antics, but Beth interrupted.

"Denton, I feel amazingly certain that in our time together, *you* will find yourself on *this* side of the table with far greater frequency than I, so for you own sake I suggest you let me apologize and explain."

Denton could not argue that for a second.

"Sorry. Please continue."

Beth nodded. "My parents are basically wonderful people – very kind, very supportive. But they are completely awful when it comes to my boyfriends."

"And fiancés," Denton offered. Beth gave him a look, and then continued.

"They are convinced that I still require their assistance in selecting a proper boyfriend, so no man I've ever dated has passed muster in their eyes. They find fault with anything they do and badger me constantly about how they're not good enough for me."

"Sheesh," Denton said as he thought about how he might fare under the Ingraham family microscope.

Not well, his brain helpfully answered.

"Trouble is, they've turned out to be right about it time and time again. You remember Derek."

Denton thought back to Mr. GQ – the obscenely attractive man Beth had been dating when they first met.

"Things had been going so well with him. He was charming, successful, handsome—"

"*Do* go on, please," Denton interjected. "Wasn't he also an Olympic gold medalist in Freestyle Hair Gelling?"

Beth blushed. "Sorry. Anyway, my father came to the states on business, so we all met for dinner. Derek was poised and polite throughout dinner. He spoke well and behaved wonderfully."

Denton finished his Coke and got up. "Please hurry to the 'but'," he pleaded.

"But when Derek went out to bring the car around, my father turned to me and said, 'Elizabeth, my dear, that man is a fraud, and – what's more, he's an idiot.'"

"Wow," Denton said. Then he mentally gave Archibald Ingraham a massive high-five.

Beth nodded. "Yes, well I was furious. And before I could regain my composure, I heard myself blurting out that maybe I happened to *like* fake, stupid men."

Denton chuckled and sat back down. "Sorry," he said. "What did he say to that?"

She shook her head. He said, 'Well, my dear, at least you have enough self respect not to try and argue with my assessment.' Then he kissed me and left in a cab."

Beth rose and began pacing across the kitchen. "And of course, he *was* right. Derek *was* all image. And he was so, *so* stupid."

Denton found himself enjoying this conversation very much. "Was he?" he asked.

Beth nodded. "It was like his entire educational career amounted to an in-depth study of ESPN and The Fishing Network."

"And the Chest Waxing Channel," Denton added.

Beth stopped and pointed at him.

"Don't get too smug, Mr. Rourke," she said. "You, too, can be a complete pillock sometimes."

Denton cocked his head. "I'm not familiar with that term," he said.

"You don't want to be," she said. "I just mean you have a tendency to get in your own way and make yourself look bad. Sometimes you don't seem capable of *not* saying or doing things which are not in your best interest."

Denton rubbed his jaw, thinking back to his last case and the number of times his mouth and brain plotted together to offer up some hilariously insulting comment aimed at someone who would retort using a well-placed punch or kick.

"And if I tell my father we're engaged," Beth continued, "what do you suppose his first question will be?"

"Whether you lost a bet or are facing deportation?"

Beth did not smile. "See … like that," she said.

Denton put his hands up. "Sorry."

Beth nodded. "The date, Denton. He'll ask for the date. And when we say we haven't decided yet—"

"He'll question my sincerity, intentions, all that good stuff," Denton completed the thought with a nod.

"Correct," Beth replied. "It will be open season on you. I do not want you to go through that. I don't want *us* to go through that."

"I don't need to be protected from anyone."

"Except yourself," Beth said.

Denton frowned. "Is that why you didn't tell him my last name?" he asked. "What does he think it is?"

"Smith," she replied.

"Great. Original."

Beth took his hands and looked into his eyes.

"My father has had some bad experiences with a few Irish folks. I wanted to ease him into all this gently."

"Why didn't you just warn me? I could have introduced myself as Lord Denton Snively of Hamptonshropshatshire Manor, or something."

"Hmmm … I guess I was afraid you'd introduce yourself as Lord Denton Snively of whatever you just said. Silly me."

Denton shrugged and tried to *not* feel like a mutant whose blue skin and third arm required a bit of getting used to at dinner parties.

Beth shook her head.

"Denton, I haven't handled this properly, I know. But please try to understand. I never *loved* Derek, but I *do* love you. I just want everything to be perfect and planned for my father this time."

Denton really wanted to huff and pout some more, but her sincerity prevented him from continued drama. He smiled.

"You'll sort this out, right?"

"Yes."

"Tell them all about me – about us?"

"Absolutely."

Denton shrugged, then leaned in and kissed her.

"Good enough for me," he said.

He rose from the table and turned to her.

"Of course," she said slowly, "you *could* help me out with all this sorting by providing a teensy, tiny little calendar number."

Denton grinned.

"Duly noted, and on the high priority list," he said. She smiled back at him, but he couldn't tell if she meant it. Maybe she had developed a defense against the charms of the infamous Rourke smile.

"So what's your plan for global family peace?" he asked.

Beth smiled.

"Easy. The three of us will go out to dinner. Tomorrow night."

The mutant shuddered.

"Can't see any problems with that," it lied.

Denton's phone rang. Desperately looking for an out from his current situation, he answered with uncharacteristic speed.

"Hello, son," Connor Rourke's Irish accent came through the phone. Denton shook his head.

"Hey, Dad, what's up?"

"We've been saying for weeks that we'll get together for dinner. How about we actually set something up now?"

Denton shrugged. "Sure, just not tomorrow night," he said. "I'm having dinner with Beth and her dad, His Royal Snootiness Archibald Ingraham."

Beth slapped him as he chuckled.

Connor Rourke did not respond immediately. After a moment, Denton heard his father's voice again, speaking slowly and very seriously.

"Archibald Ingraham," he said as though he were reading the name off an arrest warrant. "Of the Northampton Ingrahams?"

At that moment, Denton understood just how dogs must feel when they sense an impending natural disaster but can't quite pinpoint the specific danger.

"Beth, where in England did your family come from?"

Beth smiled. "Most of the Ingrahams come from Northumberland, of course," she said. "But Daddy can trace our family back to Northampton for the past four hundred years or so."

Denton turned back to his phone. "Yes, Dad – of the Northampton Ingrahams."

"Well, that's wonderful news," Connor said in a tone that indicated the exact opposite. "Congratulations son, you're marrying into the biggest den of liars, thieves, and complete bastards who ever set foot upon this earth."

Following the traditional Connor Rourke hang-up, Denton casually closed his phone and tucked it away.

Beth looked at him closely.

"Are you okay?"

"Yep!" he lied some more. "Dad says hi."

CHAPTER 12

Lyle Saunders sat in front of his computer and removed a disc from the drive. He glanced at his watch and thought about the money the next morning's haul would bring. Then he smiled.

In his time as a security guard on the overnight shift at United Alliance Bank, Saunders had seen it all – thanks to the company's decision to install high-definition hidden cameras in the executive garage with no announcement to its executive users. He recorded employees sleeping off hangovers in their cars, smoking in unauthorized areas, carrying out drug deals, having affairs – pretty standard stuff.

But nothing he'd ever seen had prepared him for what graced his monitors the past weekend.

"Jackass," Saunders chuckled to himself, thinking about his new money tree. He grabbed an empty beer bottle off his desk and tossed it toward the trashcan, missing badly.

The event had started as just a mildly amusing Friday night episode involving a clearly frantic little executive pulling into his underground parking space at far too quick a pace and at far too late an hour for anything work-related.

Saunders had laughed as the little man jumped from his car and darted down the ramp toward the elevators, his stocky little legs chugging along like fat locomotives. But he laughed even harder when the executive reappeared a few minutes later in possession of an office chair which he wheeled awkwardly up the ramp to his trunk while looking every direction through wide, panic-stricken eyes.

When the man popped his trunk, Saunders stopped laughing.

"What in the *hell?*" he said. He leaned forward toward his security monitor until he'd nearly pressed his nose against it.

Executive shows up well past working hours? Sure – happens all the time. Executive escapes with a fancy office chair? Stupid, but plausible.

Executive shows up very late at night, wheels an office chair through the parking lot and tries to transfer dead body from his trunk into that chair?

Um ... no.

Of course, dead bodies take great pride in their penchant for uncooperativeness – especially when it comes to attempts at moving them in any orderly, logical fashion. So Saunders sat riveted as he watched the man flop about clumsily, throwing all his weight into awkward pulls and lunges, trying to grasp the body from all possible angles, all while his eyes darted back and forth across the entire garage in continual fear of witnesses.

Just as Saunders started to tire of the man's wretched attempts to manipulate chair and corpse, the man maneuvered the body into a position he could work with. Bracing one leg behind the chair, the man hoisted the corpse into a sitting position on his bumper with the legs still in the trunk. Then, with a desperation heave, he pulled it over his bumper and directly into the chair.

That's when the video – in Saunders' opinion – got *good.*

Mentally and physically exhausted, the frantic and sweaty executive collapsed onto the parking lot pavement and panted rapidly. The dead body, keen on preserving the troublesome reputation of all dead kind, noted the removal of the man's foot from the bottom of the chair, and so began a hasty getaway down the inclined parking ramp.

The executive bolted upright and stared stupidly at the escaping body, unable to make any kind of noise.

At the bottom of the ramp, the chair collided with the curb and catapulted its passenger onto the ground in front of the entrance.

This caused the executive to let out a high-pitched scream as he scrambled to his feet.

Reaching into the trunk, the man grabbed what Saunders recognized as duct tape, and another item which looked like a kind of shiny blanket. He then slammed the trunk and trotted after his runaway guest, clutching the blanket to him and waving the duct tape over his head as though trying to reassure his pavement-stricken partner that he knew what to do.

While the man wrestled with body and chair, Saunders busied himself with his standard blackmail routine: pull all the day's recorded video from the target camera onto DVDs and then delete the originals from the security system. By the time the man disappeared inside with his precious cargo concealed under what Saunders decided was a tarp, he had already accessed the employee data system and run the man's plate.

"Jackpot," Saunders grinned.

Kevin Kahneman – up and coming executive at United Alliance Bank – was being a *very* naughty boy. He'd have to pay.

A lot.

As Saunders put together the DVD and the note the next day, his plan seemed to be moving along just like it always had before. But in his cursory review of the rest of the day's footage, he stumbled on to something fantastically bizarre – even by the new standards Kevin Kahneman had established.

Almost five hours before Kahneman made his spectacular film debut, his BMW sat peacefully in its parking spot, awaiting the end of another typically long day at the office. Then a car entered the lot, backed up tail to tail with Kahneman's and popped its trunk lid. A man in a large jacket and hood walked around to Kahneman's rear driver's side window and smashed it in. After reaching through the window and opening the driver's door, he popped the car's trunk release.

Saunders grabbed a pen to write down this new car's license number, but didn't even finish putting the first digit on paper before he found himself glued to the screen in stunned silence.

The hooded man opened both trunks. Kahneman's was empty.

His wasn't.

Saunders dropped his pen and watched the man hoist the dead body up from his trunk, slide it across the fenders of both vehicles, and roll it completely into Kahneman's trunk. He closed both trunk lids and then bashed out the back driver's side windows of three more cars on the same row.

While counting up new blackmail cash in his head, Saunders did note with appreciation that, in contrast to Kahneman's clown-like performance in the garage, this man's entire effort took less than three minutes.

He popped a fresh DVD blank into his system and began saving footage to it while whistling to himself. He prepared a second note with a discounted rate due to the man's lower position in the company.

Now, on the eve of a double payday, Saunders smiled through a yawn and turned off the computer. He picked up another empty bottle and tossed it toward the bin.

"Bull's-eye," he said as it connected with a satisfying clang. He headed for bed, making sure to set his alarm.

It was shaping up to be a *very* good week.

CHAPTER 13

Tuesday

Denton snaked into Fred's office unnoticed by UAB's key Communications employee, who sat engrossed in something on his monitor. Denton moved behind him and stole a glance at the screen. He smiled to himself and made a mental note.

Everyone has secrets.

He pointed at his friend.

"Fred Maxton *what* are you looking at?" he exclaimed loudly. "That's not even legal in twelve states – hey, is that a badger?"

Fred managed to jump from his seat, close his browser, and spin to face Denton in one spectacular, seamless movement.

"Stop that!" he whispered with a scowl. "That wasn't porn!"

"I know – sorry," Denton said. "I'll just clarify that loudly. One sec."

"I will kill you," Fred warned.

Denton smiled. "Relax. It's barely seven a.m. No one's here but us."

"What are you doing here this early, anyway?" Fred asked.

"I've got a lot of work to do."

"I'm sure. But what are you doing here this early?"

Denton tried to look hurt, but couldn't muster the interest to sell it. He shrugged.

"We have an appointment," he said. "Breakfast at Julian's."

Fred smiled. "Yes, right. After you."

Denton gave a mild genuflect and exited the office with Fred right behind him.

At the elevator, Denton turned to his friend.

"You know, you could have shared your secret little hobby with me," he said. "It's not exactly uncommon."

"It is around here," Fred replied. "People think it's weird – except for the people *I* think are weird – and of course they love it. But you're right. I could have confided in you."

The elevator doors opened and the two men entered.

"Blah, blah, blah," Denton said. "To breakfast!"

Fred smiled and nodded his agreement.

"GENTLEMEN, WELCOME TO JULIAN'S."

Denton and Fred stood in the employee break room down the hall from the main lobby and looked into the beaming face of Julian Chase, UAB Call Center liaison and all around awesome cook. Tall, slim, with his hair cut close and bleached to a near frost-white blonde, Julian should have looked out of place in a stuffy bank office building. But he didn't, and all of UAB's employees were thankful for it.

For reasons Julian never bothered to explain, he had chosen the third Tuesday of every month to commandeer a break room and serve an unbelievable free breakfast to employees who were willing to show up a little early for a shot at the limited, first come-first served meals. The feedback had been so positive that for several months he'd also hosted "Julian's Charity Breakfast Sale" every third Friday, with all monies collected going to local UAB-supported charities.

Denton inhaled and smiled at the master chef.

"Good morning, Julian. Smells like another stellar offering."

He and Fred sat down at a table. Fred pointed to the television.

"Can you put that on, Julian?

"No," Julian said, almost scolding Fred. "The news will continue to suck after breakfast. Watch it and be miserable then, not now."

Julian handed each of them a cloth napkin with tableware. Then he clasped his hands and smiled.

"This morning we have two options: Nutella stuffed French toast with hot maple syrup, or a special egg, cheese, and sausage tart with an apple compote topping. And of course, we have fresh Kona coffee to complement both dishes."

"Apple compote? Was that really the right call?" Denton teased.

Julian's eyes rolled to the heavens. "Contrary to what you might believe, Mr. Rourke," he said, pointing at Denton's stomach, "*that* is *not* a degree in culinary arts."

Fred laughed and unfolded his napkin. "I love this restaurant."

Denton grinned good-naturedly, but tried nonchalantly to suck in his gut just a little. "Me too. Okay, Julian, they both sound awesome. Surprise me."

"French toast for me, please," Fred chimed in.

Julian winked at the men and wandered back to a countertop lined with silver heating trays.

"So," Fred began in a tone that sounded like a tease, "how'd your chat with Beth go?"

"Oh, it was great," Denton replied. "I mean, what guy wouldn't be thrilled to find out his fiancée is hiding him from her family?"

"Ouch. You're not being a tad dramatic are you?"

"They don't even know my last name."

"Hmm," Fred's eyes moved into thinking position. Then he shook his head. "Sorry. That is a little … peculiar."

Fred wanted to reassure Denton, but the moment found itself ushered away by the introduction of a large, red-faced man whose bulging eyes had locked onto them.

"Ah, good morning, gentlemen," Marcus Rompeaux said, blotting his brow. "It's most opportune to have found you both here."

Denton looked around desperately. "Who are you talking to, Marcus?" he asked.

Rompeaux ignored the question and sat down at their table. Though Julian's monthly breakfast feasts violated numerous health, safety, and HR policies, Rompeaux turned a blind eye to the practice because he believed it promoted employee satisfaction. That and the fact that he found it positively yummy.

He stuffed a napkin in his shirt collar and draped it over his tie. "Now, I wanted to talk to you about the teambuilding exercises you'll be involved in this morning," he said as he waved Julian over.

Denton and Fred looked at each other. Denton turned back to the man.

"Marcus, you're looking at the only bit of teambuilding I'm planning for the day."

"Nonsense," Rompeaux said, still not looking at either man. "You both received the email letting you know you had been signed up for the Rocket Blaster teambuilding seminar this morning. I have your read receipts on file, so it's no use saying you never opened it, either."

Julian reappeared at the table and placed entrees in front of Denton and Fred. Then he gave Rompeaux a look of annoyance.

"Yes?"

Marcus smiled. "Surprise me, my good man."

Julian returned a smile – of sorts.

"Okay, how much of a surprise would it be if I poured hot coffee in your crotch?"

"Not much, I suspect," Denton muttered.

Julian's hostility stemmed from Marcus Rompeaux's latest HR compliance effort which aimed at terminating the charity breakfasts on the basis that they created "an unfair eating environment for lower-income employees."

Rompeaux let the comment slide and pointed to Fred's plate.

"I'll just have that, thank you."

Julian retreated from the table without providing a clear signal as to whether Rompeaux would get anything. Denton downed a bite of his breakfast tart and pointed his fork at their new table guest.

"You know, Marcus, you could really improve relations with Julian if you'd just drop this charity breakfast nonsense."

"Rules are rules," Rompeaux said. "Charging employees for food items puts those people with lower pay scales at a disadvantage, and highlights those disparities."

Fred snorted as he took a bite. "That is ridiculous. He already does *this* for free every month. The bake sale is for charity. How would he raise any money if he gave the food away?"

"It's out of my hands," Rompeaux replied.

Julian returned and dropped a plate of French toast in front of him and a pot of coffee in front of Denton. Then he whisked himself away before Rompeaux could ask for a fork.

Denton continued to chew heartily as he poured coffee for himself and Fred and then handed the pot to Rompeaux.

"Marcus," Denton said through chews, "I don't think you're looking at the longer-term effect of this decision. You've got to … oh my God, this is so good."

Denton turned to Fred, who nodded in emphatic agreement.

"Awesome."

"How's yours, Marcus?" Denton asked. "Oh, sorry. No fork."

Rompeaux smiled. "Yes, do eat up, because – as I mentioned – you'll be in the Rocket Blaster session and will need your energy."

"No can do," Fred said. "I've got multiple meetings this morning that I can't miss."

"I spoke with your boss yesterday and those meetings will be rescheduled."

Fred sat with his mouth open for a moment before finally shoving another bite into it and chewing slowly. Rompeaux turned to Denton.

"And you, Mr. Rourke," he smiled. "Your boss was elated at the idea of you attending this morning's session. So your calendar has been cleared of … whatever it is you do."

Denton wanted to argue with the man, but his food tasted so good that he couldn't stop grinning.

"Fine," he heard himself saying. "Sounds awesome."

He took another sip of coffee and avoided Fred's stare of shock.

Truth was, Denton didn't mind "sessions" like these because of the fairly straightforward expectations of the employees who attended: Let the highly paid consultants talk and talk and show their pretty presentation slides. From time to time, nod vigorously at them as though some particular point really hit home. Shake hands, eat snacks, and go home.

Events like that gave Denton plenty of time to think about other things, and today he had multiple issues he wanted to work on from Beth and her dad, to the death of Phillip Anderson, to Beth and the date, to Beth and …

Denton took a final sip of coffee and chewed on the issues. Maybe he'd just listen to the Rocket Blaster guys.

He rose from his chair with Fred following suit.

"Okay, Rompeaux," Denton said, "Fred and I are going to make this the best Pocket Buster session ever."

"Rocket Blaster," Rompeaux corrected.

"Whatever. Here you go." Denton wiped off his fork and placed it next to the man. "Don't let that get cold."

Rompeaux watched Denton and Fred depart, and then turned his attention to the used utensil, making a face as though Denton had dropped a dog turd next to his plate.

"Pass," he said to no one in particular as he tried again to flag down Julian.

"THE POINT I'M TRYING TO MAKE is that these are good problems to have."

Fred and Denton sat together in the UAB lecture hall with pen and paper out on their mini-desks. Denton tried to listen to Fred's continued attempts to make him feel better about his current situation with Beth. But as Fred started talking, Denton had noticed the colorful Rocket Blaster pamphlet on his desk and now found himself engrossed in the glossy advertisement promising increased productivity, teamwork, and overall satisfaction via the Rocket Blaster 'Soar to Success' program.

"I mean, look at me," Fred continued. "I *wish* I could pursue a relationship with someone special. But I'm here all the time, and dating someone in the Communications department is dangerous at best, and certainly stupid for a VP."

"Got it," Denton said, looking around at the dozen or so other employees scattered throughout the room. "Instead of being alone, you'd like to give your heart to someone who wants to shove you under the bed when her parents show up."

"Come on, Denton. It's *not* like that with Beth, and you know it."

Denton nodded. "You're right – I know." He waved the brochure at Fred. "This is stupid."

Fred picked up his copy and read from the cover.

"Supercharge your personal productivity and growth with the 'Soar to Success' program."

Denton nodded. "It also whitens teeth and quiets unruly children."

The two shared a quick laugh under the din of the other quiet conversations going on.

"GOOD MORNING."

Chuckles, murmurs, and all other sounds in the room halted at the voice which boomed across the audience like a command rather than a traditional greeting. All eyes immediately turned to the four men and one woman who inexplicably now stood next to the lectern, each clad in sharp, fitted business attire and standing at perfect attention.

"Where the *hell* did they come from?" Fred whispered in a barely audible voice. Denton only shook his head.

A slightly short man with a regulation flattop haircut stepped forward from the center of the lineup and approached the microphone. Instantly, the business commandos closed ranks and returned to attention. Though stocky, the audience could tell the speaker's suit covered a serious amount of muscle, not flab.

The man placed his hands on either side of the lectern and smiled.

"I am Retired Lieutenant Colonel Sam Miller, and on behalf of your entire Rocket Blaster crew, I'd like to welcome you to the very best efficiency, productivity, and development session you will *ever* experience."

"Oh my God," Denton whispered to Fred, mouth barely moving. "That guy is going to eat us."

Colonel Miller removed the microphone from its holder and stepped from behind the podium.

"Let's start by addressing audience questions and concerns."

Miller took a step forward and pointed directly at Fred, who tried to look away, but could not.

"Sir, to answer your question, we came from San Diego, California by way of the airport and a rented SUV."

Fred smiled and waved weakly as Denton snorted.

Miller's finger then moved about six inches to his left and landed on Denton Rourke.

"Sir, I have already had breakfast. And even if that weren't so, I am not in the habit of eating our clients' employees."

While the rest of the audience chuckled at his expense, Denton closed his eyes and tried to spontaneously combust.

Miller smiled. "I can't, however, speak for my colleagues. We'll just have to see where the morning takes us."

As the retired Lieutenant Colonel headed back toward the podium, the audience collectively sat up just a tad straighter in their seats.

"The time is now oh-eight hundred hours. Let's begin."

# # #

LYLE SAUNDERS WATCHED THE ANCIENT CHRYSLER approach slowly from the drive-in entrance and wondered how his first customer of the day would look. They always looked either angry and embarrassed or terrified and embarrassed. Both were fine with Saunders, and he liked the consistency that came with these jobs.

He stifled a grin at how this poor bastard's day would go. He'd pay Saunders the money and take the DVDs. Safe at home, he'd put them in his computer and find them blank, except for a text file telling them where to meet for the second – and final - payment.

Worked every time.

Saunders looked through the windshield and smiled curiously.

The driver, a large woman with big hair and dark sunglasses, waved at him as she motored slowly past and then carefully backed the car up and stopped trunk to trunk with Saunders' car, leaving room for them to make their deal between the two vehicles.

The trunk of the Chrysler popped and rose on its own. In the bed lay a single, very thick envelope.

"*Very* cloak and dagger," Saunders said, walking up to the car and picking up the envelope. He removed DVDs from his jacket and waved them in front of the side mirror so the woman could see them. She nodded, and he tossed them into the trunk and closed it, slapping the lid twice and saluting.

Saunders could not have imagined the transaction going more smoothly. As he opened the envelope for a quick peak, he started rethinking his code against blackmailing women.

But as he stared at the thick stack of grocery coupons he now owned, he suspected his change of heart might have been premature. A second later his suspicions were confirmed as the Chrysler's tires screeched under a sudden acceleration and its rear fender smashed into Saunders' legs, pinning him between the two vehicles.

Saunders screamed in pain and banged on the trunk of the woman's car repeatedly. But as hard as he pounded, the sound of the car's roaring engine continued on. He could feel the pressure continuing to increase against his shin bones, which he knew were already shattered.

"Jesus Christ, you left it in Reverse, you stupid bitch! Drive! Put the car in Drive!"

The engine returned to idle and Saunders fumbled in his pocket for his phone, already working on a story for the ambulance.

"Lose the phone."

Saunders froze. In spite of the blinding pain, he realized the woman had put the car in Park, not Drive. He remained trapped … as she'd intended.

"Lose the phone," the order came again.

Saunders threw the phone to the ground.

"It's gone! It's gone! Jesus Christ, let me free!"

"Remove your firearm and throw it on the ground."

Saunders wasted no time retrieving his gun. He waved it in the air and then tossed it toward his discarded phone.

"It's gone!" he cried out. Sweat poured down his face. He felt nauseous. "Move the goddamned car!"

The Chrysler shuddered into gear and delivered a new round of pain to Saunders' limbs. Then it lurched forward about a foot and stopped.

With no support from his mangled legs, Saunders' body slid down until the two bumpers pinned him in place again – this time at his chest.

"Oh, God, no. Please don't, please don't," he begged.

Saunders felt the car settle into Park once more. He coughed out a desperate sigh, and tried to rest against his own car's bumper.

The trunk of the Chrysler popped open again and the driver emerged and walked back to Saunders.

Saunders eyes bulged in panic.

"Are you out of your goddamned mind?" he yelled.

The driver removed the wig and sunglasses and grinned at Saunders.

"Oh yeah, you got that right," Gavin Spincer said.

"Holy shit," Saunders said.

Spincer reached into the trunk and picked up the DVDs.

"Bet these are blank," he said.

Saunders dropped his gaze as he winced and wheezed through the pain. Spincer tossed the discs back into the trunk and pointed at Saunders' legs.

"That looks painful," he said.

Saunders needed to take back control. "You're making a big mistake, asshole," he said. "I know where the real discs are, I know what you did. And I know where you live."

"Yeah?" Spincer smiled. Then he walked over to Saunders' car and got in. After a few moments, he returned and knelt down in front of Saunders'. He opened the man's wallet.

"Well guess what, *Lyle*?"

Spincer leaned in close.

"I know where you live, too."

Then he stood up and waved Saunders' garage door opener at him.

"Well, what do you say I give you a lift home?"

Saunders couldn't argue, curse, or beg. He could feel the blackout surging over him.

He welcomed it.

CHAPTER 14

Denton harbored an unhealthy distrust of many, many things – especially people. Over the years, he'd developed a, "doubt first, ask questions always" stance toward almost everyone, which made it difficult for him to talk to people, make new friends, or give travel directions to strangers.

But at that moment, Denton only hated overly friendly strangers armed with bright smiles, trite clichés, and promises of individual betterment through colorful workbooks printed and distributed by the thousands. He wished he'd been able to take Candace Covington up on her bizarrely generous offer to take his place in the event.

"Communication is the hub of all action," Colonel Miller told his band of UAB recruits.

Denton tried to shoot a look to Fred, but Fred refused to make eye contact, apparently still incensed that Denton had stolen his "ice-breaker" information sheet and listed as his unique feature that he suffered from "pig-tongue" – a disease he claimed made Fred's entire mouth swell whenever he ate bacon.

"Wouldn't you agree, Denton?" the Colonel asked his clearly oblivious recruit.

Denton turned to his commanding officer and nodded.

"Yes, sir. Do unto others before they do unto you," he said.

Colonel Miller's head cocked slightly.

"I'm not sure that's got a lot to do with the topic," he said. "But great food for thought, Denton – and a good way to end this section. Let's regroup with Lieutenant Gordon. We're about to have an awesome power collaboration session that will blow your minds!"

Denton frowned. He didn't want to collaborate with these people. He had a case to … hell, to *understand*, much less solve. He had a fiancée to placate and a future father-in-law to win over.

The two leaders stood in front of the group and smiled. Lieutenant Gordon spoke while Colonel Miller handed each person a sealed brown envelope.

"Good communication means great execution, and we're going to do some pretty unique role playing now to see how well you work – and communicate – as a team when success is on the line."

Lieutenant Gordon pointed to the group.

"Now, you are all parts of a bomber team. Some of you are bomb technicians, some of you are bomb loaders, others might be in mission control, or bomb inventory tracking – one of you is even the bomber *itself*."

Denton examined his envelope. Could he cut his wrists with it? Probably not. And besides, these guys probably all earned black belts in suturing and tourniquet application. He sighed and tried to tune back in to the Lieutenant's orders.

"Your job as a team is to get the bomber loaded with the appropriate bomb types for the mission at the appropriate point in the mission execution process. That will take coordination between the various departments, assignment prioritization, oversight, and cooperation."

"Now let's get a move on," Colonel Miller added. "UAB Team Z has already begun its exercise," he said, pointing to the opposite end of the auditorium.

Denton turned to observe the other UAB team, and watched in pained amusement as people shook their envelopes at each other and pointed frantically in numerous directions. One young woman sat on the floor, crying as she tore her paper into tiny pieces.

Denton's mouth turned upward and downward in a half grimace as he tore open the envelope. He retrieved the orders and read.

You are a bomb loader. You may only load Category A bombs. If a delivery team brings you any other category, you are to refuse the delivery.

Denton nodded and folded up the note.

"Where's the plane?" he asked loudly.

Scanning the group, he watched a single hand slowly rise into the air. Denton traced the hand downward and found it connected to the arm of one Frederick Maxton.

Denton grinned and wandered over to him.

"I'm supposed to stuff your bay with A-bombs," he said.

Fred crossed his arms and looked away.

"Are you pouting?" Denton asked.

"Pig tongue?" Fred said in a sharp whisper.

Denton opened his hands to surrender. "I'm sorry. I just got a little carried away. Forgive me … please? I'll buy you lunch. How about a nice BLT? Oh, wait, not that."

As Fred laughed against his own wishes, another UAB employee barreled up to them.

"I'm a bomb delivery team member!" he said. "What kind of bombs do we need for Mission C?"

Denton heard exactly none of the question, because his phone had buzzed as the man approached. He read the new text with interest.

Prelim. autopsy results on Anderson in. Come to the station ASAP. –T.S.

Denton pocketed his phone and looked around. Then he put his hands out to the sides of his head stared wide-eyed at the room.

"Uh oh – do you know what just happened? I accidentally accepted all the bombs from every category and stored them in the plane's cargo bay."

Denton walked away from the group and stopped to pick his jacket up off a chair.

"But then I went on break and smoked a cigarette next to them and BOOM – the plane exploded, and I was killed by the shrapnel.

That'll teach me."

The UAB group stood and watched him in confused silence. The Rocket Blaster team glared.

Denton waved and turned toward the exit.

"Sorry about that. See you at the role playing funeral. I call dibs on the gravedigger job – but only for category B cadavers!"

"Do all the jobs get smoke breaks, or just the bomb loaders?" someone asked.

"No, look …" a lieutenant began, but trailed off.

Fred's hand shot up.

"Yes?" another lieutenant snapped.

"Um, does my life insurance pay out for death by hypothetical workplace explosion?"

"Get out," Colonel Miller ordered with alarming speed.

"Right," Fred nodded. He waved and disappeared through the nearest stairwell exit, thanking Denton Rourke in song with his every step toward freedom.

CHAPTER 15

Denton practically bounced up the police station steps, taking in everything around him like a kid on his first trip to Disney World. A wave of nostalgia rushed over him and he felt the aggravation from his Rocket Blaster experience washing away.

In the months since he'd received his unofficial department shunning, not much had changed in the station. But so much had, too. He thought of the hate/hate relationship he and Russell Carlson used to share with such enthusiasm, and how a gang of giant fighting birds had helped them both find common ground and develop a decent friendship.

And Sowell, once frozen as a Sergeant doing Lieutenant-grade work, had received his long-deserved promotion thanks to that case, too.

And look how you were rewarded.

Denton rolled his eyes and pushed open the door.

Inside, the business of police work hummed with precision and the occasional loud expletive. Denton walked twenty paces down the main corridor, turned and walked ten paces left, then turned and knocked on the doorframe of Tim Sowell's office. And knocked. And continued to knock.

Sowell looked up from a file and stared at his visitor.

"That's very annoying," he said.

"I know," Denton replied, smiling and still knocking.

Sowell removed his oversized glasses and rubbed them against his tie.

"Is your plan to antagonize me into shooting you?"

"I just wanted to see what it was like to show up at someone's workplace and start bugging them for no reason."

Sowell smiled and sat back. "Would it not be easier to simply ask any of my colleagues about their impressions of your previous dozen or so visits?"

Denton kept knocking. "That's cold."

Carlson appeared, already yelling.

"Who the hell is knocking on the wall? Oh – of course."

Denton stopped knocking and smiled.

"Hello, Carlson. I'm here for all the news on Phillip Anderson. And it better be good, because I'm missing a very important … work … thing."

Sowell rose quickly and came from behind his desk while Carlson looked carefully in both directions.

"Keep it down, Rourke," Carlson said. "This case is being kept very quiet around here."

"Why?"

"Because of the UAB's connections to the department," Sowell explained. "As you know, Anderson counted numerous police officials as friends. The less they hear about this in passing, the better."

Denton shrugged. "Fine, whatever. Let's just go see the good doctor."

Carlson led the way with Denton and Sowell in tow.

"What's the mood like at UAB?" Sowell asked.

"Beats me," Denton said, wondering if he should actually know. That sounded like Fred's job. "Caldwell's given me total freedom to work on this as I see fit."

"No, he hasn't," Sowell replied.

"What makes you say that?"

Sowell looked over at his friend as they walked. "Men like that – with that much to lose, or gain – never give anyone total freedom. He's watching you closely; don't you dare kid yourself into thinking otherwise. Be on your best behavior, okay?"

"Hey," Carlson piped up. "I hate to cut the fatherly advice segment short, but the sign says we're here."

Denton felt a slight chill as he looked at the frosted glass double doors adorned with some of the most unnerving words he'd ever read.

COUNTY MORGUE
JEFFREY LEWIS, M.E.

Denton had worked with Dr. Lewis quite a bit during his first case and found him smart, organized, hard working, and insanely creepy. He felt pretty sure his uneasiness in the morgue stemmed from the doctor's practice of talking to his "guests," patting their hands, and generally treating them as though they were very sick instead of completely dead. It was that or his horrible neon ties.

Carlson knew about Denton's phobia, and grinned as he pushed open the doors.

"Welcome to the fun park, Rourke," he said.

The trio entered the bright, cold room and made their way toward Dr. Lewis, who stood next to a stainless steel examination table.

"Gentlemen, hello!" Dr. Lewis called out as he tucked the last corner of the clean white sheet covering his latest assignment into place.

"There you go, Phillip. All comfy-cozy," he smiled at the corpse.

"Lewis, you *do* know you're in charge of a morgue, not a bed and breakfast, right?" Denton asked.

"Ah, Denton Rourke," Lewis said, beaming. "It's been too long. I've missed your wit and your mind."

He stepped around the table and shook Denton's hand as he looked him over.

"And your continued rebellion against all fashion sense," he added.

Denton smirked and glanced down at his shirt. Lewis continued smiling as he circled back around the examination table.

"How have you been, Denton? I haven't seen you here since … well, goodness, since The Paladium incident? Can that be right?"

"You wouldn't think so, but yes," Denton said. "I've been okay, Lewis. How about you?"

Lewis smiled. "No major complaints, but it *has* been a bit boring lately. Hit and run death here, a slip down the stairs there, – nothing to get excited about. But now that you're here, there's hope! Nothing normal ever happens when Denton Rourke is on a case."

"I'm not sure that's the slogan I'm looking for," Denton said.

Lewis smiled. "Perhaps not. But I'll make sure to clear some extra freezer space just the same."

"Dr. Lewis," Sowell said. "Are you saying that Phillip Anderson's case isn't normal?"

Lewis scoffed.

"Hardly, Lieutenant. By the way, I *love* saying that. Too long in coming, *Lieutenant*."

Lewis pulled the sheet back and revealed the upper torso of Philip Anderson. Denton backed up a half step as though he feared contracting a bad case of death from the body.

"Don't be nervous, Denton," Lewis said with a smile. "Mr. Anderson is here to help you."

"Thanks, I feel much better already."

Lewis shrugged and began his routine.

"Phillip Anderson, fifty-four year old Caucasian. Examination reveals severe trauma to the throat, multiple injuries to the right side of the face and right shoulder, random small lacerations and abrasions found on his arms and knees."

The doctor turned to a table and picked up an item. He held it up to his audience.

"And, I'm told, a tiny phone jammed in his mouth."

"Another open and shut case," Carlson nodded.

Lewis nodded and looked at Denton.

"Like I said, I knew you'd bring me something good. Although, I'm a little surprised that Captain Levine agreed to allow—"

"Doctor, what can you tell us about the phone?" Sowell asked.

Lewis looked at the small device and shrugged.

"Non-working display model – something you'd see on any electronics store counter in the mall."

"Safe to say it didn't find its way to his mouth by accident," Carlson added.

"Very safe," Lewis agreed with an animated nod. "As to the message intended, well, that's *your* job."

"And the million-dollar question," Denton said.

"*Did* he kill himself?" Lewis guessed. Then he pursed his lips and shook his head. "Not a chance. Someone murdered Phillip Anderson – no question."

Lewis took a clipboard off the desk and read. "Among his personal effects we found his smart phone, a Rolex watch, a wallet containing four hundred dollars in fifties and hundreds, an electronics store gift card with two hundred and twelve dollars on it, and an American Express platinum card."

"So, not a robbery gone bad," Sowell noted.

"How do you know how much is on the gift card?" Denton asked.

Lewis smiled. "Just testing you, Denton. Nicely done."

"Cause of death?" Carlson pushed forward.

"Asphyxiation via strangulation."

The three men looked at each other, then back at Lewis.

"And yet," Sowell spoke deliberately, "the fact that we found him hanging from a telephone cord doesn't play into the equation?"

"Oh, it's clearly a factor in this equation. Just not in the *murder* part itself."

Carlson scratched his head and looked at Denton.

"This is your fault," he said.

Denton eyed him with amusement, and then refocused on the Medical Examiner.

"Go on," he said. "Wow us."

Lewis pointed to a thick, dark bruise running across dead man's neck.

"You can see the ligature marks left by the murder weapon."

"The telephone cord," Carlson said.

"The rope," Lewis corrected.

The men performed their collective turn and stare routine once more.

"Doc, there was no rope at the scene. Just the telephone cord," Carlson said.

"I believe you," Lewis said. "But the fibers I pulled out of Mr. Anderson's neck are from a rope – a braided, nylon and polypropylene rope, to be exact. About a quarter-inch thickness, and available in any hardware store for about ten bucks."

"So someone strangled him to death with a rope, then – after they killed him – strangled him a second time with a telephone cord and then tried to make it look like a hanging," Denton said.

"Yes."

Denton pointed across Anderson's body. "And the injuries on his face and other parts of his body – are all post-mortem?"

"I'm afraid so. He has a cracked cheekbone and a serious abrasion here on his forehead. No swelling and no bruising on either. Definitely happened after his heart had stopped. I've pulled what I could from the wounds – dirt, debris and the like. Analysis shouldn't take too long."

Denton stepped away from the table and looked at the ceiling.

"Another case involving dead people getting beat up," he said to no one in particular.

Carlson walked over and put a hand on his shoulder. "Look on the bright side, Rourke. You've been right about everything."

Turning to Sowell, Carlson smiled. "I say we bring Kahneman in for some bright light, big city questioning."

"I'd love to," Sowell said. "But this has to stay very quiet – almost off-the-books quiet. We can't bring any UAB executive personnel in for questioning without a pile of hard evidence first."

"Did you get anything from the security team?" Denton asked.

Carlson shook his head. "Nope. I put a call into their so-called "Security HQ" – a third-party vendor UAB contracts out to. I'm guessing this company was selected after coming in as the dumbest bidder."

"Ah, the marvel of efficiency gains," Lewis said.

"Yeah. Anyway, the genius I spoke to said they'd had a system glitch and footage from Friday night through early Saturday morning had been lost. No backup."

"Sounds fishy," Denton said. Then he slapped himself mentally for saying *fishy*. But no one seemed to notice his introduction of an outdated phrase, so he continued on.

"You know what we need? We need someone to go into the UAB security detail undercover. Someone big and tough, with a burly mustache and Cheeto powder under his right thumbnail."

"No," Carlson said flatly, looking down at his thumb.

"Come on," Denton pleaded. "UAB finds an employee *dead* in his office and security says, 'We got nothing,' and that's all just fine?"

"Nope," Carlson repeated.

Denton looked over at Sowell.

"Lieutenant," he said. "As trusty Sergeant Russell Carlson himself said moments ago, I've been right about everything."

"I take it back," Carlson said. "You've been an idiot."

"Someone on the inside could help us get to the bottom of this," Sowell nodded, trying to keep his patented straight face.

Carlson winced. "Lieutenant, please."

"No need to beg, Sergeant," Sowell smiled. "Your eagerness to assist is noted and your request granted."

Carlson shifted his stare back and forth between the two men.

"I hate you both," he said.

"Come on, Carlson," Denton said. "Sowell can't do it, and I already work there."

"Yeah, yeah, I know that, Rourke," Carlson grunted. "But you still owe me one for this."

Sowell smiled. "I'll reach out to the security company and work out an arrangement."

"Yeah, and I'll go tell my wife I'm working late for a few nights and see if she believes me."

"I can come vouch for you," Denton offered.

"No, thank you," Carlson said. "You've helped me out enough for one day already."

Denton smiled and turned to the table. He looked down at Phillip Anderson as Lewis recovered his body.

"So someone strangles him with a rope, transports him to his own office, then strangles him again and tries to make it look like a suicide," he said aloud. "And someone would do that, because …?"

Sowell leaned over his shoulder. "That's why you're here, Denton."

"*What* is why he's here?" a voice invaded from the double doors.

The group turned and met the scowling gaze of Harris Levine, 35-year veteran of the police force and Captain of Sowell's precinct. Denton couldn't help but notice the man's eyes seemed fixed on his position.

"Good morning, Captain," Sowell said with ease. "Denton stopped by to say hello, so Carlson and I brought him down to make sure Dr. Lewis didn't miss his visit."

"Let me know when you start believing your own bullshit, Tim," Levine said, eyes still focused on the outsider.

He walked toward Denton, who maintained a pleasant expression and eye contact with the tall, very fit man with dyed-black hair and beady blue eyes.

Denton had no reason to fear this man. He didn't work for Levine – not really, anyway. And he hadn't broken any laws … had he?

He turned his eyes from Levine to Sowell, trying to telegraph his confusion. But Sowell and Carlson had apparently discovered answers to some of the universe's greatest mysteries inside Carlson's notepad and could not tear themselves from its pages to assist.

Levine stopped directly in front of Denton and eyed him.

"The great Denton Rourke, in my very own police station," he said. "I must have done something really good today. Just here for a visit, eh, Mr. Rourke?"

"That's what he said," Denton nodded, drawing the words out slowly.

"Good, good," Levine nodded. "Because you know we no longer

hire amateurs here."

Levine's inflection made the word "amateurs" sound like something he'd found on the bottom of his shoe after using a French public toilet. Denton continued to smile.

"I was in the area and thought I'd stop in to let the guys know they were missed."

"Nobody misses Lewis," Levine snapped. Then he leaned to his left and looked at his Medical Examiner. "No offense, Dr. Lewis," he added.

"None taken, Captain," Lewis replied without looking up from his own suddenly fascinating paperwork.

Levine moved from Denton to the examination table. He wrapped his knuckles softly on the corner and looked skyward.

"Now, Mr. Rourke, I know this will seem a tad bit boring to you, but sometimes a death – even with a few odd circumstances – is just a death."

He lifted the sheet and looked at Phillip Anderson for a moment, and then let it drop back over him.

"Phillip Anderson's demise will not be a playground for theories of conspiracy, intrigue, and secret plots. His death is an absolute tragedy and very sad – very sad, indeed. And we will investigate further if warranted. But for you, it's *over.* Is that clear?"

Denton shrugged. "Like I said, I'm just here to say hello."

"Yes, well, to prevent this from becoming grossly uncomfortable for us all, I'll just go ahead and pretend that your decision to stop in for a chat with your chums during the autopsy of a man who died in your very workplace is simply a stunning coincidence."

He turned and headed for the exit, but stopped partway.

"I'll also assume you won't feel the need to stop by and wax nostalgic with my men anytime in the foreseeable future?"

"Yes, sir," Denton replied.

"Excellent," Levine nodded. He opened the door and faced the men. "Well, Denton, I imagine you've had enough of the morgue by now and would like to head back topside with Sowell and Carlson."

"Absolutely," Denton nodded.

"Good, good. Well, it was a pleasure to see you again. I wish you luck in the future. Now, this station is a little big, so let me walk you back to the parking lot."

He smiled and waved his hand through the doorway in a graceful gesture. Sowell, Carlson, and Denton lined up single file and began to march out.

"Denton!" Lewis called out from his desk.

Denton turned and watched Lewis trot over to him waving something in his hand.

"You forgot your phone – again!" Lewis said and handed him a very nice smart phone. Then he looked over at Levine.

"He loses his head down here, Captain. Can't handle all the corpses."

"What a shock," muttered Levine. "Come on, ladies, let's go."

"He's wrong, Lewis," Denton whispered. "People miss you."

Lewis smiled. "Get out of here. I'll be in touch."

Denton nodded and fell back in step with the others. Lewis watched them exit with a slight smile. He sat down at his desk and swiveled around the Anderson's table.

"Don't you worry, Mr. Anderson," he said. "He'll find out what happened to you. Trust me – you just wait and see."

Anderson said nothing in reply, and Lewis resumed his work in the sterile silence.

"DENTON, HOLD UP!"

Denton continued down the police station steps toward the street. He turned his jacket collar up against the wind and squinted into the grey light of midday.

"Rourke!" Carlson's voice called out from behind him. Denton turned and watched him stepping briskly down the steps.

"Don't trip and fall and hurt yourself badly," he suggested.

Carlson waved off the comment. "Hey, Denton, I'm sorry about that back there."

Everyone has secrets. Everyone lies. Shut up. Pay attention.

"Sorry, schmorry," Denton said. "How am I going to get paid?"

"Sowell will figure that out. You know he will. Look, he really wanted you on this case, and so did I – it was a no brainer. But the Captain wouldn't even listen to our proposal, so—"

"I get it," Denton said.

His head hurt. Captain Levine's refusal to consider a foul play angle likely stemmed from his agreement to keep this quiet for the sake of UAB. But Denton suspected the man might refuse to open a full investigation unless someone actually pushed Anderson off a building live on the nine o'clock news.

"Rourke … you okay?" Carlson asked.

Denton nodded. "I'm just tired. What were you saying?"

"I said that somebody saw something. In that garage, I mean. There's footage somewhere."

"But they said they don't record the executive parking garage."

"Yeah, well, that's what we in law enforcement call, 'A load of crap.' There's no way they're not recording down there – I don't care *what* the official line is."

"So you think they're hiding the weekend recordings?"

"Nope," Carlson smiled.

Denton looked at him without smiling.

"I'm tired and hungry, Russell. So if you don't say something coherent in the next ten seconds you're going to see me eat my own foot."

"They record that garage, no question," Carlson said. "But I believe them that the footage is missing."

Denton managed a partial smile. "I'll bet you asked them how often they've lost full overnight footage in the past couple of years."

Carlson nodded. "Four additional times in the last 18 months."

"That's a pattern."

"Yes it is," Carlson agreed. "But there's no rhyme or reason to the occurrences."

"Not yet," Denton said.

He sat on the bottom step and chewed on the information. He

squinted at the sun, which had decided to visit, and wished his sunglasses weren't sitting in his condo serving absolutely no purpose.

"Carlson, when you pull the personnel files for the UAB security team, you're going to find the same guard on duty on every one of those weekends. And you're going to find both the address and phone number on file are bogus."

Denton stood up again and aimed himself in the direction of Ford's Diner.

"And when you get his real Social Security Number, you're going to find bank accounts – probably local, with large deposit transactions within two weeks of each of those weekends."

"You think this guy's an accomplice to Anderson's murder?" Carlson called out.

"Nope," Denton replied back as he started walking. "He's an entrepreneur. And we need to see what he's selling."

CHAPTER 16

For Denton, Ford's Diner represented a shelter of serene protection against a raging storm of noise – a delicious shelter built with French fries, chocolate shakes, and the best chicken fried steak in the city. He breathed in all the familiar smells as he smiled.

Ford's had doubled as Denton's sanctuary and all round "place to think" ever since he'd met Beth there several years earlier. And while it was a longer walk from the police station to Ford's than he'd normally enjoy, today it had given him time to organize a few thoughts both case and non-case related. Plus, he now sat just a block and a quick jaywalk away from the UAB building – one of his favorite perks about working for the teetering financial giant.

Henry Sorrell – Ford's owner, manager, hospitality director, and head cashier – made eye contact with Denton. He flashed a smile and waved. Denton dropped into his usual booth and returned both gestures as Henry approached.

"Hello, Denton! How've you been?" Henry asked, pouring coffee into Denton's waiting cup.

"Hi, Henry, not bad. You?"

"The same, the same," Henry scratched his chin. "Though it has been just a bit slow lately. Hey, maybe you could come around more often, like the old days."

Denton thought about the old days, when he would visit the diner nightly, hoping to catch a glimpse of Beth who showed up sporadically with her pretty boy companion. He thought about the number of nights he sat alone, hoping she'd come by for a late night snack by herself. And he thought about the robbery attempt he foiled in the diner which lead to his meeting Tim Sowell and getting a real date with Beth. Then he thought about the obvious flaw in Henry's latest plan for fiscal growth.

"Henry, you don't charge me to eat here, so you might not find my continuous presence the revenue boon you were expecting."

Henry scoffed and looked offended. "I meant that you should come by more because we'd have time to catch up."

"Ah," Denton said. "Well that I can do, I'm sure."

"Good. I miss seeing you and Beth," he said. Henry fancied himself a bit of a matchmaker and took complete credit for initiating their relationship.

"How is she, anyway?" he asked.

Denton sipped his coffee and nodded. "She's doing well. She's really close to finishing her Master's."

"Well, tell her to come see me. She can study here whenever she needs to."

"I will, thanks."

Henry nodded. "The usual?"

Denton avoided eye contact with his belt line.

"Um, let's make it a half order. I've got to get back to work and … oh God." Denton buried his face in his hands.

Henry stayed silent and waited. Finally, Denton emerged from his quiet place and looked up.

"I've got dinner tonight with Beth."

"Great!" Henry said.

"And her father."

"Oh wow," Henry said, and then whistled. "So, it's really coming together now, huh? Meeting her dad – big step. Did you set a date finally?"

Denton cringed. "No, not yet. Still trying to get everything sorted."

Henry stared at Denton, focusing his eyes like lasers on his favorite customer.

"Denton, I'm getting impatient now. You're not getting any younger, and neither am I, frankly."

"I know! I know! I'm working on it – really. I just want to feel more secure with my job and future first. There's so much that's unknown right now."

"I understand," Henry said. "But let me tell you something. There are very few things in this world that will *ever* be for sure. Her love for you is one of those things. And yours for her is another."

"Jesus Christ, Henry," Denton chuckled. "You sound like a rejected Valentine's Day greeting card."

Henry shook his head with a smile. "Those are righteous words, young man." He turned back for the kitchen without waiting for a rebuttal.

Denton smiled and shook his head. He pulled out the phone Lewis gave him – which clearly belonged to Phillip Anderson. He turned it on and watched the screen come to life. He scrolled through the main menu, noting that he needed no PIN or other code to gain full access to the device. It seemed like an odd security lapse for a high-level banking executive.

He scrolled through to Anderson's contacts tab and opened it.

"Let's see what we've got here," he muttered as he scrolled through a few entries.

AD Air
BE Beach
CF Sands
DG Rain

Denton sighed. *Air, Rain, Sands,* … clearly the names in Anderson's list were fake – part of yet another code. He moved over to recent calls. Anderson had cleared them. Same with texts. And emails. In fact, as Denton moved through screen after screen, he realized Phillip Anderson's phone had *nothing* in it – except the contact list.

"Come on, little phone," he said. "You are the puzzle, and I am the puzzle master."

"Having a conversation with your phone might get you talked about."

Denton frowned and looked up at the smart-ass grin of Candace Covington.

"It's the only one that won't talk back," he said. He gestured to the opposite booth as he looked at her outfit.

"Let me guess," he said. "You've given up being UAB's best IT woman and are now auditioning for the role of 'Weird Homeless Cat Lady' in some community theater musical."

Candace sat down and gave him a sarcastic smile.

"*Only* woman in IT, so shut up. And there is nothing wrong with the way I'm dressed," she said. "I'm working in the basement all day, anyway – just came up to grab a to-go order for some of my team mates."

Denton nodded and returned to the phone. Candace watched him for a minute.

"Don't you have Risk and Fraud cases or something like that waiting for you?" she asked.

"Probably," he replied. "But I've got something else I need to attend to."

Henry appeared and placed a plate in front of Denton.

"So I see," Candace said.

Denton surveyed the enormous meal and wondered if Henry thought the words "half" and "double" meant the same thing.

"It's the half order," he said.

"I didn't know they did half orders on dinner for six menu items," Candace said, still grinning. She looked up at Henry.

"Hi, Henry," she said.

"Hello, dear. Your order's almost ready. Can I get you anything while you wait?"

"Just water, thanks."

Henry nodded and wandered away. Candace stole a fry from Denton's plate and watched him chewing his food and scrolling through the phone.

"So," she said, "You've been holding out on us."

"I have?"

"Uh huh," Candace nodded. "Word on you is that you're clever."

Denton didn't look up. "There is *word* on me?"

Candace nodded. "Yep. *Caldwell's little genius*," she said.

He stabbed another bite and returned to the phone.

"Not a genius," he muttered.

"I don't need convincing."

Denton looked up at her grinning face, then shook his head and refocused.

"Can you really piece whole stories together off a few seconds of looking at something or someone?" she asked.

"It's *rarely* a few seconds," he said. "It can take several minutes – or hours, or days."

"Why don't you ever talk about any of this at work?" Candace asked.

"People don't like to think someone's figuring them out all the time."

"Are you?"

Denton broke away from the phone and looked directly at Candace.

"Yes," he said. "I don't want to, but it's like telling someone not to breath. I can't *not* do it."

He took a fry, dipped it in gravy and popped it in his mouth. Candace did the same.

"Show me," she said.

"Go away."

"Come on," she pleaded. "I want to see the great Denton Rourke in action. I might look at you in a whole new light."

Denton put his fork down and wiped his mouth, staring at Candace.

He took a sip of coffee, still staring at her. Then he cut another bite of steak and resumed his study of the phone.

"Man, early fifties in a blue suit and green tie at the corner table to your left."

She scanned over and nodded. "Got him. But he's sitting with his back to us. How do you know his tie is green?"

"Irrelevant," Denton said. "The man works in finance, but is not a stock broker. He's here to meet a woman, and that woman is late – by more than twenty minutes. She's also younger – by more than twenty years. And she's not his wife."

"Ooh – he's *cheating*?" Candace whispered.

"I didn't say that. I just said she's not his wife. But yes, he's cheating. And the watch he's wearing is almost brand new – he hasn't owned it more than a week or two at the most."

"Nice," Candace said. "But you could make up whatever you wanted about that guy. We can't verify any of it."

Denton gestured toward the door with his eyes. Candace turned to see a young brunette in a stylish short skirt and blouse combo enter and make a bee line for the man in question. The man rose, kissed her on the cheek, and pointed to his watch with exasperation.

Candace giggled and turned back to Denton.

"Oh my God, Denton!" she said. Then she cast a suspicious gaze on him. "But those are fifty-fifty guesses. Man – woman, younger-older. Mistress or friend – heck, she could be his daughter."

Denton took another bite and pushed the plate away.

"Look again," he said. "I'm pretty sure she's *not*."

Candace looked over and saw the man squeezing her thigh.

"Ick," she said. "Okay, the watch?"

"Go ask him when he got it."

"You don't think I will, do you?" she challenged.

Denton shook his head. "Quite the contrary, I'm *sure* you will."

Candace popped up without another word and slowly made her way to the couple's table. Denton returned to his phone puzzle and scrolled through more names. After a few moments she returned.

"Tell me how," she said.

"What'd he say?"

"He got it this past Saturday," she said.

Denton smiled and rested his chin on his fists.

"Tell me," she repeated.

"No."

"PLEASE?" she threw a fry at him.

"No! God –" Denton looked up. "*Where* is your order?"

Candace leaned toward Denton and smiled.

"If you tell me, I'll owe you a favor."

Denton ran her proposal through his head for a few seconds. Then he took a piece of paper and a pencil from his jacket and started writing.

"Okay. You owe me a favor. I need what's on this paper, and I'll come to collect it tomorrow."

"Deal. Now spill it!"

Denton stared down at the table and started talking.

"The man arrived first, but sat with his back to the door, meaning he couldn't see his guest when she arrived. It was more important that no one in the diner or passing by on the street see him with this person."

"Not bad," Candace said. "Plausible."

"The time was 1:21 when I pointed him out to you and he'd already checked the time on his phone more than twice and stole seven irritated glances at the door. You wouldn't do that if you'd agreed to meet at 1:15, and no one agrees to meet at 1:10. They were supposed to meet at one on the dot."

"Not perfect, but pretty clever. The watch?"

"Like I said, he used his phone to check the time. He never glanced at his wrist. He hasn't worn it long enough to break the habit of using his phone as a timepiece – even though his watch is more accessible."

"Holy sh—" Candace covered her mouth and giggled.

"Yeah, yeah," he said, handing her the paper. "Tomorrow."

Candace took the paper and grinned. Then she stopped. "Hey, what about the 'not a stockbroker' bit?"

Denton shrugged.

"Stock market is still open. Henry keeps the Finance Network on for business customers. The channel has that scrolling stock ticker at the bottom. The only time this guy even looked at the television was when he asked Henry to change the channel to golf. No broker would do that until after the closing bell."

"Okay, so J.M. Coats he isn't," Candace said, stealing another fry.

"Who is that?" Denton asked.

Candace shrugged. "You know, our local genius stock broker – or *ex*-stock broker, now? He was famous when I was just a kid – was always on TV giving interviews and such. One day he's on top of the world, the next we watched him wander into a courthouse in cuffs. Lost his licenses, I think."

Denton nodded and returned to his fries. Several gravy dipped bites later, Denton stopped chewing in the middle of a bite of steak. He stared into the distance for a few seconds, and then his eyes slowly moved down and locked on Anderson's phone.

Without warning, Denton spit his bite of steak back onto the platter and grabbed the phone.

"Gross!" Candace said and made a face to match the sentiment.

Denton ignored her as he opened the phone's directory once more and scrolled. When he stopped, he held it up for Candace to see.

"Hah!" he announced.

HK Mist
IL Reeds
JM Coats
KN Flowers
LO Cloud

"Huh," Candace said. "J.M. Coats."

"Ah yes, dear Mr. Coats," Henry chimed in as he dropped a bag off in front of Candace. "Fraud, embezzlement, perjury – all the good ones. He's under 'house arrest' of sorts and can't leave the city. He hosts a series of investment seminars downtown."

"How do you know all that, Henry?" Candace asked, handing him a wad of cash.

"Beats me," he said with a wink. "Back with your change in a sec."

Candace smiled and looked back to Denton, who no longer sat in front of her.

"What …?"

"Thanks, Candace, I owe you one!" Denton said as he passed through the door and onto the street.

Candace watched him walk by the window, pecking at his phone. Henry joined her.

"He's very strange," she said. "Beth must be a saint."

"Amen to that," Henry nodded.

CHAPTER 17

Joseph Handel smiled at the perfectly coiffed young television anchor and let out his standard self-deprecating laugh.

"Well, Jessica, I wouldn't say, 'genius.' I guess I just have a … knack – I suppose – for understanding what people want, what they need, and how to deliver those things quickly."

Jessica fixed a serious gaze on the CEO of Huntsman Bank and nodded slowly, conveying a sense of oneness between them.

"I know just what you mean," she said.

She didn't. Jessica hailed from Belarus and her real first name contained seven consonants, three vowels, and an ampersand. She came to America as an aspiring model, but landed at the Financial News Network after a producer saw her in a bar, recognized her intangibles, and gave her a contract. Now she displayed her intangibles to a live television audience five days a week.

Today she had the honor of interviewing the fearless leader of one of the largest and strongest banks in the United States from a beautiful park across the street from the Huntsman Bank building. A live audience stood behind a barricade and filled in the camera space between interviewer and executive with waves and well-behaved smiles.

Joseph Handel loved these events. Canned interviews that

Huntsman paid for and subsequently controlled from start to finish. Huntsman communications writers provided the questions and the answers, and the FNN talking head simply spouted them out to him. No surprises, no gaffs.

"So, Mr. Handel," Jessica leaned in. Handel tried to ignore her intangibles as she spoke. "I hear Huntsman Bank has a secret new CD rate promotion coming out soon. Care to tell us about it here?"

Perfect.

Handel put his hands up in a "you got me" pose. "Jessica, how did you hear about that?" he asked with a laugh.

"Come on, Mr. Handel," she cooed. "What does Huntsman have up its sleeve?"

"Well... well, I guess I could announce it right now – what the heck."

The audience cheered and applauded as though on cue. Handel waved and gestured for the crowd to quiet down.

"Okay, everyone, I'm pleased to announce that today, Huntsman Bank will begin offering a new five-year Certificate of Deposit with the highest interest rate of any bank in the United States – 3.5 percent!"

The audience erupted again in a euphoric roar as though each person planned to stop into a Huntsman branch the minute the newscast ended.

As the cheering and high-fives continued, a path opened up in the center of the crowd to allow a single figure to move into full view of the camera crew.

After a brief refocus, the camera centered on the clear image of Ohnemus Parker.

Parker, in his standard light tan suit and red bowtie, smiled at the camera. Then he held up a hand-written sign about chest-high.

Hello, FNN Fans! You're #1!

A few members of the live audience read the sign and cheered louder, creating a new wave of elation on the set. Unaware of Parker's presence, Joseph Handel continued to wave and display his pasted on smile to the camera. But he knew the applause had gone on too long.

Parker continued to smile as he turned the sign over so more than a million viewers could read a second message.

UAB 5-Year CD Rates: 3.6% Have a nice day.

Neither Jessica nor her now-sweating sidekick noticed Parker and his sign. The cameraman did, but believed Parker's distance from the set might make it difficult for viewers to read the message. So he zoomed in. *A lot.*

As the audience got an up close look at the renegade CEO, Handel caught the scene on the closed-circuit feed just off screen. His entire body swiveled backward to face Parker. He looked at the man, and then his sign, and proceeded to turn purple.

Parker smiled at Handel and gave him a thumbs up.

"You're doing great, Joseph," he encouraged. "You're a natural. Keep it up!"

Jessica didn't need a television journalism degree to recognize ratings gold. She gave the camera an, "I am *shocked*" look and then turned to Handel with a smile.

"Well, Mr. Handel, it looks like you've got a real fan in your esteemed colleague, Mr. Parker. Do you want to say anything to him?"

Handel could have said any number of things. "Hi" works. "Hello" is fairly common. He could have laughed off Parker and commented on his crazy antics being a lot of fun to watch, but probably a little scary for the company he represents.

But Handel's talking points cheat sheet did not include responses to questions about an insane bastard who uses Huntsman Bank interview time to promote his own product.

So he just sat there, looking like a wide-eyed walking coronary.

Less than a hundred yards away in a UAB break room, Peanut Reilly ate her yogurt, watched her CEO on TV, and smiled.

CHAPTER 18

The footage of Handel's event hit the national networks immediately. Most chose to air the CEO's less than graceful exit, which included twenty seconds of him trying to remove his microphone while mumbling about possible SEC violations.

Denton and Fred sat in a 6th floor break room and watched as FNN repeated the key scene for the gazillionth time. A Huntsman executive got his sound bite in, expressing disappointment with FNN's handling of the debacle. Denton smiled at the footage and flipped the pages of a newspaper. Fred, viewing the incident from a public relations perspective, looked ill.

"Relax," Denton said. "Remember, they say there's no such thing as bad publicity."

"Yeah, well *they* are idiots," Fred replied hotly.

"Hey, hey!" Julian Chase wandered by. "That's no way to talk to your friend, Mr. Sour." He opened a Tupperware container and pushed it toward Fred. "Eat one of these," he said.

Fred pouted at the offer. "I don't want—"

"EAT ONE," Julian repeated.

"I'll have one," Denton said.

"No," Julian said. "You're too happy right now."

Fred grabbed a muffin and took a bite.

"There," he mumbled. "Satisfied?"

Julian nodded and extended the container to Denton, who took a muffin.

"Hey, these are really good," Fred finally came up for air. Then he looked at Denton.

"I'm sorry. I didn't mean you or anything."

Denton shrugged. "Whatever gets more of these in front of me is fine."

Fred smiled and looked up at the television again.

"Well, Handel's on every TV in the country," he said. "That has to make him happy, I guess."

"He looks puffy," Julian said. "And kind of purple."

Fred looked at Denton, who averted his eyes quickly and refused to turn back to his friend.

"You're trying not to laugh, aren't you?" Fred accused.

"Certainly not!" Denton spurted out with a shudder.

"You look like you're having a giant muscle spasm."

Denton closed his eyes tight. "That's fine," he said, unable to stop himself. "As long as I don't look puffy."

Fred watched in horror as his friend lost complete control and sat laughing quietly, tears rolling down his face. He turned to Julian, who had his back to him and whose body also seemed to convulse involuntarily.

Fred burst from his chair. "You two think this is *funny*? You think it's *funny* that our CEO goes on national television and taunts our key rival bank's CEO and makes him look like a … a …"

"Pissed off eggplant in a tie?" Denton offered.

Julian ran into the hall and burst into tears of laughter.

"Shut up!" Fred snapped. "… an *idiot* in front of millions of people! That's funny?"

Denton looked away. "Well, when you put your negative spin on it … yes. Still yes."

Fred glowered and chomped another bite of his muffin and chewed. Then he dropped back into his chair and mumbled something.

"Come again?" Denton asked.

Fred swallowed. "I said he does look puffy."

Denton nodded.

"I hope I'm not interrupting anything," a new voice said in a tone that sounded insincere.

Denton looked up into the scowl of Don Fowler.

Fred stood up and nodded at Denton.

"Well, Mr. … *Rourke*, was it? Yes, thank you again for taking the time to give me some insights into the important work your department does for the company. Good-bye."

With that, Fred rushed past Don Fowler and out of the break room. Fowler watched him head down the hall, and shook his head. Then he looked at Denton.

"You, in my office, with the paper," he said.

"Oh, that is *so* close," Denton said. "It was actually Professor Peacock, in the study, with the undercooked veal cutlets."

Fowler did not respond.

"Wait – what are we playing?" Denton asked.

"Not now, Denton," Fowler said. "Let's go."

Denton watched as his boss turned and headed toward his office. He swallowed hard and rushed to catch up. He decided against further conversation and stayed in step with Fowler until they reached their destination. Fowler opened the door and ushered him in. Denton complied and walked directly into the stern glare of Marcus Rompeaux.

"Oh come *on*," Denton said. He looked at Rompeaux. "Shouldn't you be off shutting down a Salvation Army collection kettle or something?"

"Sit down, Denton." Fowler said.

Denton complied, dropping into the chair next to Rompeaux. The HR man shifted his weight and looked at Denton.

"Do you know how long it took to schedule the Rocket Blaster team visit? Do you know how much it cost?"

"No, and no," Denton said.

"Well I do," Rompeaux sputtered. "And let me just say that you single-handedly embarrassed UAB in front of the top corporate teambuilding experts in the country."

"Oh, I did *not*," Denton argued. "Fred helped, too."

"Can it, Rourke," Fowler interjected. He came around from his chair and leaned against his desk in front of Denton.

"I like you, and Marcus here has accepted your work for Caldwell in spite of the serious corporate and personal liability potential it brings. But you step out of line again – you put even a toe over, and I *will* watch security escort your ass to the curb, where you will be more than welcome to continue your one-man stand-up routine. Is that clear?"

Denton looked his boss up and down quickly. Then he looked over at Rompeaux.

"Crystal clear," he said. "It won't happen again."

Fowler nodded to Marcus Rompeaux.

"We good here?" he asked.

Rompeaux rose. Denton saw the man working very hard to suppress a smile of satisfaction even in that moment of victory. He could not help but respect that, which aggravated him.

"Yes, Don, thank you," Rompeaux shook Don's hand. He then turned to shake Denton's. "Thank you both for your time."

Denton shook his hand and watched him exit. Fowler watched the door close and turned to Denton.

"How was I?" he asked.

"How were you?" Denton repeated. "You were an asshole," he said. "But convincing. You seemed genuinely pissed off."

"Oh, I *am*, Denton," Fowler replied, returning to his seat. "Please stay a bit longer so we can review a few things."

He leaned forward and tossed three pink sheets of tablet paper at Denton.

"First of all, turn on your phone. My phone is not your police hotline and I'm not your secretary."

Denton looked at the messages. Two from Carlson, one from Sowell, two from his father.

"Second," Fowler pulled a single piece of paper out of the pile on his desk. "What in the hell is *this*?

Denton recognized the form immediately. "It's an expense request for an investment conference here in town."

"Request denied," Fowler said, tossing the paper aside.

Denton grabbed the form. "It's a good conference, Don."

"It's *tomorrow*, Denton! Did you look at the late registration fee?"

"This is a conference on emerging trends in financial fraud and new detection strategies. It's valuable to our team."

"I see," Fowler said, eyeing his employee. "And I should send you to an all-day conference? You – the man who can't sit through a three-hour teambuilding session on site?"

Denton pondered the question, moving his eyes side to side and up and down.

"Yes."

"No," Fowler countered.

Denton didn't argue. He laid the form down on Fowler's desk and rose.

"You're right. It's a dumb idea. I just wanted to try and help you out."

Fowler chuckled. "Help *me* out?"

Denton nodded. "Yeah. I go to the conference and increase my job knowledge and gain experience I can use in my daily work. You get to check off the box on your performance review regarding your efforts to enhance the skills and productivity of your employees. Win – win."

Fowler watched Denton closely as though waiting for some visual indication of his employee's sincerity. Finally, with a sigh, he picked up the request form once more.

"You're right," he said. "This is a win-win. Send an employee to gain insights; show I'm dedicated to their development."

"Precisely," Denton smiled.

Fowler nodded. "Okay, I'll do it. I'll send Robert."

Denton shot up. "What?"

"Excuse me," Fowler said. "I need to call him."

"You cannot send Robert Moore," Denton pleaded. "Sure, he's smart and does good work, but he's boring."

"Seems like a selling point right now," Fowler picked up the phone and started dialing.

Denton put his finger down on the handset and disconnected the call.

"Don, his kind of boring isn't safe at all. It's lethal. You remember the last team meeting – when he hijacked the agenda and spent twenty minutes giving us the history of shoelaces?"

Fowler smiled. "Those plastic things on the ends of the laces are called *aglets*. I never knew that."

"We're not *supposed* to know that! We're not supposed to know any of the crap he tells us. I don't want to know about aglets, or the hourly rate at which grass grows, or the rich history of French coffee grinding. Please, Don!"

Fowler put the phone down and stared at Denton. A snorting laugh erupted from his mustache. Denton put his hands up.

"Okay, you got me, hooray—"

"You can go," Fowler interrupted. "But I know this has something to do with helping Caldwell. And I have conditions."

"Fine, agreed," Denton nodded.

"You need to hear them before you accept. First, the only item that goes on your corporate card is the conference fee. Breakfast and lunch are on your dime."

"Fine," Denton said.

"Second, you will actually *attend* the conference – the whole thing. And you'll put together a presentation for our team when you return so they can all benefit from your learning."

"Ugh … fine!" Denton agreed.

"And you take Robert with you."

"That is either a joke, or you hate me," Denton said.

Fowler smiled. "Okay, okay. But I'm serious about the other conditions. If you agree, I'll approve this immediately."

Denton raised his right hand. "I will pay for my own food. I will attend the whole thing. I'll build a presentation. I'll kick ass for Queen and Corporation."

"I wish you all the best in your endeavors," Fowler said.

Denton sat back down. Issues resolved, he switched topics.

"Ready for your interviews?"

"I think so," Fowler replied.

"Have you been getting your name out in front of leadership?"

Fowler shrugged.

"Well, I know a report I put together last week on departmental efficiency gain opportunities made it up to Erik Taberman's office. Word is he really liked it."

"Whoa – he's up there. That's great news."

"It would be if it hadn't reached him with Rampart's name on it as author."

"What? Don, you have to say something. You can't let him take credit for your work!"

Fowler kept typing.

"Nothing I can do right now. If I rock the boat, I can kiss my chances good-bye. If I keep quiet about this, Rampart might recommend me."

"I see," Denton said. "Tonight the part of Don Fowler will be played by a delusional sourpuss with powdered sugar on his tie." Denton leaned on Fowler's desk.

"Don, the guy's a weasel. He won't reward you for keeping quiet."

Fowler brushed at his tie without looking.

"I'm stuck. I have to hope Rampart does the right thing here. Raising a stink now won't fix what he did, but it will lose me that promotion – and possibly *this* job, too."

Denton shook his head. "This isn't right."

"I know," Fowler said. "But trust me – this is it. If Rampart doesn't repay all my favors this time, I'll take more drastic measures."

"Well okay, then." Denton rose and headed for the door. "I'm off to see a COO about a DOA EVP."

"Don't forget our agreement!"

Denton turned and smiled.

"Trust me, boss," he implored. He then made a very hasty exit to prevent a retort. He headed for the elevators, wondering what happened to people who called on Daniel Caldwell without an appointment. Were they turned away? Yelled at? Ushered into a vacuum tube and fired out over the city skyline?

He pressed the elevator button and waited. He'd know soon enough.

CHAPTER 19

Daniel Caldwell waved from behind his desk and stood up.

"Denton, hello!" he smiled, extending his hand. Denton shook it and smiled.

"Sorry for the intrusion," Denton said.

Caldwell shook off the apology.

"Anytime," he said. "I'm sorry to have kept you waiting."

As Denton crossed the office he caught sight of the sunset out Caldwell's window. He stood quietly and took in the gorgeous blue and orange hues accented by dark streaks of shadow. Caldwell smiled and sat back down.

"I didn't take you for the silent type, Denton."

Denton snapped out of his trance and turned toward the COO with a smile.

"Sorry. It kind of takes you away, doesn't it?"

Caldwell nodded. "Working late does have a few perks around here. That's one of them."

He pressed a button on his phone and spoke.

"Rachel, will you hold my calls for a few minutes, please? Thank you."

He turned back to Denton. "So, any progress?"

Denton shrugged.

"Well, Phillip Anderson definitely didn't hang himself. Someone murdered him and then hung his body up in the office."

Caldwell leaned backward and took the news without a word, but Denton saw his eyes twitch for just a second.

"I knew someone else had done that to him."

Caldwell took a cup off his desk and sipped. His pleasant demeanor changed.

"Motive?" he asked. "Any idea why he was killed?"

Denton shook his head. "Not yet, which is why I came by."

"Oh?" Caldwell leaned forward. "Denton, if you think there's anything I can do, just say the word."

Denton sat down across from Caldwell.

"I know I asked before, but I really think it would help for me to see everything Phillip sent you the night he died. Specifically the attachments."

Caldwell whistled. "Denton, I don't know." He rose, walked to the large window and stared out.

"I'm already taking some heat for involving you in this – nothing I can't handle, mind you. But turning over coded files from a dead senior executive?"

"His note said you would *need* those files – so they must be important. What else could he have meant?" Denton asked.

Caldwell shook his head and sighed. "Part of me knows you're right – that there are answers about his death in those files. But the other part of me won't shut up about corporate policies and non-disclosure protocols."

He looked past Denton and out the window. Then he took a deep breath and looked back at his detective.

"I will keep trying to get into them and if I do, you'll be the first person I share information with. Okay?"

Denton nodded. "I'll take what I can get."

"Thank you for understanding," Caldwell said with a smile. "Now, you don't mind me asking, are you doing okay?"

"I'm not sure I know what you mean." Denton said.

Caldwell looked surprised. "Well, it's just that … someone did murder Phillip, and word is out that you're trying to find out who's behind it. That doesn't worry you at all?"

"Well it didn't," Denton replied. "Probably because I hadn't thought about it like that until now."

"Sorry," Caldwell said. "But I find it disconcerting. I don't want you in harm's way."

"It's okay," Denton said. "Really – I'll be fine. My next step is to talk to an associate of Anderson's – a name I found in a coded contact list on his phone."

"How did you get his phone?" Caldwell asked with a surprised smile.

"Give me a little credit," Denton said with a grin.

"Of course, sorry. So why is he important?"

"I think he might have information I need to figure out Phillip's situation."

Caldwell nodded. "Well let me know if you need anything, and remember to keep it discreet."

Both men stood and shook hands.

"I will, sir," Denton said.

"How's it going with Lieutenant Sowell and the police department?" Caldwell asked. "Are you able to work together without issue?"

Denton decided elaboration and clarification could wait.

"Yes," he said.

Caldwell smiled.

"Good. I think being able to share information back and forth with the department can only help. And let me know if you need me to make a call or anything."

Caldwell looked at his watch and then leaned toward his monitor and moved his mouse.

"Well, I've got dinner plans this evening, so I'm going to log out and let you go about your business. Check in when …"

Caldwell looked up and found himself alone. A moment later he saw Denton flash by as he ran from the women's washroom corridor toward the elevators.

Caldwell chuckled and continued closing down his system.

"And I thought I was running late."

# # #

DENTON RAN IN THE DIRECTION of the restaurant, dodging slower people and keeping an eye out for a cab.

How could he have forgotten? He wanted to kick himself, but lacked the coordination to do that and maintain his current pace. He glanced at his watch and calculated his arrival time. Five minutes late. Not a felony. And since the delay stemmed from his hard work at the office, that couldn't look *too* terrible, could it?

Before he could take another stab at making himself feel better, his phone went off. He didn't stop to check it. He felt pretty certain he knew exactly who wanted to talk to him at that moment – and why.

Turning onto a new block, Denton saw the restaurant's glowing sign which seemed to be beckoning – or maybe taunting – him to run faster.

Denton stuttered to a stop at the door and yanked it open. He checked his watch again. Five minutes late. Right on time.

Panting, he moved through the entrance and scanned the bar to his right but saw no sign of Beth and her dad.

He turned toward the main dining floor and saw the pair tucked in a corner by the window. Not just any window – the window facing the street. The window Denton had just sprinted by to make his grand entrance. They both looked at him, Beth waving slowly.

Yep – they'd seen his pre-meal sprint.

Denton headed toward the table with a smile and a wave. Beth watched him the entire way. Her father continued to read the menu.

He leaned in to kiss Beth and she gave him her cheek.

"Hello, darling," he said. "I'm *very* sorry about being late. I got caught up in a conversation with our COO, and it ran long."

"It's five minutes, Denton," Beth laughed it off. "*Not* a big deal when you're working as hard as you do. Right, Daddy?"

Denton turned to meet the stone face of Archibald Ingraham. He extended his hand to the snooty statue.

"Mr. Ingraham, I shouldn't have kept you waiting, my apologies."

Archibald shook his hand. "Think nothing of it," he said. He returned to reading the menu as Denton took the seat across from Beth and her father.

A smiling waiter approached.

"May I get you something to drink, sir?"

"Scotch, please," Denton nodded.

Beth looked at him. "Tough day?" she asked.

"Not particularly. Just long."

Archibald continued to read his menu. "I would have thought your exercise routine might have put you in the mood for something more refreshing."

"Like a Bloody Mary?" Denton asked.

"Daddy, he was *trying* to get here as quickly as possible," Beth said. "He doesn't have cushy executive hours like some people."

Denton had no interest in having his fiancée and her father use him as fodder for their private argument, so he tried to steer the conversation away from arrival times.

"Well, that's the nice thing about United Alliance Bank – every day can be a little different."

Archibald put his menu down.

"You work for UAB?" he asked with a sincere curiosity that worried Denton. He shot a look at Beth before answering.

"Yes. I work in the fraud department."

"I see," Archibald nodded. "Do you like it?"

Well, it's boring to a level not measurable with current technology, and unless an employee gets murdered every week, I'm destined to eventually quit, get fired, or lose what's left of my sanity.

"Yes – it's very interesting work for a very interesting company," Denton said.

"Interesting choice of adjectives," Archibald said. "What do you find interesting about the work itself?"

Nothing. Well, lunch is nice sometimes.

"Helping the UAB customers who've had something bad happen to them. It's always something different, and that keeps things fresh."

The waiter dropped off Denton's scotch and left without asking for their orders.

"So what's the current feeling among staff about UAB's stability, given the constant rumors and the tragic events unfolding right now?" Archibald asked.

"Okay, you two are boring me already," Beth said. "I'm going to the loo. Back in few."

The two men rose and watched her walk away. When they sat back down, Archibald smiled.

"Let's change the subject," he said.

Thank God. Wait ... why?

"Sure," Denton said. He took a sip of his scotch.

"I hear you would like to marry my daughter," he said.

Denton held the sip a bit longer. Then he nodded.

"Yes. I asked her to marry me and she accepted."

"And yet you refuse to set a date."

Denton felt hot.

"Well, I wouldn't say 'refuse' is the best choice of terms."

"I'm very sorry," Archibald said, smiling. "My daughter asked you to select a date, and you have not complied with that request. Is that better?"

"Have not 'complied *yet*' would probably be more accurate."

"And when will you comply?" Archibald raised an eyebrow.

"I refuse to answer that," Denton quipped.

Archibald's eyebrows rose for a moment. Then he smiled.

"Well, you're a damn sight more clever than the last one."

"Thank you," Denton said. "But I think you'd agree this is slightly different than meeting just another boyfriend. I'm her fiancé, Mr. Ingraham. I'm going to marry her."

Archibald lifted his wine glass. "Well *that* Mr. Rourke, is very far from decided," he said, taking a sip.

Denton stood up.

"Well I guess that depends on whom you ask, Mr. Ingraham." He turned to greet Beth. "Wouldn't you agree, dear?"

Beth sat down. "What's not decided, Daddy?"

Denton watched Archibald's pale skin darken just a bit. The man took his time sipping his wine and lowering the glass. He smiled at Beth.

"Well," he struggled to buy himself time. "Your wonderful fiancé and I … we were just talking …"

"About potential rule changes in Cricket," Denton helped out. "Specifically, whether they'll change the Batting and Bowling Powerplay rules again."

"Oh, God, *please* go back to talking about work," Beth pleaded.

"Of course, of course," Archibald chimed in. "Denton and I can pick up our discussion another time."

"Indeed," Denton said.

With that, he emptied his glass and stood up.

"If you'll both excuse me, I'd like to wash up a bit."

He turned and headed toward the front of the restaurant.

Washing his face and hands, Denton wondered if setting Archibald up – and then saving him – had bought him any good will. Probably not. A dozen thoughts pushed into his head. The case, his job, Beth and her dad – everything mixed together like a giant stress smoothie. He shook his head and pushed out into the hallway.

Flicking the thoughts off his brain one by one, he made his way back to the table and sat down. A plate of fried calamari and a second scotch awaited him. He took a sip and smiled at Beth.

"Thank you."

Beth smiled back.

"So, Denton," Archibald joined in the moment. "Beth tells me that among your many talents, you do part-time investigative work."

"From time to time, but demand has been light lately." Denton took a piece of calamari.

"Denton was responsible for stopping the murders of the members of The Dash at The Paladium," Beth said.

"Ah yes, I remember reading about that," Archibald said, pouring himself some more wine. "I'm surprised you're having a tough time generating business. Didn't your previous client provide a glowing reference, given your success?"

Denton chuckled and drank his scotch. He looked at Beth, who glared at her father.

"Archie – may I call you Archie?"

"You may not," he said.

"How about Cary?" Denton tried.

Archibald snorted. "Please tell me your wit isn't your strongest point."

"It's one of … many …" Denton lost his train of thought and found his focus pulled to the window.

"How many?" Archibald challenged.

"A billion," Denton said, continuing to stare.

"Denton?" Beth touched his arm.

Denton didn't respond. He picked up a menu, held it in front of his face and let his eyes pop over the top. The table went silent as Denton watched Daniel Caldwell outside on the sidewalk laughing and conversing with a high-level Huntsman Bank executive Denton recognized from television.

Was it normal for executives from rival companies to hang out? Denton had no way of knowing.

Caldwell looked at his watch and said something to his companion, who nodded. Then both men headed off together.

Denton jumped up.

"You know what? I just remembered I have a conference tomorrow that I have to prepare for. It's an all-day thing, so I'll call you in the evening, okay? Here – for the scotch."

He pulled a wad of bills out of his pocket and put them in Beth's hand. He kissed her and saluted Archibald.

"Prime Minister."

"Denton, this is *eight dollars*!" Beth yelled.

"I know," Denton said as he walked away. "Hold on to my change. Love ya!"

Beth looked down at the money, confused. Then she and Archibald both watched Denton run by the window once more.

Archibald turned back to the table.

"You know, I think he may be on a case."

"Do you, now?" Beth asked.

"Oh yes," he said, nodding. "A case of booze."

"Daddy," she warned.

CHAPTER 20

Wednesday

Denton wandered the quiet halls of UAB and cursed the hour, the sunrise, the elevator, multitasking, bad coffee, and the general everything of life.

With the case still muddy, he'd managed to ruin Beth's dinner plan by abandoning her so that he could track Daniel Caldwell to his clandestine meeting with a Huntsman Bank executive. After watching the two men arrive at a soup kitchen, Denton started to suspect something. When his targets had finished two hours of serving food to the homeless and having their pictures taken by media types, Denton's suspicions were confirmed.

He was an idiot.

Now he had to blow an entire day at a boring conference just to get five minutes with a man who might or might not have anything solid to offer. He looked at his watch and noted the amount of time he still had before the seminar started. He'd find his own leads.

Denton made his way to the IT department and found Candace Covington sitting at her desk, quietly cursing at her computer monitor.

"Well hello, sunshine," Denton smiled.

Candace turned around in her chair and gave him a sickly sweet smile.

"Oh, good, it's Denton Rourke before my first cup of coffee.

How could I be this lucky?"

Denton started to answer, but then took a closer look at the woman, whom he'd never seen dressed in khaki capris, a white blouse, and clean, blue and white tennis shoes.

"I'm sorry, I was looking for a cranky blonde woman dressed like a cranky blonde teenage boy."

"It's funny how funny you think you are," Candace said.

"Seriously, you look great."

"Well I feel like an idiot," she said.

"Why the change?" he asked.

Candace shrugged. "No special reason. I just thought I'd try something new."

Denton scanned her desk. When he saw what he was after, he smiled.

"I'm here for two things. One – the favor."

"Right," she said. Then she gave him a look.

"I will keep my part of the bargain, Denton – and I'll do it today. But what you want is not as easy to get as you must think it is. I need a few more hours. I'll leave it on your desk later, okay?"

"Okay," he said. "And thanks again."

"You're welcome. What's the other thing?"

"Another favor," Denton said with a smile.

Candace stared back at him. "Uh, I'm paying out way bigger than you on the last favor already."

"I'll repay it – big time," he said.

She looked him up and down.

"Okay, I'm intrigued. What do you need?"

"Nothing much," he said. Then he looked away. "Just a program that can download files off a computer without the owner's consent and/or knowledge."

"Wow," Candace said. "How impressive do you think that diner performance was?"

"Tell you what," Denton said. "I'll pay out my side of the favor in advance. How's that?"

"Perfect," she said. "When?"

"Now."

"What?"

Denton extended his hand to her.

"Come with me," he said.

Candace Covington looked at him with a suspicious smile. Finally, she took his hand and rose.

"Denton Rourke, what is with you today?"

He smiled.

"Just follow me."

FRED STARED AT HIS MONITOR AND CHEWED his oatmeal slowly. Denton peeked in, smiled, and then dragged Candace quickly into the room.

"Hi, Fred," Denton said loudly and pointed to his companion. "This is Candace. Candace works in IT and hates most of her colleagues. She's smart, striking, and thinks you're dreamy."

"Denton, you son of a—" Candace suddenly shifted her scowl into a smile for Fred, who had jumped out of his seat and now stood looking at Denton with his hands on his hips.

"Denton, what are you—"

"Candace, this is Fred," Denton continued. "Fred is a powerful force on the UAB Communications team. He eats fiber, runs, and drives a very cool car. But he's secretly a complete nerd who loves computer games, can't talk to women, and – I'm guessing – owns a closet full of Star Trek action figures."

He pointed to his friend.

"And the other day I caught him trying to use his work computer to access cheat codes for Death Bringer 5."

Fred and Candace both stopped glaring at him and looked at each other. Denton pointed at Candace.

"Fred, Candace also learned to dress herself recently."

Candace slapped his arm and he yelped.

"And she hits hard. Oh, and she *loves* the Death Bringer series –

and lots of other PC games, just ... like ... *you.*"

Fred smiled sheepishly at her.

"Hello," he said.

"You're really a Death Bringer fan?" she asked.

Fred scratched his chin and nodded quickly.

"I stayed up until two last night trying to get past the Blood Mine in level seven."

Candace smiled. "I know a few tricks to get you through there. And I can show you how to access *anything* from this PC without getting caught."

Fred's eyes grew wide and his mouth fell open. Then he giggled like a dork.

"Okay, cool," he said. He scurried back to his computer. Candace nearly knocked Denton over following him to his desk.

Denton brushed his jacket sleeve and headed for the door.

"Okay, well, my work here is basically done. I'm off to the conference on fraud detection strategies or whatever. I'll see you guys later, I guess."

"Later," Fred and Candace said and without looking up from Fred's monitor.

Denton nodded with a smile and disappeared.

At the elevator, Denton hit the button, still grinning. The doors opened and he entered, patting himself on the back and praying his little plan would help his own romantic karma.

"Hold the door, please!" a voice called out.

Denton's arm instinctively reached out and complied with the request. Marcus Rompeaux waddled in and nodded.

"Thank you very – oh. Good morning, Denton," he said, pushing a button.

Denton looked at his watch. "Jesus, Marcus, what time do you get here?"

"On Wednesdays I come in early to file a number of weekly reports which are due mid-week and then leave early when possible." Rompeaux looked at his own watch. "And what on earth is *your* excuse for showing up before – good heavens – before eight-thirty?"

"I had to make a love connection," he said.

Rompeaux choked on a scoff. "I don't even want to know what that means."

"Well, don't worry, I'll be out of your hair all day," Denton said. "I'm going to a day-long fraud seminar."

"Ah, well, I did want to speak with you and Fred today, but I suppose you wouldn't mind filling him in for me later?"

The elevator stopped and the door opened.

"About what?" Denton asked.

Rompeaux stepped off and turned back to Denton with his arm across the door.

"Word came down yesterday from the HR Leadership Council. The Friday charity breakfast of Julian's is over, effective immediately. It's just not fair to charge for the food."

"Marcus!" Denton said. "The key word is *charity*!"

Rompeaux moved his arm out of the door.

"Well, now the key word is *over*. Enjoy the conference."

The door closed and the elevator carried a livid Denton Rourke toward the lobby.

# # #

JOSEPH HANDEL SMILED AT THE MORNING PAPER, specifically the Business Lifestyle insert for which he'd taken pictures and given an interview to … *what was her name*?

A tiny shred of embarrassment for still not knowing the young lady's name tried to develop, but his vanity and ego molecules vaporized it almost immediately. He looked over the picture of himself and the accompanying headline again.

HANDEL-ING THE LITTLE THINGS

CEO JOSEPH HANDEL: 'GOOD LEADERSHIP REQUIRES SERIOUS ATTENTION TO DETAIL'

Handel loved that cliché. He always kept a few handy for talking to lower level employees who seemed to always want tips on leadership. "Work hard," and "Don't cut corners," worked well, but the attention to detail bit always garnered the most sycophantic nods – especially when coming from the Chief Executive Officer of one of the strongest financial institutions on the planet.

He skimmed the article, pleased with its overall theme. He sipped his coffee slowly and started thinking through the various ways he would say "thank you" today as people called and complimented him on the positive press.

Handel's wife appeared, passing through the room. He cleared his throat and held up the page for her to see. She stopped for a moment and scanned her husband's latest newspaper coverage.

When she saw it, she covered her gasp with a quick fake coughing fit and headed out of the room very quickly.

"Nicely done, dear," she said without stopping. "I'm going to breakfast with the girls."

Handel waved behind him and brought the paper back down to give it a final look before he showered.

Then he saw it.

Joseph Handel spewed coffee from his mouth and spilled the rest of the cup on the floor as he bolted from his chair. He darted for a telephone, stabbed at its keys, and started yelling before it had a chance to ring.

"Sue them!" he demanded through coffee-infused wheezes. "Sue *everyone*!"

CHAPTER 21

Jake Mandlebaum Coats never bought into the moniker of "Wall Street Whiz." He thought the media used the phrase to describe far too many mediocre fund managers, and he knew that at the time of his greatest success, "Swindler" fit him far more aptly.

Though a savvy stock picker, Coats had earned his millions in the mid to late-90s by selling senior citizens the only kind of bonds more dangerous than junk status instruments: Fake ones. Through careful study of the highly risk-averse demographic and some well thought out planning, Coats managed to develop a simple, straightforward strategy for getting the elderly to put their money in his fictitious investments: Lie to them.

When meeting clients, Coats would caution them against investing in actual junk bonds and other risky instruments, and then sell them on safe, reliable bonds from solid, reliable companies he made up on his home computer. The plan made him a lot of money, but the money eventually made him sloppy. And when it did, Avery Thynes made him pay.

Thynes, a millionaire many times over, enjoyed spending his retirement years accepting invitations from hungry brokers eager to pitch him their investment strategies, and then see how much of their time he could waste with pointless, annoying questions. Nothing pleased him more than watching these know-it-alls turn red, lose their patience, and run out his front door screaming.

Well, nothing except JM Coats.

The old JM Coats would have vetted Thynes carefully and caught that the man's son was Daniel Thynes, owner of Thynes & Gilford Fund Management Group. From there Coats would have learned that Daniel Thynes learned everything he knew about investment markets from his father.

But he didn't. So when he presented Thynes with bogus bonds from his bogus companies, Mr. Thynes smiled and asked him to wait while he got his checkbook. Then he went to his bedroom and alerted the FBI and SEC via the technology toddler called the World Wide Web. The SEC vaporized Coats' brokerage license before he finished his first cup of tea, and the Feds cuffed him soon after his second.

Judge Barton Hoyer reviewed the indictment against Coats and noticed something curious about the man's modus operandi. As a rule, Coats never took more than 20% of a client's liquid assets. And in many cases he had called clients with legitimate stock recommendations that easily covered the money he'd stolen. Judge Hoyer said the country would have been in a far better place if all its criminals – and many of its stock brokers – would emulate the Coats model. He sentenced Coats to 10 years probation and recommended he run for mayor. Hoyer retired from the bench a week later.

"And now you're lecturing on corporate fraud prevention and investment risk," Denton finished the story.

JM Coats sat next to him on a bench outside the seminar, wearing a dark overcoat over a deep brown suit and white shirt. He smoked his cigarette and smiled at Denton.

"Those who are legally unable to do, teach," he said.

Denton smiled back, happy with how openly Coats had offered up his story. Not wanting to alarm the man by wandering up unannounced and grilling him about a murdered banker, Denton watched Coats before the seminar had begun and during the morning break. When lunchtime came, he knew that while everyone else hit the free buffet, Coats would return to his bench for a smoke. So Denton left a minute or two early and when Coats arrived, he found his bench already occupied.

Denton turned toward him, not sure how to segue into his next set of questions.

"Well, I've been enjoying this conference. I work for United Alliance Bank, and I can't wait to share some of this with my colleagues."

As Denton spoke, he noticed a twitch at the corner of Coats' mouth.

"Ah, UAB, eh?" Coats said. "I used to work with some folks there. A lot of good people, if I remember."

"Yeah, I agree. Hey, maybe you worked with Phillip Anderson – our EVP of Accounting?"

"No, I can't say that's a name I'm familiar with," Coats said.

"That's kind of weird," Denton said, scrunching his mouth into a half frown. "Because—"

A ringing from Coats' pocket interrupted him. Coats took out his phone and stood up.

"You must excuse me," Coats said with a kind smile. "I have to take this."

Denton nodded and watched Coats walk several steps away before answering his phone.

"Hello?" Coats said.

"Because I'm pretty sure he knew *you*," the voice on the phone said.

Coats turned back to Denton, who smiled at him and held up Anderson's phone.

Coats looked at him for a moment, then pocketed his phone with a chuckle and walked back to the bench.

"Okay, Mr. Rourke," Coats sat back down, "Who are you and what do you want?"

"I'm just a fraud analyst for UAB. But I've got a bit of an investigative background. Phillip Anderson died inside the UAB building last weekend, and our COO asked me to help look into the matter."

Coats raised an eyebrow. "Did he?"

"Yes, Anderson left behind a lot of unanswered questions and a very bizarre scene in his office. I'm just trying to see if I can piece together what happened."

Coats sat quietly for a few moments. Then he turned to Denton.

"Do the police know about his phone?"

Denton's internal warning system went off. If Coats did have something to do with Anderson's demise, the man might make it a high priority to remove the phone from Denton's possession, followed closely by removing the life from his body.

"Here's the thing," Denton said. "Anderson *wanted* someone to find your name. But I don't think he wanted your head. I think he wanted your help."

Coats put a new cigarette to his lips and lit it. He cast an eye on Denton as he blew smoke skyward. Then he nodded.

"Phillip Anderson and I attended business school together. He studied accounting, I focused on investment management. We weren't great friends, but we knew each other well enough. Last year, out of nowhere, he called me."

"How long had it been since the two of you had spoken?"

"Ages," Coats said. "He said he was working on a risk assessment model and wanted to talk theory with me."

The emphasis Coats put on the word *theory* peaked Denton's interest.

"What kind of theory?" he asked.

Coats gave Denton a stern look.

"Mr. Rourke, I've done nothing wrong when it comes to Phillip Anderson, I said nothing to him that anyone could construe as illegal. That said, I *am* still on probation for my past crimes, and have no interest in turning even the most remote police curiosity my direction."

Denton nodded and returned the gaze.

"I have no interest in bringing you into this at all, Mr. Coats. I swear. I'm just trying to help UAB prevent further problems, if that's possible."

"Why?" Coats challenged.

"Why what?"

Coats took a drag on his cigarette. "Why would a lowly fraud analyst – if you'll forgive the phrasing – want to help United Alliance Bank? Out of the goodness of your heart?"

"Why do men do anything peculiar?" Denton replied. "It's for a girl."

"A girl?" Coats narrowed his eyes, interested.

"Yep. We're engaged and she wants to set a date. I work for UAB, which means every day could be the last for my job, heck, for my whole *team*."

"And you think maybe if you uncover – and then prevent a serious financial scandal for the company that the powers that be will buy you a gold watch and grant you tenure?"

Denton smiled. "Something like that. I prove myself invaluable, maybe that comes in handy later."

"Well, Mr. Rourke, I admire your motives, I truly do. But the name and number of a convicted swindler in a dead man's phone isn't a lot to go on, I'm afraid."

"No, but now I also have that convicted swindler alluding to a – how did you put it – 'serious financial scandal' – I believe." Denton said. "I'll bet that means I'm on the right track."

Coats stared at Denton. "Well, you mentioned—"

"Nope," Denton answered.

The man looked at his cigarette, and then scoffed with a smile. "I'm sure you said—"

"*Nothing*," Denton helped. "Not a single word."

Coats continued to stare at Denton. Denton took Anderson's phone out and slid it across the bench to Coats.

"You can have this, Mr. Coats," he said. "I'm here to gather information, not to take names."

Coats picked up the phone and turned it around in his hand. He pocketed it and chuckled.

"At the risk of being an old fool, I think I believe you, Mr. Rourke."

He rose from the bench and turned to Denton.

"As Phillip and I talked, I got the sinking suspicion that our conversation had nothing to do with theory, and everything to do with actual action. I believed he was planning something very real."

He took a final drag on his cigarette and crushed it under his shoe.

"And I told him as much," he added.

"How did he respond?" Denton asked.

Coats shook his head. "I'm sorry, Mr. Rourke. I do believe your sincerity – truly, I do. But as I said, I am on probation. And while I'm fairly certain my conversation with Phillip in no way incriminates me, I cannot take that chance. Nor do I want to put you in a position of being forced to reveal something I think you'd otherwise keep to yourself."

Denton nodded. He stood and shook Coats' hand.

"Can you tell me *anything* else? As vague as you'd like."

"Honestly, I did not allow Phillip to get into very much detail. I told him his theory would be a very bad idea in practice, I'm afraid that's it."

Coats looked up at the sky.

"Well, Mr. Rourke, this has been a truly unique lunch break, but I do have to get back."

"Thank you. I hope you'll forgive me if I miss the second half of the seminar. I think I've got work to do."

Coats smiled. "I'll see that UAB receives confirmation of your presence for the entire event."

He turned toward the hotel, but stopped after a couple of steps. He rotated back toward Denton.

"Good luck, Mr. Rourke."

Denton waved and watched the man make his way back into the hotel. Then he turned and headed up the block.

# # #

"DON, I DON'T WANT TO pull rank here," Martin Rampart said. "But I need to review your documents before they go up the chain."

Don Fowler sat behind his desk and watched his boss trying to smile while sweating. He looked like an undernourished hyena. Fowler almost felt sorry for him.

"And remind me why that is again?" Don requested. "Oh, wait – is it because you need time to take my name out of the page headers and put in your own? Because I can do that for you and save you some time."

Rampart waved a finger at Fowler. "I told you, that was an oversight. I don't know why my admin did that, and I just couldn't find the right time to set it straight with Taberman."

"I don't know, Martin," Fowler stroked his mustache and tried not to show how much pleasure this conversation gave him. He held up a manila folder. "If Taberman loves what *you* did with that report, and you turn in the follow-up – which clarifies numerous points and provides insights only *you* – as the writer – could know, but it has *my* name on it, that could look very bad."

"Well," Rampart paused and glossed on a plastic smile. "That's just something I'm willing to do … for you."

"Martin, that could make you look bad," Fowler said. "Having you look bad doesn't make anyone look good."

He extended the folder to his boss.

"You should go ahead and put your name on this. For the good of the team."

Martin shifted his wiry frame a bit and looked closely at Don Fowler.

"You're sure about this?" he asked.

"Absolutely," Fowler nodded. "Take it. Your name should be on it. No question."

Martin Rampart's plastic smile shifted into something more snakelike. He took the folder from Fowler and nodded.

"I knew you'd make the smart move, Don. You're a smart guy – a team player," he said.

Fowler leaned forward. "Which is what that new vice president position needs, Martin. I've got the experience and the know-how, and with you backing me to Taberman—"

"Whoa, whoa, there, Don," Martin shook his head and waved the folder. "Look, I appreciate that you want to move up, but honestly, I just don't see that role playing to your strengths."

Fowler stood up. "Doing all your work for you isn't my only strength, Martin. You *owe* me this."

Martin chuckled. "You know, it would be easy for me to sit here and lie to you, tell you I'll put in a good word for you, and then torpedo your candidacy behind your back. But I'm being honest here. I think you ought to be a little more appreciative."

Fowler opened up a drawer on his desk. "Yeah, Martin, you're a stand up guy." He pulled out a black file folder and placed it on the desk in front of him. "Maybe I can learn to be as honest as you are one day."

Martin pointed at the folder. "What is that?"

"This?" Fowler said. "Oh, it's the follow-up report Taberman asked for."

"Then what …?" Martin Rampart flipped open the folder he held. His eyes widened as he read out loud.

"*The UAB Annual Report on Martin Rampart's escapades as a Corporate Imbecile and All-Around Bastard*?" he looked up. "Don, what the hell?"

"In my defense, Martin," Fowler said, sliding his folder back into the drawer. "I *did* say your name belonged on that one."

"Cute," Martin hissed. He threw the file on the floor. "Give me the other one."

Fowler chuckled and picked up the folder.

"Don't think so," he said. "Taberman expects this on his desk tomorrow morning, and I'm going to hand deliver it to him."

Martin swallowed hard and tried to resurrect his heartfelt smile.

"Look Don, I know we can come to an arrangement."

Fowler nodded. "I think we can, Martin."

"Good, good. Now how about—"

"No, no. I've already thought through the terms," Fowler said. "And they're non-negotiable."

Fowler's boss kept the smile pasted across his face.

"Sure, Don. Whatever you say. What do you want?"

Don looked Rampart over for a long moment, and then pointed

at the door.

"I want you to get the hell out of my office before I kick your emaciated ass halfway down the hall myself. And trust me, you should accept this deal, because I have a feeling if my foot connected with any part of you, your bony little body would collapse into a pile of dust. When's the last time you ate solid food?"

Martin's grin crumbled as his mouth fell open in front of Fowler. After a few seconds, he composed himself enough to walk slowly to the exit.

"This isn't over, Don," he said. "But your career is."

"Martin," Don said, sitting back down. "Implying that soon I might not have to see you every day isn't really the threat you seem to think it is."

Martin laughed. "Get rid of you? Not a chance. You'll be right here, every day, until I say otherwise. I own you, Fowler."

Fowler stood again with a look on his face that made Martin take a step closer to the door.

"Well we'll just see about that, won't we?" he said. "Now get out."

Martin sneered, but didn't say a word as he walked out the door.

Fowler dropped back into his chair and stared at his desk.

"I tried," he told no one in particular. "I really did."

He picked up the phone, held it in his hand for a moment, and then started dialing.

"Time for plan B."

CHAPTER 22

UAB's furniture inventory had not kept up with employee growth over the years. When chairs broke, the facilities team often provided helpful suggestions, such as, "sit in the broken chair." Unimpressed with this guidance, UAB's proactive employees addressed the issue by swapping their chairs with those in the facilities department. The facilities team got wise and responded by stealing chairs from remote break and meeting rooms. Notified of the growing problem, UAB's security team sprung into action by introducing a new form for guards to fill out when reporting incidents of, "involuntary chair relocation."

Shockingly, the strategy did little to prevent the corporate version of *Quest for Fire* from playing out across the UAB building's remotest break rooms. And as Denton sat alone in a post-scavenged break room with only his thoughts, an empty vending machine, and three broken chairs, he thought the issue had worked out just fine.

Denton looked out the window and tried again to push through the clouds surrounding him. He believed Coats had shared what he could, but it hadn't helped Denton move any closer to hard facts.

He turned on his mobile phone and looked at the missed call counter which registered double digits. Several from Beth, who likely wanted to find out when she could stop by and kill him, a handful from Sowell, and a couple from his father. He turned it back off and stuck it back in his pocket.

"Looks like you're a bit troubled," a voice said from behind him.

Denton's heart jumped and started beating faster. He didn't turn around immediately, as he felt fairly sure he knew the voice. Instead he nodded slowly.

"Well, I just bought a CD at Huntsman Bank, but now I hear we have a higher rate," he said.

Footsteps brought the chuckling voice closer, and Denton turned to watch Ohnemus Parker sit down next to him.

"I have a feeling that's not really your problem," he said. "Why don't you tell me what's on your mind? I'm a good listener," Parker said.

Denton smiled back, hoping he didn't look terrified.

"It's a lot of stuff, and it's complicated," he responded.

Parker leaned back still smiling. He waved a hand at Denton.

"Well, then never mind," he said. "What would I know about complicated matters?"

Denton chuckled and looked at the man carefully. Then he smiled and shook his head.

"Okay, Mr. Parker, you asked for it."

Parker clapped his hands once. "That I did."

Denton sat up straight.

"I think one of the cleaning ladies here is purposefully closing the men's room when I most need to go, my boss thinks I'm slightly insane, the COO asked me to look into Phillip Anderson's death but he won't share all he knows with me, and Anderson himself reached out to a disgraced stock trader for advice on *something* which of course could be nothing, but I know it's not nothing. It's something."

Denton took a breath.

"And my fiancée desperately wants me to set a wedding date, but I've been afraid to do it because of the company's uncertain future, even though she says not to worry about it. And her father loathes me, so I can't see how being unemployed will score me any points."

Denton sat back and watched Parker. The CEO nodded, interlocked his fingers and put them under his chin.

"A member of the cleaning crew is after you," he said.

"Basically, yes."

"Well, I can't understand why your boss might think you were losing it," Parker chuckled.

"I'm not sure how to take that from a man who goes out of his way to publically agitate his major corporate nemesis."

"Well, I can't let dear Peanut have all the fun," he smiled. "Do you think I went too far?"

Denton shook his head. "Nope, it was perfect, and a lot of people enjoyed it. But I worry about the timing. Most of your employees have a lot more time and heart invested here than I do. Embarrassing Handel could make things worse."

Parker nodded at Denton and looked out the window.

"I think about the people here all the time. I think about what the end of UAB would mean to them. I think about Phillip's death and how that could – if it's possible – make things worse."

He turned back and fixed his hard blue eyes on Denton.

"This company is special. There are wonderful people working here. So have some fun while you roam these halls. Have fun until it's time to get serious."

"And when's that?"

Parker smiled and stood up. He walked to the door and turned back to his curious employee.

"Sometimes the good guys win, and sometimes they absolutely do lose – no two ways about it. But no matter what side of the equation you find yourself on, you've got to have some fun. And if that fun comes at the expense of 'the bad guys,' well, that's just a bonus."

Denton shifted in his seat.

"Mr. Parker," he said slowly. "Is this your way of saying it's over, and that the fun you're having with Handel is your version of going down swinging?"

Parker shook his head. "No, Mr. Rourke. It's me being serious."

"That makes no sense," Denton said. "And how do you know my name?"

"I'm the CEO," Parker smiled. "I know everything."

"Ah. Then I assume you've got solutions to all my problems?"

"Sure … set the date. If you become unemployed, you'll get another job. If that doesn't bother her, don't let it bother you. As for her father … well, if you marry her, you win. And I'm sure you can always find ways to have some fun with him, too."

"And Phillip Anderson?"

Parker gave him a non-committal shrug.

"Well how about that. It turns out I don't quite know everything. But you're resourceful. You'll figure it out."

Denton cocked his head slightly and smiled. "Let's hope you're right about that, too."

Parker nodded and turned for the exit. Denton watched for a moment, and then jumped from his seat.

"Mr. Parker!"

Ohnemus Parker stuck his head back in the room and looked at Denton.

"What if … what if nothing works?" Denton asked him. "What if everything collapses?"

Parker blinked at the question and chuckled softly.

"Why, you *rebuild*, of course."

With a wink, Parker disappeared, leaving Denton to his thoughts. Denton watched the doorway for a minute and then turned back to the window with a slight smile.

"I'm resourceful," he repeated.

After a couple of minutes of what started as quiet contemplation of the case but accidentally morphed into an internal debate about whether he'd look good in a hat, Denton bolted to his feet.

"Come on, Candace," he said and trotted out of the break room.

DENTON MOVED ACROSS THE 6th floor quickly, making no eye contact. He reached his cubicle and scanned his desktop for a gift from Candace.

A clean white envelope stood out among the stacks of folders and files. He picked it up and read Candace's writing.

Here's the info. Tool coming later.
I don't want to know why you need this.
--CC

Denton pocketed the envelope and started planning. Since he'd promised Fowler that he'd attend the entire conference, he figured running into the man now might create trust issues between them.

He peeked over the cubicle wall and into his boss's office. Seeing it unoccupied, he bolted straight past, took a hard right, and moved swiftly toward the safe haven marked, "men's."

Head down, he pushed through the door and closed himself in a stall. He opened Candace's envelope and started reviewing the report.

"Boring … boring … bor-hello …"

Denton reread a few lines. Then he laughed quietly.

"This will do – nicely."

Before he could think more about it, he found himself looking left to right and surveying his surroundings with a bit of confusion.

How did I get into this restroom? Where's the crazy stalker woman?

Denton put away the report and left the stall. He washed his hands and looked in the mirror, making sure to ignore his clothes, his hairline, and basically everything else.

Out of the restroom, Denton made a dash for the exit. But he slowed his race to freedom as he passed the break room and saw a maximum crowd crammed together, watching the television. Denton looked up to see the current FNN graphic featuring a large and ridiculously clear picture of Joseph Handel from the morning paper's article. Over the picture, a headline glowed.

CEO: Chief Executive Oblivious?

Denton glanced at the picture of the Huntsman Bank leader and immediately saw the problem. As the fearless CEO of one of the largest financial companies in the world, a photo of you leaning against your desk with a confident yet somehow humble smile produces great results. But when the photo shows you're blissfully unaware that your desk has been emblazoned with a rival bank's logo in shiny gold lettering, viewers tend to shift their perceptions of your expression from "all knowing smile," to, "clueless grin of an idiot."

Denton looked around at the smiles and chuckles, and took in the general good mood of the UAB employee audience. Maybe Parker knew what he was doing. He listened to the FNN reporter who spoke as stock footage of Handel waving to cameras and speaking from behind various podiums played.

"... as the Justice Department rejected outright Joseph Handel's request for an immediate inquisition into the visa status of German photographer Niklas Zot. Additionally, a member of the American Board of Bankers who wished to remain anonymous told FNN that while they found Mr. Handel's angst justified, the ABB could not prioritize the issue ahead of growing consumer debt losses, rising mortgage foreclosures, and basically everything else going on in the world of finance."

The screen then cut to a shot of the FNN desk anchor, with a photo of a smiling Ohnemus Parker in the right corner.

"Meanwhile, United Alliance Bank CEO Ohnemus Parker, who is reportedly on vacation, held his own press conference where he denounced Huntsman Bank's use of *his* bank's trademarked logo in the newspaper. He vowed to post the picture on billboards across the city along with a hotline telephone number to collect anonymous tips from anyone who might have information on how this bizarre incident occurred."

With that, FNN gave viewers a look at one of the new billboards already in place. As promised, Handel's grinning face against the gold UAB logo stood in 14 by 48-foot glory next to a major highway. The words "Let's get a Handel on the truth!" screamed out from the top of the sign, with a toll-free phone number plastered across the bottom.

Denton immediately recognized the number as the same one Parker had given out as his "investor hotline" the week before, and which most people now knew as Joseph Handel's direct corporate line.

Shaking his head with a smile, Denton left the now raucous

crowd to their high fives and laughter as his mind focused on the singular errand he had to handle before enjoying a quiet evening at his condo.

As he pushed through the UAB exit, his phone rang. He looked at the screen and gulped as he read Beth's name. Even the ring sounded angry. She deserved an explanation for his awful behavior at dinner, but Denton needed time to create one that might prevent their conversation from ending with her calling him an ass. So he apologized internally and moved this thumb to the Ignore button.

However, Denton's brain had other plans, and directed his thumb to select Answer instead. Denton stopped in his tracks and stared wide-eyed at his phone. Then he glared at his traitorous digit, which offered no defense for its behavior.

"Hello?" Denton could hear Beth's voice in the earpiece. He lifted the phone quickly to his ear.

"Hi, Beth!" he said. Did he sound excited enough?

"Denton," Beth said, not sounding excited at all, "I've been calling you all day."

"I know, I know – sorry. I had that conference today and then I headed back to the office to do some research."

"Research?" Beth asked.

"Just work stuff. Nothing major."

"Well, we need to talk," Beth said.

"Definitely," Denton agreed. "How about I come by tomorrow during—"

"How about now, Denton?"

Denton moved the phone from his ear and gave his thumb another dirty look. He returned to the call.

"Beth, I know I owe you some face time, but I'm exhausted and I just want to head home tonight."

"That's totally fine," she said.

Denton paused. She sounded sincere.

"Really?" he asked.

"Absolutely," Beth replied. "I'm already here, so hurry on home."

Denton grimaced. "Okay, sounds good. I've got a stop to make and then I'll be there."

Denton put his phone away and headed down the street, begging his brain for some fresh material to present on the stale topic of his perpetual idiocy.

# # #

ACROSS THE STREET FROM THE exuberant UAB break room, the live-action version of Joseph Handel paced violently across the floor, moving quickly from one end of the office to the other, and then turning at the wall and repeating the process over and over. In the past, people called this "intensity." But now he seemed to stomp so hard with each step that at times the words, "temper tantrum," might have formed on the lips of some – mainly those who no longer cared about steady employment.

"Well then who *can* I sue?" he asked the small man sitting on the leather couch.

John Pinsler ate another of Handel's $12 dollar a pound French chocolates as he watched the sunset near its finale. He shrugged.

"It's *your* picture, Joseph," Pinsler mumbled between chews. "The reporter took the photo in your office, and you consented to its use."

"But I didn't see that logo!" he yelled.

"I would probably stop saying that if I were you," Pinsler suggested.

Of course, if I were you, I'd open my eyes when I walk into my own office. Dickhead.

"Why did I ask you to come up here?" Handel fumed and resumed his pacing.

"Presumably because you knew your attorneys would bill you to listen to this nonsense," he said. "Whereas I will happily sit here and watch you fume and fuss for nothing more than a few of these marvelous little treats."

Handel stopped and turned to Pinsler, glaring.

"You're enjoying this, aren't you?"

"Yes," Pinsler replied as he sat back. "Very much. Why?"

Handel stared a moment longer and then turned away without comment. Pinsler's amusement faded as he took another chocolate. He knew the importance of maintaining composure and patience when a multibillion-dollar deal neared fruition, and he also knew how to spot a man nearing the edge of a breakdown. With some people the signs were subtle but still easy to identify if you knew what to look for: A bit of rambling from a CEO who normally spoke with impressive succinctness, or maybe a new physical habit, like rubbing one's neck when a topic came up. Some gained a little weight, some lost it. The symptoms varied by leader.

However, picking up on Handel's stress did not require such keen awareness. Pinsler only needed to know that a man in his 50s didn't normally stomp around his office looking like an enraged toddler who may have just shit his pants.

Though he enjoyed it very much, Pinsler turned off the taunting valve and tried to ease the man's psyche.

"Not much longer now, Joseph," he said. "Before you know it, you'll own that logo and everything else at United Alliance Bank."

"None too soon, I'll tell you that!" Handel erupted.

Pinsler rose with a smile. "*Relax*, Joseph. It's all set. How long have you known me?"

Handel looked at Pinsler. He scanned the man's weird white suit, peach shirt and darker peach tie.

"A long time," Handel said finally.

"And how many deals have we done and how much money have we made? Don't bother counting, it wastes time – plenty."

"Plenty."

Pinsler nodded. "This is no different. We're talking about a matter of days now. *Singular* days. Agreements have been met, deals are almost done. Just sit tight, stay off the television, do not comment to anyone. In a few days, the big story will hit, no one will care about any of this. You can watch the adulation pour in once more."

Handel liked the sound of that. He thought of his name in the papers again – this time getting the adulation he deserved. He forced himself to smile for his guest.

"Fine," he muttered.

"Good, much better," Pinsler said. "Now, I've got a brief bit of business in Miami, but I'll be back tomorrow evening. I'll call you then."

"Hence the outfit?" Handel asked.

"What do you think?" Pinsler asked with a fashion runway turn.

Handel's eyes narrowed just a bit as he looked the man up and down.

"You look like a big, stupid daiquiri," he said through his pout.

Pinsler smiled. "Sweet, strong, and cold. Sounds about right."

With a nod, he left the room quietly. Handel turned back to the window and fixed his hateful gaze on the UAB building, which seemed to grin back at him.

"I still think I should sue someone," he said.

# # #

MARTIN RAMPART LOOKED UP from the desk and glanced at the door for the third time. Satisfied at the silence, he resumed his desperate after-hours search.

Drawer after drawer gave him nothing. He looked across the desktop again, moving every piece of paper individually. He flopped back into the chair and looked around. He would show Don Fowler who was boss – literally and figuratively. He fumed as he thought again of the gross insubordination the man subjected him to earlier.

He needed to deliver that report to Taberman. If Fowler did, Taberman would have a few questions – first among them: What was he paying Rampart to do? And however interested Martin Rampart himself was to hear the answer, he couldn't risk the scenario playing out like that.

Rampart grabbed a steel letter opener off the desk and moved to the file cabinet on the opposite wall. After finding the top drawer locked, he slid the opener into the side of the cabinet and jerked it up in down in harsh strokes as he tried to break the lock.

After several minutes of prying and turning, he felt the lock mechanism start to give. He smiled at his progress and started working more carefully. One wrong twist and he could move the latch back into place.

Rampart's full attention on in his efforts in amateur corporate espionage allowed the office door to open without his awareness. As the cabinet lock finally gave in to his repeated pressures, the door closed without a sound.

Rampart pulled the filed cabinet open and grabbed a stack of folders out. He turned back toward the desk and felt his heart jump as he screamed and dropped files across the floor.

"Jesus *Christ,* lady! You scared the crap out of me!" Rampart screamed in embarrassment for how he knew he must have looked. He eyed the broken file drawer and the folders and papers scattered at his feet, and tried to force a reassuring smile to his face.

"Not that I feel the need, but I can explain this if you've got any concerns."

Without allowing a response, he knelt down started gathering file folders into his hands.

"We have a standard review process here. All reports require—"

Something bit Rampart on his neck. He dropped the files again and slapped at the pain.

"Son of a—!" he yelled. He rubbed the spot on his neck and staggered to his feet. As he tried to fight the sudden dizziness, something much larger bit him on the other side of his neck. He fell once more as he put his hand up to the new wound and felt something warm and wet covering his palm. He brought his hand in front of his face and saw blood – a lot of blood. He noticed with some curiosity that it matched the splatters of blood now appearing across the wall and on the floor around him.

Rampart tried frantically to rise, but found his legs would not cooperate. He slapped at his face as a gray haze formed in his eyes and blurred the room. His chest felt heavy and he seemed to be forgetting how to breathe.

"Help me," he pleaded. But with the muscles in his face no longer working properly, his cry for help sounded more like a wheezing, muted moan. He dropped face down into a pile of crimson-stained paperwork.

"Well, shit," a disappointed voice said from high above Rampart.

"Eh – close enough," the voice decided.

As Rampart's world spun past him in darkening shades of purple and red, he felt himself being rolled onto his back. What was this weird woman doing to his mouth? He tried to mumble a protest, but his throat betrayed him.

Rampart heard the office door open and footsteps moving away. He wanted to wonder why the door had not closed again, and why he couldn't breathe. But he needed sleep. He could think about … what was it? Whatever it was, he could do that tomorrow, or the next day … or …

CHAPTER 23

Denton hiked the large black bag up on his shoulder and approached his condo with mild fear. Like most people in a serious relationship, Denton hated arguments. But his disdain for the occasionally loud and frequently pointless back-and-forth sessions stemmed from a slightly different place than many other people.

Denton believed most couples' arguments invariably boiled down to two people trying – and failing – to explain why they're right about one thing or another without somehow implying the other is rabidly idiotic for thinking otherwise. But for Denton, arguments invariably boiled down to him trying to explain that *Beth* was right about one thing or another, but that he had a *really* good excuse for whatever idiocy he'd been accused of that time.

So now he had devised a new strategy – one he suspected would rank toward the top of the "Dangerous and Stupid Man Moves" list.

He would blame Beth ... and/or her dad, depending on how the discussion evolved. He'd put her on the defensive – make her explain his behavior – and her own, for that matter.

Without allowing for a rebuttal from his brain, he opened the door, dropped his bag in the entryway, and strode in with confidence.

Beth sat on his couch with a glass of red wine. She wore a white halter top, a pair of black Capri pants, and a look of stern expectation.

"Hi, honey," he said, closing the door. "Glad you could make it."

"Are you, now?" she asked without looking amused.

Denton sat in a chair across from her that he estimated fell just outside her swing radius.

"Yes," he said. "I wanted to give you a chance to apologize and explain your behavior of late."

Beth stared at him. "I don't know how much wine you *think* I've had, but I assure it's not nearly enough to find you amusing right now. What on earth is going on with you, Denton? Do you know how stupid I felt last night?"

"Having also spent time with your father, I think I can say yes, I do."

Beth put her glass down on the coffee table.

"This is *not* about my father," she said.

"Isn't it though?" Denton replied. "He clearly takes great pride in making me feel like an idiot."

"Well you're clearly making it easy for him to do."

Denton continued to push forward with his ridiculous plan.

"I think it's *you* who's made it easy for him. You didn't tell him anything about me until he got here – not even my *name*. Yet somehow he's supposed to trust me with his daughter and – maybe even – *like* me?"

Denton stood up. "And let me tell you something else: he's not stupid. He knows you've been light on the facts until now, and I'm sure he thinks the reason I've been kept a secret is because there's something about me he *should* dislike. After all, if you actually thought I was great, you'd have told him all about me a long time ago."

Denton walked into the kitchen and grabbed a beer from the fridge. As he tossed the cap into the trash bin, his brain caught up with all the crap he'd just finished saying. He took a sip as a thought entered his head.

That wasn't brilliant improvisation. It's probably true.

He walked back to the den and took a seat. Beth watched him sit down, and then lowered her eyes.

"Oh my God, Denton," she said quietly. "I think you're right. This whole idea that I could make things better by keeping you separate from my parents only made things worse."

Denton's mind raced.

Am I winning? No, you don't 'win' something like this. Oh yes, you do. Now shut up – pay attention, she's still talking.

"I'm really sorry, Denton. I never meant to make you feel like you were anything less than wonderful. I feel horrible about this."

Needing a moment to craft a proper response, Denton took another sip of beer and nodded. Then he rose from his chair and planted himself next to her on the couch.

"I know you didn't – I know that," he said. "Your heart was in the right place."

Denton Rourke: Master of the Moment, King of the Conversation. Able to sway a woman's intuition with a single thought.

Beth put her hand in his. "And this conference – that's really why you ran out of the restaurant?"

"So it would seem," Denton said slowly.

"Okay, good," Beth smiled. "Because lately you've been acting a lot like you did when you got deep into the case with The Dash, and I was worried you were getting involved in the UAB problems and hadn't told me."

"I can see what you mean," Denton replied.

She squeezed his hand, and then rose and headed for the kitchen. She pulled the cork on the wine bottle and poured another glass.

"But I have no reason to think you'd hide that from me."

Denton Rourke: Master of Morons, King of the Idiots. Governor of the Guilty Conscience.

Denton shifted uneasily in his seat and took another sip as Beth sat back down next to him.

"Beth," he started, "you know how you kept me a secret from your parents in an attempt to do something good, but that it just didn't work out quite like you thought?"

"Well, since we just discussed it, yes, I do remember."

"And of course, I said I understood and didn't hold it against you."

"Thank you?" Beth's eyes narrowed as she brought the wine glass to her lips.

"I mean, it's not uncommon, you know. Sometimes good people try to help a situation by doing things that in hindsight look less than brilliant."

Beth looked at him for a moment. Then she leaned over and kissed him on the cheek.

"I sense you have an example you'd like to share?"

Denton tapped his brain for some phrasing that would sound better than, "I'm on the UAB case, and I didn't tell you." Within seconds, his brain complied.

"I'm on the UAB case," he said. "And I didn't tell you."

Beth looked him up and down, and turned away.

"Dammit, Denton," she drug his name out in a scolding tone.

Denton stood up quickly. "But wait – I let you explain yourself. Don't I get the same opportunity?"

Beth nodded without making eye contact.

"Knock yourself out."

Denton moved back to the chair and tried to get her to face him.

"When they found Phillip Anderson – our senior accounting exec – dead in his office, Sowell and Carlson showed up and they asked me to take part in the investigation."

"And you agreed."

"No – even though the guy's death looked ridiculously suspicious, I told them I couldn't help," Denton said. "At first."

Beth smiled. "But then?"

"But then our Chief Operations Officer, Daniel Caldwell asked for my help. Beth, the COO sat me down and asked me to investigate. I'd been worried that taking on another case might put my job at risk, but now the company is asking for my help. With all our jobs in danger right now, I thought if I helped solve this, I'd become a valuable asset to Daniel – valuable enough to be kept on if UAB were to merge with another bank."

Denton moved back over to the couch and sat down next to her.

"And I just figured that kind of stability would mean we could … you know … pick a date and get going on this wedding."

Beth shook her head at Denton. Her eyes now red, she smiled.

"Denton my dear," she said. "You're such an ass."

Mission complete.

"When you were on the case with The Dash, you were – among other things – kidnapped by thugs and nearly blown up by an insane person. Do you think I was worried about your *salary*?"

"Not really."

"Not at *all*," she corrected. "I'm not worried about you losing your job. I'm worried about losing *you*."

"I know you were," Denton said. "But really, this time, I'm really safe. I work in a very big, very secure building with lots of potential witnesses. It's far safer than skulking around dark alleys looking for clues."

"I suppose that's something," Beth said, still not sounding quite convinced.

"Besides," Denton continued, "I can't bear the idea of not being able to do my part to support our marriage. And I don't want your father to ever introduce me as his unemployed son-in-law. *Ever.*"

"Denton—"

"And, if I'm really honest," Denton said, "I don't think I *can* stop. Beth, something's wrong at UAB – very wrong. I can help, I know I can. And this kind of thing, well … it's all I've ever been any good at."

Denton's last few words came quietly, and the two sat hand in hand without speaking. Beth stared at his profile, while Denton stared at the bag of chips on the kitchen counter.

A few peaceful moments later, Beth patted his leg and stood up. She walked to the counter and tossed the chips to him.

"I'll make you a deal," she said. "You do as I've asked repeatedly and *stop* worrying about money, and I'll do my best not to worry about your investigation."

Denton opened the bag and popped a chip in his mouth.

"Deal."

"And no more secrets – from either of us."

"Agreed," Denton continued to chomp, now with a smile on his face.

"*And* you'll come to dinner Saturday night with my father and me."

Denton groaned and ate another chip. "Do you acknowledge that my saying yes indicates that I *must* love you very, very much?"

Beth smiled. "I do."

"Fine."

Beth's smile widened and they both felt their tensions evaporate from the room. She dropped back onto the couch and leaned against him.

"And don't worry," she said. "You'll have backup this time. I called your dad and asked him to join us."

Denton stopped chewing.

"What?"

"I thought it would be a good idea for the two of them to meet, so I called and invited him. He was very excited – said he wouldn't miss it."

"I'm sure," Denton said, already trying to figure out if he could super-glue all the doors of Connor Rourke's house closed with him inside until Sunday.

"So what's in the bag?" Beth asked.

Denton looked over at his giant black bag and shrugged.

"Special project materials," he said.

"Okaaaay," she smiled. "What about the case?"

"Anderson's death looked like a suicide, but it's a murder – and it didn't even occur at the office. His body was brought to the office after the crime."

"Brought back to the safe, secure office," Beth added.

"Yeah," Denton breezed by the comment. "The guy left behind an ambiguous email and some encrypted files. The AVP of accounting is acting weird and likely knows more than he's saying. And today I met a reformed Wall Street scam artist whom Anderson contacted last year, but he wouldn't tell me much because he's still on parole. Caldwell – though he wants my help – won't let me see the files Anderson sent him before he died because they could contain highly confidential company material."

"Sounds like those files might be a key to finding out what's going on."

"Right," Denton agreed. "That's why I'm going to steal them."

Beth nodded.

"Yes, brilliant. I see you've already stopped worrying about your job security."

"I don't have a lot of choice," Denton said. "I've got all these puzzle pieces in front of me, but no idea what the picture is supposed to look like. I think those files will give me that guide."

Beth kissed him on the cheek again and whispered in his ear.

"I'm sure whatever plan you come up with will be completely ridiculous … and successful. Just be careful."

Denton nodded. "I will," he said, and kissed her softly.

The piercing sound of a mobile phone dissolved the moment.

Denton threw his head back and watched Beth jump from the couch and grab the offending gadget.

"Hello?" she said. She looked at Denton as she spoke again. "Oh, hi."

"See, this is why I don't turn my phone on," he called out loudly.

Beth put a finger up and listened. She nodded and said, "Okay, I will."

She disconnected and looked over at Denton.

"That was Sowell," she said. "He's been trying to reach you for hours."

"What for?"

"He's on his way to pick you up," she said. Then she dropped into a chair and began flipping through a magazine.

Denton sat up. "Now? Why?"

Beth didn't look up from the page.

"Seems there's been another murder and he'd like your help at the crime scene … since you *work* there."

Denton froze in place. Beth looked at him and nodded with an insincere smile.

"That's right – someone was murdered in your *very* secure building, on *your* very safe floor."

Denton frowned at the unfortunately timed news which made his, "I'm safe at work" speech fairly worthless. He wondered what would have happened had he chosen to remind her that he enjoyed the very protective company of Tim Sowell and/or Russell Carlson. Likely both men would have shown up at his condo and taken turns shooting him.

"Sorry," he said. "I still promise to be careful. And when we catch this guy, I'll tell him how rude he is to interfere with our relationship."

"Sowell says they're bringing in a suspect now," Beth said somberly.

"What?" Denton said once more. He recognized with a tinge of guilt the slight irritation he felt at not playing a major role in the man's capture.

"They have a suspect," Beth repeated, "and he needs your help."

Denton didn't care for that sentence at all. Beth's grammar did not lend itself to mistakes.

"The suspect needs my help?" Denton asked.

Beth looked up at him.

"Denton, it's your boss," she said. "They're arresting Don Fowler."

CHAPTER 24

Denton stood outside his condo holding his near-empty beer in one hand and a large black bag in the other. He pouted as he thought about how he and Beth had finally broken through the tension and shared a moment from a recent past when things were simpler, issues were smaller, and kisses were longer.

Then Sowell and Fowler and some dead guy had ruined everything.

Denton took a swig from his bottle and waved at the unmarked police cruiser slowing in front of him. The driver's window slid down and Sowell's soul-boring eyes and gigantic eyeglass frames focused on Denton.

"That's illegal, you know," Sowell said, nodding toward Denton's adult beverage.

Denton looked at his beer and shrugged. "So's lying to your friend and arresting your friend's boss."

"No it's not," Sowell said. "But I defer to your overall point. Please get in. We need your help."

"No kidding."

Denton strolled around to the passenger side and got in. The car pulled away from the curb and into traffic, its occupants riding in silence.

Denton finished his beer and stared out the window at the city lights. He thought about Beth. And he thought about Caldwell … and all of UAB.

Sowell kept his eyes on the road as he spoke first.

"Denton, you deserve an explanation for my not being entirely truthful with you."

Denton shook his head. "I don't need an explanation," he said. "Your boss never wanted to hire me, but you did it anyway without telling him."

"That about covers it," Sowell agreed.

"What I deserve," Denton said, turning to his friend, "is to have you trust me with that kind of information. Do you know how much easier I could have made this on you?"

"Denton, you were already so apprehensive about helping out, I didn't want to throw anything else at you that might push you away."

"Well, then, *that* makes it okay."

Sowell shook his head. "No, it doesn't – obviously. But I hope you understand something, Denton. I didn't ask you to join the case because I felt I owed you something, or because we're friends."

"You asked because I work at the scene of the crime," Denton said.

For the first time Denton could recall, Sowell took his eyes off the road. He shot an annoyed looked at Denton.

"Don't be an idiot," he said and returned his focus to the traffic. "I asked you because this case *needs* you. It needs your ability, your vision."

"My style?" Denton suggested.

"No one needs that," Sowell said quickly. "The point is that I'm sorry I didn't fill you in fully, I wish I had. I know Caldwell asked you to assist, so I'm sure you're going to continue looking for answers. I just want you to know that Caldwell or not, we'd be backing your involvement, Carlson and I."

"Do you mind?" Denton said. "I'm trying to sulk over the ways I've been wronged by people around me. But between your sickly sweet apology and Beth's kissy-face sincerity, it's not easy!"

"Really?" Sowell smiled. "Please, go on."

"No," Denton said. Then he redirected the conversation. "I assume you already know you've locked up the wrong man."

"I suspect you're right, yes," Sowell said. "But I need you to tell us why it's not him."

"Who's the victim?"

"Fowler's boss, Martin Rampart."

Denton pulled off a beautiful double take.

"Of course."

Sowell nodded his agreement. "Stabbed to death in Fowler's office earlier this evening – a few hours after several employees heard the two of them arguing loudly about promotion opportunities."

"Oh, perfect."

"Exactly. And with the suicide angle dissolving around Phillip Anderson, the Captain is eager to move this forward so he can show some progress to the chief."

"Who cares if he's got the right man?"

Sowell shook his head. "It's not like that. Remember, he sees a frustrated employee who feels he's been passed over once too often, who witnesses saw arguing with his boss just hours before the man is found murdered in his upset employee's office. That sounds a lot like motive and opportunity."

Denton shrugged. "I guess. What's Fowler's alibi?"

"He says he was at the movies."

"Well, he wasn't," Denton said flatly.

Sowell jerked his head toward his friend.

"What?"

"Total lie," Denton said. "When can we see Mr. Pants on Fire?"

Sowell chuckled and turned toward the highway.

"He's still being processed. You won't be able to talk to him for a couple of hours still."

"So straight to the UAB crime scene."

"Yes. I'd like you to take a quick look – as an employee who has spent a lot of time in there—"

"And *not* as an amateur detective who does not work in any way, shape, or form for the department."

Sowell smiled and nodded.

"Your boss is lucky to have you on his staff, Denton."

Denton stared out the window.

"Let's see if he agrees later tonight."

Sowell glanced over at Denton, whose gaze remained fixed on the glow of the city lights against a pitch black sky. He smiled.

"He will."

Denton turned toward him.

"Do you think I'll get a raise?"

"From the department?" Sowell snorted. "No."

"I mean from Fowler and UAB."

"Ah," Sowell replied. "In that case, no."

Denton shrugged and turned his attention back to the skyline.

DENTON STARED AT THE PURPLE AND green sky, then at the rows of moon-lit buildings, and finally at the passing giraffes.

"Did you see that?" Denton asked Sowell.

Sowell did not shift. "No."

Denton pointed out the window. "Giraffes," he said. "There are giraffes out there."

"What of it?"

Denton stared at him. He turned back to the window and watched another one lope by in a fast yet hopelessly graceless fashion.

"*What of it?* Sowell, I've grown accustomed to watching your car get passed by joggers, dog walkers, and small children on bikes, but wouldn't you say it's a bit odd to see wildlife running past us on a downtown street?"

Sowell shrugged. He scratched the head of the small monkey sitting between them.

"Nothing's normal in this case, Denton."

"When the *hell* did you get a monkey?" Denton demanded as he scooted himself up against the door.

"Denton, what is the matter with you? I don't have a monkey."

Denton wagged a finger at Sowell. "Then what do you call—"

The monkey made a brief yet sharp noise. Unsure of what the beast's utterance meant, Denton retracted his accusatory digit quickly. "Tim, you honestly expect me to just accept what you're saying?"

"Yes."

"In spite of the fact that I can see – and, quite frankly – *smell* an entirely different story?"

Connor Rourke reached up from the rear seat and slapped the back of Denton's head.

"I told you, son – everyone has secrets, and everyone lies. You're too trusting. Now sit down, shut up, and *pay attention.*"

"Your father's right honey," Beth said. She patted Connor's shoulder. "You really should follow his advice."

Denton turned to the back seat's annoying occupants.

"Didn't you once say my father had the sense of a block of concrete?" he asked Beth.

"Denton!" Sowell scolded.

"No, I said he had the etiquette of a caveman," Beth corrected. Then she turned to Connor. "He's still not listening."

"Maybe another smack will help," Connor suggested.

Denton felt a succession of rapid blows to his cheek.

"Denton!" Sowell repeated. "We're here."

Denton opened his eyes and pushed Sowell's hand away.

"Okay, okay!" he sat up and blinked. Sowell looked at him.

"You were asleep," he said.

"Yes, I gathered you weren't hitting me for the sheer fun of it," Denton replied. "I'm glad your car is free of obnoxious animals and/or family members."

"Do I want to know what that means?"

"No."

Denton looked around, and turned back to Sowell.

"Why are we in the executive garage?" he asked.

Sowell gestured toward the exit. "Reporters got wind of a potential second murder," he said. "They've staked out the main entrance."

Denton got out of the car and followed Sowell through the garage entrance. As the two men entered the main lobby, Denton stopped and looked around.

"Where is everyone?" Denton asked, noting an extreme lack of police presence.

"We *are* everyone," Sowell replied. "The rest of everyone is upstairs at the crime scene. Captain Levine asked that this be kept as quiet as possible."

"Of course," Denton said, certain that were he to give the vending machine on 5 the valiant kicking it so desperately deserved, the discrete Captain Levine would order the entire precinct to descend on UAB and subdue him using – if at all possible – deadly force.

Denton followed Sowell to the elevator and they rode to six without speaking. When the doors opened, Denton again followed Sowell to Fowler's office in silence.

Sowell stopped at Fowler's doorway and gestured to Denton.

"After you," the Lieutenant said with a slight smile.

Denton entered the room and looked around quickly. He watched the forensics team and wondered how they could move through their tasks with zero eye contact or conversation past the occasional grunt. Maybe they were part zombie.

Denton shifted his focus to Martin Rampart's corpse, still lying where it had fallen hours earlier. The blue tint now forming in his skin matched his eyes – which had locked in a hard stare to the right, as though trying to get a good look at the pool of dark blood congealing on the floor directly below their owner's head.

"Good thing he's dead or he'd be *very* uncomfortable," Denton said.

One of the forensics team members looked over at Denton. Sowell shook his head.

"So, anything out of place?" he asked.

Denton scanned the room with a slow nod.

"Well … yes, I think so," he replied. "First, Fowler is a bit of a slob, but he's *never* left dead bodies in the middle of his office floor – so that's odd behavior. Also, he's always had a strict rule about not letting blood dry on his walls or congeal on his floor, so this is very unlike him."

Sowell humored his friend.

"Anything we can *use*?"

Denton pointed at Rampart.

"The raised mark on the left side of his neck," he said. "Is that from a hypodermic needle?"

"Excellent deduction as usual, Denton!"

Denton turned to see Dr. Jeffrey Lewis enter the room holding a syringe and wearing an ear-to-ear smile.

"Dr. Lewis," Denton said, raising his eyebrows. "It's certainly a surprise to see you out among the living. Aren't you worried one of your other guests might ring for room service or something while you're gone?"

"It's a chance I'm willing to take tonight, Denton," Lewis replied with a smile.

Denton made a face at Sowell as Lewis pocketed the syringe and pointed at Rampart's body.

"Any idea what was in the syringe?" Sowell asked.

Lewis shook his head. "Not yet, I'll have to get it back to the lab and run some tests. Give me a couple of days."

"Did you find anything else?"

Lewis shrugged. "Does Mr. Fowler have long blonde hair?"

"Not quite," Denton said.

Lewis pulled a seemingly empty sandwich bag from his pocket.

"Then we also found some strands of hair that we should test as well."

Denton nodded as Lewis put the bag away.

"Now," Lewis said, still smiling. "Guess how he died."

"Advanced yoga without stretching – broke his own neck," Denton suggested.

Lewis's smile faded as he stared at Denton. He looked down at Rampart's contorted body. Then he furrowed his brow and looked back at Denton.

"No," he said. "No … what would possibly lead you to think—"

"*Joke*, Lewis," Denton said.

"We're a little short on time," Sowell said. "How about you just give us the basics?"

Lewis shrugged.

"Okay. He choked to death."

Denton and Sowell turned to each other and then back to Lewis.

"Naturally," Denton said. "This is actually starting to make sense. Big, burly Don Fowler concocted a brilliant plan to lure Rampart into his own office so he could kill him via a clean and quick lethal injection. But in a fit of impatience, he then stabbed his boss in the neck, adding a bit of unfortunate mess to his previously perfect murder."

Denton knelt next to Rampart's body.

"*Then* Fowler decided the combination of injected poison and deep bleeding wounds still weren't killing Rampart quickly enough, so he *choked* the man to death."

Sowell and Lewis said nothing as Denton stood up and gestured at one of the larger blood stains.

"And naturally, all that choking and stabbing and poisoning made Fowler tired. So he figured he'd just leave the body, the blood, and potentially incriminating evidence all over his own office and take off with some blonde woman who I guess had waited patiently while he worked."

Lewis smiled once again. "I didn't say someone choked him, Denton. I said he choked."

Denton rubbed his eyes. "Fine, good, great. Choked on what?"

"On this," he said and extended his hand to Denton.

Denton looked down at a black, non-working demo of a very small mobile phone.

"Oh hell," he said and started dreaming of alcohol.

"Exactly," Lewis continued. "The deep stab wounds or whatever was in that syringe would have done the trick, but it looks like this little bugger just beat them out."

Denton scanned the room's carnage again. He walked over to Fowler's chair and glanced over the mess left on the man's desk. Then he moved to the broken file cabinet, took a black folder out of the top drawer, and turned to Sowell.

"I'm done here."

"That's *evidence*," Sowell said as he reached toward him.

"You can't have it," Denton said and clutched his new possession like a child with a candy bar. "Not yet."

"Fine," Sowell said. "I didn't see anything."

"Deal."

"No. No *deal* – I don't even know what you're talking about."

Denton nodded. "Okay, okay. Let's just go."

The two men waved good-bye to Lewis and headed out of Fowler's office. They reached the elevator and Sowell punched the down button and focused on the red digital display above the doors.

Denton shook his bag.

"You go ahead to the station," he said. "I've got a little work to do here first. I'll catch a cab when I'm done."

Sowell kept his eyes on the display. "I don't want to know," he said.

Denton looked at his bag and then back at Sowell.

"You don't?"

"No."

Denton made a face and shrugged.

"Well," he whispered and tapped his jacket pocket, "would you like to look at some stolen crime scene evidence?"

Sowell turned and stared hard at him for a moment, and then walked away.

"I'm taking the stairs," he announced.

"Want me to join you?" Denton asked, still watching the floor counter.

"I do not," Sowell said.

Denton smiled to himself and listened to the stairwell door swinging open.

The elevator opened and Denton hopped in.

"So, I'll just meet you at the station then?" he said to himself as the doors closed.

CHAPTER 25

Denton arrived at the police station following a supremely irritating lesson about cab drivers and their lack of interest in having odd people in their cabs after midnight who ask to be taken to jail. As he rode to the station in the back of a patrol car, the officer explained that people who request delivery to the steps of a police station between one and six in the morning have almost always just completed some bit of severe naughtiness – the kind of thing where 9 out of 10 times the witness reports include phrases like, "… and then I realized he'd been shot," or, "… and that's when we saw his head was missing."

Apparently these rather violent folks often freak out post incident and want more than anything to go the police and receive absolution from their ghastly sins. But halfway to the station they typically realize the gravity of that plan, freak out again, and wish in the exact opposite direction of law enforcement strongholds.

That's perfectly fine for would-be felons driving their own vehicles, but the request to change destinations in the dead of night never sits well with cab drivers. So a lot of yelling from both parties usually takes place and generally ends with a panicked driver abandoning his cab after his panicked passenger wins the argument by trying to jam a blood-stained weapon of some sort through the driver's steel grated partition.

So three consecutive cabs had pulled up to a shabbily dressed man who held a black trash bag and asked to be taken to the police station. The first two drivers asked him what he had in the bag and when he answered, "I'd rather not tell you," they both drove away.

The third also drove away, but had helpfully radioed the police, given them the disheveled man's description, and theorized that his black bag probably contained someone's head. Denton's black and white ride to the station arrived three minutes later.

With the night's lesson complete, the officer let his unwilling pupil out in front of the station doors.

"What *is* in the bag?" the officer asked as he got back in his car.

"It's a secret," Denton said once more.

The officer nodded. "Well, if you thought cabbies didn't like that answer, wait until you try it *in there*."

Denton watched the officer drive away. Then he sighed and headed toward the entrance.

Before he had time to come up with a horribly unbelievable answer to the question of his bag's contents, Denton saw Sowell waiting for him at the front. He thought that behind the man's standard poker face of uncommitted disinterest he could see a hint of amused judgment.

"Cabs don't like me," Denton said.

"I can't fathom why," Sowell said. "Come on. Let's go see your boss."

Denton followed Sowell through the station, both men trying to make the trek as quietly and inconspicuously as possible. A few nods and generic greetings later, they stood in front of a sour looking, grey-haired desk sergeant. His eyes telegraphed boredom and annoyance, and for some reason the man had locked his angry frown and bushy mustache on Denton.

"Holy..." Denton trailed off as Sowell stepped forward and signed the log.

Denton leaned in close to the Lieutenant.

"Sowell, is Carlson aware you have his dad trapped down here in booking?" he asked.

"Yes," Sowell said and kept writing.

Denton's mouth fell open. He shifted his position and tried to watch the sergeant out of the corner of his eye while pretending to find something profound in the DIAL 9-1-1 wall poster. Then he shook his head and leaned toward Sowell.

"You're lying, right?"

Sowell put the pen down and nodded to the sergeant. The sergeant returned the gesture and pressed a button on his desk. Denton heard a brief buzz and watched Sowell pull open the barred entrance to the cell unit.

"After you," he said.

Denton walked in, still staring at Sowell.

"He's not wearing a name badge," Denton said.

Sowell walked down the dim corridor ignoring his friend's accusatory stare.

"The desk sergeants have a desk nameplate," he said.

"Yes, but I doubt seriously that his name is actually *Sergeant Mary Ortiz*!"

Sowell chuckled. "He must have forgotten to switch it out at shift change. That's crazy Russell, Sr., for you."

"Stop it," Denton hissed.

"Well, well – isn't this an unexpected and unpleasant surprise," a voice sounding appropriately unpleased joined the conversation. The two men turned to find the voice attached to the equally disagreeable face of Captain Harris Levine.

Denton smiled. "Well, look at the two of us, Captain. We've finally found something we can agree on."

Captain Levine ignored the comment.

"Why are you here, Mr. Rourke?"

"I'm here for the Scared Stupid program."

"It's *Scared Straight*," the captain corrected.

"Yes – that one. I need a good talking to before I head too far down the wrong path."

Levine gave up and turned his attention to Sowell.

"Why is he here, Lieutenant?"

"Don Fowler is his boss, sir," Sowell replied.

Levine looked at the ceiling and smiled.

"Ah yes, of course. How could he *not* be here to see him?"

He turned back to Denton.

"Your boss is the prime suspect in a rather gruesome murder."

"Yes, well, for some odd reason he thinks he's innocent. Not sure why, really. Maybe because he has an airtight alibi, or because he has no motive, or it *might* be because you wouldn't know a serious suspect if he walked into your precinct wearing a scarf knit from his victim's hair."

Denton turned to Sowell. "No offense, of course."

Sowell said nothing as Levine continued to engage Denton.

"Since I know better than to discuss open cases with members of the general public, I'm going to simply let you know you have about five minutes to talk to Mr. Fowler before I have you thrown out of here."

"I'll send along your love and find out where you need to send the apology bouquet tomorrow."

Levine turned without acknowledging Denton and disappeared around a corner.

"Thin ice, Denton," Sowell said. "He can make things difficult."

"He can't do anything to me," Denton said.

"I wasn't thinking about *you* this time."

Denton turned to Sowell.

"Of course," he said. "Crap – Tim, I'm sorry. I just—"

"I know," Sowell stopped him. "It's all right."

"Jesus *Christ*, could you two have your man moment some other time?" Fowler's unmistakable growl asked.

Denton approached the next cell and looked in on his boss, who sat on his cot and watched them with a scowl.

"Wow, it's like watching an angry, mostly shaved ape," Denton said.

Fowler stood up and approached the bars.

"Yeah, an ape that'll pull your arms off, beat you with them, and then fire your sorry ass."

"I did not think you could look any more irritated," Denton replied. "But here we are."

Denton smiled and reached through the bars. Fowler shook his hand and managed to almost smile.

"How are you doing, Don?"

"Well, I'm in in *jail*," Fowler said, gesturing at his surroundings. "So I've had better evenings."

Denton nodded and looked at the weary man. Then he looked closer. Still grasping Fowler's hand, he turned his own hand slightly underneath his boss's.

Fowler dropped the handshake.

"Look, Denton, don't worry about me," he said. "I'm fine in here. You just go out there, find the killer, and they'll set me free soon enough."

Denton's eyebrow rose.

"May I see your feet, please?"

"What? No!" Fowler snapped.

"Permission to see the defendant's feet!" Denton called out.

"Denied," Sowell replied without changing his tone.

Denton shot a look of surprise at the makeshift judge. Then he turned back to Fowler and winked.

"I know where you were. And it wasn't the movies."

Fowler's expression softened a bit.

"Denton, please ..."

Sowell stepped forward. "Mr. Fowler, if Denton can get you out on bail, I suggest you let him help. Captain Levine will not let you stay in the precinct jail for long. He will transfer you to central lockup before the night is over."

Before the conversation could continue, a tall, well-dressed man with a brown leather briefcase appeared from nowhere in particular. His eyes conveyed general fatigue and boredom as they gazed at the piece of note paper in his hand.

"Hello, I'm Winston Davis, the state-appointed attorney," he said. "Which one of you is Donald Barclay Fowler?"

Denton looked at the man closely. "Well, I hope it's not *me*," he said.

Fowler cleared his throat, and Winston Davis turned to him and waved.

"Of course, of course. Sorry – very long day."

He fumbled with his briefcase and retrieved a thin manila folder.

"I'm afraid I haven't had a chance to fully review the charges—"

"That's okay," Denton said. "This one's going to be easy."

"Oh? And why is that?"

Fowler gripped the bars. "Denton, don't you have somewhere else to be? Anywhere else?"

Denton ignored his boss and put an arm around the tired attorney.

"I'd like to point out that your client's hands are magnificently soft and supple, and his cuticles are just *too* well-kept for a man of Mr. Fowler's … *burly* nature."

Winston Davis tried to smile politely and worked hard not to roll his eyes.

"Um, okay," he said.

And as you no doubt already noticed, Mr. Fowler also has the dried remnants of fresh wax in his left eyebrow."

"Right. Well, thank you, mister …?"

"Rourke. Denton Rourke."

"Yes, well thank you, Mr. Rourke. I'll certainly note that," Davis said, giving every indication that he intended to do nothing of the sort.

"Good," Denton said. "Because being a super smart attorney with nothing but your client's best interests in mind, you've no doubt already connected the dots here and are preparing to have his credit card transactions from this evening pulled.

"Have I now?"

"Yep," Denton nodded. "Because that's how you'll prove that at the time of Martin Rampart's murder, Donald Barclay …"

Denton turned back to his boss.

"*Barclay*? I love that."

"I may yet kill someone tonight," Fowler warned.

Denton refocused on Winston Davis.

"… Fowler was having a mani-pedi miles from the UAB campus."

"Dammit, Denton!" Fowler said. "Go away, please."

The attorney gave Denton a long, tired stare. Then he looked past him to his client.

"If this is true, we can access your bank account online and I can probably have you out on bail in an hour."

Fowler gave both men a red-hot glare before finally lowering his head.

"Fine," he mumbled. "Pull my Amex transactions. You'll find a charge to a manicurist."

Winston Davis produced a pen and made some notes. Denton looked over the man's shoulder.

"You're looking for a charge to Madame Cho's – they cater to metrosexual men and offer manicures, pedicures, and – only coincidentally in my client's case—"

"*My* client's case," Davis corrected.

"— massage therapy."

"Denton," Fowler said.

"Though I believe they call it, *deep-muscle stimulation.*"

"Denton!"

Denton turned to Fowler and winked. Then he smiled.

"But, Mr. Davis, when you find his transaction, you'll only need to see the pittance of a tip he left to know he just had his hands and feet – and eyebrows – serviced."

"Why keep this from us, Don?" Sowell asked.

"Because all this primping is for the interviews he has tomorrow with another company," Denton said. "He was afraid his real alibi might tip UAB management off to his plans, which could put his current job in jeopardy, so he made up the story about the movies."

"Denton," Fowler tried to interject.

"Problem was," Denton continued on, "Fowler didn't know who was dead when the police questioned him – he didn't even realize he was suspect number one until he'd given them his lame excuse. By the time he realized the gravity of the situation he'd already lied to the police and didn't know what to do about it."

"I *can* speak for myself, you know," Fowler said.

Denton spun toward his boss.

"Then *do it*, Don! Because frankly, I'm tired of piecing together the facts from the accidental tidbits of truth you and everyone else leave lying about."

Denton walked to a nearby bench and dropped down with a pout, leaving Davis and Sowell to stare at each other. Fowler watched him for a moment before turning to the lawyer.

"He's right," Fowler said. "I didn't know Rampart was the victim until they were arresting me, and I didn't know what it would look like if I changed my story at that point."

Fowler looked to Sowell. "I've never been in jail before, and I didn't know what to do. I really figured you guys would uncover the truth quickly enough that it wouldn't be an issue."

Sowell nodded. "I appreciate the faith, but trust me – you need to get out of here now."

Winston Davis handed Fowler his pen and a piece of paper.

"Write down your card details and I'll get this taken care of."

Fowler complied and handed back the paper and pen. Davis pocketed the information and nodded. "Okay, I'll be back soon."

He turned to leave, and stopped in front of Denton.

"Thank you," he said.

Denton nodded and watched the man slip away.

"Of course, there is still a slightly concerning matter," he said, still staring down the hallway.

"You mean that someone might want to kill me, and they're not particularly worried about collateral damage?" Fowler asked.

"Yep," Denton nodded. He stood up and walked back over.

"I'll have a couple of officers assigned to you," Sowell told Fowler.

"I don't need police protection," Fowler growled.

"Missed a dose of your reality medication, did you?" Denton asked. "Come on, Don. Someone out there wanted you to occupy a very different room at this station – one where no one cares that it's cold and dark and run by a weird doctor, because they're all too focused on how dead they are to notice."

Fowler looked at the two men and then smiled at his colleague.

"Denton Rourke, you're my hero," he said. Then he turned to Sowell.

"Okay, fine, give me a couple of bodyguards. Make sure they know how to play poker."

"I'll see what I can do," Sowell said.

"And they all lived happily ever after," Denton said.

Sowell looked at him. "What about the file folder?"

"The file folder?" Denton asked.

Sowell looked at Fowler and then leaned in to Denton.

"The *evidence* from his office?"

"Ah. It was nothing. I didn't even take it out of the building."

"Denton," Sowell's voice carried a quiet threat.

"Tim, I *swear* to you, I left it right where it belonged – at UAB."

Sowell took a deep breath and put his hands up.

"Fine, fine. Now, can I take you home, or would you and your mysterious trash bag prefer to try and scare people on the train?"

"Yeah, what's with the bag, Rourke?" Fowler chimed in. "What's in there?"

"Leftovers," Denton said. "Now hush or I'll tell the guards you're lonely and need a roommate."

"Wouldn't it be simpler to just tell us at this point?" Sowell suggested.

Denton tilted his head and smiled at both men.

"You know what? No."

He placed the bag on the ground and reached in.

"It'd be simpler at this point if I just *showed* you."

Still grinning, Denton pulled the contents from the bag, thrust it forward, and shook it toward his interrogators.

Dead silence overtook his friends. Sowell turned away, removed his glasses and cleaned them with the edge of his sweater. Fowler just stared, mouth open.

"Denton, what the hell are you doing with those?" he finally asked.

Denton dropped the newly revealed secret back into the bag and clasped it tightly.

"Bet you wish you could have one for the night," Denton said.

Fowler scoffed. "Just go catch the bad guys, please."

Denton turned to follow Sowell to the exit.

"And Denton," Fowler called out. Denton turned back to see his boss displaying a facial expression slightly lighter than a scowl.

"Thanks," he said.

Denton smiled and nodded. "You're welcome."

Fowler watched the two men turn the corner. He listened to the large security door as it opened and then closed in the distance.

Finally alone, Fowler returned to his jail bunk and sat on the edge.

"Keep it together, Donald Barclay Fowler," he told himself. "Not long now."

Swallowing hard, he repeated those words over and over in his head and listened desperately for the opening of the security door and the return of Winston Davis.

# # #

"DON'T YOU FEEL BAD?"

Gavin Spincer stopped smiling and regarded Tonya Garza. His mouth turned downward a bit as he wiped the sweat from his large forehead.

"I tell you an incredible story about missing the target and hitting an even *bigger* one, and that's what you ask?"

He scoffed and shook his head at her.

"Why should I feel bad? Getting Rampart was just as good – better, really."

"I mean about *killing* these people!" Tonya cried a little louder than she'd wanted.

Spincer crossed his arms and continued to stare. Then he scratched his neck as he pondered her follow-up question. Finally he shrugged.

"Rampart got off easy, especially compared to … well, never

mind. There's plenty of time for that story later."

He clapped his hands together.

"Okay, good chat – glad we got to do this," he said. "But now I need you to do something for me, okay?"

Tonya said nothing, but nodded slowly.

"Don't worry," he said. "I don't want you to *do* anything, jeez. I just need you to give me your honest opinion on something."

"Okay," she said, turning her head and wrinkling her brow.

Spincer gave her a thumbs-up.

"Great. Stay there and I'll be back in a few minutes."

Tonya watched him leave the room. She closed her eyes and said another prayer.

After several minutes, Spincer's voice came through the door.

"Close your eyes, please," he said. "Seriously, no peaking, I don't want this ruined."

"They're closed," she said.

She heard the door open and the creaking of the floorboards as he walked toward her.

"Now don't look yet. Remember, I need your honest opinion, but be nice-honest, okay? I mean, if you feel like you need to criticize, just try to be constructive, okay?"

"Yes," she said, not wanting to ever open her eyes again.

"Okay … open your eyes … and say hello to Gadsden the Mighty's disguise!"

Tonya turned her head to the side and opened one eye slightly. As her brain started to register the image, both her eyes popped open wide and took in the full vision of a proudly smiling Gavin Spincer.

Tonya stared in complete silence for several seconds and then dropped her head straight down and burst into uncontrollable sobs.

Spincer's smile faded. He raised his hands up in confusion.

"What? Is it the straight razor? Is it too much? I was going to go with the butcher knife since it's more versatile for stabbing and slashing. But that's *so* overdone, isn't it? For visual effect, the razor is much more menacing, right?"

Tonya made no attempt to respond and continued to cry.

Spincer pouted and crossed his arms.

"Okay, look – this is not what I meant by constructive. I worked hard on this, but I'll go back to the knife, all right?"

He walked back to the door and opened it. Then he turned back to his prisoner.

"Don't cry, please? Look, I'm heading out right now to complete the side mission, and then I can finish the final quest on Friday. I promise you on Friday evening I can share the entire story of my adventure with you. And it'll have a happy ending. You'll see."

He waited a few moments longer in the doorway to see if Tonya would respond. After what he swore was a nod of agreement, he backed out silently and locked the door behind him.

In the hallway, he heard his mind replaying his promise to Tonya.

I can share the entire story of my adventure with you.

And he tried – but failed – to drown out the follow-up.

But I can never let you leave.

CHAPTER 26

Thursday

Marcus Rompeaux could not breathe. He could not move. He felt fairly certain that were he to attempt to scream out, he'd find himself incapable of that as well.

I'm being murdered, he thought. *Murdered by Denton Rourke.*

Sweat welled up on top of his head and ran down his temples. He wanted to wipe it away, but his hands would not release the vice-like clutch they had created around his briefcase. Only his eyeballs continued to move properly, and they already had a full agenda of darting rapidly from side to side, surveying the scene in front of their owner's face.

Rompeaux had sensed trouble from the moment he crossed the UAB lobby and ran into a large, neon yellow poster which read:

HR PRESENTS: M. ROMPEAUX'S
"JOYS OF SEA LIFE" EXHIBIT
HR OFFICE FROM 8:30AM – 8:32AM
(*VIEWING MANDATORY*)

His heart had jumped as he quickened his pace toward the HR corridor. But as he made the turn, he had to slow down to pull the multiple signs inviting everyone to his office off the walls. Then, just thirty feet from the HR offices, Rompeaux stopped dead when he saw the main door propped wide open.

I was surfing in privacy mode. I know I was. I checked. And besides, I had approval.

Marcus Rompeaux had been called many things by his colleagues, but whatever they wanted to say about him, he followed the rules, he always had. He knew he had nothing to fear in terms of his job, but that thought didn't make him feel any better as he reached the HR door and peered inside.

"Nice work, Marcus," a passing employee offered. "Very ... special."

Rompeaux wanted to yell that he had approval, but his brain had frozen in place. In fairness, if anyone walking into their office to find two dozen stuffed dolphin and whale toys on display in grossly inappropriate and highly inaccurate sexual positions across their desk would likely suffer from brain lock. And if someone had also hung a banner announcing that the person had watched 26 different dolphin and whale mating videos on the internet that month and that they, "put the *hump* in *humpback*," they'd likely suffer full body paralysis – or burst into flames.

After what felt like an hour to Marcus Rompeaux, he heard his breath exhale loudly from his chest, and realized he had control of his appendages once more.

"I had approval!" he yelled to the employee who by then was back at his desk, telling everyone he knew about the display.

Rompeaux pulled the block out from under the HR door and closed it with pronounced vigor. Then he stumbled over to his desk and pushed the entire display off with a desperate swing of his arm. After noting the very unsatisfactory lack of dramatic noise made by shoving stuffed animals off a desk, he knelt down in the center of the pile and started throwing them one by one over the high wall of the one unoccupied cubicle in his area. After 24 frantic throws, he leaned against his desk, panting.

Looking up, he sighed as he read the banner again. He rose and carefully maneuvered his body on top of his desk, taking care to keep his weight over the legs, and ripped down the banner. After making his descent back down to the floor, he crumpled the offensive advertisement into a giant ball and stuffed it into his trash can. He stomped it as far down as possible, thinking of Denton with every crash of his foot and running through possible scenarios for dealing with the man's antics. After several minutes of filtering out ideas he deemed impractical and/or illegal, he settled the perfect course of action.

He would tell on Denton Rourke.

And so, twenty minutes later, Rompeaux stood at Denton Rourke's desk looking very pleased. Far more pleased, he noted, than Denton himself actually looked.

Denton sat with his back to Marcus Rompeaux as he studied a file with one hand on his chin and the other holding a red pen.

Rompeaux cleared his throat. Denton turned, saw his visitor, and dropped his pen with a roll of his eyes.

"Great, Marcus – perfect – just what I need. Let me guess, you found out I donate to the Volunteer Firefighters Association and you're here to lodge a fairness complaint on behalf of the Amateur Arsonists Union?"

Rompeaux's smile did not waver.

"Very amusing, Denton. Almost as amusing as the stunt you pulled in my office."

Denton stared at him stone-faced and irritated.

"Marcus, it's not that I don't enjoy trying to make sense of your every utterance, but I don't have time right now for this game. What do you want?"

"Feigning ignorance won't save you this time," Marcus erupted. "I've already alerted Daniel Caldwell to your antics. This time you've gone too far – TOO FAR!"

Rompeaux tried to cover his suddenly loud speech with a cough. Denton looked around and then returned his frown to his accuser.

"Lower your voice," he said. Then Denton leaned forward in his chair and spoke in a whispered tone.

"Clearly you're really angry about something, and you obviously think I'm involved – which is honestly a pretty fair assumption most of the time. But right now I've got a pile of work – work you know I loathe – to finish. My fiancée's snooty, judgmental, and disapproving father is in town and trying to impress him is proving impossible, and someone tried to kill my boss. I'm *booked*, Marcus. So if you've really told our Chief Operating Officer that I'm involved in some sort of offense against you, you'd better be ready to explain to him that you have nothing on which to back up your claim."

Denton glared at Rompeaux a moment longer and then turned back around, and resumed reading the file.

Rompeaux stood and blinked rapidly, watching Denton's back.

"You … you really don't know?" he asked.

"Don't know and don't care," Denton clarified.

Rompeaux scratched the side of his head and bit his lip.

"I just thought … well, you know."

"I know, I know – and I can't blame you. Just please fix this, okay?"

Rompeaux nodded and started backing away. "I will, I will. I'm the head of HR for your department, and I'll make sure this misunderstanding is corrected."

Denton nodded. "Good, because I'm going to have a whale of a time finishing all this as it is."

For the second time that morning, Rompeaux froze.

"What did you say?"

Denton turned to him.

"I said I'm going to have a hard time getting through all this as it is."

"No," Rompeaux pointed at him. "You said *whale*. I heard you."

Denton's eyes narrowed again. "Marcus, what is the matter with you? Yeah, I said I'm going to have a *whale of a time*. So *what*?"

Rompeaux smiled uneasily. "I'm sorry, I'm sorry. Just one of those mornings already. I'll take care of this."

"Perfect. Wonderful. Thank you," Denton said. He turned back to his file.

"Now that we're past this hump, I can get back on track. Maybe

I'll finish before the Dolphins play tonight."

Marcus Rompeaux felt the blood rushing to his face as his eyes bolted open.

"You said *humpback*!" he said. "And you said *dolphins*!"

He raised a stubby finger and pointed it at Denton's back.

"You did this!" he said.

Denton placed his pen on the desk and turned slowly to face Rompeaux once more. His solemn expression gave way to the slightest smile.

"Oops," he said.

Denton's phone rang. Both men looked at the display which showed the caller as D. CALDWELL.

"Oops *indeed*!" Rompeaux said as he stormed away.

Denton picked up the phone.

"Good morning, Mr. Caldwell. What can I do for you today?"

"Well, I need to kill you," Caldwell said, "so would you mind coming up here? I want to conserve my energy."

"Okay," Denton heard himself saying. He hung up the phone, locked his computer and walked toward the elevator, wondering if Ohnemus Parker's pranks ever landed him in the principal's office.

# # #

DENTON STEPPED OFF THE ELEVATOR and walked toward the receptionist. Rachel saw him coming and shook her head.

"Go right in, Mr. Funnyman," she said.

Denton waved feebly and plodded along, trying to think of a proper explanation – something that would help Caldwell to understand that he had absolutely no choice but to turn Rompeaux's desk into a set piece from some bizarre, aquatic-themed porno flick.

Just say that. It'll work perfectly.

Denton tried to glare at his brain as he knocked on Caldwell's door. He heard the man's voice order him in and he complied, closing the door behind him.

Caldwell sat behind his desk with his hands clasped. He brought his forefingers to a point and rested his chin on them. Denton waved and sat down across from him.

"Denton," Caldwell spoke slowly. "This is very difficult. You have put me in a very difficult position."

"I'm sorry. I know—"

"You *don't* know," Caldwell corrected. "You can't possibly know – can't have an inkling of just how hard it was to watch Marcus Rompeaux barge in here, panting, and deliver his tale of desk violation – to look at the pictures of stuffed animals he brought me – and maintain my composure!"

Denton smiled, but the look on Caldwell's face shut it down.

"No, Denton. This is *not* funny. I don't have the luxury of bursting into laughter when a Human Resource department head gets pranked."

Caldwell rose and looked out the window behind him. He put his hands on his hips and shook his head.

"It's none of your business, of course," he said. "But Marcus has been helping a local school teacher – a woman with whom he has a new relationship – with an educational video she is building for her sixth-grade biology class. He received corporate approval to use his work computer, and even took vacation hours for the time he spent on the project. So in spite of how amusing it may have seemed, he's not some kind of …"

"Purveyor of aquatic erotica?" Denton offered.

Caldwell turned back to meet his eye.

"Two employees have *died* here, Denton – one just last night. Of all people, how could you have thought this was the right time for such a thing?"

"I'm sorry," Denton replied. "I didn't want to make light of what's happened. It's just … well, Rompeaux canceled the charity bake sale – and he seemed to take such joy in it so I wanted to—"

Caldwell put a hand up.

"Rompeaux didn't shut it down. That came from senior HR leadership. And I'm ignoring the decision," he said. "I'll risk a fairness complaint, whatever the hell that is. So the breakfast is a go."

He sat back down and stared at Denton.

"On one condition," he said.

"Name it."

"Leave Marcus Rompeaux alone," Caldwell said.

"Deal," Denton nodded.

"And apologize to him. *Sincerely*."

Denton stopped nodding.

"Far be it from me to correct the Chief Operations Officer," Denton said. "But that seems like *three* conditions."

"Your protest of the actual number is noted and dismissed. Do we have a deal?"

"May I sit here for a moment and act like I'm giving serious consideration to refusing?"

"Certainly."

Denton drew in a deep breath and let it out with a stern bend in his brow. He stared out the window at the city skyline and shook his head.

"Okay, you have a deal," he said finally.

"Well done," Caldwell said. "Your contemplation seemed genuine."

"Thank you," Denton said. "Anything else?"

"Well, since you've had time to put together a rather elaborate joke at Marcus Rompeaux's expense, I'm guessing you've also had time to work on the case? Any updates on Phillip's death?"

"Well I've scratched Martin Rampart off my suspect list," Denton said.

Daniel Caldwell stared back without a smile. Denton shifted in his chair and wondered if Caldwell's continued silence meant Denton should try another answer, or if the man simply needed a few moments to work through the pros and cons of throwing him out the window.

"Have I made a mistake here, Denton?" he finally said. "It's okay to say I have. I'm a COO, but that doesn't mean I'm infallible. If this is too much for you, there is *nothing* wrong with saying so. It was always a lot to ask, and—"

"No. No, it really isn't. I'm sorry. I just get a little nervous when giving out bad news."

"Bad news?"

Denton stood up and walked to the silver serving tray and its alluring pitcher of super-water.

"It's just that … well, I don't know *a lot* yet, but it looks like Phillip Anderson might have been caught up in something illegal."

"Phillip Anderson," Caldwell said, his mouth turning downward. "Involved in something illegal." he repeated. "Any idea what he might have been up to?"

Denton shook his head.

"I'm not sure yet – and I'm not even sure he actually did anything wrong. But in the past year he's been in contact with someone very iffy."

"What kind of iffy?"

"The criminal record for financial fraud kind."

Caldwell took in the news without showing emotion, but Denton saw something in his eyes.

"But you're not *sure* right?" he asked.

"No, not at all sure. But Daniel … he did run our accounting department."

Daniel Caldwell let out a deep sigh. He nodded toward the pitcher.

"Fix me one, too, will you?"

Denton took two glasses and filled them. Caldwell joined him and took a sip.

"It doesn't seem like him, Denton. I just can't believe he'd risk all our futures on something illicit."

"I trust your judgment," Denton said. "And I don't know if he's done anything wrong, let alone anything involving his role here."

Denton took a sip and looked over at Caldwell.

"I think it would help if I could see everything he sent you that night," Denton said.

It would help me not have to steal it from you this evening.

Caldwell gave him an apologetic look.

"I'm sure you know what I'm going to say," he replied.

"Something about the risk being too great, even though we're of like minds that there are answers in those files?" Denton said.

"Exactly."

Damn.

"I understand," Denton lied. "Just thought I'd ask again."

Caldwell returned to his desk.

"So apart from the financial scheme angle, there's no indication why he and Rampart were killed?" he asked.

Denton shook his head. "Not yet. And I'm afraid that's another issue."

Caldwell tilted his head slightly. "How so?"

Denton paced the floor.

"*If* Phillip had some sort of financial plot in mind, he most certainly did not have Martin Rampart as his accomplice. I think these two men were murdered because of something else – some other connection. So there's the case to uncover what – if anything – Phillip Anderson was up to, and there's the case to find out who killed both these men, and why."

"Well that's just wonderful," Caldwell said. "Complicated, clouded, and nowhere near resolved."

"I'll get it figured out," Denton said. "I will. It's what I do."

Caldwell looked over at him and smiled. He reached out and shook his hand.

"Thank you, Denton. This is way beyond what I expected we'd be asking of you, and I do appreciate your efforts. I hope you understand my concern about Marcus."

"I do, and you're right. Bad timing on my part."

Daniel walked Denton to the door.

"Well, I know you'll make it right. And Denton, I know you have experience with murder investigations, but *please* be careful with this. Peter and I will make ourselves available whenever required, so don't hesitate to reach out if you need anything."

"I will, thanks."

Caldwell gave him a final wave as he made his way back to his desk. Denton turned and headed for the elevator hoping something down on six would help distract him from his next visit to Marcus Rompeaux.

CHAPTER 27

After a successful trek back to six without running into his HR nemesis, Denton sat at his desk and stared at the wall in front of him. His eyelids felt heavy, and so far the free coffee from the break room had only served to double his restroom use. He swiveled around and glared in the direction of the break room. Maybe that's why they didn't charge for it. It tasted terrible and did nothing to stimulate brain activity. Maybe it wasn't coffee at all.

Denton ran his hands down his face and thought about the morning's events. His prank had been a daring success – as long as he didn't count his ill-timed deployment, the scolding from Caldwell, or the now-required apology to Marcus. At least Julian Chase had found the news of his charity breakfast's resurrection something to celebrate with a hug and a promise that it would be, "glorious."

His mind tripped and fell onto the case and he swore he could hear himself groan. Reviewing the situation with Caldwell provided Denton with a raw realization every answer he found only resulted in more questions. Two murders, hazy leads. A possible financial scheme with potential ties to UAB management, yet so, *so* little to go on. For the first time, Denton wondered whether Caldwell had gotten it right. Maybe he *was* in over his head.

"Well, good morning Mr. Grouchy Face," Candace Covington's

voice announced.

Denton looked up to find Candace's face smiling at him over the wall. He turned as she came around and entered his cubicle.

"Well, look at you," he said. "From storm cloud of loathing to beaming ball of sunshine," he said.

"Thanks to you," she said. "You did a great thing, Denton. I can't thank you enough."

She leaned over and kissed him on the cheek. Then she stood back up and switched out her smile for a far sterner look.

"And it's a good thing you did, Denton. Otherwise I'd be convinced of your complete and utter bastard-ness right now."

Denton rolled his eyes. "Ignoring that you're making up words, what have I done?"

"I heard what you did to poor Mr. Rompeaux," she said.

"Okay, also ignoring pretty much all of that sentence," he replied. "I admit it may have been a bit over the top," Denton said.

"Over the top, huh?" Candace said.

"*And* I'll be apologizing in a severely very sincere fashion in a matter of minutes, okay?"

Candace looked at him sideways, and then uncrossed her arms. The smile returned.

"Okay, good enough for me."

"Thank heavens for that," Denton replied. "Now, I assume your presence means you've got something for me?"

"And then some," Candace replied, reaching into her pocket.

She brought out a small, red flash drive and held it out. Denton reached for it, but she pulled it back.

"It'll cost you a favor," she said.

"I thought I'd already banked enough favor points by getting you acquainted with Fred. He already likes you – what do you need, a marriage proposal in week one?"

"Like I'd ask *you* for marriage help of any kind," she replied. "No, I need some manual labor assistance."

"Nope."

"Please?"

Denton cringed at Candace's ability to stretch the single word into a ten-second, ear shattering beg.

"Jesus Christ, okay!" he relented.

Candace smiled and clapped. "Yay! Thank you!"

"I'm warning Fred about your evil power," he said. "What do you need, and when?"

Candace leaned against his desk. "A few of the folks we lost last week left tons of crap at their desks, and one guy wasn't here that day, so no one's cleared out any of his stuff yet."

"So?"

"So now my boss has told me that I have to get all those desks sorted – and for the weirdo's desk I have to separate trash from valuables so they can mail his crap to him."

"The weirdo?" Denton asked.

"Weirdo and slacker," she said. "And – by the way – he was the IT contact for *your* unit – your whole organization structure, really."

"I thought you were our contact."

Candace shook her head. "That's because Superfreak hardly ever came to work and when he did, he'd disappear for hours and leave his work for the rest of us. Unless, of course, one of your execs needed help, in which case he'd rush right up to the 28th floor to save the day and book some face time. Fat load of good that did him."

She gestured across the entire sixth floor.

"That's why I'm always up here helping you guys out *and* trying to manage the escheatment project at the same time."

"Fowler and I were just talking the other day about how good a person you are," Denton smiled.

"Whatever. Anyway, his desk is gross – like he was. And because we're doubling up on the number of departments we support, I have to come in at six-thirty tomorrow morning to get all this done before I'm knee-deep in project testing. We go live on Monday."

"Tomorrow?" Denton asked. "Oh, no, Candace. Look, seriously, I would help you out, but with Fowler out for a couple of days I'll already be here working through our back-dated files all morning."

"You can go help her in the morning," Fowler said.

Denton and Candace turned to see Don Fowler standing in the doorway reading an open file folder. He looked up and smiled at Denton.

"I officially give you the morning off. I've got a handle on our backlog."

"Oh, that is … *wonderful*," Denton said. "And, if I could just add … what the hell are you doing here?"

Fowler winked at Denton and walked away. Candace smiled and extended the flash drive again. Denton snatched it away and waved it at her.

"This toy better be good," he said.

Candace nodded. "It's better than good. And it's *not* a toy."

She hopped off his desk and pointed at the drive.

"Now listen, Denton. This is *not* for amateurs. You plug this into any USB port and it will automatically download files. It targets documents – like spreadsheets, word processor files, and emails."

"Nice. How long does it take?"

Candace shrugged. "That depends on the amount of data on the machine. Could take two minutes or it could take thirty. It's best to plan for longer."

"Great."

"Now, in the drive directory you'll find some other tools – including a program called a Shredder."

"Right," Denton said. "A program designed to permanently wipe files from hard drives to prevent confidential information from being stolen."

"Color me impressed," she said. "But this is a hacker's version. It's designed to allow you to cover your tracks instantly. You double click it, and boom – you've just turned your machine into an expensive paperweight. No failsafe, no warnings, no 'Are you sure' messages before it starts. You click it, everything is destroyed – even files on cloud storage sites. And when it's done turning the files to vapor, it will over-volt the system BIOS."

"And all that stuff means the data is gone?"

Candace picked up the manila folder on Denton's desk and

dropped it in his trashcan.

"Still using that," Denton said.

Candace ignored him. "That is *gone*," she said. "Using the shredder is like taking that file, burning it in the parking lot, collecting all the ashes and putting them through a paper shredder, and then taking those pieces and firing them into space."

"Wow," Denton said.

"And then destroying space in its entirety."

"Why the hell would you give *me* something like that?"

"It was on the drive when I got it, and it can't be removed. So I figured I'd better warn you."

"Consider me warned," Denton said.

"You can rename it to anything you'd like, so if you want to go in and call it, *Do Not Click This Ever*, that might help."

"Got it."

Candace patted him on the shoulder and headed out of his cubicle. "Only other rule is simple: If you somehow manage to wipe out UAB with this drive, you and I never met."

"Understood," Denton said.

"Good," she smiled. "Okay, super spy, I'll see you bright and early tomorrow. Bring your muscles."

Denton watched her leave and then bolted from his chair and made his way down the hall toward the conference room. He pushed through the door and stared at Don Fowler, who sat alone at the long table next to a stack of file folders.

"How'd you know I was in here?" Fowler asked.

Denton tapped his chin and looked skyward.

"Gosh, let's see … you're technically not supposed to be here, which means you need a place you can work without calling attention to yourself. Your office is off-limits since it's now a crime scene, and this is the only conference room on the floor that has frosted glass. That means people can see that it's not available, but can't see that it's occupied by everyone's favorite murder suspect."

"Sorry I asked," Fowler said. "How's it going?"

Denton sat down and looked at his boss.

"Don, what are you doing here? I know you've got a lot on your mind, but it's really in your best interest *not* to forget that someone is trying to kill you."

Fowler shrugged with a smile.

"Well, I would have stayed home today," he said. "But Erik Taberman called me."

"Taberman?" Denton said with mock surprise.

"Yeah. Someone put a copy of my efficiency proposal on his desk last night. He looked it over and asked to see me."

Denton smiled. "Well, well. What crazy luck. Deserved, to be sure."

Fowler nodded. "Yes, quite the surprising good fortune, wasn't it?" He closed the file in front of him and looked at Denton.

"Thank you, Denton," he said.

Denton shook his head. "Don't look at me," he said. "I'd have to be crazy – or not that interested in my job – to sneak into an executive's office after hours."

"Of course, what was I thinking?" Fowler said.

Concern about an outbreak of male bonding grabbed hold of Denton, but a knock at the conference room door spared him the task of making up an excuse to leave.

Both men turned and watched Russell Carlson enter the room. Dressed in the new UAB security outfit, which consisted of a pistachio green button down shirt with brown accents and dark green pants, the now-undercover police officer telegraphed a very clear message to Denton: *If you say a word, I will kill you.*

"Hello UAB security officer whom I have never met," Denton said. "What can we do for you?"

"Can it, Rourke," Carlson said. "Fowler and I have met."

"Right, sorry. What's up, Carlson?"

"Could I have a few minutes of your time alone?" Carlson asked.

"No problem," Fowler offered. "He was just leaving anyway. Maybe you can escort him to his next appointment. In HR."

"You heard about that?" Denton asked.

Fowler chuckled. "Wow. You really don't know how a corporate office works, do you?"

"I'm still learning," he replied. Then he turned to Carlson. "Okay, I guess I'm all yours, officer."

Carlson nodded to Fowler and followed Denton out.

Fowler smiled and shook his head at their departure. He glanced at his watch, and then rose. He adjusted his tie and he too headed for the door.

"Showtime," he said and strolled out toward the elevators.

# # #

RUSSELL CARLSON SHOOK HIS HEAD as he and Denton walked through the lobby toward the HR corridor.

"Security here is a joke," he said. "The only thing these guards could stop is efficiency."

Denton nodded. "They do like their forms," he said.

Carlson gestured to the grey-haired woman sitting behind the main lobby security desk.

"Look at her – she's sixty-three years old and uses a cane to walk fifteen feet to the bathroom," he said. "Who is she going to deter – a *seventy*-year old with a walker who's bent out of shape about account fees?"

The woman made eye contact with Denton, and he waved at her. She smiled, put down her knitting needles, and waved back.

"What about our mysterious overnight guard?" Denton asked.

Carlson shook his head. "His name is Lyle Saunders. The company hasn't been able to reach him since we found Anderson," he said. "So far, tracking down his residence has been a long dead end process. His two most recent addresses are empty lots and the third is a post office box that hasn't been checked in months. He saw something – maybe a lot. He knows what happened to Anderson, I'm sure of it."

The two men turned the corner into the HR corridor. As they approached Denton's destination, he stopped and looked Carlson up and down.

"I'm sorry, Russell, but what *is* this outfit? None of the other guards are wearing it."

"It's the new uniform. Everyone's got them already, but they're wearing the old blue-on-blue versions until they fall to pieces – for obvious reasons. I feel like an idiot."

"Well don't," Denton said with firmness.

"Thanks," Carlson replied.

"You're welcome. I'm sure *looking* like an idiot is painful enough."

"Yep," Carlson said. "I'm going to kill you when this is all over."

Denton smiled. "Come on, if you can't laugh at yourself, who can you laugh at?"

"You," he said. "When I'm killing you."

Then Carlson pointed toward the Human Resources door.

"I think you'd better handle the rest of this journey on your own," he said.

"Don't you want to stay?" Denton asked. "I might need protection."

Carlson shook his head.

"You're on your own. I've got to make my rounds and fill out some paperwork."

With that, Carlson waved a quick good-bye and left Denton alone. Denton watched him disappear around the corner. Then he wandered the rest of the way down the hall and stopped in front of his destination.

"Be sincere," he said. His brain seemed to accept the order rather quickly, and something struck Denton.

He actually did feel a little sorry about what he'd done.

A little.

"... BUT I'M AFRAID THAT, DUE TO BUDGET constraints, we have no choice but to eliminate your position. There's no need to return to the building, as your personal effects will be forwarded to your address of record. Also, security will no longer allow you past the lobby.

We wish you the very best in your future endeavors and thank you for the work you have done for United Alliance Bank."

Marcus Rompeaux hung up the phone and made some notes on a piece of paper.

"What the hell are you doing, Marcus?"

Rompeaux turned in his chair and looked at Denton Rourke.

"Ah, hello, Denton. I was just taking care of some unfinished business with some layoffs."

"You're laying off people over the phone? That's pretty awful."

"It's worse than you think," Rompeaux said. "I'm laying them off via *voicemail*."

"What?"

The HR lead nodded and waved toward the papers on his desk.

"Per HR policy, when affected employees do not show up for work on the day we're doing a layoff, I have to call them. If they don't answer, I have to leave a message."

"Jesus, Marcus," Denton shook his head.

Rompeaux sat up in his chair. "Do you think I *enjoy* this, Denton? *Any* of this? Do you think I actually revel in bringing people in here – or *calling* them and conveying the news that they are no longer employed? Well I don't. I hate it. But it's a requirement of my position, so I don't have the luxury of just making smart remarks and leaving the task incomplete."

Denton put his hands up. "That's fair, I withdraw my judgment."

He pulled up a chair and sat down.

"So, Marcus, I came here to apologize. I'm sorry I … uh, *decorated* your office. It was childish and unwarranted. I'm really sorry."

Marcus Rompeaux nodded. "Thank you, Denton. I appreciate you coming down here to say that. I'm sure it wasn't easy."

The lack of smugness in Rompeaux's voice shocked Denton's system, and he suddenly found himself continuing the conversation.

"Well, Caldwell made me," he admitted.

Rompeaux chuckled. "I'm sure he did. But you took it seriously, so thank you all the same."

Denton nodded and rose. Marcus reached out his hand, and Denton shook it.

"It's not easy, you know," he said, "being the 'bad guy who ends people's employment, who cancels charity bake sales."

"Well that's back on, so no worries," Denton said.

"Yes, I heard. Well, you seem to have won that round, Mr. Rourke."

Denton watched as Marcus Rompeaux's lips formed a nearly imperceptible smile followed by the slightest wink from his right eye. Denton nodded and waved as he moved to the exit.

Back in the corridor, Denton barely had time to think about how Marcus Rompeaux had not gone out of his way to make the apology difficult or embarrassing for him before Russell Carlson's bright green figure appeared once again.

"Oh, boy!" Denton said, once again looking at the man's uniform. "I'll have a double scoop of Rocky Road in a sugar cone, mister!"

"Ha, ha – eat me," Carlson replied. "Sowell's here."

"What for?"

"We found Lyle Saunders."

Denton turned around and looked at the HR office, and then back at Carlson.

"How long was I in there?" he asked. "What happened to the endless dead ends and misdirection?"

"We just followed the smoke," Carlson replied.

"The smoke?"

"Yep," Carlson nodded. "His house burned down last night … with him inside."

Denton closed his eyes and opened them skyward.

"Of course it did."

"Yeah. But Sowell wants us to check it out anyway."

"Well I'm glad I haven't had lunch yet," Denton said. Then he gestured toward the lobby. "Lead the way, officer."

Carlson grunted and handed him a piece of paper. "That's the address, he said. "We can't be seen leaving together, so you have to get your own ride. We'll meet you there."

Denton nodded and waved as Carlson departed. Then he stood in the corridor a bit longer and wondered how a request to be driven to a burned down house might go over with a cab driver. Maybe he'd leave out that detail.

Finally comfortable with his plan for incident-free transportation, Denton made his way across the lobby and out of the UAB building. In his preoccupied state, he missed the pasty face of Kevin Kahneman as the man pushed through the adjoining doors and staggered into the lobby.

The security guard put down her knitting and gave the disheveled AVP a thorough once over. Sensing her disapproval, Kahneman ran a hand through his hair and checked his tie, which seemed to be missing. He fumbled in his jacket pocket, found his ID, and waved it from a distance he felt would keep the smell of alcohol from reaching her. Then he displayed a ridiculous smile and moved off toward the elevators.

Once inside, Kahneman selected the 40th floor and leaned against the wall.

He reviewed his plan and saw no flaws. The past few days felt like a blur, partly because so much was happening and partly because he'd obscured most of the week's events via a rather indelicate use of alcohol.

His binge started at an abandoned drive-in theater where he finished most of a bottle of bourbon while waiting for a blackmailer who never showed up. Returning home, he consumed large amounts of vodka and waited for the inevitable call to reschedule the money drop. After several hours of shifting his blurry gaze between the silent phone and an oft-empty glass, he quit waiting and passed out.

The next morning he cured his hangover with a large tequila sunrise and made his way to UAB in time to hear two employees gossiping about Phillip Anderson's death and its rumored connection to, "another employee."

Unaware the rumored connection referred not to Kahneman himself but rather to the newly deceased Martin Rampart, the alcohol-fueled exec assumed someone had uncovered his deeds in the UAB executive parking garage. So, not having much interest in being arrested in his workplace, prosecuted in court, and man-handled in prison, Kahneman made an immediate exit from the building. Soon after he found himself in front of a large bottle of anti-anxiety medicine, commonly known as, "booze."

The elevator slowed and Kahneman snapped back to the present as the doors opened. He stepped out onto the floor and stopped to give himself time to remember his plan.

Oh, yes. It was all about leverage now. Kahneman started forward across the floor.

He'd spent most of the week worrying about the police and that bastard with his salacious DVD. But as the week wore on with no knock at his door from the authorities and no phone call from the blackmailer, Kahneman's thoughts had returned to his lost fortune and what he could do to get it back.

And the answer came to him. *Leverage.*

Kahneman realized that Anderson's scheme – as brilliant as it seemed – could not have succeeded without help from another UAB executive. And while it could have been any number of executives, Kahneman felt certain he knew who Anderson had put his faith in.

My knowledge is my leverage. My leverage will make me rich ...

Then he stopped and looked around.

... if I can find this asshole's office. Where am I?

After a sympathetic admin explained he had spent the past few minutes wandering around the 14th floor, Kahneman returned to the elevator and found the actual button for 40. He smiled as the elevators closed.

Soon I'll be ... I have to use the restroom ...

CHAPTER 28

Denton stepped out of the cab, mildly pleased with the overall travel experience. He blinked hard in the bright sunlight and surveyed the row of simple yet well-kept houses surrounding the smoldering shell of Lyle Saunders' abode.

Ignoring the smoke still billowing from the roof, the charred brick and blackened windows, the security guard's home still stood out among its peers. Denton trudged through the overgrown lawn which weeds had long ago taken ownership of and forced the grass to move away to safer yards.

Reaching the front porch, Denton surveyed the area further, noting the peeling paint, the thick dirt coating the windowsills, and the rusting rain gutter that threatened to fall on him at any moment. All in all, Denton felt with some certainty that only by the slightest of margins did the house burning down represent a devaluation of the property.

Russell Carlson met him on the porch.

"Looks like the case is heating up," he said with a smirk.

"No, no, no," Denton said. "Don't do that."

Carlson smiled. "I can't help it. I'm on fire."

Denton put his hand up. "Before this officially becomes a nightmarishly bad buddy cop movie, please tell me what you have learned so far."

Carlson bowed slightly and ushered Denton into the house.

"First floor is safe – as safe as it can be, anyway. After you."

Denton ducked under the police tape and met up with Sowell as he surveyed the remains of the living room. He pushed his jacket sleeve across his nose as he adjusted to the powerful smell of burnt woods and melted plastics.

Carlson navigated through the maze of debris and stood next to a scorched metal armchair. Though burned black, the chair had carried out its prime directive quite well in spite of the blaze, as evidenced by the fact that it continued to proudly hold the remains of Lyle Saunders firmly in a sitting position. Eager to get in on the recognition, the handcuffs used to keep Saunders in place had also held up marvelously.

Carlson flipped open his notepad and read.

"Lyle Saunders, thirty-seven, single. Primary occupation: security guard at UAB – overnight shift. Secondary career: kindling."

"Russell," Sowell said without smiling.

"Sorry, L.T.," Carlson said.

"One question before I throw up, please?" Denton asked pointing downward but looking to the ceiling. "Why are his legs on the floor?"

Carlson shook his head. "We're not sure yet, but it looks like someone tortured him before lighting up the house. Depending on the damage inflicted pre-fire, there may not have been much to keep them connected after the heat and flames started to melt the fat and sinews—"

"Got it, got it, got it … stop talking now," Denton begged.

Carlson closed his notepad. Denton looked again at Lyle Saunders' body and filed the grim scene away alongside the others he'd amassed over the past year or so.

"Denton," Sowell said. "We found a lot of high-tech recording and video transfer equipment in his bedroom."

"And a safe," Carlson added.

"Which was opened and empty," Denton said.

Sowell smiled. "Yes, save for a couple of DVDs."

Carlson looked at Denton. "You called Saunders an entrepreneur before. I can't see him making much by selling recordings of incidents he caught going on at UAB."

"Me either," Denton said, staring out at nothing. "He made his money *not* selling them."

"Blackmail," Sowell said.

Denton nodded and paced across the floor.

"It explains the random dates that footage went missing. Saunders only lifted the video feed when he found an executive doing something *really* worthy of keeping quiet."

Carlson snorted. "Who are these people who think in this day and age that they can still do that kind of stuff and not get caught?"

"Think about it," Sowell said. "A secure parking garage for the company's top executives – all of whom believe it's the last refuge for privacy in a world of recorded phone calls, monitored emails, and digitally tracked comings and goings."

"And who can – and would – pay to make ugly situations go away," Denton said. "But it looks like one of Saunders' customers decided to leave a little negative feedback about the service. They tortured him until he gave up the safe combination, took his inventory, and put him out of business."

"And shut down a crucial lead," Carlson added.

Sowell nodded his agreement and looked over at Denton.

"Sorry we seem to have wasted your time here," he said. "Can I drop you back at work?"

"No, but you can take me to Ford's," Denton said. "I need to think through some stuff, and that requires assistance from my loyal, steadfast, and trusty sidekick."

"How can you think about Boston cream pie right now?" Sowell asked.

Denton shrugged. Then his eyes opened wide and he pointed out the front doorway. "We should hurry. Henry only makes one per day and I don't want to risk missing a slice."

"Well, then, I'll run the siren all the way there for you."

"Really?"

"No," Sowell rolled his eyes. "Come on."

Denton followed him out of the burned out tomb and into the bright daylight.

# # #

KEVIN KAHNEMAN STOOD IN FRONT of Daniel Caldwell and Peter Markung and let them digest what he'd just said. Daniel and Peter exchanged glances and then the COO looked at Kahneman and shook his head.

"I'm sorry, but what did you just say?" he asked.

"You heard me," Kahneman said, his voice shaking just a bit.

Caldwell nodded. "Well, yes, I heard you, but I couldn't understand you. Have you been drinking, Kevin?"

Kevin Kahneman did not like this direction at all.

Screw them – I must stay on the offensive.

"Don't try to change the subject, Caldwell. I know what you and Phillip Anderson are up to! I know all about your murderous scheme of embezzlement and … and … murder – and everything."

Kahneman trailed off and spent a few moments staring at the top of a building outside Caldwell's window. Then he refocused.

"…and you're going to cut me in as a partner, or I'm going to blow the whistle on this whole operation!"

"*Whole operation*?" Caldwell said. "*Our murderous scheme*?"

He looked at Peter Markung, whose expression did not provide any clarifying details. He looked back at the AVP.

"Kevin, what in the hell has gotten into you?"

Kahneman shook his head and then pointed a finger at the two men. Then he flopped down in one of Caldwell's chairs. Caldwell nodded to Peter, who walked over to the wet bar and poured a tall glass of water. He handed it to the rambling man. Kahneman took a long drink and then glared again at his hosts.

"I had my own plan, you know. I've been on to you for months, and I made a plan for myself so that you wouldn't be the only one getting rich."

Kahneman stood again.

"Kevin," Caldwell said. "I hate to sound like this, but … I'm *already* rich."

Kahneman ignored Caldwell's excuse.

"But then … then he died. He *died.* And it all went away."

Oh God. Am I crying? I think I'm crying. This isn't going at all well.

"Excuse me," Peter Markung said. "Would you like a tissue?"

"No!" Kahneman wiped his face hastily.

Caldwell rose and fixed his hard eyes on Kahneman.

"Kevin, I think I've been more than patient," Caldwell said. "You storm in here unannounced – and drunk – and accuse me of financial crimes and *murder*, and then threaten me with blackmail? Can you tell me why I should be anything other than grossly offended by your behavior?"

Kahneman stared at Caldwell through wide, tired eyes. He found himself impressed with the man's ability to convey extreme displeasure while maintaining a calm, professional appearance.

Not like you. I cannot believe you cried. Cry baby.

"No, sir," Kahneman heard himself say.

"I see," Caldwell said. "Well, can you think of any reason I should *not* have you tossed from the building this very minute?"

Cry baby Cry baby Cry baby CRY BABY!

Kahneman jumped from his seat.

"No, no, no!" he said.

He walked quickly toward the door and turned back to Daniel Caldwell.

"I want … fifty million dollars in cash by tomorrow," he said. "Otherwise I'm going to the SEC, the FBI, and the CIA."

"How about the YMCA," Markung suggested. "You can dry out there."

"We'll see how funny that is tomorrow," Kahneman snapped.

With a final dramatic turn, Kevin Kahneman departed, leaving Daniel Caldwell staring, mouth open. He watched as Peter walked over and closed the door.

"*That* is Phillip's second in command?" Caldwell asked.

Peter shook his head. "I'll straighten this out with him tomorrow."

"See that you do," Caldwell said. "He can't be in the building in that condition, Peter. Can you imagine if the press got hold of *him*?"

"I know," Peter replied. "Any word from Denton Rourke?" he asked.

Caldwell chuckled without pleasure. "He *says* he's getting closer to the answers. But I don't know."

"He'll get there," Peter said.

"Oh? And what has turned you into a believer?"

Peter shrugged. "Just a hunch."

"Well, he's running out of time," Caldwell said. He sat back down and turned toward the window.

"We all are," he added.

CHAPTER 29

Denton sat in his usual booth at Ford's Diner and stared at the most alluring piece of pie he'd ever seen.

"Henry, this is simply profound," he said.

"I'll take that as a compliment," Henry replied. "Whoops – forgot to get you a fork. Be right back."

Denton watched him disappear into the kitchen and then turned back to his dessert. He smiled at its thick chocolate top, its moist cake and cream center, and its severed and charred legs smoldering on the floor.

"Dammit," he muttered as he forced Lyle Saunders from his mind.

He looked back over his shoulder and saw Henry assisting another customer. He shrugged with a smile. The fork would come. Until it did, Denton felt content to take solace in the peace and quiet the diner afforded him.

"Hello, son."

Denton looked up and watched Connor Rourke slide into the booth across from him.

"Dad, what are you doing here?"

Connor fixed his deep green eyes on his son and smiled.

"Can't a father drop by to see his boy at work?"

"I'm not *at* work, Dad," Denton replied.

Connor nodded and pulled Denton's plate in front of him.

"So they told me across the street. I figured I'd try here."

Connor looked at the pie and then up at his son. Still very aware of the lack of utensils, Denton gestured at the plate.

"Please, have some," he said. "I insist."

"Thanks," Connor said. He pulled a fork from his overalls pocket and stabbed a very healthy bite.

"Good God," Denton said. "You carry your own *fork*? What kind of … wait a second."

Denton pointed at his father and cocked his head.

"You went to my office. Why?"

Connor took another bite and chewed slowly.

"Because I wanted to talk to you. And since you won't call me back, I figured I needed to try a little face to face time."

"Sorry, Dad," Denton said. "But I really don't have time to entertain your tales of the Rourkes and Ingrahams. Whatever the gripe, I'm sure it's ancient history."

"Denton, listen—"

"No, you listen, Dad - please," Denton cut in. "Things have been strained enough between Beth and me with the wedding stuff."

"You mean your refusal to pick a date," Connor clarified. He took another bite and shook his head. "Women and their outrageous demands."

"Thanks for that," Denton said. "Anyway, having her dad here isn't helping, and the last thing I need is for you to start digging up tribal folklore and igniting a new feud."

"They took what was ours, Denton."

"I don't know what that means, and if whatever it is happened more than a hundred years ago, I don't want to know. You should let it go."

Connor watched his son and continued chewing. Then he looked down at the plate.

"I suppose you could be right," he said.

"Will the wonders never cease," Denton declared. "Now look, Dad, will you *please* promise me that you'll be on your best behavior Saturday night? No talk about past slights, no challenging Archibald to a sword fight. Just dinner and pleasant conversation. Okay? Please?"

Connor finished off the pie and smiled while he chewed.

"Okay, son. Best behavior."

"Thank you," Denton said as he breathed a little easier.

"But I want you to promise me that when you have just a few minutes you'll do a quick profile search on Archibald Ingraham."

"Dad!"

"Just a quick profile search," Connor said. "They're going to be family, you know. You ought to learn at least a little bit about their background."

"Fine, fine, I will – I promise."

Connor smiled, stood up, and gave him a wink.

"No, you won't," he said. "But I have a feeling I'm going to get to say 'I told you so,' later, so that will be nice."

He turned for the exit and met Beth coming in. Beth broke out into a big smile and gave Connor a hug.

"Hi, Mr. Rourke," she said. "How are you? I haven't seen you in awhile!"

"I'm doing well, dear," he said, returning the smile. "And you're looking as lovely as ever. I am looking forward to having an evening of just dinner and pleasant conversation with you and your father on Saturday night."

Connor turned back to Denton.

"How was that?"

Denton shook his head. "Brilliant – except for all of this part right now."

Connor shrugged, waved at the two of them again and departed.

Beth watched him leave with a laugh and then joined Denton on his side of the booth. She kissed him on the cheek and pointed at his empty plate.

"Was it good?"

"Probably," he said. Then he smiled back at her. "And just what is it that brings you to my secret headquarters?"

Beth shrugged. "I was in the area and thought I'd see if the most handsome fellow for ten blocks was here."

She turned and looked over her shoulder. "*Is* Henry around today?"

Denton flicked her thigh and she squealed. She leaned in close to him.

"So when does your clandestine mission begin?" she asked.

"Very soon," he said. "My target will be out most of the afternoon attending a fundraiser for local underprivileged children. That's when I'll strike."

"Huh," Beth said as she nodded and leaned back in the booth. The two of them stared straight ahead for several moments. Then Beth turned back to him.

"Had to be a fundraiser for needy kids, did it?"

"Right?" Denton said. "I feel dirty pulling this while he's off trying to save the community."

"Well, maybe it's a front for a ring of ultra-evil villains who secretly kick puppies and conduct human sacrifices."

Denton looked at Beth. "Elizabeth Ingraham, I like the way you think."

The two smiled at each other, and Beth kissed him again.

"Just be careful, Mr. Bond," she said.

"Do you have *any* idea how sexy that sounds with your accent?"

Beth scooted out of the booth and turned to him.

"Yes," she said. Then she waved and departed.

Henry wandered back over and handed Denton a fork.

"And when's that wedding date again?" he asked.

"Slow down, Henry," Denton said. "Rome wasn't built in a day."

"No, you're right."

Denton watched Beth through the window until she turned the corner. He looked up at Henry who continued to stand at his shoulder.

"Why do I feel like you've got a 'but' to add?" Denton asked.

"Because I do," Henry said and slid into the booth opposite Denton.

"You're right, Rome wasn't built in a day. But you're not looking at this correctly, Denton."

"What do you mean?"

Henry banged lightly on the tabletop with his forefinger.

"This *is* your Rome, Denton," he said. "It's not waiting to be built – you two built it over the past few years. Now you have to maintain it – take care of it … make sure it gets the improvements it needs to stay strong."

Henry stood up and cleared away Denton's empty plate.

"You know your history, I'm sure," he said. "So I don't have to remind you what happened when Rome's keepers failed to follow that path themselves."

Denton looked up at the man and smiled.

"Henry, you always know just what to say to make a stressful situation even more taxing."

Henry smiled back. "I do what I can. Say, how was the pie?"

Denton's smile wavered as he looked at the plate. "I don't know," he said. "It was taken apart while I wasn't looking."

Henry turned for the kitchen. "Well, I'm sure that's not appropriately symbolic in any way at all," he said.

Denton shook his head and scooted himself out of the booth. At the door, he turned back.

"Henry," he called out.

Henry's head popped out from the kitchen.

"Thanks," Denton said.

Henry nodded with a smile. Then his head disappeared again.

Moments later, standing on the sidewalk outside the diner, Denton turned toward the UAB building and squinted.

"Am I actually going to steal corporate files from the man who hired me?" he asked.

An answer swirled around him in the breeze.

Yes.

A SHORT WALK LATER, DENTON found himself riding in a UAB elevator once more. He ran his hand over the jump drive in his pocket and tried to think of something to focus on during his climb skyward. Given the very simple instructions Candace had given him for using the tool, reviewing his plan took all of ten seconds.

"Plug it in. Wait. Remove it. Leave," he repeated. He looked at the counter and watched it move past the 21st floor. He thought about whistling. Then he thought about Phillip Anderson. Then he thought about the decline and fall of the Roman Empire. Soon after that, he thought that he might actually hate Henry.

Before he could pursue that idea any further, the elevator opened and ejected him into the heavens of the UAB building. He strode quietly across the empty foyer toward Caldwell's office, impressed with the smoothness of his execution.

"Hi, Denton," Rachel said.

Denton performed a bizarre stutter-stop in mid-stride but managed to keep moving. He waved and spoke quickly.

"Hi, Rachel, I know he's not in so I'm just going to leave him a message. I won't be a second."

"You can leave it with me, if you'd like."

Denton picked up his pace.

"No, no – it's double super private. Not that I don't trust you but I promised to make sure …"

Denton quit talking after he realized he'd put so much distance between himself and Rachel that he was now yelling at her.

Continuing with his, 'breeze in and breeze out' plan, Denton plunged right through Caldwell's door, closed it quickly behind him, and headed straight for the man's computer.

He sat down at Caldwell's desk and plugged the flash drive into the USB port. The drive's green light came to life and blinked rapidly. Denton smiled.

Good sign. Blinking light is a good sign.

"Denton, what the hell are you doing?"

Denton looked up into the very irritated face of Peter Markung.

Bad sign. Angry right-hand man is a bad sign.

CHAPTER 30

Denton found it difficult to gauge the gravity of Peter Markung catching him in Daniel Caldwell's office. Normally when Denton got in trouble during a case, he faced someone with a gun, or a knife, or some other dangerous tool that could break him into small pieces. But Peter Markung simply stood in front of him with his hands on his hips, looking severely disappointed. Denton knew better than to take that as a good sign, suspecting the man's giant forearms and sizeable knuckles could probably complete the "break him into pieces" task quite nicely on their own.

But he *did* register a small bit of hope when Markung went back to the door and closed it quickly. He walked back over to the desk, looking alarmed.

"Denton," Peter started. "Again – what the hell are you doing? Do you have *any* idea what would happen to you – and frankly, to *me* if you got caught in …"

Markung's eyes caught sight of the flash drive plugged into his boss's computer.

"You're stealing files?" Markung said a bit too loudly for Denton's liking.

"Peter, I need them. I told you – I need to know everything Anderson sent Daniel."

"Jesus Christ, take that out right now! I have my own copy of the email – with the attachments. I'll get you what you need."

Denton pulled the flash drive out immediately and put it back in his pocket. Markung pulled out his smart phone and started clicking through screens.

"He's going to fire me," he muttered as he continued to type. "He'll probably arrange to have *you* melted down and used as glue for our company envelopes."

Markung tapped the phone screen a few more times and then looked at Denton.

"It's in your email," he said.

Denton smiled. "Wouldn't it have just been easier to give that to me when I first asked?"

Markung frowned. "Why would a different day of the week make it easier for me to go behind my boss's back and do something I know he does not want done?"

Denton nodded. "Of course, you're right. Thanks Peter. I really do appreciate it."

"I don't care if you appreciate it," he said. "Just make what I've done worth it."

"I will," Denton promised. "Thanks again."

Markung continued to not smile.

"Please get out of here."

Denton headed for the exit without another word.

"And good luck," Peter said without turning to him.

Denton continued out the door with a quick wave as he passed into the hallway. He didn't dare make eye contact with Rachel for fear that she'd somehow be able to discern from his face that he had been up to no good.

He got in the elevator, pressed the button for the 6th floor, and watched the doors close. As he started down, a thought grabbed him and refused to let go.

He *had* been up to no good. And he didn't like it.

For the rest of the ride, Denton ignored himself and focused on his next steps. He would go to his desk, forward Peter's email to his laptop, and spend a quiet weekend piecing together whatever information Anderson had folded into the attachments he sent to Daniel

Caldwell before his death. And he'd take a break from this brilliant plan to have a wonderfully peaceful dinner with his beautiful fiancée, her displeased father, and the highly combustible Connor Rourke.

Nothing at all could go wrong.

The elevator opened and released Denton onto the 6th floor just as the echoing laughter in his head started to fade.

"Denton!" Fred's voice called out from the break room. Denton waved and joined his friend at a table.

"Where've you been?" Fred asked.

"Back on the 40th floor," Denton said.

"Nice. Did you manage to drop my name while you were up there?"

"No, but I think I managed to make a guy violate his principles just to help me out."

"You do have that effect on people."

"Not all people, though," Denton replied. Then after a moment's contemplation, he actually smiled.

"Hey, here's something fun," he said. "Yesterday I had no trouble using the restroom!"

"Most people don't consider that something worth celebrating after their third birthday," Fred said. "But sadly, I know to what you are referring. So now I'm the weird one."

Denton nodded vigorously and grinned. Fred continued.

"Yeah, I meant to tell you that I think she got transferred or fired, or quit. I saw her replacement yesterday while I was having coffee in the break room."

"Whatever the reason she left, it wasn't me," Denton said. "I never reported her behavior to anyone."

"Well, I hope to hell this new lady cleans the restrooms like mad. Because she is … uh, well, she is really not attractive."

"Fred."

"Ugly, really."

"Fred!"

"Hey, I'm just warning you so you don't do a double take when you see her. She's actually, physically, scary."

Denton shook his head. "I don't care if she has two noses with matching mustaches underneath and forgets to clean the restroom for weeks," he said. "If I can use the facilities in peace, I'm happy."

"She's also not very bright," Fred added.

"Oh? Did the two of you compare SAT scores?" Denton asked.

"No, no. It's just that I saw her barge right into the men's room, and then knock on the *women's* door and announce herself before entering."

"I got it," Denton said. "I will be on the lookout for a woman who is part circus freak and part Matt Damon."

"You leave Jason Bourne out of this," Fred warned with a pointed finger.

Denton grinned and went to the coffee pot. He poured a cup of black goo and walked back over to his friend.

"Okay, I've got to go to my desk and deal with some emails. Then I'm headed home."

"A tad early, isn't it?"

Denton shrugged. "I've got a long day tomorrow."

"Ah – you remembered your promise to Candace? Nice."

Denton gritted his teeth, as he had most certainly *not* remembered his agreement to act as her hired help in the obscenely early hours of Friday morning.

"Of course," he said. "Can't wait."

With a nod and a wave, he left his friend and headed for his desk. Fred turned back to the television and listened to the Financial News Network anchor as she reported on new rumors that a prominent negotiator for their sister company, United Alliance Insurance, had arrived in town.

"We do not comment on rumors and speculation, Sally," Fred told the anchor as he sipped his coffee.

# # #

GAVIN SPINCER SAT IN THE QUIET darkness and stewed. After several hours of tossing and turning, he'd given up on sleeping and sought to clear his busy mind by sorting through a few outstanding issues.

His quest would come to a successful conclusion in a matter of hours, and though one enemy had eluded him, he knew that wouldn't matter once he vanquished the big boss. Once he'd sent him to the fires of hell, Gadsden the Damned would claim total victory.

But then what?

Spincer shifted uneasily on the couch and rubbed his face with his hands. For all his work and planning, and in spite of his success, he still had a problem.

Though it had taken a few days to realize it, he felt really good about no longer working for UAB. He felt alive, and unchained. And he recognized that his arch enemy, the vilest fiend of them all, had actually set him free.

And now he would kill him.

Gavin breathed deeply and sighed as other issues lined up for face time with their master. First, though it started as nothing more than a way to move about UAB unnoticed, Gavin had no choice but to admit that he really liked his job cleaning toilets in his old building. He loved the very straightforward work and its basic solutions. He didn't have to spend hours troubleshooting an issue with customers who called for his expert assistance every time they kicked the power cord out of the wall. He didn't have to listen to his colleagues talk about the stupid new music they downloaded, or endure their chatter regarding the latest clubs.

You walk into the bathroom. If it's dirty, you clean it. The end.

But could he really seek full-time work as a janitor?

Certainly not.

Gavin could not discount the serious pay drop and the major plunge in professional rank between IT Specialists and janitors. But pay and social rank issues aside, Gavin could not shake one thing – the thing that negated the fact that he really liked cleaning.

He really liked killing more.

With each victim, Gavin had felt something inside him slipping into place in a kind of perfect fit. One or two murders and you can still probably walk away from the work. Three makes it harder. But Friday would make it four murders. Four murders … that's serious career development. And when you have the chance to do what you love, well, that's every employee's dream.

Gavin nodded in the dark. He stretched back out on the couch and felt more relaxed. Four murders provided a path from which he couldn't turn. He closed his eyes and smiled.

Besides, Tonya Garza would be five. And once you have five, is there a point in discussing another vocation?

CHAPTER 31

Friday

Denton hated a lot of things. Some days he hated most things. And by general rule he hated every single thing about early mornings. Waking up, turning on lights, smiling at people – all hate-worthy.

One notable exception to the rule: fresh brewed coffee from Ford's Diner. So as Denton backed through the front entrance of UAB at an hour of the morning he normally reserved for hiding his head under the pillow and yelling at alarm clocks, he counted the two large cups of black brew in his hands as the day's saving grace.

Steadying himself, Denton picked up the pace and scooted quickly across the lobby. By some stroke of luck, he managed to get to the elevator without having to deal with roughly thirty ounces of hot black coffee escaping their containment units and seeking political asylum on his shirt and pants.

The doors opened with their usual pleasant ding, but not before Denton's nostrils picked up the scent of bacon, cheese, and various other dishes. He felt his mouth watering as he entered the elevator and used his elbow to press the basement level. As the doors closed, he felt a momentary pang of jealousy for Marcus Rompeaux, whose office sat directly across the hall from Julian Chase's smorgasbord.

At the basement level, Denton stepped out into a dark, depressing hallway which helped him forget all about the breakfast buffet upstairs. He made his way to Candace Covington's desk but upon arrival found yet another item to add to his ever growing hate list.

"What the hell are you doing here?" Denton demanded as he placed the cups on Candace's desk.

Fred Maxton looked up from his newspaper and smiled.

"And a joyous good morning to you, too, sunshine," he said. He eyed the coffees and reached for one. Denton slapped his hand.

"Not for you," he said.

Candace appeared and hoisted her own mug with a smile.

"Thanks, Denton, but I already got mine, too.

Denton looked at both of them. Then he placed a careful hand on each of the coffee cups.

"Not for *either* of you," he clarified.

Fred and Candace looked at each other and giggled. Denton took his first sip of the strong black elixir and shook his head.

"Okay, let's get this done so I can leave and you two can go carve hearts on trees or whatever."

# # #

TONYA GARZA KNEW SHE COULD not wait long, but she had to make sure Spincer had really gone. She held her breath and tried to focus.

For a long time after he'd left the room she could hear him replaying that answering machine message over and over. Finally, the recorded voice had gone silent and she'd heard the front door slam shut. She hadn't heard anything since then.

Tonya took a deep breath and convinced herself to start. She didn't know how long he'd be gone, but she knew when he got back he would kill her.

This has to work.

The previous evening, Spincer had agreed to cuff her hand to the side of the bed frame instead of the headboard so that she could lie down properly. When he unlocked it, she told him she could secure it herself, and went about connecting her cuff to the side rail.

When she finished, Spincer looked at her and made a face like a disappointed parent. He inspected the cuff and realized immediately that Tonya had tried to leave it unlocked.

With a quick squeeze, Spincer shut the cuff tightly around the side rail and then pulled on it several times to confirm its strong connection to the frame.

"You'll have to do a little better than that," he said as he left the room.

Now Tonya had to find out if that diversion would equate into having "done a little better."

Having spent several days examining every aspect of her prison, Tonya knew there was no removing the cuff from the side rail. However, she also knew that the side rails connected at the headboard and were removable.

Tonya lay down on her side with her legs facing the head of the bed. In a single impressive motion, she coiled both her legs up to her chest and fired them hard against the large steel headboard. Not sensing any change in her situation, she repeated the process.

With the screeching sound of metal against metal, the side of the headboard collapsed and the bed tilted toward the floor. Tonya gripped the side rail and pulled up hard. Another groan from the joints and the rail came away in her hand. Choking back tears of relief and anger, she slid the cuff off the end of the rail and let it drop to the floor.

Moving quickly, she grabbed the lamp off the end table, ripped the cord from the wall and approached the bedroom door. For the first time, she thanked God above that she'd dated a man who turned out to be an amateur thug. Until now, she believed she'd learned absolutely nothing from the man – except for several rather embarrassing lessons in how bail bonds work.

But now she remembered something he'd said about breaking and entering. He maintained that for the most part, people either put strong locks on weak doors or weak locks on strong doors."

"Pick the weakest part and take it out," she whispered.

She looked at the very old and very strong door. Then she eyed the fake brass locking doorknob and compared it to the real brass lamp she held.

If he's still here, I will probably die in the next few minutes. If he's not … I'm going to kill him.

Tonya Garza said a quick prayer, raised the lamp high above her head, and brought it down hard on the doorknob.

# # #

DENTON TRIED TO KEEP HIS MIND off his current foray into manual labor by focusing on the case. But since that involved his failing company, a murderer targeting employees, and a bunch of files he'd acquired in a somewhat devious fashion, it didn't really help.

"Put your back into it," Candace said.

"Put a sock in it," Denton replied. "How long have we been at this?"

"Eight minutes!" Candace said. "You need to get more cardio."

"Unless that's a new Italian pasta dish, I'll pass."

"Come on," she coaxed. "You want to get in shape for the wedding, don't you? Now, I forget … *when* is that again?"

Denton's thoughts shifted from wondering about the case to wondering what it would be like to push Candace Covington down the elevator shaft.

JULIAN CHASE SURVEYED HIS HANDIWORK and smiled. As he scanned the two full tables of festive, edible joy, a small kitchen timer rang out.

He removed the basket from the bubbling fryer and carefully shook off the excess oil. Then he turned the basket over and watched the round, crackling treats roll onto the awaiting platter. As he began arranging his famous deep-fried sausage breakfast balls into a decorative pyramid, a throat cleared behind him. Julian turned to see the front desk guard standing in the doorway.

"Hello, Officer Daniels," Julian said. "How are you this morning?" As he spoke, Julian tried to slide his body slightly to his left in order to block the guard's view of his hot oil fryer – an item most guards would recognize as a pretty serious violation of the, "Do not bring items to work that could burn the building down," code.

"Good morning, employee," Daniels said. "I couldn't help but notice the smell of all things breakfast coming from this room."

Julian nodded. "That's right." He stuck a toothpick into a sausage ball and handed it to the guard.

"Here, try my hot saus … my breakfast sausage balls."

Daniels accepted the offer and ate the sausage in just a few bites. Then he nodded.

"Delicious," he said. "They taste very fresh."

"Well … that's because I fry them at home and then immediately seal them in an airtight Tupperware container until I get them here."

Daniels nodded again and poked his toothpick into another.

"Sounds like a lot of effort," he said as he popped the second breakfast ball into his mouth. He turned and headed for the exit.

"I'd have used the fryer behind you," he added. "But you're the cook."

Julian's eyes popped wide open as Daniels turned back to him and smiled for just a moment. Then he waved a finger at Julian.

"I'm off duty," he said. "Officer Blint is at the desk now, so be careful. He's a 'by the book' kind of guy. But he's also an idiot. If he asks about the fryer, there's a fifty-fifty chance you can get away with telling him it's a fish tank."

"Duly noted," Julian said. "Thanks."

Julian watched the guard leave and couldn't help taking their conversation as a very good sign for his charity breakfast. He looked across the hall at the door leading to HR, and stuck his tongue out at a hidden Marcus Rompeaux.

GAVIN SPINCER SAT IN HIS CAR and watched the United Alliance Bank campus from a parking lot not a thousand feet from the entrance. He felt no need to rush. Rushing only led to mistakes. He took the time to review his brilliant plan once more, and smiled as he thought about just how much he liked his disguise. So simple, so deadly.

How does one bring a plastic jug full of kerosene and a portable propane torch through the front door of a Fortune 500 company HQ?

Simple: Be someone no one looks at – someone no one even *wants* to look at, and let human nature take care of the rest.

Spincer scolded himself for the smiles. This was not the time for smiling. He forced himself to stop imagining the look on Marcus Rompeaux's face when he discovered it was he, Gavin, who would kill him. And he further forced himself to quit imagining the fat HR man's final, desperate cries for mercy as the flames engulfed his body.

He reset his game face and focused once again on the UAB building.

Almost there. Keep it together. This mission is almost complete.

Gadsden the Damned started the car.

"WE'RE NEARLY DONE," Candace announced through grinning teeth.

Denton gave her a quick thumbs up, and then cast a not so positive look toward Fred, who continued to sit at an empty desk sipping coffee and reading his newspaper.

"I hope our work isn't disturbing you, Prince Maxton," Denton said.

Fred offered a royal wave. "Perish the thought, my good man," he said. "You may carry on."

Candace smiled and pointed at the cubicle directly across from the one Fred had usurped.

"Now we say our final goodbye to the king of the weirdos," she said.

Denton looked at the work station in question. A half-dozen used coffee cups decorated the desktop and created a Styrofoam trail leading to a long-expired plant. An assorted variety of crumb types provided a special non-hygienic accent to the overall grime motif.

Denton shifted his focus to the myriad of hand-drawn pictures pinned to the cube walls. Most depicted swords, knives, mythical creatures, or scantily clad women with swords, riding mythical creatures.

"Wow," Denton said. "What are the odds this guy does not have a girlfriend?"

"He does have one," Candace said as she pointed to the frame on his desk. "Sort of."

Denton moved the empty potato chip bag out of the way and picked up the frame.

"Egads!" he said.

The picture showed two men standing on either side of a rather large woman who, in spite of her jet black hair and large sunglasses obscuring much of her face, was easily the ugliest woman Denton had ever seen. And he said so.

Candace slapped him on the back of the head.

"Idiot," she said. "That's *him*."

Fred joined them. Leaning over Denton's shoulder, he looked at the picture and pointed.

"That's her," he said.

"Him who – her what?" Denton asked.

"That's the new cleaning lady," Fred said "The ugly stupid one."

Candace slapped *him* in the back of the head.

"No, genius. That's Gavin. That's my IT creep."

SECURITY OFFICER RALPH BLINT smiled at the hideous cleaning woman and quickly found a blank piece of paper and made it the most important thing in his world.

As he furrowed his brow and pretended to scribble some notes on the empty page, he wondered how many more days he would have to endure her morning arrival. If the company had a discrete back entrance for use by important guests and visiting senior executives, could they not also open it up to the stunningly gross?

Oh God, what is she doing? Is she …? Shit.

He pushed his paper away and watched as she walked directly to his desk.

"Mmm … it smells delicious in here today," she said.

Blint cringed at her cackling voice. He opened a drawer and rummaged for nothing in particular.

Oh that's great. Already ugly and now she smells like kerosene.

"Yeah, they're having a charity breakfast in the break room back there," Blint replied without looking up.

"Sounds wonderful," she said. She hoisted her backpack over her shoulder. "Well, have a nice day."

"Just a second, miss," Blint said.

Yeah, it's GOT to be "Miss."

She turned back to him and smiled.

"You're here awfully early today," Blint said. "Cleaning staff aren't supposed to arrive before eight a.m."

She gave him a pleading, pouty frown.

"I got on an earlier bus this morning by mistake," she said. "Do you think you could make an exception for me today?"

Before Ralph Blint had a chance to host an internal debate on the matter, she smiled again and batted her eyelashes at him. That sealed the deal. He wanted her to go away.

"Yeah, that's fine. Go ahead. But this time only, okay?"

"You are a dear," she said.

Blint watched her slowly head down the HR hallway.

"And you are a freak," he muttered.

FRED TURNED TO CANDACE with his finger still pointing at the picture.

"*That's* Gavin Spincer?" he asked.

"Yes," Candace nodded at him. "Why a man would display a picture of himself in drag at work is beyond me. But that's Gavin."

"And he's cleaning our restrooms now," Denton said. "In drag."

Fred reached into his pocket, and a moment later began slapping his clothes all over.

"Where the hell is my phone?"

Candace shook her head. "I don't get it. How the hell could this weirdo get a job with a cleaning company and get assigned to the office that just let him go?"

"That's what I intend to find out right now," Fred said, now digging into his sport coat pockets.

"Fred," Denton shook his head slowly at his friend. "Come on. We know the answer already."

Fred stopped fumbling with his pockets and looked back and forth between Candace and Denton.

"He *couldn't.*"

Denton nodded. "How do you know about Gavin Spincer, anyway?"

Fred shrugged.

"Whenever there's a large layoff like last week's, I get a list of the people we contacted by telephone and ended up leaving a message about their termination."

"You leave that on someone's voicemail?" Candace asked.

"*I* don't do that!" Fred said. "But it happens. Anyway, we keep a list of those people we left messages for to make sure we really do speak with them. Spincer's name was on that list – and then we added him to a second list."

"What second list?" Denton asked.

"The list of ex-employees who make threats against company personnel. Spincer called the company operator last weekend and said he'd be leaving us a message soon. Of course, we haven't heard anything from him."

"Yes, we have," Denton said.

Candace and Fred looked at him as he shook his head and looked at Candace.

"Spincer supported my department. But I'll bet he supported Accounting, too, didn't he?"

When Candace confirmed with a slow nod, Denton bit his bottom lip and closed his eyes.

"He's already left messages with Martin Rampart and Phillip Anderson," he said. "Tiny little phone messages."

"Holy shit, Denton," Fred said.

"Who left Spincer his layoff message?" Denton asked, already running for the elevator.

"Rompeaux did," Fred replied, following Denton.

Denton hit the call button over and over again. He yelled to Candace.

"Call him. Call, email, instant message – whatever it takes. Tell him to get out of his office."

Fred shook his head. "Rompeaux is an HR department head," he said. "His number's unlisted and his email is a generic mailbox."

The elevator opened and the two men jumped in.

"Then call the front desk," Denton said. "Tell security to go down to his office and get him."

Candace nodded and grabbed the phone as the doors closed on Denton and Fred.

CHAPTER 32

Marcus Rompeaux sat at his desk and filled out forms while trying to ignore the intoxicating aroma sneaking into his office from Julian's breakfast party across the hall.

He sighed, marked another piece of paperwork off his list, and moved it from one pile to another. As he began on his next form, the office door opened and Rompeaux turned to see who could possibly need him so early in the workday.

He mumbled a quick "good morning," at the incredibly weird cleaning woman and immediately turned back to his paperwork, thankful that he would not have to work very hard to avoid looking at her.

As he heard the door close, Rompeaux felt a pang of guilt for his behavior. He imagined that most people reacted to her as he had, and she no doubt knew why. So Marcus Rompeaux decided to be better than most people.

He turned back to her with a pleasant smile.

"It's a bit early to get started, isn't it?" he asked. "I've hardly had a chance to make a mess yet."

"Oh, don't worry," she said. "It's going to get plenty messy in here."

Rompeaux looked at her closely.

"Are you—"

The woman ripped off her wig and her sunglasses and sneered.

"That's right! I'm Gavin Spincer!"

"Oh," Rompeaux said. "No, I was just going to ask if you were *okay*. You seemed a bit unsteady. But there's no need to be nervous or anxious about your lifestyle or your clothing choices here, Mr. Spincer. United Alliance Bank and all its approved vendors fully support diversity in the workplace. So if you've experienced any sort of trouble, you just tell me and—"

"You don't get it!" Spincer began waving wildly. "I'm *Gavin Spincer,*" he repeated.

Rompeaux sat back in his chair and cocked his head slightly.

"I'm sorry, Mr. Spincer," he said. "Do we know each other?"

Gavin took a turn at staring in wide-eyed, jaw-dropping disbelief.

UNITED ALLIANCE BANK SECURITY code 188-7.0 expressly forbade a security officer from leaving the lobby without a second officer remaining at the front desk.

Security specialist Ralph Blint knew that. And he would have taken great pleasure in reading the exact verbiage of the code to Candace Covington had he not been otherwise engaged and unable to pick up the ringing phone.

Still reeling from his latest encounter with the woman he now referred to as, "Mop Bucket Medusa," Blint now found himself watching as two men he recognized burst out the elevator and ran toward him. Blint steadied his clipboard.

"There is *no* running within—"

"Ugly, fat cleaning woman!" the unkempt one yelled. "Has she come through here?"

Blint, now in fully stunned silence, simply nodded his head and pointed in the direction of the HR corridor. The men ran past him and made their way around the corner. Unsure of exact protocol, Blint simply stood and stared after them until the elevator dinged again and a guard wearing the new uniform design stepped out and broke into a run as well.

"I got this one, Ralph," the new guard said. "Call the police and start the paperwork!"

"How did you get a gun?" Blint yelled out after the man.

Receiving no reply, he stared at the hallway and then at the elevator for a few more moments. Then he walked back around the desk and picked up the now quiet phone. But before he could dial, Blint dropped the receiver to the floor and watched in dumbfounded shock as a short, visibly angry Hispanic woman dressed in the jeans and white button down shirt of a very fat man, burst through the front door and flashed by the desk, leaving a trail of angry Spanish ranting in the air behind her.

Christ, it's not even eight o'clock yet!

"Excuse me – excuse me – hey!" Blint protested.

Blint's commanding voice stopped the woman in her tracks. She turned toward the security officer and shot back a fiery look which Blint swore he actually felt hit him in the chest. He shook his clipboard at her.

"Don't think I won't report this, missy," he said. "I've got the form right here!"

After a moment of considering Blint's warning, the woman smiled. Then she made her thoughts about his forms fully evident via the delicate use of her middle finger and a fresh burst of shouting in Spanish.

The one-two punch stunned Blint long enough for the ill-clad young woman to turn tail and disappear down the corridor toward HR. Blint tried to give chase, but took only a single step before looking back at the desk phone which had started ringing again. He swayed back and forth as he looked at the phone and then down the hallway.

Surely the "do not leave your post" edict allowed for reasonable exceptions, didn't it?

GAVIN SPINCER RECOVERED FROM his enemy's insulting question

and ripped open his backpack. He pulled out a large, white bottle and brandished it at the man.

"You fired me on a *voicemail*!" he shouted, face reddening. Then he grabbed the mini propane torch with his free hand and fired it up. "And now you will pay for your insolence."

Marcus Rompeaux sat back in his chair and raised a single forefinger into the air.

"First of all, Mr. Spincer, I have laid off a lot of people in my time and I can tell you that I derive no joy from it."

He raised another finger.

"Secondly, I only use the telephone as a means of communication when an employee does not show up for work as scheduled. Believe me, Mr. Spincer, I would have much preferred to sit with you and talk through the entire situation, to help you create a transition plan and review your employment options and your next steps, face to face."

Spincer opened his mouth to speak, but didn't say anything. Rompeaux gestured to an empty chair.

"Right now this is just a minor incident stemming from a simple miscommunication. So why don't we sit and talk about this before it becomes something worse?"

Spincer stared at his foe and wrinkled his brow. He looked at the chair and then at his weapons. His head swirled, and his legs itched.

"Mr. Spincer, are you okay?" Rompeaux asked. "Gavin?"

Spincer's face pinched up in a near contortion and then relaxed into a vile grin.

"Call me Gadsden," he said. "And believe me, it's already 'something worse.' Just ask Phillip Anderson, Martin Rampart, and that nosy guard Lyle Saunders."

"Mr. Spincer—"

"CALL ME GADSDEN!"

Rompeaux pushed his chair as far back against the wall as possible as Spincer closed in.

Gavin Spincer looked down at the bottle of kerosene and realized he needed two hands to pull out the stopper. He growled as he tried to manipulate both the torch and the bottle.

"Help!" Rompeaux screamed.

"Shut up!" Spincer screamed back. He put the bottle to his mouth and bit down on the rubber stopper.

"Help!"

Spincer pull down hard on the bottle and the stopper gave way with a dramatic burst of kerosene. Spincer spit the top from his mouth and held the torch away from his other hand. He swirled the now-open container.

"Still plenty for your baptism," he said.

"Baptism? Awesome – I love the wine and cracker part of church!"

Spincer spun around to find Denton Rourke giving him a grinning wave. Fred Maxton leaned over Denton's shoulder.

"That's *Communion*, idiot."

"WHO THE HELL ARE YOU?" Spincer demanded as he turned his head rapidly from side to side, trying to keep tabs on both Denton and Marcus Rompeaux.

"Fire safety warden," Denton said. "And you, sir, are in direct violation of our 'No propane torches without marshmallows' policy."

"You're not a fire warden," Spincer said. "You're an idiot."

"That doesn't really matter, does it?" Denton said. "It's over – put the torch down."

Carlson appeared in the doorway, gun drawn and tracking on Gavin Spincer.

"Put it down, Spincer," Carlson commanded.

Spincer backed up toward Rompeaux.

"He's going to burn!" he said. "He has to pay!"

"You spark him and you'll be dead a second later," Carlson said.

Denton kept his eyes on Spincer.

"I think he knows that, Carlson," he said. "He's going to do it either way."

Carlson surveyed the scene a moment longer, and then pulled back his gun and raised up his hands.

"Okay, Gavin, let's all just take a step back."

"A step back would be smart, officer," Spincer said, pointing to the large, darks stains covering the floor. "I've made quite a mess over here."

Carlson shook his head. "Look, Gavin—"

"Enough talk! If you and those two morons know what's … Tonya?"

All eyes shifted to Tonya Garza, who stumbled in from the hallway. Panting, she stepped forward.

"Tonya," Spincer said. "You … you came for me?"

Tonya nodded slowly.

"I sure did," she said.

Without another word, Tonya strutted forward toward her former captor.

"Ma'am, stop!" Carlson yelled.

Spincer smiled as she approached with speed. "Careful, baby, I spilled some—"

Tonya Garza grew up with four older brothers who all fought in Golden Gloves and took great pleasure in teaching their little sister everything they knew. So when she clenched her hand into a cocked fist and released the full weight of her body into a hard right cross, the smiling Gavin Spincer never saw it coming.

But he felt it.

"No!" Carlson yelled as he bounded forward and pulled Tonya toward him. As Spincer spun backward and stumbled, Rompeaux bolted from his seat, immediately fell, and crawled his way to the others.

Tonya's room-spinning punch, combined with a prolonged period of kerosene fume inhalation left Spincer without much sense of direction or balance. The group watched as he attempted to steady himself by grabbing and leaning on the back of Rompeaux's now empty chair.

The chair, sensing far too many pounds of pressure being exerted on it, wheeled itself away from the punch-drunk man. As he fell, Spincer threw his hands out toward Rompeaux's desk, dropping both bottle and torch on the way down.

Spincer's clothes lit up immediately, along with a large portion of the floor between himself and his shocked audience. Carlson pushed the group back into the hall and they split on either side of the doorway as the heat and flames raged.

Ralph Blint arrived with his clipboard. He saw Tonya and pointed at her.

"There you are. I've got form 915-A here, and you're going to fill this out."

Realizing that no one was looking at or listening to him, Blint stepped in front of the HR office doorway and looked in. For a moment the security guard stood in stunned silence. Then he watched as a giant flaming mass rose from the floor, unleashed a roar of pain and anger, and ran directly toward him.

Blint screamed and turned tail back toward the lobby, nearly breaking his shoulder against the fire extinguisher bolted to the hallway wall. Denton and the rest of the group held their positions and watched as Spincer barreled blindly out of the HR office and ran directly into Julian Chase's charity breakfast break room.

Julian saw him first and gasped as he wondered how to deflect his diners' attention from the fiery intrusion. But the human flambé caught the immediate attention of everyone when he collided with the sausage ball table and fell to the floor.

As his patrons ran screaming for the exits, Julian watched the table collapse on the man and thought that perhaps he really should have moved his hot oil fryer to a safer location.

Unable to convey his intense agreement with Julian's assessment, Gavin rolled around in the grease fire, screaming as he tried desperately to stand up.

Marcus Rompeaux fought through the exiting crowd, ripped off his jacket, and threw it over Spincer in an attempt to extinguish the flames. Unfortunately, during Rompeaux's time as Spincer's prisoner, his jacket had accumulated quite a bit more kerosene than he realized

– until his jacket burst into flames on top of the man.

Rompeaux fell backward with a high-pitch scream as his shirt cuffs lit up. All eyes watched as the HR leader rolled his round body end over end away from the makeshift pyre, stopping only when he hit the other buffet table, which dumped a large volume of scrambled eggs onto his chest. Rompeaux remained on his back, panting, and tried to scrape the food off.

Carlson pushed his way in carrying the extinguisher and emptied its contents over Gavin Spincer. The flames surrendered to Carlson's attack and a still fell over the room. He knelt down next to the smoldering mass for a moment and then rose again and shook his head.

"He's dead."

Tonya Garza sobbed softly against Fred's shoulder.

"It's over now," he said. "It's all over."

Ralph Blint reappeared, still rubbing his shoulder. He looked at the scene with wide eyes.

"Jesus, Mary, and Joseph!" he said.

Denton approached the guard and joined him in looking over the room.

"Do you have a form for this?" he asked.

"Oh, I hope not," Blint replied.

But fearing they might, the guard retreated from the room with soft footsteps, leaving the group to their shocked silence.

CHAPTER 33

As Denton surveyed the carnage, a large number of guards appeared in the doorway. He looked over at Fred, who nodded his okay while still holding Tonya. Then he turned his attention in the direction of a series of sad, earnest grunts coming from the second breakfast table and saw the wobbling body of Marcus Rompeaux as he worked to roll back onto his stomach so that he could get up. Denton trotted over to lend a hand.

Rompeaux happily accepted the help and once standing, wiped himself off a bit and looked at Denton with a sad chuckle.

"I don't suppose I'll be able to live this down, will I? 'Saved by Denton Rourke,'" he said.

Denton smiled. "Tell you what – you don't say 'I told you so,' about the breakfast fiasco and I won't say anything about what went on in your office," he said. "*Or* about you secretly being a hero."

"Deal," Rompeaux said, shaking Denton's hand.

"Besides," Denton said. "You did most of the work – staying calm and keeping him talking. This could have been a lot worse if not for that."

Denton looked around the room again and added, "Well, worse for *you*, anyway."

Rompeaux nodded his appreciation.

"Denton," Carlson called out amid a sea of guards who clearly needed his direction given the situation. "It's going to get real hot in here – real fast. Why don't you all find somewhere quiet to lay low?"

Rompeaux nodded and gestured toward another exit.

"We have a private conference room for HR meetings just down the hall. We can use that."

Denton waved Fred and Tonya over and the three of them followed Rompeaux out.

When they hit the hallway, Fred put a hand on Denton's shoulder.

"Hey, I've got to head to my office. There's no way this isn't getting out – or isn't already out. I need to prepare the team for a media barrage and get an update to my bosses."

Denton nodded his understanding. "All right – we'll catch up later."

Fred departed and the remaining three entered a clean, quiet meeting room with half a dozen comfortable chairs and a modest conference table.

Tonya sat down and Denton took the chair next to her.

"Are you okay?" he asked.

She wiped a lingering tear from her cheek and nodded.

"I will be, thank you," she said.

Denton nodded and faced the table.

"And, I'm sorry," Tonya added.

Denton did not look at her.

"For what?"

Tonya smiled. "You know."

Denton turned and smiled back at her. He wanted very much to hear the explanation, but more pressing matters weighed on him.

"I can't believe it's finally over," Marcus said from his seat.

Denton sighed. "It's not."

Two pairs of eyes riveted their full attention to him. Marcus spoke first.

"What can you possibly mean? He murdered those people, he admitted it. And he tried to kill me, too!"

Denton put up his hands.

"I know, Marcus – and you're right about the murders. That's over."

Marcus sighed.

"I think," Denton added.

Denton stood up amid a duet of protests.

"Spincer's plot of revenge against those he saw as responsible for his termination has clearly ended," he said. "But you saw Spincer. There's no way that man hoisted Phillip Anderson's dead body up over his desk."

He sat back down and rubbed the back of his head.

"Something else is going on here."

As Rompeaux scooted forward in his chair and prepared to respond, Carlson opened the door and looked directly at Denton.

"Get out of here," he said.

"What? I haven't even had breakfast yet," Denton said.

Carlson waved him out into the hall. "No jokes. Get out. Sowell is coming."

"Good," Denton replied.

"No, not good," Carlson corrected. "Captain Levine is with him."

Denton bolted from his seat. "Russell, you have to *lead* with that kind of information! Come on, let's go."

Carlson pushed the door wide as Denton waved a hasty good-bye to Tonya and Marcus.

"Get on the nearest elevator and go *anywhere*," Carlson said.

"Good plan," Denton said.

But at the corridor's curve they ran into a stoic Tim Sowell and a far-too jovial Harris Levine. The four men stopped and took turns staring at each other.

"Well, nearly a good plan," Denton said under his breath.

"WELL, WELL," CAPTAIN LEVINE SMILED, "I suspected I'd find you here."

Denton smiled back.

"Really? You deduced that I'd be at my place of employment on a weekday morning? How *did* you piece that intricate puzzle together?"

Marcus Rompeaux appeared at Denton's back.

"What's going on here?"

Denton turned to the HR leader.

"Well, Marcus, as you know, I was simply minding my own business, trying to get some breakfast when out of nowhere you and this nice security guard – Roscoe, is it?"

"Jesus," Carlson rolled his eyes.

"Anyway – the two of you spilled into the break room in some kind of fracas with a crazy man."

Denton pointed at the police captain.

"And this man seems to believe that being hungry in one's workplace is a very serious offense. I hope he doesn't find out what our employees do in the restrooms here. It's probably a felony in his book."

"Can it, Rourke," Levine snapped. He turned to Sowell. "Lieutenant Sowell, you're suspended pending a full investigation."

Sowell nodded and stared straight ahead. "Yes, sir."

"Hey!" Denton felt heat moving up his spine. "You can't suspend him because I was in the wrong place at the wrong time!"

"No? Well how about I do it because of the phone call I received yesterday evening from a certain UAB employee who wanted to thank me for allowing you to take a major role in this investigation? Would *that* be okay with you?"

Denton turned to Marcus Rompeaux and glared.

"Son of a bitch," he said. "I thought you and I had turned a corner or something like it – and you go and do *this*?"

Marcus raised both his hands up in defense.

"Denton, if you never believe another word I say as long as we work together, please believe me when I tell you I never said a word."

"He sure didn't," Levine nodded. "Which is something you'd better believe I'll be taking up with Daniel Caldwell later."

Levine looked past Denton and Marcus.

"Sergeant Carlson, secure the crime scene and do not allow any unauthorized personnel access to the area. Is that as painfully clear as it sounds to me?"

"Yes, sir," Carlson said.

"And get out of that ridiculous costume!"

Without waiting for a response, Captain Levine turned his back to the group and headed back toward the lobby.

"Enjoy your vacation," he said as he brushed by Sowell without stopping.

Denton watched him march down the hall. Then he approached Sowell.

"What are you going to do now?" he asked.

Sowell looked at Denton for a moment, and then smiled.

"Like the captain said, I'm going to take a vacation."

"This isn't right," Denton said.

"Well, technically he is right," Sowell said. "But I won't give him the satisfaction. And I do have a lot of vacation hours saved up."

Denton made a face, but couldn't argue with his friend's assessment.

"Besides," Sowell continued, "the more important question is what are *you* going to do now, Denton Rourke?"

"You're Denton Rourke?" a guard heading their direction called out.

"Yes?"

"Mr. Caldwell rang the front desk, looking for you. He wants to see you in his office."

Denton waved his acknowledgment and smiled at Sowell.

"I think we'll have that answer pretty soon," he said.

The two men shook hands and Denton headed toward the elevator once again.

CHAPTER 34

Denton breezed through the executive floor waiting area without a word as Rachel found herself immersed in phone calls from various media outlets. He reached Caldwell's office and opened the door while knocking. Caldwell stood behind his desk, hands on his hips and a frown on his face. He stared at Denton as though he'd known the exact moment his door would open.

"And I told you already that we do not comment on rumors," Caldwell said.

"What rumors?" Denton asked.

Caldwell turned his profile to Denton and pointed at the small Bluetooth device in his ear.

"Oh," Denton said loudly. "You mean the rumor about the guy who exploded in a break room?"

Caldwell cupped his hand over his earpiece and turned away from Denton.

"That's really it – no additional comments. There will be a formal communication to the press as soon as possible."

Caldwell ripped the earpiece out and tossed it on his desk.

"You are not helping," he said.

"Oh – you mean the way you helped me by alerting Captain Levine to the fact that Sowell had hired me without getting department approval? Why would you do that?"

"Gosh, I don't know, Denton," Caldwell said, scratching his chin.

"Maybe I'm just an incredible asshole. Or maybe I did it because I didn't know you and Sowell were working behind Levine's back *because you never told me.*"

Denton swallowed and shifted his feet.

"Ah, yes. Well, what's done is done. I forgive you."

"It doesn't matter now," Caldwell said. "It's over."

"But it's not," Denton said. "This guy is only part of the puzzle. He doesn't have anything to do with Anderson's files and anything he might have been up to."

"So this guy just happened to kill our Executive Vice President of Accounting?"

"No," Denton shook his head and walked toward Caldwell's desk. "Spincer was a psycho looking to avenge his termination. He was an IT employee who supported Anderson's line of business. He didn't know or care about anything Anderson may have been up to."

Caldwell shook his head and put both hands out in front of him.

"This is out of control, Denton! We've got a transvestite nut job with an employee hit list—"

"I don't think Gavin Spincer was really a transvestite," Denton said. "I think it was just his disguise."

"Well I'm sure the Cross Dresser's Union will be relieved, but that's hardly the point, is it? This is not for you or me or anyone here to investigate anymore. This is for the police – real police with real handcuffs, real guns, and real backup."

Denton shook his head. "But there is something else going on," he said.

Caldwell lowered a forceful hand down on his desk.

"Denton – I'm telling you that this is over!"

"And I'm telling you that you're wrong! They're going to chalk this up to a disgruntled employee on a psycho rampage and that'll be that. And what they don't investigate could affect our future!"

Caldwell stared back, exasperated. After a few moments, he smiled faintly and shook his head.

"How long, Denton? How long am I supposed to disregard the board, our HR team, and the police so that you can chase the invisible bad guys?"

"One more day."

Caldwell looked at Denton. He turned to the window and gazed out at the darkening clouds.

"That's about all I can afford you anyway," he said.

Denton looked at him closely.

"Meaning?"

Caldwell took a deep breath. "Meaning … just hurry, Denton. Whatever you're going to do, please do it quickly."

He took a business card out of his pocket and wrote on the back. He handed it to Denton.

"I'm hoping you don't need this, but if you get into a situation you can't handle, call that number. It's my private line."

Denton took the card and pocketed it.

"Thank you."

Caldwell nodded. "Do you have everything you need?"

Denton nodded. "I think so."

"So, now you *don't* want those files I've been reluctant to share?"

Denton felt every hair on his head stand up.

Everyone has secrets. Everyone lies. Even you. And he knows it.

"Um … I don't know how to answer that," he said.

Caldwell gave a shrug and an easy smile. "Peter told me – he couldn't stand it, apparently."

"I'm sorry, I should never have made him do that."

"No one makes Peter do anything. Whether he wants to say or not, he clearly thought I was wrong. So now it's up to you to prove I was."

Denton stood up. "I'll do my best."

"Good," Caldwell said. He rose and shook Denton's hand with a smile.

"You're suspended for the day," he added. "Get your stuff and go home. You need to be somewhere quiet and devoid of all this chaos if you really intend to crack Anderson's puzzles. Escheatment accounts are inherently complex and tricky on their own, so you can imagine what happens when someone like Anderson uses them as his puzzle playground."

"Understood," Denton said, thinking of the headaches the subject had given Candace of late.

"And I mean it, Denton," Caldwell said. "Get out of here. I might pay a surprise visit to six later and if I find you loitering, I'm going to have Fowler assign you to work exclusively with Robert Moore."

Denton shuddered at the thought of nonstop lectures from Moore on riveting topics such as 16th century glass blowing techniques, and the invention of dirt.

"Okay, I get it. I'm out of here," he promised.

"Good. Okay, I won't delay you any further. Good luck, call me if you uncover anything or if you need help. And really, Denton, be careful."

Denton headed for the elevator and the 6th floor, taking great care not to make eye contact with Rachel, whose phones continued to ring.

"She deserves flowers," he thought out loud. "Most of the women in my life probably deserve flowers."

The doors opened and he stepped in. Instinctively, he stole a glance at Rachel who made instant eye contact. The look on her face gave Denton a chill.

"Lots of flowers," he said to himself as he hit the button for six and stared at the ceiling.

SITTING IN THEIR USUAL 6TH floor break room, Fred and Denton drank the usual bad coffee and stared at the usual television set. However, instead of their usual Financial News Network show, the TV now provided them with a golf tutorial on avoiding the dreaded "three-putt." Both men found the change unusual.

Fred nudged his pouting friend.

"Come on," he said. "You did a great thing today. You saved someone's life – maybe more than one."

"The case isn't solved," Denton said without looking up from his laptop. "There's more to it, and I need to get out of here so I can work it out before it's too late."

Fred took a sip of coffee and stared at the television.

"I'm sorry about your car," he offered.

Denton nodded his thanks and wondered whether Caldwell would believe that he really had tried to comply with the man's evacuation order.

After grabbing his laptop, Denton had headed straight for the first floor, intending to leave post-haste. He crossed the lobby thinking about the single positive aspect of coming into the building at the crack of dawn to help Candace: his fantastically close parking spot just a few feet from the entrance.

But the pleasure of the convenience evaporated as he reached the exit and found the entire first row of employee vehicles blocked in by a dozen mobile news vans which had delivered a bevy of screaming newscasters, intrusive microphones, and nosy cameras to the company's doorstep.

Unable to get out, Denton now found himself back on six watching a well-dressed man on television talk about long-distance putting and the importance of speed versus aim.

"No one believes me, Fred," Denton said.

"Denton, try and see it from the average person's perspective," he said. "You just stopped a real life killer – someone murdering employees in our building. That is *huge*. People are desperate to feel safe again, but you're trying to convince them they're less safe than ever because of some secret plot which may or may not actually exist."

"So you don't believe me either," Denton stared. "I never considered you average."

Fred smiled. "I'll tell you what," he said, pointing at Denton's laptop, "If anyone else dies, I'll believe you – *and* – I'll come over tomorrow morning and help you go through every spreadsheet and document file you've opened."

"And?" Denton said.

"And I'll bring beer," Fred said. "What do you say?"

Denton stared down the main hallway off the break room and

tried not to think about the one thing that refused to quit bugging him. Then he took a long drink of his coffee and stood up.

"What's the time frame?" he asked Fred.

"Beg pardon?"

"The time frame," Denton repeated. "If someone else dies over what period of time?"

"Um … the rest of the day?" Fred said.

Denton nodded. "Deal."

He closed his laptop, tucked it under his arm, and slapped Fred on the back.

"I win," he said. "See you tomorrow around eleven a.m.?"

Fred narrowed his eyes and shook his head. "What are you – oh, no. No, no, no – come on!"

Fred threw his hands up as Russell Carlson walked in and waved.

"Hey, Denton," Carlson said.

Denton looked his friend up and down.

"The plainclothes look fits you a lot better," he said.

"You *cannot* be here for what he thinks you're here for," Fred insisted. "Can you?"

"Does he think I'm here to tell him we found Kevin Kahneman?" Carlson replied.

"Where?" Denton asked.

"At home, in his garage."

"Doing what?" Fred asked.

Carlson looked over at him. "Being dead in his car next to a near-empty bottle of sleeping pills. Lewis is on his way over there."

Fred looked back and forth between Denton and Carlson. "Do you think he was Spincer's last victim, or maybe in cahoots with him?"

"*Cahoots*?" Carlson asked.

Denton nodded. "Yes, apparently the crime took place in 1887. We'll make inquiries at the Livery and the Blacksmith, then make our way back around to the Cobbler."

Fred got up and made for the exit.

"See you tomorrow," he grumbled.

"Where are you going?" Denton asked.

"Back to my office. The communications team for our parent company took over the handling of all media for this, but I'm hoping they'll reach out and ask me to assist in *some* function."

"Don't forget the beer!" Denton called out.

Fred muttered something unrepeatable, and Denton shrugged. Carlson looked closely at him.

"You okay?" he asked.

"I'm just tired," Denton said. "Have you talked to Tim?"

Carlson shook his head. "I called, but he's not picking up. Maybe he's taking the vacation bit seriously."

"I hope so."

Denton looked at the television once more and then back at Carlson.

"Okay, I've got to get out of here. I assume you have a super-secret police exit strategy – one that doesn't involve tear-gassing the reporters out front?"

"Sadly, I do," Carlson said.

"Lead the way."

Carlson complied and the two men made their break for freedom.

# # #

FORD'S DINER ONCE AGAIN WELCOMED Denton into its peaceful world of fried food, sugar, and all things bacon-related. Denton wasted no time sliding into his booth and Henry wasted no time in bringing him a menu and a cup of black coffee.

"Good to see you again so soon," Henry said as he poured.

"And it's good to be seen again," Denton replied. "Just the coffee, Henry."

"You got it," he said. Then he gestured at the television. "Let me know if you need something stronger."

Denton looked up and saw Financial News Network buffoon Russell Banfield talking to the camera and wearing his patented "grave situation" face. Of course, Denton had to admit that Banfield's choice of facial expression really worked well as he stood in front of the UAB building with a dozen police car lights flashing behind him.

Turning from the television, Denton opened his laptop and went back to work on Phillip Anderson's files. He tried to focus on the numbers and tabs and get a feel for a pattern, but a singular issue refused to stop tapping him on the shoulder: while still sitting in the UAB break room, he'd cracked Anderson's access code to the attachments in less than a minute using Candace's flash drive. Now Anderson's email revealed two spreadsheets of vague financial data. Now he sat looking at two spreadsheets of financial data … and he hadn't told Caldwell.

And he didn't plan to.

Denton sipped his coffee. If he told Caldwell, the man might take the files away, or have to report to a higher authority that he'd exposed confidential data to a peon. No, after careful consideration, he knew the right thing to do was to hide this information from his employer until he knew what the hell he was looking at. And that might take a while.

He tried again to study the rows of numbers and letters contained within. Then his mind wandered to the menu Henry left on the table, and then to the small crack in the booth vinyl, and also to how many yellow cars passed his window.

And then to Tim Sowell's suspension.

Denton tried not to think about how his mind had prioritized that list of thoughts. He took out his phone and turned it on. He dialed Sowell's number and watched Henry press a button on the remote which brought Russell Banfield's voice to life.

When Sowell's voicemail came on, Denton hung up and pocketed his phone again. He sipped his coffee and watched Banfield, who now smiled for his audience.

"Joseph Handel's office has reported that while the tragedy unfolding at UAB is heartbreaking, the Huntsman CEO will speak as planned this evening at Western University where he will receive an honorary degree in Humanities."

Denton rolled his eyes away from the television and mocked Banfield's exciting narrative.

"After the ceremony, Handel plans to save the entire planet from a giant asteroid by hurtling his ego into space on a direct collision course with the global killer. Then he'll juggle two panda bears and a wombat to raise money for world leprosy awareness. I just love him *so* much!"

Denton caught the couple at the next table eyeing him with concern. Not wanting Henry to lose potential paying customers, he decided he'd be better off muttering to himself in the privacy of his condo. He smiled at the worried patrons, then grabbed his laptop and exited.

CHAPTER 35

Joseph Handel sat in the small waiting room behind the stage and rehearsed the ending of his speech.

"Be strong," he said. "Face your challenges head on and stand firm. Share your vision with those around you, and let it guide your actions."

He looked over at Oscar Hall. The aide produced the expected smile in return.

"Very nice, sir," Hall said to his boss. "You're going to kill them."

Joseph Handel nodded his thanks, but did not share the man's opinion.

"Is the teleprompter ready?" he asked.

Hall smiled again. "Yes, sir. I've spoken with the university's head of Audio/Visual, and he will handle your presentation personally – no students or department interns."

Handel returned to his note cards feeling a slight bit of relief. Few outside his personal circle knew that the ability to speak in public with natural grace and charm came to him almost as easily as the ability to physically take flight. Every word had to appear with painstaking perfection on a glowing screen to the side of the podium so he could read it verbatim.

"Sir," Hall started, "are you sure you want to keep the part about UAB?"

The CEO bristled at the mention of the rival bank's name. After the morning news reports, Handel had punched up a few lines on UAB's troubles and given them to his Communications team to tweak, which meant, "Make this hastily scrawled crap into something coherent." They had complied.

"Yes," he said. "It stays in. They created the mess they're in, now they have to sow it."

Hall returned to typing on his laptop without comment.

"You don't approve?" Handel challenged.

Hall looked up slowly as he tried to pick the right words.

"Well, people may think it's a little bit of kicking them when they're down."

"Well it's not," Handel said. "Kicking someone when they're down is more like … okay, I've got it. Take you, for example. It would be like me taunting you about my six-figure bonus."

"I'm not sure I follow – that seems like it would just be tacky."

"Normally, sure," Handel said. "But here I am, waving my big fat bonus check in your face when you don't even have a job."

"What?" the aide's eyes widened.

"That's right – you're fired. Get the hell out of here before I start complaining about my income tax rate."

Without further discussion, Handel returned to his note cards while Oscar Hall collected his papers and headed for the exit.

"By the way," Hall offered at the door, "you're as natural on stage as a cadaver, but only half as interesting."

"Sticks and stones," Handel replied without looking up.

Hall exited, missing the outbreak of cold sweat on Handel's forehead that he helped create.

"Be strong," he began his big close once again – this time without looking at the cards. "Face your challenges on your head … shit."

A student stuck his head in the room.

"Five minutes, Mr. Handel."

Handel nodded and watched the door close once more. He tossed the cards on the floor.

The teleprompter had the whole thing captured anyway.

I AM ACTUALLY GOOD AT THIS, Handel's inner voice declared as the teleprompter signaled 90 seconds left.

True to Hall's word, the university A/V manager had performed splendidly, with the speech displayed in a large, easy-to-read font which scrolled in perfect pace with Handel's speaking. The Huntsman CEO had not suffered even a single miscue, and to the audience he appeared comfortable and natural behind the podium. Even when he used the murders at UAB to take a cheap shot at Ohnemus Parker, he had made it sound like sincere concern for the employees and their families.

Time for the big, "Be strong" finale. All right, Western U, prepare to be dazzled.

Handel smiled with ease as his eyes picked up the first line.

"Get hard!" he said. "Get very hard!"

Was that right? Just keep reading.

"Face forward with emotional erectness and length. Let your vision splash across those around you, and hold it in a firm grip as the eruption guides your actions."

Handel shook off the quiet snickering and read the final line.

"Thank you, students and faculty of Eastern University."

As the snickering gave way to not-so subtle boos, Handel waved, walked off stage, and headed for his dressing room as quickly as possible.

A few minutes later, Handel's stomach attempted to turn itself inside out as the Stage Director stood in front of him and explained the university had no A/V teleprompter team, and that he thought Handel's people had provided the equipment and the manager – who no one could locate.

Through a tightly locked jaw, Handel heard himself ask the question he didn't want an answer to.

"What did this A/V guy look like?"

The stage manager kind of shrugged.

"I don't know – a little bit of an older guy. Tall, thin … wiry gray hair. Very nice guy."

Handel turned to tell Hall to go make sure the video was not distributed. But the words evaporated as he saw – and remembered – that his aide had long ago departed.

"HOW IS IT ALREADY ON THE NEWS?" the still-fuming Joseph Handel demanded into a telephone as his limo sped away from the university. He listened to the response while watching FNN, who had received a clip of his "big finale" before he'd even gotten out of the building.

Done with listening to the person on the phone, Handel started shaking his head.

"I don't give a good god damn if I should be calling you. Have you seen the clip? I look like a demented pervert!"

He listened some more, turning off the TV in the process and opening a crystal carafe of scotch. After a quick pour and a deep drink, he resumed his head shaking.

"No! No more excuses. I've waited long enough, I want this finished. I agreed to your terms and I've played by your rules. You owe me a company, and it had better be on my desk on Monday morning tied up in a bright red bow!"

He listened again and his eyebrows moved ever so slightly skyward.

"Is that so? See – that's all I wanted to hear. Next time why don't you start with that?"

He ended the call with a forceful push of a button and briefly longed for the days when he could slam his phone down to make a dramatic point. With the TV turned off and his call over, Joseph Handel sat in furious silence and stared out at the night. The semi-peaceful moment did not last, as he realized he could hear something coming from the driver's radio, followed by the man's laughter.

Handel glared at the partially open partition and stared into the driver's mirror.

"For the sake of your tip, you'd better be listening to a comedy show up there," he warned.

"Sorry sir," the man said as the partition started to rise.

Handel stopped it with his set of controls.

"No, no, driver," he said. "What are you listening to that's got you so tickled? I could use a good laugh."

His tone told the driver that Handel had no interest in discovering new comedy.

"Well, if it makes you feel any better, it's *not* your speech, sir."

"Good."

"Not exactly, anyway."

Joseph Handel did not know what that could possibly mean.

"What could that possibly mean?" he demanded.

"Someone took the audio and made an internet music mix. Satellite radio stations picked it up."

With that introduction, the driver turned on the passenger cabin speakers so Handel could hear his voice combined with synthesized pop music and a clever drum beat.

Get hard! Get – get – get hard!

Firm grip, Firm-a – Firm-a – Firm-a – Firm grip.

Eruption … Eeeeeee-ruption.

"Catchy," Handel said with a pout. He felt tired – too tired to yell at the driver or even ask that he turn down what – knowing his luck – would turn into a Top 40 hit within the week. He smiled just a little and relaxed in the seat. Parker had won a lot of pointless, silly battles, and Handel would never try to deny that fact.

But on Monday morning Handel would win the war. And when he did, he would make sure Parker stood right next to him so they could both smile for the press and the public.

Parker's smile would convey graciousness in defeat, where Handel's would … well, naturally it would convey an appreciative humility considering the circumstances. And it would communicate optimism for the future strength of Huntsman Bank. But he planned to spend the weekend practicing in front of a mirror so that when he shook hands with Ohnemus Parker and looked directly at the man, his smile sent an important personal message.

Gotcha, you fucking prick.

He refilled his scotch glass, drank it down and closed his eyes. Within moments he drifted into a twilight sleep as the radio soothed him with the rhythmic sounds of his own voice.

# # #

DENTON STARED AT THE SCREEN and continued to search for a pattern to the numbers and letters in front of him.

Q1 Y1	Q2 Y1	Q3 Y1	Q4 Y1
-1.2	-0.93	-1.43	-0.82
Q1 Y2	Q2 Y2	Q3 Y2	Q4 Y2
-1.73	*Denton*	*Rourke*	*Sucks*

Sensing from the screen's aggressive taunts that it, too, wanted to take a break, Denton closed the laptop and rubbed his eyes. Two spreadsheets, one labeled Company A and the other Company C. Both showed quarterly measurements of … something. He took another sip of his beer and wondered why his pizza had not yet arrived.

He picked up the phone and called Pincole's. Owner Joe Turino answered pleasantly, and then explained that he could not deliver Denton's pizza until he actually called in an order. Denton thought about it for a moment and realized Joe was right. He thanked him and told him he'd call back.

He tossed his empty bottle in the trash bin and retrieved another. As he popped the cap, he heard the lock on his front door turning. Knowing only one other person had a key, Denton took a quick drink, brushed his hands down his shirt as though they possessed the mighty power to eliminate wrinkles, and trotted into the living room.

Beth came through the door with a smile.

"Hello, darling," she said.

Denton beamed a grin back at her and followed it up by closing in with a kiss.

"Hey there," he said. "This is a nice surprise."

"It wasn't going to be," she said as she moved past him and dropped onto the couch. "Originally I intended to come here and just kill you on sight."

Denton backed up a step and tried to think. Then it hit him.

"Oh my God, Beth," he said. "I'm so sorry – I should have called you."

Beth nodded. "You're damn right, Denton. It's one thing that you didn't call to tell me how your stealth mission turned out, but it's another for burning bodies to start showing up on the news and not hear a word."

"You're right. You're totally right. The aftermath was a blur, but that's not an excuse. I'll figure out how to make it up to you, I promise. I'm really glad you came to find me."

Beth looked down at the couch and ran her finger over the upholstery.

"Well … I *wanted* to not come, but I had to get out of the house," she said.

Denton joined her on the couch. "Why's that?"

She rolled her eyes. "My father – he's been on the phone – my phone – taking business calls since early this morning. He has not hung up for more than a couple of minutes at a time all day."

Denton snapped his fingers. "I just remembered I called you at home multiple times today but got your busy signal. I was starting to get worried."

"Don't push it," she warned. "You're cute, but you're not that cute."

"Sorry, please continue."

She shrugged. "Basically I just got sick of listening to him drone on while the Financial News Network blared across my television."

"And so you sought refuge at Castle Denton."

"Something like that," she smiled.

"Well, do you want to grab a bite? I haven't eaten yet."

"Really? Are you working on some kind of Guinness world record?" she smiled.

Denton shot her a look. "Don't push it, yourself. You're cute, but you're not that cute, either."

"Yes, I am," she said.

"I know. So, food?"

"In a bit," she sat back on the couch. "Tell me what happened."

Denton obliged, trying to share only the high points regarding the aftermath, the official police perspective, Sowell's suspension, *his* suspension, Anderson's sneaky files, and the time limit ultimatum from Caldwell.

"And that about covers today," he said.

"Well I have to admit, that's a pretty good excuse for not calling."

"Yeah … but it really isn't," he said. "And I really will think of a good way to make it up to you – and soon. But right now my brain is stuck on figuring out what Anderson is trying to tell me before UAB refuses to support this investigation any further."

"I understand that," she said. "It's okay."

He scratched the back of his neck. "That and trying to figure out how to get Tim off suspension. All he's tried to do is help UAB from the start. And this is the reward for thinking slightly outside the box."

"You know," Beth started, looking at the ceiling, "I might know someone who could help out."

"With what?"

"With Tim's situation – and maybe with your need for UAB support or at least time to investigate."

Denton took a deep drink from his beer and tried not to bite off the end of bottle.

"Who's that?"

"My father," she said.

Be nice. Be nice. Be nice.

"Aha. And how might Lord Fancy Pants be able to assist?" he asked. "Does he own UAB?"

Beth shook her head and waved the idea away. "Good heavens, Denton – no. Nothing like that. He's just … involved at higher levels."

Denton did not smile.

"How is he 'involved' with the company I work for?"

Beth readjusted on the sofa and looked at him. He read her eyes.

Everyone has secrets. Everyone lies. Shut up and pay attention.

"Well, it's a bit complicated," she tried.

"Well, let's try to simplify it a bit," he said. "Does your father work for UAB in some high-level capacity?"

Beth bit her lip and smiled apologetically.

"Sort of?"

Denton sat back, took another drink, and chewed on that answer.

"Sort of," he repeated as he stared at the far wall.

After a few more moments of pondering, he turned to Beth and smiled.

"Right," he said as he rose. "Good-bye."

Beth watched him collect his keys.

"Denton, please don't be angry."

"Why would I be angry? My fiancée's father is probably my boss's boss's boss or something higher, but we don't really know because it's complicated."

He jammed his arms into his jacket and yanked it around him.

"I should be elated," he said. "Oh, except that the man *hates* me."

"I know you two didn't hit it off, which is why I didn't want to say—"

"You're wrong, Beth. It's *not* really that complicated. In fact, it's actually very simple. When I don't provide detailed information about something you might find concerning, I'm a total jerk. When *you* do it, you're some kind of saint."

"Denton …"

Denton waved her off as he snatched his keys from the countertop and yanked open the front door.

"Sorry, Saint Elizabeth, but I've had about all the complications I can handle for one day. I'll see myself out now."

"Denton this is *your* flat," she said.

"Yes, yes *of course it is*!" Denton said from the doorway. "But I've never done this before, and I got so caught up in the dramatic yelling and storming around that I didn't think about that until just now!"

Denton looked at his keys, and then his feet. His voice softened a bit.

"And seeing how I'm past the point of recovery, and since I'd never throw you out … I'm just going to go."

Denton turned to close the door and Beth called out.

"What about tomorrow night?"

The door closing paused. Denton's head reappeared, and he looked at her.

"I wouldn't miss it," he said in a tone that clearly meant something far different than, "I'm looking forward to it."

With that, Denton closed the door without slamming it. Beth kept her dazed stare focused on the door for a long time. When she finally accepted that Denton wasn't standing out in the hall trying to figure out how to come back in gracefully, she closed her eyes, and let the tears well up and pour over.

As she got up to go in search of tissue, her phone rang. She blinked at the caller ID showing Denton's smiling picture.

She answered and held the phone to her ear.

"Denton?"

"Hey," Denton said, sounding down. "I'm sorry."

"No, Denton—"

"Let me finish, please."

"Of course, sorry."

"Thanks. So, I'm acting like an ass, I didn't mean it when I called you Saint Elizabeth. I'm just tired. It's been a very bizarre week and a horribly long day. I'm just tired. I'm really sorry."

"I'm sorry, too, Denton," she said.

"And … well, there's really no way for me to say this without sounding like a jerk, and I really don't mean it in a bad way … but would you mind leaving while I'm still out?"

"Um … sure?" Beth said.

"I'm not mad at you or anything," Denton said. "I just need to turn my mind off for awhile. I've got another long day tomorrow before we all get together."

"It's okay, Denton. I understand," she said.

"Thanks."

"Here's a thought," Beth's voice picked up. "Tomorrow night … we go to dinner, drink whatever we need to get through it, ditch 'the dads' afterward and come back here for dessert. How does that sound?"

"That sounds *awesome*," he said.

"I love you, Denton Rourke."

"I love you, too, Beth."

The pair ended the call with Beth wondering if he hadn't said her full name because he was afraid he'd start an argument about the wedding, and Denton wondering if he could order a pizza delivery at the counter in Pincole's and then catch a ride back to his condo with the driver.

CHAPTER 36

Saturday

Denton's alarm clock greeted him in its dutiful way by blasting out a steady siren-like noise at a volume loud enough to have awoken him if he'd been two blocks away – and dead. With his eyes closed, he turned and performed his patented clock punch which would render the noisy villain permanently silent. For eight minutes. But as his hand came down and hit only the top of his nightstand, his brain reminded him that he'd hidden the alarm clock before he'd gone to bed.

He struggled out from under his covers and demanded an explanation from whichever side of his brain concocts his ridiculous strategies. As the noise continued, some faint thought memory bounced through his head. Something about hiding the clock from himself so he'd be forced to get up and start the day when he intended to, not 16, 24, or 32 minutes later.

Denton made his way to the one electrical outlet on the opposite wall. He took both cords he found there and yanked them out of the socket.

"Take that!" he said.

At least, he thought he said that. He couldn't hear himself over the alarm's continued blaring.

He gritted his teeth and pulled the source ends of both cords toward him, discovering almost instantly that the non-alarm clock cord belonged to his floor lamp, which he watched become his *former* floor lamp as it hit the ground and broke into several pieces.

He followed the other cord to its end and found, lodged under his TV stand, a screaming alarm clock which also had the word "former" stamped all over its cheap plastic case.

An hour later, with coffee in his belly and the alarm clock in his toilet, Denton sat at the kitchen table and stared at Anderson's spreadsheets once again.

No matter how many times he told himself the spreadsheets might hold the key to a financial scandal set to destroy UAB, he could not get excited about studying quarterly financial numbers. Just saying "quarterly financial numbers" made him want to take a nap.

Daniel, my dear friend ...

"Shut up," Denton ordered.

I hope you will find my final words of some use.

"Yeah, and I hope you bring me some doughnuts, puzzle boy."

He took another sip of coffee and looked over at the door, as though perhaps a magic pastry elf might show up and grant his fried, sugary wish. But the door did not offer any indication of elves, fairies, or other mystical creatures bearing food, so Denton grabbed a coat and headed out in search of breakfast.

Twenty minutes later, with a box of doughnuts in one hand and a cup of fresh black coffee in the other, Denton bounced toward home chewing wildly, sipping slowly, and smiling.

I've included attachments you'll need ...

"Don't care," Denton sang as he approached his building.

Besides, Denton justified between bites, he couldn't find anything to study anyway. The Company A spreadsheet looked just like the Company C spreadsheet. Except for the numbers. If they were performance figures, then Company A's numbers looked decent. But Company C's figures looked much more like UAB's with all the minus signs and such.

Company C's figures look much more like ...

"Go away!" he demanded. "I'm saving that crap for Fred!"

"Denton Rourke saving doughnuts for me?" Fred fell into step and opened the building door for Denton. "Do my eyes deceive me?"

"Your ears and your optimism definitely do," he said as he entered the building. "You're early."

Fred shrugged as they walked across the lobby and stepped into an open elevator car.

"I figured I'd get a jump on these files and this beer."

The elevator closed and pulled them skyward.

"Just because?" Denton asked. "I'd say either you came by early in the hopes of waking me up with your ridiculous knocking."

"That would make me a total bastard."

"Which you're really not," Denton said.

The elevator opened and the men walked to Denton's door. As he entered, Denton smiled.

"*Or*, you have a date tonight which you planned without remembering your prior engagement. Because as the owner of an emaciated dating history, you're just not used to having Saturday evening plans beyond sitting in your boxers eating leftover chow mein noodles and watching *Saved by the Bell* reruns."

"That's not quite accurate," Fred replied.

"Sorry, I forgot … *all alone*. Better?"

"Much. Yeah, so, Candace wants to celebrate the escheatment project completion. The final testing went perfectly and it goes online Monday."

Fred pulled a 12-pack of Smithwick's out of his backpack and stuck it in the fridge. Then he started a fresh pot of coffee. He looked over at Denton.

"I take it from your doughnut binge that you're getting nowhere with the spreadsheets?"

Denton sat back down at the table and shrugged.

"There's not much to them, and I don't even know what I'm looking for."

He took another bite of a doughnut and frowned at the table.

"Fred, this may be the easiest bet you ever had to pay out on," he said. He paused before his next thought, and then finally looked at his friend.

"There may *not* be anything nefarious going on here at all. I could be totally wrong."

Fred came and sat across from him. He reached carefully for the box of doughnuts. When Denton didn't slap his hand with a steel spoon, he opened it and grabbed one.

"Well, Denton, it'd be the first time, wouldn't it?"

"The first time I've ever been wrong? Hardly."

Fred shook his head and took another bite.

"No, the first time you sensed something fishy, *really fishy*, and it turned out to be absolutely nothing."

"Oh … I'm not sure. Possibly."

"Okay then," Fred turned the laptop around and pulled it to him. "Let's not assume Denton Rourke is losing his touch just yet."

Denton watched his friend studying the screen and smiled. He'd shown up for Denton in a pinch. He'd brought beer.

And he'd used the word *fishy*.

Denton pushed the box of doughnuts next to Fred.

"The rest are yours," he said.

Fred didn't look up but shook his head.

"No thanks, I'm getting ready to switch to beer."

Denton looked at his watch. "It's 10:30," he said.

Fred smiled. "Yeah, I know, and I'm looking at stuff for UAB – technically. This'll be like drinking at work."

Denton looked at him for a moment and then deemed his logic acceptable. He retrieved two beers from the fridge and popped the tops. He handed one to Fred and raised his own.

"Sláinte," he said as they toasted.

"Tru dat," Fred replied.

"I will hit you with a bottle if you ever say that again," Denton warned.

Fred smiled and continued to look at the spreadsheets. Denton sat back down with Phillip Anderson still pestering him.

I hope you'll find my final words of some use.

"Yes, yes, as do I," Denton muttered. He took a sip of his beer and read the letter again. Then he read it again.

And then something happened.

Denton grabbed a pencil and started writing on a piece of scrap paper. When finished, he looked at his creation.

USE SEE REVEAL BE STILL BEST TIME TO CONVERT

Denton read the line several times over. Then he rubbed his eyes and dropped the pencil.

"Just the breakthrough we've been looking for," he muttered.

"What is it?" Fred asked, looking at the paper.

"I think it's a key," Denton said. "It's from Anderson's email. It's his last words – that is, the last words from each sentence in the letter."

"What do you suppose it means?" Fred asked.

"Not sure yet," Denton said. "It might just mean I'm desperate."

"Use, see, reveal. Be still. Best time to convert," Fred repeated from the paper.

"Yeah, I know. It's muddy."

Fred shrugged and returned to the spreadsheets. After a couple of minutes he chuckled.

"I tell you one thing: I *wish* Company A's numbers were ours. We'd been in a hell of a lot different position right now."

"Amen to that," Denton said. "Here's to Company A."

The two clinked bottles and drank. Denton smiled as he finished his drink, but then stopped suddenly and stared at Anderson's message.

USE SEE REVEAL BE STILL BEST TIME TO CONVERT

Denton choked on his beer as he slammed the bottle down and grabbed his pencil. Fred watched as his friend wheezed as he scribbled across another piece of paper.

"Fred, where's the Company B data?" he asked through a cough.

Fred looked at his friend. "We haven't found anything for a

Company B," he said.

Denton cleared his throat loudly and smiled as he put his pencil down. He turned the paper around and pushed it in front of Fred.

"Perfect choice of words," Denton said.

Fred looked at the paper once more.

USE ~~SEE~~ REVEAL ~~BE~~ STILL BEST TIME TO CONVERT
USE C, REVEAL B. STILL BEST TIME TO CONVERT

Fred looked up at Denton and smiled. He flipped to the Company C spreadsheet, shaking his head.

"No way," he said. "Seriously?"

"I think so," Denton said. "Anderson wouldn't have skipped from A to C."

Fred made a few clicks of his mouse, furrowed his brow a bit, and then looked at Denton with a stupid grin.

"One second," he said. Then he grabbed his phone and pressed a button. After a few moments, he smiled fully.

"Hi, honey. Uh, quick question. How do I find hidden tabs in a spreadsheet? Invisible or hidden? I don't know – both."

Fred started clicking while nodding at the phone with the occasional "uh huh" thrown in. Then suddenly his face lit up.

"Got it! Thanks, Candace!"

He ended the call and turned the laptop to Denton.

"May I present Company B!"

Denton looked over the page with excitement, and then frowned.

"What the hell is all this?"

Fred looked at the rows and rows of data which looked nothing like Company A and Company C.

Acct	Time Opened	Number	Amount
1	13:19:20 EST	TBD	$10,125,425.25
2	15:45:35 EST	TBD	$8,216,174.63
3	12:23:54 EST	TBD	$9,587,892.23
4	18:41:39 EST	TBD	$11,234,456.98

"Wow," Fred said, shaking his head. "This goes on for … a hundred rows."

"My brain hurts," Denton said. "Whose accounts are these?"

"No clue," Fred offered. "Here, try this brain juice," he said, handing Denton another bottle.

As the men started their second beers, Denton reviewed the Company B sheet another dozen times without really digesting much.

"Anything?" he asked Fred in desperation.

"Well," he started. "No. Not really. Not yet, anyway."

"Well, Candace knows every inch of this program," Fred said. "Maybe there's more hidden info we haven't found."

Denton shrugged. "Maybe you can take my laptop and the two of you can review it tonight at her place."

Fred looked at him with excited eyes.

"Denton, are you serious? That would be awesome."

"Are *you* serious?" Denton asked. "Of course I'm not. I don't want my laptop near either of you."

"Fine," Fred said. "Okay, this seems like a break point. I guess we can … turn on college football?"

Denton smiled. He picked up his beer and the letter and gestured Fred to the couch.

"Right this way," he said. "And I grant you full rights to the remote."

"A better man the world has never known," Fred bowed. Then he grabbed the remote, dropped onto the couch, and propped his feet on the coffee table.

As Fred flipped through a number of football pregame shows and drank his beer, he stopped on the Financial News Network. Both men watched as FNN replayed the final moments of Joseph Handel's speech from the previous day. As the sound bite ended, Fred sighed.

"He's going to kill all of us," he said with a laugh.

Denton watched his friend with a smile.

"Well I'm pretty sure that violates all sorts of hostile work environment codes."

Fred's relaxed demeanor didn't change. He flipped away from FNN and settled on another sports channel.

"He'll have them removed," he said. "Or he'll prepay whatever the fine is so he can take his time plotting our murders. I wonder if he'll kill us slowly, one by one, or in bunches."

Denton noted – with a slight bit of personal shame – that he missed the version of Fred Maxton who, upon the delivery of unfortunately amusing news about Joseph Handel, could be counted on to break out in hives, drop into an ashen-faced stupor, or fall prey to some other panic-filled malady.

"You sound very different," Denton said. "I don't like it. Do you at least have hives?"

Fred smiled and resumed his channel flipping.

"Thank you, Denton," he said.

"For?"

Fred kept smiling. "For using your powers for good. Candace is fantastic."

"The two of you do seem to be a very good, albeit weird fit."

Fred finished the last of his beer and nodded his agreement. He went to the kitchen and grabbed two new bottles.

As he sat back down on the couch, the pregame show ended and players took the field.

"Finally," Denton said. "Go … who are we supporting?"

Fred shrugged. "The Smithwick's All-Stars."

"Go, Smithwick's All-Stars!" Denton cheered. The two toasted once more and settled in.

"STAY TUNED FOR THE SECOND game of our college football double-header!" the announcer pleaded to the television audience.

The audience in Denton's condo stared at the screen without indicating whether they planned to comply. As commercials took over, Denton rose slowly and retrieved a trash bag from the kitchen. Kneeling in front of the coffee table, he and Fred wrangled their herd of empties into the bag. Denton winced at the noise created by the colliding bottles, but tied the bag and returned it to the kitchen.

Fred called out.

"Since I'm now officially required to believe that Kevin Kahneman did not fall victim to Gavin Spincer, why *did* someone kill him?"

Denton made his way back to the couch and let gravity take him down.

"Why is anyone who works in high executive levels of a major company killed? It has to be about money."

"Or a woman," Fred suggested as he used the remote to flip away from the commercial break.

"Or a woman with money."

"Or the need of money … for a woman."

"We could do this all day," Denton said. "I may not know Kahneman's part in this—"

"Denton," Fred said.

"— but I think the answers are in those spreadsheets. I know I'm beating a dead horse, here—"

"Denton," Fred poked Denton with the remote and then pointed at the television screen.

Denton turned his attention to the screen where a Financial News Network anchor sat speaking with a guest at the news desk. Though Fred had the sound muted, the title bar at the bottom gave them a pretty good indication of the current topic.

BREAKING NEWS
HUNTSMAN BANK TO ACQUIRE UAB

"Turn it up!" Denton said.

Fred clicked the remote and the anchor's voice sprung to life.

"… during a private meeting as soon as tomorrow, some sources suggest."

"Oh shit," Fred said.

Denton leaned forward toward the TV and listened to Banfield.

"… had been plagued by …"

Daniel, my dear friend.

"… facing a revolt by remaining board members …"

I hope you'll find my final words of some use.

"Christ, not *now*," Denton said. He turned to Fred, who sat dumbstruck.

"You didn't know this was coming," Denton said.

"No," Fred replied barely above a whisper.

"How can the lead communications guy for our main site not know?"

"Because he's out," Fred said. "Because Huntsman's comm. team is taking over."

Denton looked at his friend.

"No, Fred. No, it doesn't mean that for certain."

"… talking to us now from Huntsman Bank headquarters is Aaron Voss, head of Media Relations and Communications for Huntsman. Aaron, talk to us about this takeover."

Aaron Voss smiled warmly and shook his head.

"Well, Jeff, let's just start with the fact that this is not some kind of forced 'takeover.' UAB has had some financial issues of late, as we all know, and Huntsman Bank found itself in a position to help. Obviously we'll be acquiring the company and its assets and liabilities, but beyond the financials, this is a chance to bring a large pool of very talented employees from a company with a rich history in the banking industry into the Huntsman bank family."

"Now tell them that in the end, it's the customer who wins," Fred muttered as he took a final swig from his beer.

Voss continued. "This will lead to the sharing of best practices and the development of new efficiencies which will ultimately translate into a better experience for our customers. And at the end of the day, they are the reason we're here, Jeff."

Jeff the anchor put on his "hard question" face.

"So Aaron, let's get to the hard questions. Did I hear correctly that you were in the shower when you received the news about this final chapter in the Huntsman / UAB saga?"

Fred killed the sound once more as Aaron's face conveyed confusion and mild annoyance at the question.

Denton looked at him and searched for the right words to help ease the pain his friend clearly felt. But he didn't search for very long, as he knew those words didn't really exist at that moment. So he thought of the next best phrase.

"Come on," he said, standing up. "Let's go get hammered."

Fred's glum face turned toward Denton's big, mischievous grin. Denton started nodding and gesturing toward the door with his eyeballs.

Fred turned and looked at the door. The glumness faded behind a decent-sized smile.

"Why the hell not," he said. "It'll be like sitting in a bar on a workday."

Then Fred pointed at Denton.

"Are you going to change first? Your pants and shirt don't match."

Denton grabbed a light jacket from his the entryway closet and put it on. He opened the front door.

"There – it hides the shirt color," he said. "Better?"

"Not even a little bit."

Denton shrugged and ushered Fred into the hallway and down to their new appointment at Kennedy's Pub.

CHAPTER 37

Two hours and many drinks later, Fred and Denton watched the television in Kennedy's and found FNN's coverage of UAB's impending demise much funnier than it had seemed previously.

"What do you suppose Marcus Rompeaux will do now?" Fred asked.

Denton sipped his drink and shook his head. "Dunno. But you know what? He handled himself really well yesterday. He impressed me."

"Me, too," Fred agreed. "Wow, he can ruin our fun without even trying."

"I know," Denton sighed. "I wanted to make a joke about him being banned from working at Sea World, but now it just seems mean. What a jerk."

"We should call him," Fred suggested.

"You go ahead," Denton waved his permission. "My phone is off."

"Big surprise. Why do you even carry one?"

"If you don't have a mobile phone, people think you're weird," Denton replied.

"Well, I hate to tell you … never mind."

They looked up at the television and watched Russell Banfield loft a softball question to a fat man in a three-piece suit wearing glasses too small for his face and a beard too … *beardy* for anyone. The words, "Market Analyst" appeared after the man's name.

"Well, Russell, let's call this what it is: An emergency rescue. A salvage operation."

"And let's call you what you are," the bartender chimed in through his thick Irish accent. "A bloated, hairy, idiot."

The assessment elicited cheers from Denton and Fred, and he smiled at his new fans.

"Another, Denton?" he asked.

Denton looked at Fred. "You?"

Fred looked at his watch and shook his head.

"No can do," he said. "I'm having dinner with Candace in … 30 minutes."

"Come on," Denton said. "That's like … half an hour from now."

"Okay," Fred smiled.

"Neither of you fellas is driving, are ya?" the bartender asked with his forefinger pointing back and forth at Denton and Fred. Both men smiled back at him and shook their heads.

"No, sir," they said in unison.

Satisfied, the bartender nodded and refreshed their rounds.

"I REALLY DO HAVE TO GO NOW," Fred insisted.

"Yes, that's probably why we're out here waving at cabs," Denton replied with a grin.

"Taxi!" Fred yelled. As one pulled to the curb he smiled and turned to Denton. "At long last – victory."

Denton nodded to his friend and opened the cab door for him.

"Indeed, I look forward to the made-for-TV special about Fred Maxton's three-minute ordeal with trying to hail a cab."

He poured Fred into the seat. Fred gave the restaurant name to the driver and turned to Denton.

"All things considered, it's been a good day hanging out with you."

"Same here," Denton nodded. He closed the cab door and leaned toward the open window. "Hey, congratulate Candace on the escheatment project. Have a good time at dinner."

Fred smiled, gave him a thumbs up, then sat back on the seat.

"You, too," he said as the cab pulled away.

Denton chuckled.

Was that funny? It seemed funny.

As he turned and began his brief stroll toward his condo, something told him to try calling Tim Sowell again. He turned on his phone and hit the Favorites button, but got no further before the phone rang out and showed a call from a local restaurant whose name looked vaguely familiar. He shrugged and answered.

"Hello?"

"Denton?" Beth said.

"Oh, hi, Beth!" he said. "Guess what? I think I'm out of a job, but I made a breakthrough in the case. If there is a case, that is. What do you know about escheatment rules?"

Beth did not respond immediately, so Denton swayed a little from side to side and waited.

"Denton … are you coming?"

"Of course," he said, now trying to remember where he was promising to arrive. Then Fred's parting words fired a shot of mild sobriety and severe panic into his system.

You, too. And by "You, too," I'm referring to YOUR *dinner with Beth, her father, and* YOUR *father.*

He turned in the direction of the restaurant name from his phone and started running.

"I'm five minutes away," he guessed.

"Well hurry, please," she said. "Your father seems very agitated – probably because you're twenty minutes late."

"Oh, I sure hope that's it," he said.

"What?"

"Nothing, sorry – see you in just a few!"

He hung up and tried to find the right pace which would deliver him to the restaurant at maximum speed with minimal vomiting.

Five minutes later Denton found himself once again panting in front of a restaurant window. He pushed through the door and followed his bladder's directions to the restroom.

Once he'd complied with its orders, Denton washed his face and did his best to wipe away the large amounts of sweat he'd produced by drinking vodka instead of Gatorade prior to his recent cardio exercise. At least he felt a little steadier now. A little.

He did what he could with his hair, and when he finally felt he had upgraded his appearance to, "Looks like hell," he nodded and made his way back to the hostess stand. Once there, a friendly woman with kind eyes smiled at him.

"Hi, can I help you?" she asked.

Denton looked at her closely.

"Maybe. Are you allowed to kill me?"

The hostess eyed him back. "I don't think so, but I can check with the manager."

"Denton!"

Denton looked past the hostess and saw his father glaring in his direction. He shook his head at the young woman.

"Too late, they've caught me. You had a chance to save my evening, but *no-o-o*."

"Sorry," she offered with an amused smile. "Next time, call ahead."

Denton flashed a quick grin as he moved past her. But the grin ran and hid as he arrived at a dead-silent table of unhappy, irritated faces. Though no one made actual eye contact with him, he waved generically as he sat down next to Beth.

He leaned in to kiss her, but she made no move to reciprocate. Denton realized immediately that Archibald's eyes had risen up and locked on him from a perfect vantage point just above the menu. In mid-lean, Denton switched actions and continued across Beth until his arm reached the salt shaker. He grabbed it and pulled back, placing it next to his empty plate.

"This looks great," he said, still smiling.

No reaction. Denton picked up the water glass in front of him and drank.

Could this night get any better? Maybe if I got hit by a car …

"Denton," Connor Rourke spoke up between sips of scotch. "I hope you don't mind that we ordered appetizers without waiting any longer."

"Yes, Dad, I think we all know I'm late," he said. He looked at his audience again. "You all have my apologies."

Connor shook his head and resumed his angry sipping. Archibald cleared his throat and stirred his hot tea with far more interest than the refreshment would normally deserve. Denton looked over at Beth and pleaded with his eyes, but she refused to acknowledge his gaze. Sensing danger, his natural instincts kicked in and he found himself turning to her father.

"So, Mr. Ingraham," he began.

Archibald looked up in surprise at hearing his name.

"How's the tea?"

He looked down at his drink and curled his lips downward. "I have no idea how one is supposed to drink this," he said and resumed his stirring.

Denton stared at the man's cup for a moment. Then he pointed at it. "Lift with the handle."

Connor scoffed, but neither Ingraham said a thing. Denton finished his water, looked over the gloomy group, and rose.

"Where are you going?" Beth asked.

Denton looked himself over in mock surprise.

"Aww, man. The guy in the shop said this invisibility potion would last for hours. Total rip off." He jerked his thumb in the direction of the bar. "I'm going to see if by any luck I can get a double hemlock before happy hour ends."

Connor raised his glass. "Bring me back another scotch will you?"

Denton's eyes narrowed and he nodded as he turned from the table. Beth stood and followed him to the bar.

"Denton, have you been drinking?"

"Not *near* enough."

He placed his order and turned to her.

"Did you know about this?" he asked.

"Did I know *what*?" she replied.

"About UAB. Did your father tell you what was going to happen?"

"No, Denton, he didn't," she said, hands on her hips. "I'm not even sure he knew before last night."

"He knew *something.*"

Denton's drinks arrived and he dropped some money on the bar.

"I'm sure he just loves this," he said, taking a sip. "Before he just didn't like me on principle, but now … now he can shake his head at the unemployed loser you've hooked up with."

"He's not like that, Denton," she said. "He isn't happy about anyone losing a job – not even you."

Denton remained unconvinced.

"I can't believe you didn't kiss me," he said.

She looked at him with her head cocked, and then moved in and kissed him hard. Pulling back, she smiled at him.

"And *I* can't believe how much you smell like a distillery."

"I ran here," he said. "I *ran* for you … twice in the same week."

"My hero," she teased.

"Are you aging that scotch another year on the bar, son?"

Denton cringed at his father's voice pierced his skull.

"We'd better get back," Beth said. "Your dad's hardly spoken since we arrived. He barely even introduced himself to my father."

"That is strange," Denton murmured.

The two made their way back to the table. Denton's warm, boozy courage bubbled up again.

"So, Mr. Ingraham," he tried again.

Archibald looked up from his review of the wine list and waited for Denton's next utterance.

"I see Mrs. Ingraham didn't make the trip with you," he said.

"Yes, you do see that," Archibald replied and returned to the wine list.

Beth frowned at her father and turned to Denton and Connor.

"Mom doesn't like air travel very much, so she doesn't come for short trips very often."

"But maybe someday in the future she'll have a special event to come for … if difficult decisions can ever be made," Archibald said, still studying his wine list.

"Ah, yes," Connor chimed. "And do you imagine a lot of the Ingraham clan would make it over for the blessed event – if it ever gets scheduled?"

Archibald shrugged. "I imagine a few aunts and uncles, Elizabeth's brother and a few others would make the trip."

Connor sat back in his chair and finished off his drink. "Better watch your wallets, people," he muttered.

Archibald took off his reading glasses and looked at Connor.

"Just what is that supposed to mean?"

Beth stared at Denton, who found himself preoccupied with an amazing speck of dirt under his fingernail.

Connor leaned forward and stared back at Archibald with particular hardness.

"It means any time you get more than a couple of Ingrahams in the same room, the Rourkes find themselves relieved of their valuables."

Beth's eyes went wide as Denton's fingernail established itself as the most fascinating item in the restaurant.

Archibald stared at Connor. "Honestly, Mr. Rourke –"

"Careful with that word, Mr. Ingraham. Make sure you know what it means before you use it further."

"Now see here!" Archibald protested. Connor rose from his seat suddenly and pointed an angry finger at Beth's father.

"No, *you* see here, you land-stealing British dandy. Maybe you don't know your family's history, but I haven't forgotten it – none of the Rourkes has."

"Okay, Dad," Denton implored. "Enough."

Connor shook his head and finger together without taking his eyes off Archibald.

"Is there a problem here?" a waiter stopped and asked, casting a concerned eye at Connor's angry finger wagging.

"You'd better believe there is, fella," Connor said. "This man's family stole our land," he said.

"What?" the waiter asked.

"Beg pardon?" Archibald said.

"Denton?" Beth said.

"Double scotch please," Denton said.

"That's right," Connor continued. "The Ingrahams spent the better part of three decades infiltrating Ireland and taking land from its rightful owners by hook or by crook."

"Oh my God, Dad," Denton said.

"They'd buy land from the desperate or ignorant, at fractions of its worth. And when they met a family they couldn't trick into selling – such as the Rourkes, well they just stole it."

Two additional waiters arrived with one tray of calamari and another of egg rolls. The original waiter used their departure as cover for his own hasty retreat from the intense conversation.

"Hooray, food!" Denton said. "Let's not talk anymore until this food is gone … along with me."

"Mr. Rourke," Beth said. "This can't be true. Surely there's more to the story."

Connor looked at her.

"There most certainly is."

Denton finished his drink and tried to take solace in the fact that no one could possibly still care about his tardy, drunken arrival.

Connor continued.

"Devlin Rourke refused to sell to the neighboring Ingrahams – who'd already taken land from the O'Toole family for a fraction of its value. So John Ingraham took matters into his own hands."

Connor sipped his scotch and continued.

"Over the next ten or so years, Ingraham had workers come in during the dead of night and gradually move the Rourke property fence lines inward. They started at the farthest points of the property so that by the time Devlin got wise to the scheme, Ingraham had already bribed surveyors and parish leaders to remap the area and sign off on forged sale documents."

"Dad," Denton said. "When was this?"

"The mid-1600s," Archibald answered for Connor.

All eyes turned to look at Beth's father. He looked over at Beth and then back to Connor.

"I wasn't aware you were *those* Rourkes," he added.

Denton turned back to his father.

"You're holding a grudge from what … three hundred years before you were born?"

"They stole our land – our heritage – right out from under Devlin Rourke as he slept!"

"As he *slept one off* is more accurate," Archibald replied.

Beth shot her dad a nasty glare.

"Excuse me?" Connor said with an eyebrow rising.

Archibald dabbed the corners of his mouth with his napkin and turned to his accuser.

"As it happens, Mr. Rourke, I *do* know our family's history. Far better, I'd say, than you know your own."

"Daddy, stop it," Beth said.

Archibald didn't acknowledge her request.

"It may shock you to know this, Mr. Rourke, but in spite of the conflicts between their countries, Devlin Rourke and John Ingraham shared a deep friendship for many years. However, Devlin was a habitual drunkard, and a gambler, and over the years he fell into a rather sad pattern. He would lose any money he had, accumulate mounds of gambling debts, and then ask John Ingraham to purchase some of his land so he could settle his bills."

"Who wants to talk about something else?" Denton asked with his hand raised. "How about politics? Religion? Medical testing on Koala bears?"

Archibald turned to him.

"The only part of the story your father has even remotely accurate is that John Ingraham always purchased the land farthest from the Rourke homestead – and that was so Devlin's family wouldn't know. Of course, as the cycle continued and their land holdings dwindled, they eventually figured it out. That's when Devlin Rourke created his ridiculous story of late night land grabs, effectively cursing the Ingraham name and forcing John put his land in the hands of a few caretakers and return home to England."

Connor's green eyes burned through Archibald's head.

"What a surprise that your version of events puts the Ingrahams on a pedestal of virtue looking down at the pitiful Rourkes."

"My version of events is captured very accurately in notes from the 1600s which we still have in our collection."

"I'm sure," Connor said. "You'd have to write all this bollocks down to keep your stories straight."

Archibald picked up an eggroll, looked it over, and put it back down.

"The notes I refer to are *from* Devlin," he said. "They're a series of thank you letters he wrote to John after each purchase. In each he promises it will be the last and assures John that he'll buy the land back just as soon as possible."

"How about charades?" Denton tried.

Archibald picked up his tea finally and took a sip.

"Of course, he never could keep that promise, so Devlin Rourke died with empty pockets and an empty bottle and his former friend John Ingraham died owning a sizeable amount of land in an unwelcoming country and an undeserved reputation as a vile swindler and thief."

Denton looked down at the table and realized the waiter had as some point deftly slipped another drink in front of him. He raised it up to the silent group.

"A toast. To family … and burying the hatchet."

But neither the two Ingrahams nor the elder Rourke joined in, and Denton drank to the notion alone.

He looked at his father. Connor continued to stare in Archibald's direction, but his eyes had softened.

Beth looked at Connor.

"Mr. Rourke, I'm so sorry – about all of this."

Connor looked at her and nodded, but said nothing. Then Beth turned and gave her father a look of such profound anger that Denton wondered if the man's head might catch fire.

Archibald must have held roughly the same concern, for his triumphant scowl faded away to something more courteous. He turned to Connor.

"Mr. Rourke, I do apologize. Family histories tend to be fuzzy at best. Perhaps the real truth of the Ingraham-Rourke saga falls somewhere in between your recollections and my own. Either way, I'm sorry I used this forum for its delivery."

With that, Archibald turned his eyes quickly to Beth. She nodded her approval and he returned to his tea.

"Well," Connor said, picking up his glass and staring into it, "I don't suppose I gave you much choice."

Archibald simply smiled back appreciatively. Connor took a sip, and continued with his head low.

"I'm sorry for being such an arse tonight. And if your story is even half-accurate, then I owe you and your family an even larger apology. I won't blame you if you want to leave, but if you will stay, I would like to buy you all dinner."

Beth's smiled warmly. "You're very gracious, Mr. Rourke."

"Please, call me Connor, for God's sake. And no, I'm not. I'm an idiot. You're the gracious ones for staying this long."

He waved at a waiter and smiled.

"Now, Archibald," he said. "With your permission, I'd like to change topics."

"By all means," Archibald said with an amused smile.

"Great," Connor said as he turned to look at Denton.

"Let's talk about my son."

All eyes fell on Denton.

"Yes," Beth and Archibald agreed.

Denton looked at his empty glass and smiled at the group.

"Is the option to leave still available?"

Connor pulled a small black notebook from his pocket. Denton read the printing on the front and went cold.

"No," Connor said with a smile as he opened the 18-month pocket calendar.

CHAPTER 38

Denton stared at the calamari which had long ago shed the "warm and tender" status it boasted upon delivery and had settled into the "fried rubber bands" phase of its life cycle.

He didn't care. The entrees hadn't arrived, so he planned to eat every single morsel off the cold rings platter if he had to. Whatever it took not to say a word.

"I mean, how do you show up thirty minutes late to a dinner with your own father, your fiancée, and *her* father whom you've barely met?" Connor said.

Denton kept chewing, which suited Connor perfectly, as he'd presented the question as a general topic of conversation to the group.

"Connor," Beth said gently. "He *has* been working quite a lot lately."

"I'd say the only thing he worked on today was liver damage," Archibald added, much to the joy of Connor. Even Beth giggled a little.

Denton spiked another bite and resumed chewing.

"We can get to his clothes and his job prospects and his overall awkwardness in a bit," Connor said. "Right now, let's talk about dates."

"And why it's so hard to pick one," Archibald said.

"Calendars *are* tricky for some," Beth jumped in.

"Now wait a minute," Denton spoke up, spitting bits of rubber onto his plate, "I've made it very clear that I just wanted to build up some job and financial stability."

"Try not killing your paying clients," Archibald offered with a smile as Connor laughed and Beth gave him a "shame on you" smile.

Something in Denton's head turned off. He stood up and turned to Archibald.

"Yes, you're right – I blew up my last client and haven't been able to get more detective work. But rather than be an unemployed jack-ass chasing a dream, I took another job so that I could be a productive part of the marriage."

Then he leaned on the table and pointed at Archibald.

"I took a *shitty* job at your *shitty* bank so that I could help take care of your daughter. But you didn't even have the decency to tell her why you were really in town or warn her about what was happening at UAB – what was going to happen to her fiancé's job."

"I … I couldn't," Archibald said, leaning back in his chair.

"Son," Connor said.

"And you," Denton turned to his dad. "Yeah, I showed up late. But you tried to start a fist fight with my fiancée's father over a centuries-old land feud you were never a part of and don't even have factually correct. But you arrived *on time*, so that's okay."

You're yelling.

"I said sorry," Connor tried.

"Denton," Beth said. "It *was* more than half an hour – and that's twice this week."

He turned to her.

"Yep – and both times I was late because – you're going to love this Archie – I've spent the week trying to stop a murderer *and* uncover a possible financial scandal in the hopes of proving my worth to a bank your father knew was already history."

You should really stop talking now.

"What financial scandal?" Archibald asked.

"None of your business," Denton snapped. "Besides, who cares, anyway? I've been attacked by a psychotic employee on fire, tricked into manual labor by the new queen of escheatment coding, and caught trying to steal files from a COO's computer, just to try and stay employed. And it turns out that all the while I was engaged to the woman whose family owns half of Ireland!"

"Not half," Beth said flatly.

"Denton," Connor said. "Son, I told you to do a little research."

"And I told *you* not to bring all this up tonight! That's all I asked. But could you keep the peace for the sake of someone else? Of course not!"

Denton picked up his glass and nodded at the stunned table.

"So you people can point, and scold, and laugh at me all you want, but I'm not the asshole here."

Stop right there. Just stop. You can still recover if—

"You all …"

Denton realized his audience now included several tables around them, which was a larger crowd than he felt comfortable addressing. He sat back down and smiled.

"So where were we?"

Archibald looked at his watch and presented a polite smile to the table and stood up.

"Well, if you'll excuse me, I'm afraid I do have to be on my way," he said. "I have quite a long day tomorrow."

Denton desperately wanted to retort, but felt wiped out suddenly.

Connor stood and Denton followed suit. Archibald shook Connor's hand and smiled.

"I'll be here a few more days," he said. "Let's find some time to talk."

Connor nodded. "I'll get your number from Elizabeth."

Archibald patted Denton on the shoulder as he passed.

"Denton."

Beth rose. "I'll go with you, Daddy."

"I'll walk you out," Denton said, reaching for Beth's hand.

She slapped it away. "Like bloody hell you will," she hissed.

She moved around him and hugged his father.

"Good-bye, Connor," she said.

Connor smiled back. "Thanks for putting up with an old idiot tonight."

"Don't worry about it," she said as she turned to glare at Denton. "I'm used to it."

Denton watched Beth and Archibald make their way to the front door and then turned to his dad. Connor looked at him like he'd put a fork in his nose.

"Are you *trying* to win the Moron of the Century award?" he asked his son. He pointed to the front door. "Go get her, jackass."

Denton turned and walked quickly through the restaurant and out to the curb where Beth stood alone.

"Where's your father?" he asked.

"You mean *Archie*? He went to get the car."

"Beth, look, I'm sorry. Things got a little heated in there—"

"You knew about your father's grudge?" Beth cut in. "You knew what he thought about the Ingraham name?"

Denton tried to look a few moves ahead, but found his brain unwilling to assist.

You're on your own, asshole.

"Well, yes. I mean, I'd heard his rant the other day."

"Why didn't you say something to me?" she asked. "We could have had this all sorted before it came to this – before it played out here in the restaurant, and before my father spent his first meal with your father *embarrassing* him."

"Beth—"

"You let him blindside us, Denton. Why?"

"Beth, I asked him not to bring it up. I didn't know he felt this strongly."

"*Bollocks*, Denton," she said. "You avoided the issue because it was difficult. It's just like the date thing."

"Maybe my microphone wasn't on in there," Denton said.

"Oh, yes, we all heard your little song and dance. Poor, put-upon Denton Rourke – always in the middle of some selfless act that just happens to make him look like a total ass. No respect for poor Denton Rourke – King of the Martyrs."

"Hey."

"Grow up, already," she said.

"I *am* grown-up, thank you. And frankly, that suggestion doesn't carry a lot of weight when it comes from a woman who's so afraid to displease daddy that she gave her fiancé a *fake name*."

"This again?" she said.

"What's the matter, were you afraid if he found out I was a Rourke he might take away one of your castles?"

Beth's eyes shot open wide and then narrowed in a flash. She shook her head slowly.

"Oh you are some piece of work," she said.

Archibald arrived with the car. Beth stepped to the door and turned back to Denton.

"If this is your idea of being grown up, then I suspect you'll be growing old alone with your father."

"There are worse things than that," Denton said.

Beth opened the door and got in.

"Not for him!" she said. Then she made an offensive British gesture at him and slammed the door.

"Hah! I don't even know what that one means!" he called out.

When the car disappeared around the corner, Denton went back in and sat with his father. He sipped his watered-down drink and stared at the four entrees which arrived in his absence.

One of the entrees had already come under attack from Connor Rourke, who shoveled pasta into his mouth while smiling at his son.

"Is it at all possible," Denton started, "that you adopted me?"

"No," Connor said and went back to chewing.

Denton nodded and picked up a fork. He pulled a chicken dish in front of him.

"Couldn't you have sold me to gypsies when I was a baby?"

Connor shook his head. "Tried that, but they wouldn't take you unless I threw in the television. That was the seventies – we'd just gotten it."

"I'm glad this amuses you," Denton said. "Nice performance tonight, by the way. Interesting interpretation of *best behavior*."

"Says the man who stood up and called his father, his fiancée, and her father assholes?"

"I never finished that statement."

"Ah, good," Connor nodded. "So now we're stupid, too."

Denton shook his head. "This was a disaster. She's really angry."

Connor wiped his mouth and both his arms on the table. He looked at his son.

"Denton, if you're not ready for marriage, then just tell her. Sure, she'll dump you on the spot, but you know … you're probably better off without her anyway."

Denton stared at his father and wondered if while he and Beth argued in front of the restaurant, the man had managed to suffer some kind of massive head trauma.

"First of all, I'm *very* ready to get married. Second, what planet are you living on? In what alternative universe can you envision me better off *without* Beth?"

Connor smiled and took a stab of pasta and mussels.

"Show, don't tell," he said.

"Dad, I'm tired," Denton said. "What do you want here?"

Connor chewed. "So, you're saying you're absolutely ready to marry Beth and can't even imagine life without her?"

"Yes."

"And you've told her this?"

"Uh, *YES*."

Connor nodded and took another bite.

"So how large is the gap between what she hears from you, and what she sees from you?"

Denton thought about the question for a few seconds. As the answer came to him, he didn't want to respond. He looked down at the table.

"I'm scared, Dad," he said.

Connor nodded and continued chewing.

"Nothing wrong with that," he said. "What's scaring you exactly?"

Denton scratched his fingernail back and forth across the table cloth. "Up to now, I told myself it was about my job and all, but I guess that's not an issue anymore. But I'm just as scared as I was before. I'm afraid of screwing it up."

"Oh, you're going to screw it up, son," Connor smiled. "You're a Rourke."

"Thanks … very inspirational."

Connor took a sip of his drink and chuckled.

"Denton, there are two paths in front of you. On one path, you travel with Beth at your side. And you hit rough patches, you screw up, and you fall down. Then you get back up – together. This path rewards you with a life filled with unimaginable joys, but at the risk of possibly losing it all if you hit an obstacle you cannot overcome."

He dipped a breadstick in the pasta sauce and took a bite. He waved the rest of it at Denton.

"The other path you take alone. It's safe, the road is smooth, and your falls never create much impact. That path rewards you with safety, consistency, and protection from any chance of being hurt … because it prevents you from ever being loved."

Denton rubbed his eyes. "You and mom have been divorced for almost 15 years, Dad. You've never gone on a single date since then, have you?"

"No."

"And you still think path one was the way to go for you?"

"Of course," he answered. "Some of the happiest moments of my life have been with your mother – and with you. How could I look back – even now – and think I'd have been happier if I hadn't pursued her and instead had sat around on my fat arse blubbering about stability, and timing and … what else have you been saying?"

Denton chuckled. Then he blew his nose and looked at his father.

"I hate talking to you," he said.

"Well, get used to it, my boy. Because at this rate I'm all you're gonna have."

"Okay, I'm convinced," Denton said with a smile. "Path one it is."

He looked at his watch and shook his head.

"Okay, Dad, I've got to get home," he said, standing up.

Connor rose, dropped several large bills on the table and looked at his son.

"After you."

The two walked out into the cool night breeze. Denton buttoned his jacket.

"Split a cab?" Connor offered.

"Nah, I'm going to walk. I need the air."

Connor nodded and the two men hugged, with Denton holding the hug far longer than normal. Connor kissed his son on the cheek and smiled at him.

"You've got this in you, Denton," he said. "No question about it."

"Thanks, Dad," Denton smiled. "I'll talk to you tomorrow."

A cab pulled to the curb next to Connor and Denton turned to walk.

"Oh, and Denton?"

Denton turned back to his father. Connor opened the cab door and looked back at his son.

"About your mom and me."

"Yeah?"

Connor shook his head and smiled.

"We're not divorced."

Then he slid inside the cab and drifted into the night.

CHAPTER 39

Sunday

Denton took another sip of coffee and leaned back on his couch as slowly and methodically as possible so as not to further anger his body which had awoken him very early in the morning to start enacting its revenge for the previous night's alcohol-induced activities.

On top of his pounding headache and upset stomach, Denton had risen to discover his calves and quads had joined forces with his temples in the struggle against their master's behavior. And they'd happily seen to it that each step toward the coffee maker came at a painful price.

Not wanting to miss out on the fun, the television added to Denton's pain by losing the remote and leaving itself locked on a channel preparing for hour one of an all-day billiards tournament. In no condition to get up, Denton settled in and tried to make the best of his punishment. By the second hour of coverage he'd surmised that the object of the game had something to do with hitting red and white balls around the table until the audience fell asleep or one of the players either died of old age or killed himself.

He shifted slightly and tried to shoo away the nagging thoughts flying through his head. He needed to call Beth and apologize. No, he needed to stop by and apologize – with flowers. He had to call Archibald and apologize as well … no flowers for him, though.

As hour number two concluded and the announcer promised more billiards action coming his way, Denton groaned and forced himself into a sitting position. Rubbing his head, he stood and put his hands out for balance. Once steady, he made his way to the kitchen table, slid into a chair and opened the laptop.

He looked again at the quarterly financials for Company A and Company C and noted that compared to televised snooker, all those numbers looked positively fascinating. He looked at Anderson's secret message, focusing on the still un-deciphered portion.

STILL BEST TIME TO CONVERT

Before Denton could take another stab at it, his front door exploded with loud, non-stop knocking. He staggered to his feet trudged to the door.

"Shut up! Who is it?" he demanded.

"It's Fred, let me in!"

Denton looked at his bare wrist.

"What the hell are you doing here so early?"

"It's eleven a.m., jackass. Let me in!"

Denton looked around for a clock, but didn't see one. Fred started knocking again. Denton flung the door open.

"Okay, okay! What?"

"I think I've got something," Fred said as he pushed past Denton and made his way to the table. "Oh, good, you've got it open."

"Please come in," Denton said to the hallway. "Would you like some coffee?"

"Just get over here," Fred said from Denton's chair.

Denton closed the door and staggered over to the table. Fred looked at him excitedly.

"Now, I think the key … wow, you look terrible."

"Focus, please," Denton said.

"Right, sorry. So we've got two companies here, A and C. Company A's quarterlies go back three years. But company C's only go back two years."

"Right – with A's numbers being a company far stronger than C."

Fred clicked over to the Company C spreadsheet and pointed at various quarterly results.

"Denton, I looked it up … these are *UAB*'s numbers from the past three years. Company C is UAB."

"So who is Company A?"

Fred clicked back to the Company A spreadsheet.

"That's what's weird, Denton," he said. "I think Company A is *also* UAB."

"That doesn't make sense," Denton said. "The quarterlies are different."

"For the most recent two years, that's true. But the extra year on Company A – the quarterlies from three years back … they match our reporting exactly."

"So …" Denton said.

Fred looked at him and then shook his head.

"I don't know. I thought I had something, but now that I'm talking it out, it's not coming together. Company C shows UAB's last two years of quarterly earnings, and Company A shows our earnings from three years ago. I don't know what it all means."

Denton looked at Fred for a moment, and then back at his scratch paper with Anderson's helpful message.

STILL BEST TIME TO CONVERT

"Christ," Denton sighed. "If Anderson weren't already dead, I'd kill Mr. 'Eschew the Superfluous' myself."

"Getting to you a little bit?"

Denton pinched the bridge of his nose and grimaced.

"Why would a guy known for eliminating anything without a specific purpose use a riddle to lead us to a hidden spreadsheet full of pointless crap?"

"He wouldn't, would he?"

"Exactly," Denton nodded. He clicked over to the Company B sheet and pointed to the screen.

Acct	Time Opened	Number	Amount
1	13:19:20 EST	TBD	$10,125,425.25
2	15:45:35 EST	TBD	$8,216,174.63
3	12:23:54 EST	TBD	$9,587,892.23
4	18:41:39 EST	TBD	$11,234,456.98

"Yet here we are with a list of accounts and dollar amounts and *account opening times*? If that's not useless information, then what is it? Hell – look at it – it's in Eastern Standard Time. We don't even have an office in the Eastern time zone, so why on earth … would …"

Everyone has secrets, everyone lies. Shut up, sit down, and pay attention.

Denton turned to his friend.

"Fred, would you kindly take the quarterly numbers from the last two years of Company C – the weaker company, and subtract them from Company A's quarterlies for the same period?"

Fred nodded and after a series of clicks and keystrokes, he turned to Denton.

"Done."

"And if you add up all the account balances on the company B page, how much is that?"

As Fred entered an auto sum formula into a box, Denton wrote something else on his piece of paper.

"Voila," Fred exclaimed. "And … oh my God."

"How long are the new escheatment holding account numbers?" Denton asked.

"Six digits," he said automatically. "Eleven if you count the new escheatment prefix."

Denton pushed his scrap paper in front of Fred.

"Is this the prefix for the escheatment accounts?"

Fred looked at it, and then looked at Denton.

"How could you know that?" he asked. "No one knows that yet – we haven't given it out."

Denton turned the paper over and let Fred read again.

STILL B - EST TIME TO CONVERT

"E – S – T," Denton said. "Fifth letter, nineteenth letter, twentieth letter. Five-one-nine-two-zero."

"Our new prefix," Fred nodded. Then he shook his head.

"I don't get it," he said. "What the hell does this mean?"

"Those aren't account opening times," Denton said. "They're account numbers. All they needed was the new routing prefix."

Denton stood up and grabbed his phone. He picked his jacket up off the floor and fished through it until he found a business card. He turned his phone on and dialed the number.

"Daniel, it's Denton."

"Denton?" Caldwell sounded frantic. "Where the hell have you been? Do you know I've been calling you?"

"No," Denton said. "Look, you have to stop the sale. The numbers are bogus."

"Bogus? What's bogus?"

"Anderson's financial reporting," Denton said. "UAB has performed far better than what he's reported for the last twenty-four months – much closer to analyst expectations. He's been hiding company profits in dormant accounts and reporting lower earnings in order to drive the stock price down."

"What?" Caldwell almost shouted. Then he whispered.

"Denton, are you sure? Do you have proof – something I can show the board?"

"Yes. I cracked Anderson's files. I've got everything down to how much he hid each quarter and the account numbers he used to stash the money."

The line was quiet for a moment. Then Caldwell spoke.

"Denton, we do not have a lot of time," he said. "The acting board meets in … forty-two minutes. Can you get here with those numbers?"

"Yes, but Daniel, there's something else."

"What?"

"Anderson could never have pulled this off by himself. He *had* to have someone high up the chain of command to assist with account access and reporting issues."

"Do you know who it is?"

"I think so," he said. "Where's Peter?"

Caldwell paused again.

"He quit, Denton. Yesterday – by *email*, for God's sake."

"What?"

"Denton, I told you how Kevin Kahneman barged into my office drunk and started raving about conspiracies and threatening to go public with his information?"

"Yes."

"Well, I told Peter we couldn't have Kevin wandering the building in such a state, and he said he'd take care of him."

"That's dangerously vague," Denton said.

"It would seem so now," Caldwell agreed. "All right, look, we're in the rooftop conference room on the 42nd floor. Take the elevator up to 41, and the escalator to 42."

"We have a rooftop conference room?"

"Yes, it allows VIPs to helicopter in and out without drawing unwanted attention. The building is on lockdown, but I'll make sure security lets you in. I had Peter's building access revoked yesterday after I got his email, but *be careful* all the same."

Denton's caller ID flashed, announcing Dr. Jeffrey Lewis trying to reach him. Denton ignored it.

"Okay, I'm on my way."

"Please hurry Denton," Caldwell said. "I can stall the UAB negotiator for a *little* while, but the guy's a snooty stuffed shirt and he's not going to put up with me floating some conspiracy story without backup. He's got complete autonomy from United Alliance Insurance to accept any deal he sees fit at any moment, and the board will likely follow his direction. He already looks bored with all of us, so move it."

"Will do."

Denton hung up and made his way to the bedroom. After a couple of minutes, he emerged wearing pants and shoes. He looked at Fred.

"Well, we haven't figured out what Anderson would gain by sinking the company yet," Denton said. "But what we do know might help keep UAB afloat while they figure it out."

Denton pulled on his jacket and grabbed the laptop.

"You know," Fred said, "there's a more important question here."

"What's that?" Denton said as he headed for the door.

"If Anderson felt guilty and wanted to come clean and maybe save UAB, why did he send all this escheatment account info to Daniel Caldwell in code? Look how much time he wasted. I mean, didn't you say Daniel hated his riddles and brain teasers?"

Denton stopped mid-stride and stared straight ahead. Then he closed his eyes tight and mumbled to himself for a few moments. Then he opened them and turned back to Fred with a grin that concerned his friend slightly.

"No," Denton said. "That's not what I said."

"Are you okay?" Fred asked.

He nodded at his friend as he stuck his hand in his pocket and retrieved his phone.

"Yes. I think so. Probably."

"Probably?"

Denton shrugged at his friend. "We'll find out," he said.

"Should I come with you?" Fred asked.

"No," Denton said. "Stay here, go to Candace's whatever, but stay away from the building. If anything happens, I need someone out here who knows what went on."

"Jesus, Denton."

"Relax," Denton smiled and shook his phone at him. "I'm calling for backup."

Denton headed out. As he reached the door, he turned back to Fred and spoke into his phone.

"Carlson, hey, I need you … yeah, you wish. Look, I'm headed to UAB …"

Denton waved to Fred and left. Fred looked at the door with his head shaking. Then he grabbed his phone and called Candace.

MOMENTS LATER AT STREET LEVEL, Denton finished his call with Carlson and waved down a cab. He jumped in and gave the driver the address. Then he flipped open his laptop, plugged in Candace's flash drive and went to work.

No traffic on Sunday meant a twenty-minute ride at most. He'd fiddled around in his condo for ten minutes, so that left him roughly another ten to get in the building and up to the 42nd floor conference room. If Caldwell could stall Mr. Snooty Stuffed Shirt for just a few minutes, they'd …

"Oh, God," Denton said.

In a single swift movement Denton pulled his phone out, pressed a button, tucked it between his ear and shoulder and resumed his work on the laptop.

"Beth! It's me – this is an emergency. What does your father do?"

"Denton Rourke, I am *not* speaking to you—"

"Beth! Hate me later! WHAT DOES YOUR FATHER DO? EXACTLY?"

Beth recognized Denton's serious tone.

"Well, I don't quite know *exactly*. He's a legal liaison for the United Alliance companies."

"Would it be safe to say he's a *negotiator*?" Denton asked.

"Well, yes," Beth replied.

"And that he's at the UAB building right now to complete the Huntsman acquisition deal?"

Beth didn't respond immediately. Then:

"Denton, how did you know—"

"Okay, thanks. You may resume hating me now, but I'm really sorry about last night and I want to talk about it later. Iloveyoubye."

He hung up and resumed banging away on his keyboard.

"Shit!" he yelled.

"What is wrong?" the driver asked.

"Oh, nothing," Denton said, still working furiously. "My fiancée's father is either part of a criminal conspiracy to sink a Fortune 500 company, or a dupe who's in a lot of danger right now."

"I see," the man said. He offered no additional thoughts on the subject.

After a few more clicks, Denton pocketed his tools and closed the laptop. He checked his watch and then stared out the window.

He had fifteen minutes.

CHAPTER 40

As promised, the front desk guards let Denton right in and led him directly to the elevators without issue.

He rode up in complete silence, except for the sound of his heartbeat pounding in his ears. He felt the laptop shaking in his hands. He took a deep breath and tried to steady himself. He'd faced a lot of things in the past year and had fought through some pressure packed situations. But nothing like this.

Today Denton had to either bust Archibald Ingraham, or impress the hell out of him.

Denton's phone ripped through the silence and made Denton jump a foot in the air. He fumbled the contraption out of his pocket and banged on it angrily.

"Good God, what?"

A light chuckle came through from the other end followed by the very amused voice of Dr. Jeffrey Lewis.

"Well, hello to you, too Mr. Happy Face," he said. "Are you busy?"

"Not for the next two minutes, no."

"Good, I wanted to update you on Kevin Kahneman's – ahem – suicide."

"I'm ready," Denton said.

"If Mr. Kahneman is a suicide, he's the first victim I've seen who used someone else's hands to strangle himself."

"Murder," Denton said with a nod.

"Oh yes," Lewis said. "He had extensive bruising around his throat and a crushed windpipe. The pills he supposedly swallowed were stuffed into his mouth post mortem. Most of them never made it past his throat."

The elevator dinged and deposited Denton on the 41st floor. Denton walked quickly across the expansive lobby and toward the escalator.

"I'm about out of time, Lewis," Denton said. "Any last tidbits?"

"A couple of curious notes. Under his bandaged hand, Kahneman had a pretty severe abrasion. I took tissue samples and the wound contained traces of oil and pavement asphalt – just like the wound on Philip Anderson's head."

Denton slowed his walk as he digested that idea.

"Anything else?"

"Well, he tried to fight off his attacker," Lewis said. "He had a lot of material under his nails. Hair and skin from another party, and something else … one second."

Denton hit the escalator.

"Oh yes," Lewis continued, "hair, skin … and under one nail we found tiny particles of yellow-dyed silicone. I'm not sure what that's from yet."

Denton sighed. "I'll bet you lunch it came from one of those physical fitness bracelets people wear."

"Really? What makes you so sure?"

At the top of the escalator, Denton stared at the imposing figure of Peter Markung, dressed in a dark blue suit with a red tie. Denton glanced at the yellow fitness bracelet on the man's left wrist, and then at the black, military-grade knife he'd chosen as a final accessory.

"Just a hunch," he said. "Thanks for the help, Lewis."

Denton hung up the phone and put it away.

"Well, this is certainly a surprise," Denton said. Then he cocked his head and frowned. "Bad news, Peter – it looks like neither Anderson's nor Kevin Kahneman's deaths will be ruled suicides – and after all your hard work. Shoot."

Markung smiled. "Put the laptop down."

Denton complied. "It really is over," he said. "I figured it out. You won't get away with it."

"We'll see about that," Peter replied. "Who else knows what's on that laptop?"

Denton almost chuckled. "You can't possibly think I'm going to tell you."

Peter Markung's smile turned scary.

"Honestly, I *hoped* you would refuse," he said. "It'll be a lot more fun making you tell me."

With a flash of his left arm, Peter swung the butt of the knife across Denton's cheekbone. Denton had tried to lean away, but took most of the blow. He spun backward two steps and fell into the down escalator stairs.

Markung removed his jacket and put the knife down. Then he stepped into the stairs behind Denton.

"See? Isn't this better?"

Denton tried to rise, and Markung kicked him in the back of the leg. Denton collapsed again and rolled to the bottom of the escalator. Markung jogged down after. He grabbed Denton by his jacket and pulled him to his feet with one hand.

"Should I ask again?"

Denton's cheek throbbed and his heart pounded hard in his chest.

"What – you've had enough already? Some Iron Man you are."

Markung punched Denton in the stomach so hard that he started to black out.

"No no," Markung said as he slapped Denton's face repeatedly. "You stay with me. Let's go back up and start over, okay?"

Markung pulled him into the up escalator and slammed him down against the metal stairs. When he landed, Denton fired his foot up into the man's crotch. Markung groaned and began to fall forward on top of him. Denton managed to put his other leg up and catch the man's chest with his foot.

"Christ!" Denton moaned as Markung's full weight slowly pushed Denton's knee toward his chest. "How much do you weigh?"

Markung braced himself against the hand rail and punched Denton with his other fist. Denton pushed him back hard with his leg and scrambled upward.

Reaching the top, Denton tried to run, but fell on his face as Markung grabbed his ankle and dragged him backward.

Markung's face burned red with anger and his eyes suggested he might not care anymore whether Denton told him anything. He might just want to kill him.

Denton kicked out with his free foot and caught Markung in the temple. Markung smiled and yanked harder on Denton's ankle, effectively dragging him back to the escalator. Markung got to his feet at the top of the escalator and pulled Denton back up with one arm. With that same arm, he threw Denton back down the up escalator stairs. Denton hit them halfway down, landing hard on his back.

The stairs dragged him straight back to Markung. Denton scrambled to turn himself around as Markung watched him approach. Denton couldn't get to his feet and instead reached the top on all fours. Markung smiled as he knelt in front of the escalator, got eye to eye with Denton, and crashed his fist across his jaw, punctuating the right cross with a howl.

Denton flew backwards down the escalator once again. He hit hard and once again struggled back to all fours. His head swam and he saw blood dripping into the steel teeth of the stairs. He tried to shake away the dizziness as he gripped the railing with both hands and pulled himself to his knees. Exhausted, Denton leaned against the side and watched Markung's sadistic smile again getting closer.

Peter Markung resumed his kneeling position at the top and waited.

"I can do this all day, Denton," he yelled. "How about you?"

"Actually, I've got somewhere to be," Denton panted.

He reached the top and Peter cocked his right shoulder once more.

As Markung swung forward, Denton ducked under the punch, grabbed the man's tie, and jammed it into the staircase teeth as they rotated under the grate. Then he scrambled over the man and collapsed on the floor next to his laptop.

Markung's muscles bulged and burned as he tried to remain in the pushup position while the whirring metal stairs pulled more and more of his tie in. He tilted his neck upward and away as much as possible and his whole body shook as it attempted to defy the hungry churning below.

Though Markung's arms started to shake, Denton watched as the man managed to move his knees under him and get on all fours. Denton scooted back a bit further as Markung seemed to be loosening the escalator's grasp on him. He reached his left hand out toward Denton, who made no attempt to assist. A second later, he realized that had been the smart play, as Markung had not been asking for help.

He'd been reaching for his knife.

Markung gripped the weapon tightly and pulled his head further away from the gears below him, grinning wildly at Denton.

Without warning, Markung's convulsing right arm gave out and he collapsed face first onto the grate with a guttural cry. An unnatural popping sound came from his neck as his body bounced and shook against the still grinding escalator. After a few more disgusting seconds, the gears gave up their attempt to pull him under and ground to a halt.

Denton sat in the eerie silence and watched smoke billow out of the machinery below Markung. He felt his jaw and surmised that though very sore, he didn't think Markung had broken anything. He crawled around the floor, collecting what he needed, and then forced himself to his feet. He continued toward his destination, taking deep breaths to try and clear his head. After a minute or so of staggering forward, the conference room doors wobbled into focus in front of him.

When he reached them, he gripped the handle and closed his eyes for a moment. Then he nodded and burst into the room with a bright grin.

"Hello, everyone!" he announced. "Who ordered the large pepperoni with anchovies, extra financial fraud and a side of industrial grade embezzlement?"

All seven people in the room turned their grim faces to Denton's without comment. Daniel Caldwell stepped over to him.

"Denton! Thank God you're here," he said.

"Well, Mr. Caldwell," a voice from the table chimed in, "that's certainly a phrase I never expected anyone to utter … *good Lord* man, what happened to you?"

Denton looked past Daniel Caldwell and smiled.

"Hello, Mr. Ingraham," he said. "Good meeting?"

CHAPTER 41

Denton surveyed the rooftop conference room and found it pretty much as he'd imagined. A short entryway tiled in black marble gave way to a sunken meeting area furnished with the longest cherry wood and lacquer table in the history of civilization. The table ran nearly the length of the room and stopped just short of the back wall. The wall, a singular pane of glass with one door leading to the helipad provided an amazing view of the city. Black leather chairs surrounded the table and, to Denton, looked *really* comfortable at that moment.

Well, except for the six chairs currently occupied by the various grave stares and scowls, all pointed his direction. Five of the perturbed faces sat together on one side of the table. Four men, one woman all wearing suits of varying colors and all unknown to Denton. The sixth face, of course, belonged to Archibald Ingraham, who sat directly across from the other five and focused his gaze of perpetual disappointment on him. Denton thought he saw a dose of genuine concern in the man's face as well.

Caldwell looked at Denton closely.

"Mr. Ingraham's right, Denton. Are you okay?"

"Yeah, yeah. I just fell down the stairs a few times."

"Did you bring the account numbers?"

"Yes," Denton replied. "Did you tell them?"

Caldwell's smile revealed a mix of apology and discomfort.

"It's a little complicated, Denton," he said.

Denton stepped down to the table.

"You bet it's complicated, Daniel," he said. Then he addressed the group.

"Now, ladies and gentlemen, I called you all here today to discuss something very important: Having your parents spayed or neutered."

"Denton, what on Earth is wrong with you?" Archibald asked. "Are you *still* drunk?"

Caldwell joined Denton at the table.

"Denton, you've obviously had a very difficult week," he said. "Why don't you give me the account information we discussed and then go home and get some much deserved rest? We can work all this out in my office tomorrow morning."

"Now *that* would be complicated," Denton said. "Since you won't be here tomorrow. Or any other day, now will you?"

Caldwell looked around the table and then chuckled. "I don't think I'm following you."

Denton slapped his hand on top of the table.

"Oh give it *up*," he said. "You're right – it's been a long week. I'm tired, and irritated, and I know what you're up to, Daniel."

"Denton, really," Archibald said.

Denton pointed at Caldwell. "You told me you had no idea what Anderson could have been sending you. But yesterday you warned me about the complications involved in escheatment account coding."

He turned to the table and waved his flash drive.

"Well guess what kinds of accounts Anderson sent to Mr. Caldwell here. Anyone? If you said, 'Escheatment Accounts,' you've just won a trip to sunny Bangladesh."

He pocketed the drive and turned back to the COO, who frowned but said nothing as he walked over to his chair and stood next to his briefcase and laptop.

"And that makes perfect sense, really," Denton continued. "What better place to hide money you two were going to embezzle out of the company than in dormant accounts no one cares about?"

"Where is Peter?" Caldwell asked.

Denton furrowed his brow and put a finger on his chin. "Peter … Peter … oh, do you mean the hulking psycho who murdered Kevin Kahneman to keep him from screwing up your plan? The guy who you sent to Anderson's office over the weekend after you got his email?" Denton asked.

He fixed his eyes squarely on Daniel Caldwell.

"Well, I'm afraid he won't be much help to you now. He's down by the escalator … tying one on."

Oh my God, that was so James Bond.

"Anyway," Denton continued, "when Peter found Anderson dead in his office he quickly set it up to look like a suicide in the hopes of keeping the police and various federal agencies from sticking their noses in too far – as they might with a murder. Then he took Anderson's computer in order to control the flow of information."

"To whom?" Archibald asked.

Denton shook his head and stared at Caldwell with a burned smile.

"To me," he said.

Then he waved away his anger.

"But where was I? Oh yes, the great plan. Anderson cooks the books, hides the profits in dormant accounts and establishes transfers out of UAB to offshore banks."

Denton pointed at Caldwell's laptop. "You had the passwords and routing instructions, Anderson had the account numbers. Put them together and you're ready to go."

Denton turned to Archibald, whose eyes were widening with every sentence.

"Then Anderson grew a conscience and wanted out of the deal. But he went ahead and sent his dear friend Daniel the account numbers he needed … sort of. He sent them in his own cryptic way and Daniel needed someone to help him get to the account numbers."

He swung back around to Caldwell.

"You didn't send me rushing across town today to stop the acquisition signing," Denton said. "You don't care about that at all. You are out of time and you need those account numbers today."

"I don't know how you can say that," Caldwell said. "Of course, I'm not sure how you can say *any* of this really."

Denton made a face and shook his head. He addressed the room once again.

"Because tomorrow his own pet project – the automated escheatment system – goes online. And those dormant accounts where Anderson stashed the money will automatically disperse their funds to the state. And if that happens, there won't be anything he can do to get all that money back."

Denton sat down at the head of the table and looked at Caldwell.

"You know, I have to applaud the way you teased me with Anderson's mysterious files, but refused to let me see them. By the time Peter handed them over, even I thought decoding the account numbers was my idea, not yours. It was very clever."

Denton leaned forward and shook his head.

"But not nearly as clever as what Phillip Anderson did to you."

Denton took a moment to look around the table. Expressions remained unchanged, except for Archibald's, which took on a confused tint.

"Do you know why Phillip Anderson put the account numbers into a coded puzzle instead of just giving them to you outright in the first place?"

Caldwell frowned. "Enlighten me."

"Because he wanted to give you a chance to do the right thing," he said. "But he also wanted to make sure that if you didn't, that you'd go down hard."

The five faces across from Archibald shifted from irritated to confused and concerned.

"You told me you didn't *hate* Anderson's brainteasers. You just weren't any good at them. Anderson knew that, and he knew you'd have to involve someone else in order to get access to the account numbers you needed. He even recommended someone to help you out."

Denton smiled as he cocked his head.

"Me," he said. "He wanted someone to get those account numbers … just not you."

Caldwell flipped the latches on his briefcase and smiled at Denton.

"And yet you brought them to me anyway," Caldwell shook his head. "Not a very smart move, Denton."

"Come on," Denton said. "It's finished, Daniel – unless you'd care to try and explain yourself to these fine people here."

Caldwell looked around the room and then back to Denton with a bit of nervousness in his face.

"Well," he said. "I suppose I should give it a shot."

He turned back to the board members, lifted his briefcase lid, and smiled.

Denton's brain kicked into high gear and ran through the week with him once more.

Oh, shit.

He jumped from his seat.

"Ladies and gentlemen," Caldwell began.

They know.

"I need the account numbers Mr. Rourke is referring to in order to pay the outrageous bribes I promised you all in order to secure your approval of the sale of UAB to Huntsman."

"What?" Archibald's jaw dropped.

Caldwell pulled a silver gun from his briefcase and pointed it at Denton.

"Well, now, Denton," he said. "What do you say we make this takeover a little more hostile?"

CHAPTER 42

Caldwell grabbed Denton by his jacket and shoved him against the wall.

"Everyone, if you'll make your way to the helipad, our ride will arrive shortly."

As the group rose, Caldwell pointed his gun at Archibald.

"Not you, Mr. Ingraham," he said with a smile. "Please come and join the brilliant Denton Rourke."

"I wish people would stop saying that," Denton said.

"So do I," Caldwell agreed. "Not to worry, they'll soon be saying, 'The dearly departed Denton Rourke.' That has a much nicer ring to it."

Archibald rose and took his place next to Denton.

"Come on, Daniel, let him go," Denton said. "He's not involved in any of this."

Denton looked at Archibald. "That's right, isn't it?"

"Of course it's right!" Archibald said.

Caldwell hit Denton across the face with his gun and watched him crumple to the floor with a groan.

"Loose lips, Denton," Caldwell said.

Archibald leaned down and helped Denton back to his feet.

"Christ," Denton said. "Doesn't anyone *shoot* those things anymore?"

"Soon enough," Caldwell nodded.

"Really?" Denton looked at him. "You can't contract this kind of thing out?"

Caldwell shook his head. "Not on such short notice. Besides, it's good for the boss to do some of the heavy lifting sometimes."

"That's quite the work ethic for a thief."

"And aspiring murderer," Archibald added.

"Gentlemen," Caldwell sighed as he watched his board members walk out the platform, "you make this sound like some kind of smash and grab robbery by a common street punk. It's so much bigger than that."

"It always is," Denton said. "You had to have the acting board involved. You needed the takeover to go through so that by the time the dust settled and all the assets were transferred, any monetary or account discrepancies could be chalked up to system errors during the merger of two giant company platforms. It would take months – maybe longer – before they discovered the truth."

"If ever." Caldwell smiled. "And that's just part of the process. Denton, do you have any idea what it *really* takes to siphon off two billion dollars in profits and make it look like a loss?"

"No."

"Actually, not as much as I thought going in, to be honest. Anderson really handled all the math, so you can ask him for the specifics. Oh, sorry – of course you can't. How stupid of me."

He pointed the gun at Denton.

"Now, the flash drive, please."

Denton's mouth opened without words. He looked at Archibald, and back to Daniel. He chuckled with a nervous smile.

"Come on, you think I *really* brought you the account numbers?"

"Yes," Caldwell said. "Quickly, please."

Denton frowned but took the drive out and extended it to Caldwell.

Caldwell snatched it from him and gave it a once over.

"So this is what two billion dollars looks like," he said. "Isn't technology wonderful?"

He backed away from the two men and reached his laptop. He

opened the lid and plugged in the flash drive. After a couple of clicks, he looked up at Denton.

"You've got dozens of files on here," he said. "What am I looking for?"

"Hopefully a clean conscience," Denton suggested. "In which case you'll want to just let us go now."

Caldwell scratched his chin. "Nope, that's not it."

He pointed his gun at the two men once more.

"File name, Denton – now. Or would you like me to shoot your fiancée's father right in front of you?"

Denton rolled his eyes over to Archibald, who smiled awkwardly.

"We were talking earlier," he said. "He must have put two and two together."

"Really? And just what the hell were you talking about that let him put this together?"

"Well, in my defense, I didn't know all of … *this* at the time."

"NOW, Denton," Caldwell ordered.

Denton looked over at Caldwell. "Jesus, Daniel – it's not that hard to figure out. It's the one titled 'Account Numbers Decoded'."

Caldwell nodded. "I see it, thank you."

The muted yet unmistakable roar of helicopter engines and blades reached them. Caldwell looked out onto the helipad and smiled as their ride landed. He snapped his laptop shut and held it close as he returned to Denton and Archibald.

"Now, gentlemen, let's go out and enjoy the glorious view from the helipad."

The two men marched toward the exit. Denton's stomach started jumping. As Archibald pushed the door open, Denton slumped against the wall.

"I don't like heights," he said, turning to Caldwell.

"You'll be on the ground soon enough," Caldwell replied. "Until then, hold on tightly to Archibald."

Denton turned to the man and held his arms out in a pre-hug formation.

"Really, now," Archibald protested.

"I can't help it!" Denton said.

"The actual helipad is more than two hundred and fifty feet beyond the door," Caldwell said. "Now move!"

He shoved Denton into Archibald. Denton grabbed the man and held on. Archibald helped him through the door and onto the deck.

No longer blocked by the thick glass, the deafening noise of the helicopter engines pulsed into their ears. Denton latched on to Archibald as they moved toward the helicopter. He tried to focus on the solid and sturdy concrete below his feet, but when they were close enough to feel the wind from the raised chopper platform, his legs buckled. He slid down Archibald's body and clutched the man's pant leg.

"Jesus Christ, Denton," Caldwell yelled as he started laughing. "This is pathetic!"

Denton mumbled something inaudible.

Caldwell leaned in. "Say again?"

"Peter had a ..." Denton yelled.

"What about Peter?" Caldwell knelt down. "What did he have?"

Denton leaned closer, rolling his eyes in frustration. Then he swung around fast and slammed his hand into Caldwell's arm.

Caldwell howled and stumbled backward, falling to the ground and dropping his gun.

"A knife," Denton yelled.

But Caldwell didn't hear him, as he found himself distracted by the 4-inch blade sticking through both sides of his forearm.

"Run!" Denton yelled to Archibald.

Archibald complied, sort of. In his panic, he ran toward the helicopter.

"Jesus Christ, Archie!"

Denton ran after him, grabbed him by his tweed jacket and spun the startled man around.

"Away from the bad guys! *Away* from—"

Gunfire erupted from behind them and shards of concrete shrapnel flew past their heads. Denton held on to Archibald and pulled him toward a large metal transformer box on the far side of the helipad platform.

"Get behind it!" Denton called out.

Archibald nodded his understanding, but a moment later collapsed, dragging Denton to the ground with him still several feet short of safety.

"I believe I've been shot, Denton," Archibald announced loudly through heavy breathing.

Denton turned to see Caldwell running up the helipad toward a beckoning pilot, but still pointing the gun at his two escapees. He looked down at Archibald.

"Where, Mr. Ingraham?"

"Upper left thigh," Archibald answered. "Denton, get yourself to safety."

Denton looked at his father-in-law to-be as another gunshot rang out and ricocheted off their intended shelter. He grinned at the man.

"Like bloody hell I will," he said.

He moved around Archibald, grabbed him under his arms, and pulled the man slowly as more gunshots rang out.

Denton lost his grip and fell on his back with a groan. He struggled to sit up and he saw Caldwell leaning out of the helicopter, lining up another shot. But the pilot, for some reason very eager to leave, pulled him back into his seat.

Denton recovered and resumed pulling Archibald.

"Denton, desist!" Archibald demanded. "I'm slowing you down," he said. "Good lord, man, I'm shot!"

"Yeah, well … you'll have to do better than that," Denton said. With a final lurch and an exhausted moan, he dragged Archibald behind the transformer box and collapsed.

"Because I am, too," he said.

As he watched the tail of the helicopter slowly rise, Denton tried to ignore the pain coming from below his right shoulder.

DANIEL CALDWELL GRITTED HIS TEETH and glanced at the gash in his forearm where his former lackey's knife had recently resided. Still holding his gun, he cursed Denton Rourke and reopened his laptop.

"Fly!" he yelled at the pilot, noting the helicopter's failure to rise more than a few feet off the helipad.

"I have to wait for the wind to die down, sir," the pilot explained.

Caldwell ignored him. He opened the directory for the flash drive and found the file he needed.

ACCOUNT NUMBERS – DECODED

Caldwell double-tapped the pointer pad and smiled to his passengers.

"We're in business, everyone."

No one replied. A moment later, his laptop screen started flickering. As Caldwell clicked random keys in furious confusion, a bright light flashed out from the machine's air vent, and he smelled smoke.

He looked again at the pilot.

"Why are we not airborne?"

Then a sickening weight hit the pit of his stomach as the screen went black.

"My laptop!" he screamed.

He ripped the flash drive from the machine and looked at its now-scorched connecting hub.

"Don't worry about it," a voice behind him yelled.

Caldwell turned in his seat to see a smiling man waving a badge at him.

"Where you're going there are plenty of laptops you can use," Russell Carlson said. "No *computers*, of course, but I think—"

Still looking at Carlson, Daniel Caldwell shot the pilot in the kneecap and jumped the short distance back to the helipad.

The pilot screamed out and clutched the wound as the helicopter pitched hard to the right. The passengers grabbed on to the nearest handrails while Carlson tried to get hold of the flight stick.

Caldwell landed solidly and kept low as the helicopter spun and swayed slowly above him. He hopped off the raised platform and fired another shot at the bird as he walked slowly toward the transformer box.

"Denton Rourke!" he called out.

"I'm right here, dumbass," Denton yelled back.

Caldwell turned away from the helipad and the transformer box and saw Denton sitting against a concrete barrier not fifteen feet from him, squinting into the sun. Denton waved at him as he approached.

"Hey," Denton said, breathing heavily. "Do you have any idea what it *really* takes to get a criminal to destroy his own assets and make him look like an idiot?"

Caldwell seethed. "You son of a bitch."

"Actually, not as much as I thought—"

The remark turned into a scream of pain as Caldwell knelt down and jammed the barrel of his gun into Denton's bullet wound.

After a few seconds of listening to him, Caldwell stood up and smiled.

"Oh, I'm sorry, Denton. Did that hurt?"

He grabbed Denton by his bad arm and dragged him across the ground toward the roof's edge, firing random shots at the helicopter which now rose and sank in jerky, awkward lurches.

Within a few feet of the edge, Caldwell let go of Denton, who hit the concrete with another scream. Caldwell checked the gun's clip, nodded and slammed it back into the handle.

"Don't worry. I doubt you'll feel this one at all!"

"I've heard that before," Denton called out.

Caldwell backed away a few paces and wiggled the gun.

"I'm afraid your little stunt with the knife has forced me to use my left hand to shoot you. Hopefully I won't miss too many times. I need to save a couple of bullets for Archie over there."

"He prefers Archibald, dickweed."

"Enough," Caldwell said. "Good-bye, Denton!"

"I THINK I GOT IT!" Carlson shouted to his terrified passengers as he got himself adjusted in the Co-Pilot seat. He pulled hard back on the stick as though it were a train conductor's brake.

"Shit!" Carlson and – in fact – everyone on board screamed.

DENTON ROURKE WOULD ARGUE that only slightly less terrifying than being aboard a helicopter piloted by a man with no flight experience and zero natural ability is being on the ground within a few feet of said chopper and its cursing, uncoordinated non-pilot.

For when Carlson attempted to land the helicopter by turning it upside down three feet above the ground, the ornery machine slammed its landing skids into the very edge of the helipad and then tried to buck the novice pilot out by jerking its cabin upward to the sky while driving its tail down into the ground no more than ten feet from Denton's position.

Daniel Caldwell would have agreed with Denton. But he'd had his back to the helicopter as he prepared to shoot Denton from about … ten feet away – and thus had missed the entire aerial calamity.

Denton did his best to cover his head as the blades came apart with a scream of bending metal, broken gears, and exploding pavement. As debris flew around him and the engine whine grew closer, Denton stayed still and focused on a simple idea.

I have got to stop working for criminals.

After what felt like an hour, the engines stalled and the air started to settle. As the noise died away, Denton moved his arms from over his head and looked at the helicopter with its cabin still pointed upward into the air and its rear blades anchoring it to the rooftop.

As a sea of blue police uniforms poured onto the helipad, Denton looked down and saw that Daniel Caldwell had dropped his gun during the chaos. Then he noticed the careless man had also dropped an arm, both feet, one of his legs, and most of his internal organs.

"Came apart under pressure," Denton said.

That's not James Bond; that's just gross.

"Rourke!" Carlson called out as he came running. He stopped in front of Denton and pointed at the helicopter.

"Did you see that? Did you see—Jesus … is this Caldwell?"

Denton nodded. Then Carlson saw the gunshot.

"Denton, how bad is it?"

"I don't know, Carlson," Denton said with his eyes closed. "How much of this blood is mine?"

Carlson knelt down and pulled back Denton's jacket to reveal the wound. He closed the jacket back up.

"Too much," he said. "Just sit tight, we'll get you taken care of."

Denton's eyes popped open. "Mr. Ingraham!" he shouted.

"I'm here," Archibald called out. He looked out from behind the transformer box and waved.

"Carlson, help me," Denton said, extending his good hand.

Carlson grabbed him under his arm and pulled him to his feet. The two made their way to Beth's father, Denton leaning most of his weight on Carlson. Denton looked down at him, still squinting and shielding his eyes.

"Are you okay, Mr. Ingraham?" Denton said.

"Please call me Archibald," he said. "The bullet went clean through. I'll be fine."

Carlson nodded. "Stay put," he said. "I radioed the station and we've got medical help on the way."

Denton smiled at him and steadied his balance.

"Land the helicopter, stop the bad guy, save the passengers and the negotiator … not bad at all, Carlson."

"Yeah, well, they didn't hire me just for my good looks."

"Denton," Archibald said.

Denton looked down at him.

"You dragged me behind this silly metal box and then took a position in the direct line of fire of that madman."

Denton nodded. "Yes."

"You were trying to draw attention away from me."

Denton tried to smile.

Archibald looked down at the ground.

"What a damn fool thing to do," he said.

"Yeah, he's stupid like that sometimes," Carlson added.

"Sit with me a moment, will you, Denton?" Archibald asked.

With Carlson's assistance, Denton slid down and leaned against the box with a groan.

"I'll be right back," Carlson said. "We'll get you both to the hospital in half a sec."

Archibald nodded and watched him depart. Then he turned to Denton.

"Denton, you should know that as a rule I do not approve of the men Elizabeth chooses to date."

"I've been told," Denton said. His body felt heavy.

"Yes, well. I'd like you to know that I'm proud – very proud – of the man she's chosen to marry."

"Thank you," Denton said. "But I think she's the one you should tell. Your opinion means a lot to her. Are you cold? I'm freezing," he slurred.

Archibald chuckled.

"In spite of your inexplicable behavior, I believe you to be smart, kind, brave, and a good person."

"Well," Denton closed his eyes to shield them from the light which grew more intense. "They say daughters are attracted to men like their fathers."

Archibald smiled. "Quite," he said. The he looked at Denton and frowned.

"Denton?"

Denton's eyes did not open.

"Denton!" Archibald slapped him several times.

"Christ, yes – I'll get a calendar," Denton mumbled.

Then he slid away from the metal box and lay unconscious on the ground.

CHAPTER 43

Denton liked floating. Floating was fun. He felt so light – weightless, really. Movement came effortlessly and without pain.

"Mr. Rourke."

Floating is too noisy.

"Mr. Rourke, are you awake?"

Just be still. They'll leave.

"Nurse?"

Floating, floating ... float— what in the hell is that stench?

Denton shook his head side to side and swung his arm at his nose. Then he screamed out in pain as he stretched the gunshot wound in his chest.

"What? What?"

"Ah, Mr. Rourke, you're with us at last."

Denton opened his eyes and looked at the gray-haired man in glasses and a dark gray suit with a blue tie who sat next to him. He glanced past him at a very large hole in the door through which he could see scenery flying by at a pretty decent speed. His brain joined his body in its newly awakened state.

"Am I in a *helicopter*?"

"A Helivac, yes. You're on your way to Roosevelt Memorial Hospital. You gave us a bit of a scare on the UAB rooftop."

Denton opened his eyes and looked at the man.

"Who are you?"

The man smiled. "My name is Andrew Binder." He held a government identification card in front of Denton.

"I'm the Secretary of the Treasury for the United States of America."

"You smell terrible," Denton said.

Binder chuckled. "That's the smelling salts, I'm afraid. I'm sorry, but we don't have much time so I needed you conscious."

"I'm off duty," Denton said. "No more cases right now."

Binder smiled. "Mr. Rourke, a lot has happened since we left that rooftop, and you and Fred now have important choices to make about your futures."

Denton's eyes opened fully again.

"What?"

"Relax, it's really a very easy decision," he said. He opened a file folder and looked at it briefly.

"Now, Denton, I'd like to help you remember what happened at United Alliance Bank."

"I already remember what happened."

"I mean what *officially* happened."

Denton nodded.

"Yes, of course … no, wait … what?"

"Denton, the sale of United Alliance Bank to Huntsman bank will go through."

"But UAB's been making money!"

Binder shook his head. "Unfortunately, that doesn't matter anymore."

"How can it not matter?"

"Denton, UAB has been – was, one of the most beloved banks in the country – trusted by its customers more than Huntsman by a wide margin. But the past two years of dismal earnings eroded that trust. And now, with this week's news that the company employed a psychotic who went on a killing spree inside the building, UAB is finished."

"But now we know the truth," Denton said. "UAB was making a

profit."

Binder shook his head.

"If word gets out that for *two years* UAB's earnings reports – and therefore their stock prices – have been bogus, and that in addition the current banking regulations still missed a senior executive colluding with a board of directors to steal billions of dollars from their customers, UAB will *still* sink. But it will take with it all the work we've done to rebuild a little bit of consumer confidence and hope in our financial markets."

Binder patted Denton's arm. "Please understand that neither version of the truth will save UAB now," he said. "I'm sorry, but it's just too late. I'm asking you and Fred to help us make the best of an awful situation."

"I don't know," Denton said. "I'm not sure this feels right."

Binder smiled and raised a finger to the air.

"Ah – well that's why I'm here – to help you review your options."

He opened his file and read.

"Option One – Denton Rourke is lauded as a hero who used his brilliant mind to foil an undisclosed financial scandal at United Alliance Bank. The SEC and the Department of the Treasury are now investigating, but no further details are available."

Binder turned the page.

"As a reward for uncovering and reporting the issue, the United States will issue Mr. Rourke a tax-free cash reward equal to ten years of his current annual salary."

"What?"

"*And* Mr. Rourke's chances of *ever* being audited by the IRS will inexplicably fall to zero."

"Fred gets this, too?"

"Let's just say Mr. Maxton was last seen dropping next year's 1040 tax form in his shredder and doing a little dance."

Binder put the file back in his briefcase and retrieved a second one.

"Now, I am required to offer you the second option as well."

"Okay."

Binder pushed his glasses up and read.

"Option Two – Denton Rourke blows his status as a hero by routinely demanding that people listen to his wild stories of conspiracies involving earnings manipulation, escheatment account transfer fraud, and corrupt senior leaders. The press represents them as the ravings of a shell-shocked lunatic and Mr. Rourke's reward – and all hopes of a real job – evaporate. And after ten straight years of IRS audits, Mr. Rourke and his squeaky clean conscience accept the fact that eleven years straight is just around the corner."

He closed the file.

"Any questions?"

"One," Denton said. "Can you send my reward via direct deposit?"

Binder smiled. "We already have."

Denton closed his eyes. Then they popped open again on their own.

"Wait," he said. "Are the board members involved getting this deal, too?"

Binder shook his head. "They're going to jail for short terms for various crimes outside the UAB world. Their reward for silence is not getting fifty years apiece."

The Treasury Secretary stood up and moved out of the way, allowing a nurse to take his spot at Denton's bedside.

"I'm going to give you something for the pain, Mr. Rourke," she said.

"Can I have something to drink?"

"I'm afraid not," she said. "You're going into surgery as soon as we land."

Denton had many questions about his surgery, and his friends, but they would have to wait.

Because he really liked floating.

# # #

JOSEPH HANDEL STEPPED OUT of his limousine and walked across the underground parking garage toward the shadowy figure. As he closed in, the man stepped into the light and smiled.

"Well, hello, Joseph," Ohnemus Parker said.

"Don't give me that bullshit, Parker," Handel said. "Let's just get this over with."

Parker smiled again and put up his hands.

"Okay, Joseph, okay. Whatever you say."

Joseph frowned and shook his head. He looked around to make sure he had walked far enough from the limo so that they could not be heard. Then he leaned forward a little bit.

"I'm sorry," he said.

"Sorry for what?" Parker asked.

"Oh, come on!"

"Now, Joseph, Mr. Binder was very specific about this. You are sorry for *what*?"

"I'm sorry for colluding with Daniel Caldwell to take over your company. But I swear – and Ohnemus, I mean this – I swear I didn't know he was cooking your books. I didn't even talk to him until a year ago, and that's the truth."

Parker smiled. "I believe you, and you are forgiven."

"Your turn," Handel said.

"Ah yes," Parker removed a sheet of paper from the pocket of his white suit jacket.

"Joseph," Parker read with sincerity and warmth, "I am sorry for allowing you to be photographed in front of the UAB logo and making you look foolish in front of millions of people. Furthermore, I am sorry for stealing your thunder and your CD rates in front of millions of people. Also, I'm very sorry for manipulating your teleprompter and making you look fooli—"

"Enough, enough, you're forgiven, shut up," Handel growled.

Parker smiled and extended his hand. Handel looked at it as though checking for a joy buzzer, then shook.

"Don't forget your promise to Binder," Parker said.

"I know, I know. All UAB employees keep their jobs and their pay for a minimum of one year and receive at least a year's salary as severance if they're let go after that time."

"Very good – and …"

Handel rolled his eyes like a scolded child. "And I will not take any cheap shots at UAB's recent issues, its leadership, or its people at my sign unveiling this week."

Then he pointed at Parker.

"And *you* won't screw with the event. It's *my* building now, Parker, so don't—"

"Make you look like a fool in front of millions," Parker finished the thought. "I agree."

Handel nodded. "Well … okay, then. I guess that's that. So, what are you going to do now?"

Parker looked skyward and took a deep breath.

"You know, I'm not sure yet. I'll just get out there and have a little fun, I suppose."

"Well … good luck."

Parker smiled at Joseph Handel.

"You, too," he said. "Have fun at the sign unraveling."

"*Unveiling*," Handel corrected as he walked away.

Parker watched the man get back in his limo and drive out of the garage. Only when the car had disappeared down the street did he let his smile fall.

CHAPTER 44

Denton's doctors proclaimed his surgery a great success and patted themselves on the back. When Denton finally awoke two days later, he proclaimed the post-surgery painkillers a great success in their own right, and spent a couple of days smiling at everyone with no clear reasons for doing so.

As the afternoon of day three turned into night, the hospital cut Denton's painkiller dosage and his memories came back for a visit. He remembered Tim Sowell coming by on his own to discuss his reinstatement and the formal apologies Captain Levine had to make in front of the mayor just prior to his taking early retirement.

Carlson had stopped by, too. He talked about a forthcoming commendation, or a raise, or something positive.

Fred and Candace were there, and Fred was saying something about money. And his dad had come by every day – several times, Denton thought. He'd smiled a lot and told him he was proud of his son. Did Connor have another son?

And of course he remembered Beth. She'd visited the first night. He remembered seeing her through blurred eyes, and though he couldn't talk, he had tried.

Denton moved his shoulder a bit and winced at the pain, which some doctor at some point told him would linger for … some amount of time.

He closed his eyes again and tried to relax, telling himself things would be even clearer by the morning. And when morning arrived, Denton sat up as best he could and waited for clearness. And breakfast.

Breakfast arrived first, delivered by a stone-faced nurse in pink scrubs with a confetti pattern. She placed the food in front of him and picked up his chart.

"Hi, Anna," Denton said with a smile. "I am awake."

"That's wonderful, Mr. Rourke," Anna said without looking up from the clipboard.

Denton lifted the lid on his breakfast, and then put it straight back down.

"Okay, so I've been kind of out of it for a few days," he said. "What's the word around Roosevelt Memorial?"

Anna's eyes stayed focused on the clipboard as she wrote something.

"Why don't you go ask your Brit friend down the hall in 704?" she suggested. She slid the clipboard back into its holder and looked at him.

"After all, he knows *everything.*"

Denton watched her leave and smiled as he imagined Archibald Ingraham instructing the nurses on proper bedpan etiquette. He took his time moving his legs over the side of the bed and stood up. His chest still hurt – a lot, but he could manage. He shuffled over to the closet and found his clothes.

Sort of. He eyed the items with suspicion. They looked like they would fit, but were not what he'd been wearing when he got shot.

Oh yeah.

White button down shirt. Dark blue jeans. Light black jacket.

Black shoes.

This is Beth's doing.

Denton dressed himself and tried not to scream when he slipped his right arm into his shirt. He repeated the process with the jacket. For some reason, it seemed impossible to reach down to his feet without eliciting blackout-grade pain from his wound, so he plodded down to Archibald's room barefoot.

Arriving at the door, Denton peeked in, but then barged into the room when he saw Connor Rourke leaning over the railing of the man's bed, speaking quietly.

"Dad, don't kill him!" Denton pleaded.

Connor turned and Archibald looked over at him.

"You're in a hospital," Denton said. "They'll just revive him anyway."

Connor grinned and walked up to his son. He gave him a hug which cost Denton all the air in his lungs.

"What are you doing out of bed, Denton?" Archibald asked.

"I heard six or eight nurses talking about heading down to your room so they could take turns practicing rectal thermometer insertion skills on their favorite patient."

Archibald allowed himself a brief chuckle. "With my luck, they couldn't even get that right."

Denton smiled. "How are you, Mr. Ingraham?"

"Please, call me *Archibald*, Denton. And I'm doing well. Full recovery expected and I'm being released shortly."

"Excellent, glad to hear it."

Connor smiled and slapped Denton's good shoulder.

"Okay, son, I've got to run take care of a few things, but I'll come back to see you in a bit." He turned to Archibald.

"And if I don't see you before, I'll see you next week."

"Next week?" Denton asked.

"Yep," Connor said. "In Ireland. Just some land stuff we're working on."

With a wink, Connor departed and left Denton alone with Archibald. Denton looked to the man for an explanation. Archibald smiled and sighed.

"As I said in the restaurant, the truth of the Rourke / Ingraham feud is hard to pin down," he said. "It's true that Devlin Rourke never bought back the land he sold to John Ingraham. However, it's not clear if that was because he never had the money ..."

Archibald paused. Then he looked out the window.

"...or because John Ingraham demanded double the value to sell it back to him."

"I see," Denton nodded.

Archibald looked at Denton and smiled.

"Yes, well, your father and I are going to spend some time in Ireland. We'll walk the land, tell some stories, and see what kind of transfer agreement we can dream up."

"Well, well," Denton said with a smile. "I'm unconscious for a few days and the whole world changes."

"Indeed," Archibald said with something other than levity in his voice. He looked at Denton.

"Denton—"

"Denton?"

Turning around, Denton saw Beth in the doorway.

"What are you doing here?" she asked as she approached her father's bedside.

Denton hugged her and she returned it, but released quickly.

"I just came down to see how your father is making out," Denton said, still smiling at Beth.

"Yes, I'll be right as rain in no time," Archibald said. "Thanks to you, Denton."

"Daddy stop it," Beth said.

"Elizabeth …" her father pleaded.

Beth stood up.

"Denton, I would like to speak to you outside, please."

She moved past him and out the door without waiting for an answer. Denton watched the door close and then looked back at Beth's father. Archibald made eye contact for a moment, but then found a sudden and severe interest in the nutritional information insert that accompanied his breakfast. Denton headed out into the hall and found Beth standing by the coffee maker in a waiting area across the hall. He walked as quickly as he could, preparing his apology as she crossed her arms and frowned at his approach.

"Beth, I'm so sorry. I've behaved horribly and I have no right to make you suffer and stress—"

"Here," Beth said, extending her right hand.

Denton looked down at the engagement ring she held, and then looked into her eyes.

"Beth, come on. I really am sorry. Really."

"And I really believe you – really. But that's neither here nor there any longer. I'm leaving the U.S."

"You're what?" Denton's head swam. "What are you talking about?

Beth looked at him. "I'm leaving the country, and I'm leaving you, Denton. I'm tired of waiting, I'm tired of the excuses."

"But … at UAB …"

"You saved my father, Denton. I'll always, *always* be indebted to you for that. You don't know what that means to me. But you and I aren't going …"

Beth's voice caught in her throat. She looked down, put her hand over her mouth, and choked off a single sob. Then she took a deep breath, blinked at the ceiling, and looked back at him. She extended the ring again.

"You and I aren't going any further."

"Beth, don't do this," Denton begged. "I'll do anything you say. I already picked a date – April third. I'll move it up or back or whatever you want. I know I've been an idiot—"

"No, Denton," Beth said firmly. "You've just been *you*. And I've waited for you to be something else. *I've* been the idiot."

Denton couldn't respond. His knees felt gummy and his brain seemed to spin without any direction.

"But … your Master's degree. You're not done yet."

"I've spoken to my counselor and she's reaching out to a number of universities in England. I should be able to finish without an issue."

"When did you do all that?" he asked. "How long—"

"Take the ring, Denton," Beth said. "I've got a plane to catch."

"What – today?" Denton said a little too loudly.

"Yes. So here," she put the ring in front of him again.

Denton's world continued to collapse in front of him. How could she leave him? Why wasn't his apology working? Without knowing what else to do, he decided to keep her there by being himself.

"No," he said. "I refuse to take it back. I got it for you because I love you and want to spend the rest of my life—"

Beth turned and dropped the ring into the waiting room coffee pot. Denton stared wide eyed as she looked at him.

"If that were true," she said, "we wouldn't be here, now would we?"

She brushed by him and disappeared around a corner. Denton watched her go, numb from the neck up. A man with a Styrofoam cup approached, and Denton grabbed the coffee pot away and took it into the men's room. He poured the coffee into the sink and collected the ring. Then, after depositing the empty pot in front of a slightly confused man, he made his way back to Archibald's room and knocked softly. Archibald's voice came back in reply.

"Come in, Denton."

Denton entered and collapsed into the chair next to Archibald's bed. The man looked at him with tired eyes.

"I'm so sorry," he said. Denton knew he meant it.

"A friend once told me British women are known for their patience and understanding of even the most frustrating of situations," Denton suggested.

"Then I would venture to say your friend has never kept a young British girl waiting for her future to begin," Archibald said with a sad smile. "I can't tell you how awful I feel about this. I spoke to her for you, I really did. I told her the same things I told you on that rooftop."

He stopped for a moment and turned his eyes toward the ceiling.

"But she appears to have made her mind up."

"Can I change it?" Denton asked. "I picked a date – April third."

Archibald's eyebrows rose.

"Her grandmother's birthday?"

Denton nodded. "She always talks about how much she meant to her. I thought that'd be nice."

Archibald stared at Denton for a long moment. Then he turned toward the window.

"I'm sorry, Denton. I truly believe I would have enjoyed having you as my son-in-law."

Denton's throat tightened as he tried to digest Archibald's words.

"Me too," he mustered. Then, "Take care of yourself, Mr. Ingraham."

"*Archibald*," he said, "Please. And you do the same."

Denton nodded quickly. He backed a few steps away from the man who would have been family, then turned and wandered into the hallway.

# # #

HENRY SORRELL SMILED at Denton as he came in the door. Then he took a good look at his friend and altered his emotion.

"Denton, are you okay? Are you supposed to be out of the hospital? Did you walk here in that rain?"

"No," Denton said. He walked past his normal booth and took his old seat at Henry's bar counter. He grabbed a menu and pointed at the TV.

"Can you turn this up?"

Henry looked up at the FNN coverage and shrugged.

"Sure, Denton. I didn't think you'd want to watch this, but it's your call."

Denton continued to stare at Joseph Handel, who stood in front of the UAB building and prepared to officially change its name.

Henry dropped off a milkshake, still watching Denton closely.

"Denton, do you need me to call anyone? Is Beth coming?"

"She left for England today," Denton replied.

"Ah, very nice. When's she coming home?"

"She's *going* home, Henry."

"Okay, so when's she coming *back*?"

Denton stared at the screen.

"She isn't."

He turned to Henry.

"I did it, Henry," he said. "I let Rome fall."

Henry slung the dishtowel over his shoulder, walked around the counter and joined Denton.

The door chimed and Fred Maxton approached. He put a hand lightly on Denton's shoulder.

"I got your text," he said simply. Then he sat down on the other side of his friend.

On screen, Joseph Handel smiled and read from his teleprompter.

"… and today we embark on another great adventure as the Huntsman Bank family welcomes our newest member, United Alliance Bank."

Tim Sowell and Russell Carlson appeared behind Denton.

"Denton, would you care to guess why we're here?" Sowell asked. "I'll give you a hint: it involves a call from the hospital and a patient who took his painkillers and walked out."

"Shh," Denton said as he pointed at the screen.

Carlson shrugged at Sowell and both men found barstools of their own as Handel continued.

"…so let me just say to both our new employees and our new customers alike that gone are the days of reckless management, of mediocre performance, and dangerous working environments. Because now you belong to Huntsman."

As the smattering of applause quickly faded, Handel waved over a man in a hardhat who gave him the remote switch which would trigger the drop of the vinyl banner covering the new Huntsman sign over the main entrance.

"What an ass," Fred said.

"I see a few extra parking tickets in his future," Carlson said with a snicker.

Denton wasn't listening. Without a word, he stood up on his barstool and climbed onto the counter.

"Denton, what are you doing?" Henry asked.

Denton walked up the television and stared as Handel babbled on.

"And now, if you'll direct your attention to the banner behind me, I'd like to present the new Huntsman Bank Tower!"

Denton pointed at something on the screen.

"Gotcha," he said. Then he scooted back down off the bar and sat down once more.

Handel turned and pressed the button. The vinyl banner dropped away on command and revealed the new Huntsman logo. The new sign stood in tall, majestic letters of dark green and silver and shone against the light of the early sunset.

Then it exploded.

Then it fell off the side of the building.

And then it landed on Handel's limousine.

In the ensuing commotion, the FNN producers forgot to turn off Handel's live microphone, and the Huntsman CEO treated the million-plus audience to a fascinating show featuring his colorful, four-letter descriptions of police officers and firefighters whom he did not believe were moving their "fat asses" quickly enough, followed by open weeping at the sight of his precious limo crushed below the flaming Huntsman logo.

As the counter at Ford's erupted in laughter and back slapping, Denton watched the man in the hardhat walk away from the scene, his wiry gray hair sticking out the sides of his helmet. Though he couldn't swear, he thought he saw the man wink at the camera as moved off screen.

Henry turned off the TV. All eyes turned to Denton.

"So what happens now?" Henry asked.

No one spoke. And for a long time no one moved.

Finally, Denton rose and headed for the exit. He stopped at the door and turned to the gang at the counter.

"What does anyone do when everything collapses?" he asked. Then he answered.

"They rebuild."

Without further discussion on that matter or any other, he left Ford's Diner.

Once on the rain-splashed pavement, Denton took as deep a breath as he could, turned toward the sunset, and started walking. He passed block after city block without stopping, and as one mile turned into two, Denton felt his head starting to clear. When two gave way to three, his mind dumped all its baggage. And as he began mile four, Denton Rourke found himself focused on a singular thought – the one thing in the world he knew to be completely true and absolutely undeniable.

I should have taken those shoes from the hospital.

ACKNOWLEDGMENTS

Once again, a large group of wonderful, supportive people exceeded expectations and helped make this novel a reality.

Performance bonuses are awarded to Nikki Folsom, Lesli Hicks, Nathan Kuntz, and Angela Nowicki.

Nikki and Nathan were forced to endure a very early and terribly rough draft and were both able to provide much-needed insights and perspectives. Lesli and Angela took editing to a new level and caught the countless typos, missing words, and odd bits of misplaced story I left lying about. These four made the book readable. Really.

KJ Feder Delgado agreed to handle the graphics and design work this time around and had to put up with helpful feedback like, "Is that blue enough?" Not only did she deliver a fantastic cover, but her incredible efforts allowed me to spend more time focusing on getting the story, "just right." I couldn't have asked for a better collaborator.

Specific roles aside, it's impossible to imagine working through this book without the support I've received from a host of friends and family who all seem to know just when to reach out with a word or two of encouragement.

Thank you all.

ABOUT THE AUTHOR

Ian O'Regan continues to amaze those who know him by occasionally managing to focus long enough to produce book-length insanity. The Louisiana native lives in South Texas with his family. He is working on the third Denton Rourke novel.

Mr. O'Regan kindly reminds fans that a great way to pass the time between books is to refer the current titles to friends and family. And by, "refer" he means, "make them buy their own copies."

You can contact him via his website, www.ianoregan.com, which is updated almost every month.

www.ingramcontent.com/pod-product-compliance
Lightning Source LLC
LaVergne TN
LVHW041101080826
845145LV00007B/1647
9780615737850